SORCERESS OF THE DRYADS

Book Two

Legend of the Singer

Kaarathlon

Areaer Novels

EPOCH OF THE PROMISE: Dawn
Unseen
EPOCH OF THE PROMISE:
Vision's Light
EPOCH OF THE PROMISE:
Wings of Healing
EPOCH OF THE PROMISE:
Darkness Bright*

Return of the Dragonriders

DragonBirth
DragonWing
DragonSword

Legend of the Singer

Other

Kingdom of Light

Children of the Dryads
Sorceress of the Dryads

Dragon-Mage
Heart of Fire*
Scars of Fire*

Standalone Novels/Novellas

The Gifts of Faeri
Kindred of the Sea
Gryphon's Escape

* Not yet available

[YOUNG ADULT FICTION] / fantasy / epic
[YOUNG ADULT FICTION] / social themes / friendship
[YOUNG ADULT FICTION] / coming of age
[YOUNG ADULT FICTION] / animals / mythical creatures

Summary: When Tara-lin finds herself in a position of influence in the elven nation of
Elethri, she must discover herself and stay true to her nature in a position where her
choices and actions will affect the lives of those she has never known, without their
consent.

Cover art by Raina Nightingale and Midnight Rose.
Cover design by Raina Nightingale.
Edited with Taylor Blake.

www.enthralledbylove.com

Forward

Welcome back again to the conclusion of Tara-lin's story.

Sorceress of the Dryads is a bit different from *Children of the Dryads*, in ways that so far none of the Areaer novels are. It's a bit more introspective, closely following Tara-lin's development, her questions, doubts, and internal journeys and discoveries, along with a plot that has a different structure and development than most plots I have seen. I hope you enjoy it thoroughly!

Find the magic within yourself and stay true to your nature! And encourage others to be true to find their magic and be true to their nature, every one unique!

Only in this way will we escape and conquer the Nightmare. Never let it crush your nature! Never compromise who you are!

-Raina Nightingale

PS. I promised that, after the *Legend of the Singer Duology,* we would get back to dragons! So let me tell you a little of what to expect. There's a dragon or two, and a few drake-lizards on the sidelines of *Sorceress of the Dryads,* but in my opinion that doesn't count for much. But keep an eye out for Corostomir and Aderan! Their story is told in *Kindred of the Sea* (if you haven't read that one already), and there's a dragon – and magical dolphins – in that book. Also watch out for *Heart of Fire,* book one of the Dragon-mage Quartet, coming April 2023. There are *lots* of dragons in that one, if the name doesn't tell you enough already!

There is also the possibility that I might sometime write an anthology about Tara-lin and some of the people in her life, especially if anyone is interested. You can find me and contact me at www.enthralledbylove.com

PPS.

I referred to a weapon in a ship battle as a cannon. Those who care about world-building may be curious as to how that fits with other things. It's not precisely a cannon but it has a similar use; if you want info-dumping, contact me. If many of you are interested in this, I'll make a page about it on my website.

Golden on the wings of eternity
White on wings of the dawn
Soul of this world
Heart of another

Golden on the wings of eternity
Silver on breath of time
Heart of ages
Shield of the morning

Sun on edges of never-ending night
Roots deep through winter's cold
Hold to the life
In the sun-earth's heart

Sun on edges of never-ending night
Roots drink deep of earth's life
Water of life
Through the withering blaze

Golden on the wings of eternity
Dreams reborn out of ice
Of thousand eyes
In the heart of dawn

Map of Ellenesia

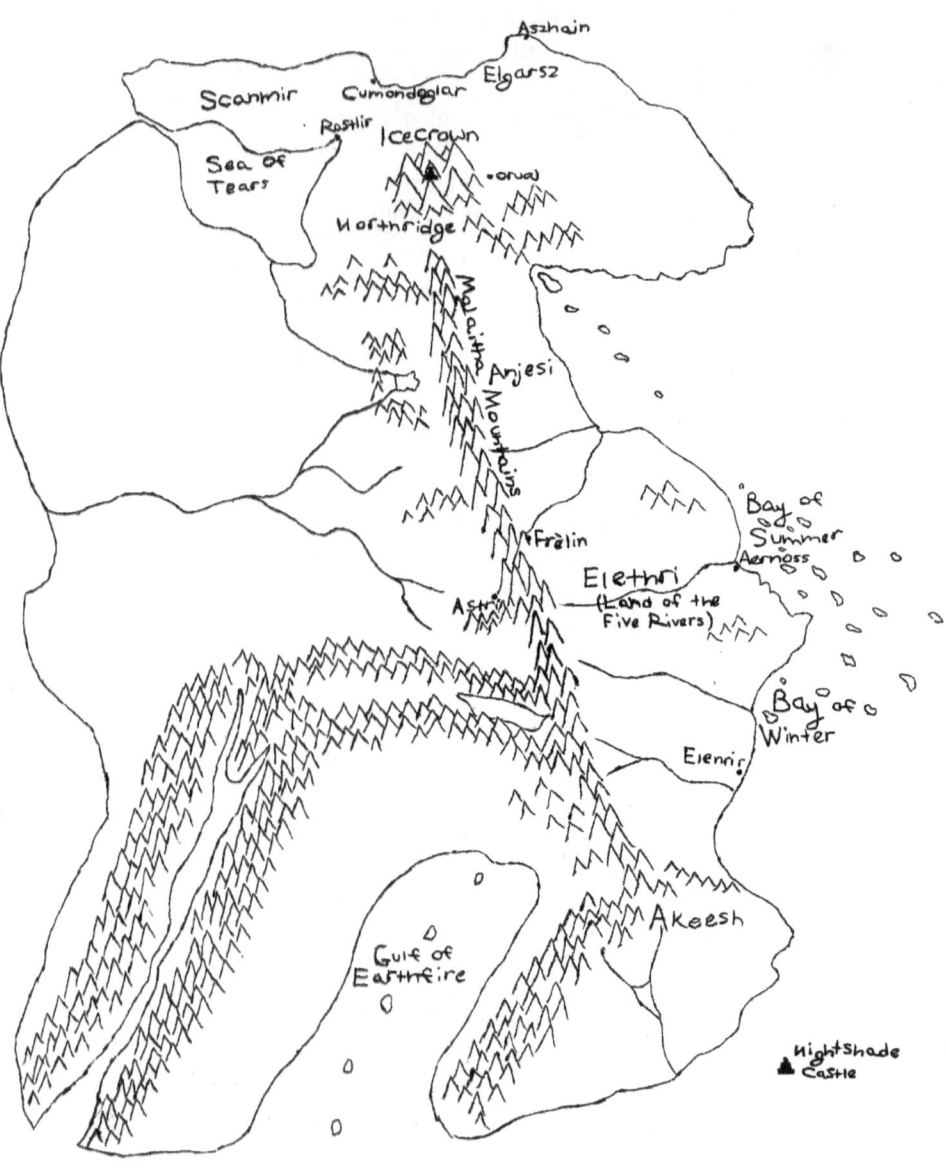

Aszhain

Elgarsz

Scanmir   Cumondoglar

Rostlir   Icecrown

Sea of
Tears   Ionau

Northridge

Malaitha Mountains

Anjesi

Frelin   Bay of
Summer
Elethri   Aernoss
(Land of the
Five Rivers)

Astri   Bay of
Winter

Elennis

Akeesh

Gulf of
Earthfire

Nightshade
Castle

Table of Contents

Heir – 1
Magic of the Dryads – 11
The Palace-Tomb – 18
Truth in the Warded Room – 27
Call of the Forest – 36
Magic of the Trees – 42
This Night Together – 50
The Coronation – 57
Lizards and Dragons – 64
Speech of the Dryads – 74
Shadow of Night – 83
Magic of the Elves – 92
Across the Malaitha Mountains – 93
Land of the Five Rivers – 107
The Warded Forest – 116
Between Fear and Laughter – 124
Warfare of the Dryads – 132
Lure of the Sorceress – 138
Song of the Storm – 146
Not Destroyer, Healer – 156
The Song in Your Blood – 166
Taste of Victory – 174
A Gryphon's Wisdom – 182
Bounds of the Song – 189
Fire and Ice – 198
The Wild Ones – 207
Resolution – 216
Epilogue – 211

Chapter One – Heir

"Eldazìn has returned."

"I'll be there in a moment, Keller," Tara-lin called back. She and Keller had married two years earlier. It was now about ten years since they had come to this valley, and Keller had, more or less, fully recovered. Tara-lin was sure he would never be completely normal, but he was no longer subject to fits of irrationality or violence. All in all, he was sane and reasonable.

Tara-lin descended the pine, climbing down its roughly evenly spaced branches. Before they were even considering marriage, Keller had revealed to her that Falkur had once expressed to him, "You're a wizard, boy. Why don't you want to help me?!" Keller had not even understood what kind of help Falkur wanted, but the wizard had then proceeded to beat him. Keller rarely spoke about his childhood, so Tara-lin had been surprised at the revelation. It had, however, made perfect sense to her. She had long been confused about how a blast had struck her, and two orcs, in the halls of Nightshade Castle, but now she knew the answer. Keller was a wizard and, inexperienced and untaught as he was, had generated it in his terror.

Tara-lin was certain she already knew some of Eldazìn's news. The elf had appeared six or so years earlier and revealed himself as the "Assassin." He had not meant that he had actually performed assassinations, but that he possessed unmatched skill in stealth, infiltration, and weapons of assassination (the Elethrian term, 'Night's Edge' was clear about that, referring to the skills, not whether or how they were used). He had run the only thing that could be called Elethrian Intelligence, but it had been small, unofficial, relatively impromptu, and nameless. One of the remaining legacies of their dryadic ancestry was that the elves tended to be a very peaceful people, disinclined to killing and war and to most political intrigue, and thus Elethri was, in many ways, very different from the human countries, even though it appeared to be headed in the same direction as they had all gone. It had taken Eldazìn a long time to find the valley, and he had brought with him the spouse of that princess of the royal house whom Lìrulin had found in her flight from Elethri ten years earlier. Eldazìn had been too late to save the lives of the King and Queen and others, but he had contributed to the princess' escape as well as that of her spouse, Oranë. He offered his services to the elves, and few humans, living in the valley.

At first, Tara-lin and Alis had discussed with him how they might help girls to escape who, like Alis, did not want to marry or join monasteries. Then, when it was revealed that Keller had wizardry talent, Tara-lin asked Eldazìn if he would acquire volumes on wizardry and how to develop the talent since, as she had said, "There is no wizard we can trust to invite here and teach Keller, so we will have to do the best we can in other ways, but none of us know anything, and dryads know nothing about this, so they cannot teach him as they taught me." Eldazìn had been relatively successful, and Keller had mastered a variety of simpler spells. Tara-lin did not know much about the art, but she thought it was probably good progress for someone who had to learn entirely from books. She knew she could never have learned how to sing as she could now from books, however well written they might be.

Now, Eldazìn was returning with a report on the state of the elven civilization below them and whatever he could glean about the leanings of the populace. Tara-lin already knew some of what he would tell her. The dryads below were languishing, their life drained by the power Anakrim drew from them. He had promised to teach the elves their lost secrets of magic, but he had really given them power that would, ultimately, serve only him, at the expense of the lives of their trees. The deterioration of the forests of Elethri had begun many years ago, but it had accelerated in the last several months. Tara-lin hoped that would wake many of the elves up to the trick by which they had been taken in. She had learned from the dryads that the lives of the elves were tied to theirs and to the health of the trees. Not quite dryads, the elves yet needed the forests – and the dryads themselves – in a way humans did not. If the forests languished and died, so would the elves. She hoped their minds were not too blinded by the Nightmare to see their foolishness before it was too late.

Tara-lin swung herself down from another branch and leaped lightly to the ground. Once again, the dryads wanted her to try to help them, and the whole world with them. The damage being done was even greater now, in Elethri, than it had been ten years ago, in Icecrown.

Tara-lin ran lightly down the slope, leaping over some branches and bramble. There was a clearing on the edge of a little lake where they typically gathered. Before she saw them, she heard voices speaking softly. She could already guess who would be there. In addition to Eldazìn, there would be Tara-lin's father, Eldor, and her mother, Lìrulin, the previous Valor Knights Namdon and Cuthlin, Keller her spouse, and several other elves, including either Oranë or his spouse, Elisa. Alis might or might not be there.

When everyone was present, Eldazìn began. "The trees are dying. Many of the elves are morose and depressed. I think that if they felt less morose and sickly, they would be more inclined to think through what is going on and, possibly, rebel, but, as it is, many of them feel too depressed and ill. Others associate any deterioration they feel within their own bodies with the deterioration of the forests, and any depression with their love for the ailing trees. It seems that many of them see King Anakrim, as he styles himself, as the cause of the forests' ailment. Interestingly, many of them are young. Some of them are outspoken, but I have reason to think there are far more who are deeply suspicious or reclusive than there are who are outspoken. I expect a great deal of turmoil. The morose and depressed elves seem willing to follow Anakrim's lead anywhere, even if they are given to a great deal of grumbling, and may resist any movement to depose Anakrim. I don't know how Anakrim plans to respond to that portion of elven society which sees him as the problem. Some of them have almost religious reasons for their opposition, believing that the Elethrian forests are unwilling to be ruled by one with human ancestry. Others believe his magic is to blame, even though it appears very similar to the ancient and lost magic of Elethri which did no harm. Many have no clear reason. They simply see a correlation."

"Thank you, Eldazìn," said Tara-lin. Several others repeated the sentiment.

She looked around, then said, "The dryads want me to do something, again. Dad, do you remember when I was talking about how people with special talents always have to do exciting things and have exciting lives? This is worse than I thought. I'd like to ... just live a quiet life. Visit gryphons with Alis." She glanced at Keller and smiled. "Instead, I seem to be right in the thick of things yet again. Why?!" She made a sound to express her frustration, then went on, "Do you think those elves who are, at best, deeply suspicious of Prince Anakrim would support us if we marched to depose him?"

"What are you thinking, Tara-lin?" asked Lìrulin.

"You don't know, Mom? I thought the dryads would have told you, too. The dryads want me to take them right into Frèlin. We've been thinking and talking about a lot of things. The dryads really appreciated my comment, years ago, about pitying Anakrim. It has given us an idea, but it's not one I can share with you. I'm not sure I understand it myself, but I'm a lot more used to dryadic magic now. I can't say I'm comfortable with the ... ideas we have, but I'm willing to try. However, we will need some ... well, we will need not to be attacked at every step by overwhelming odds."

"It's not improbable that you would be supported, Tara-lin," said Eldazìn. "Those who think Anakrim's humanity is at the root of the problem would thrill at your talent of singer. They might not even object to being ruled by you, believing that your song is a clear mark that the forests favor you. However, those who think Anakrim's magic is to blame may be suspicious of all magic, including the ancient song, not certain if it is, in fact, the ancient song, or only something like it."

Tara-lin barely kept her tongue in check while Eldazìn finished. "Ruled by me?" she gasped.

"It's high time that you acknowledged that you are a Princess of Elethri by marriage, Tara-lin," said Oranë.

"You and Elisa are Prince and Princess, too," said Tara-lin.

"It's not the same. Elisa is a distant cousin," said Oranë.

"He's right," interjected Keller. "We've never talked about it. I never even thought about it until just now, and it feels horribly strange, but I, and not Anakrim, should be the Crown Prince –" He paused, seeming to struggle with his words, "– the King."

Tara-lin wheeled to face him. "What?!"

"I'm Mom's – Ithrìl's – firstborn, Tara-lin. To begin with, Falkur was very interested in me. I don't want to talk about it, but when Anakrim was born ... that interest turned to hate." The pain in his eyes was dark and sharp. Tara-lin knew that, while he knew now that his mother had not abandoned him, at the time he had felt abandoned, even though something in him had refused to believe that she could abandon him. He had been taken from her and from the light, never to see her again, and not to see the light again until ten years ago.

Tara-lin put her hands over her face and sighed. "I *never* wanted to be the Queen of Elethri!"

"I never wanted to be King of Elethri, either," said Keller, laughing. "But I was born."

"You don't understand!" said Tara-lin. "I know nothing about ruling. Neither of us do. Nothing about managing nations and politics and crime and law and all that stuff!"

"I admit the prospect is ... without substance to me," said Keller.

"Wait!" said Eldazìn. "What are you two thinking?"

"I told you, I and the dryads have a plan, but I can't tell anyone what it is. We'll all, including myself, just have to wait and see it," said Tara-lin.

"You said something earlier about your plan requiring that we're not faced with overwhelming odds," said Eldazìn. "The magic of Anakrim seems, by itself, to be an overwhelming odd."

"I will be bringing the strength of the dryads," said Tara-lin. "Keller has mastered some spells which, while simple by the standards of wizardry, may also be invaluable. There *is* of course some risk. Perhaps everyone with small children should stay behind, for even if we fail, this valley may remain safe for a little while longer. But, if we fail, this whole world will languish, if someone or something else does not step in." Tara-lin did not share something else which had occurred to her while watching Keller struggle with wizardry, which was that there might be a dryadic element to wizardry – one greatly altered by the workings of the human mind, and therefore of vastly different power and scope, but still based in good measure on underlying dryadic magic. Perhaps, there were wizards at all because, as the dryad Aumoura had once told her, a few of the off-spring of human and dryad pairs had, instead of mating with each other and forming the elves, mated with other humans and disappeared into the mass of humanity, introducing a tincture of dryad blood into the human race at large.

There was silence, as the others considered what Tara-lin had told them. She spoke again. "But I will *not* be Queen of Elethri. I cannot be Queen."

"What would you have, then?" asked Eldazìn.

An idea struck Tara-lin. "You!" she said. "You should be King. I think you would know what to do and how to do it well."

"I have no claim," said Eldazìn. "And I have never aspired to rule anymore than you have, Tara-lin. You may have my advice whenever you ask for it, and you may ignore it whenever you do not desire it, but I have no claim. I am merely an ordinary elf."

Tara-lin growled. "I *can't.*"

Again, silence hung over the group. In an attempt to ease the discomfort, Tara-lin said, "But that doesn't mean I won't do what I've already proposed and work with the dryads." She rose. "Is there anything else we need to discuss?"

"Yes," said Eldazìn. "We will need to discuss the logistics of marching on Frèlin with a host of dryads. Since it is you and Lìrulin who know the dryads, and you and Keller who know the magic you will be using and therefore what you might require, you will need to be part of that discussion."

"Fine," said Tara-lin. "We'll talk about that tomorrow morning. Anything else?"

For a moment no one said anything. Eldor looked up at her and said, "I love you, Tara-lin."

"I love you, too, Dad," said Tara-lin. "For now, I need to go. I'll talk to you and Mom soon, though."

Tara-lin ran.

She headed for the canyon-like walls of the valley. She wanted to speak with Alis. She would talk to her mate, Keller, later. She did not want to talk to him right now. There were times when she felt like a child. She doubted the dryads would have any advice for her on this new problem thrown in her face.

Tara-lin reached the cliff-like walls and began to climb them, throwing all her nervous energy into the effort. She was hanging on when a voice above her suddenly asked, "Tara-lin, what are you doing?"

Tara-lin almost lost her footing. "Coming up here," she panted. She continued to climb, scrambling up the incline. Finally, she dropped herself down on a ledge. Alis stood next to her, and beside Alis stood her mighty brown beast, the gryphon Kushon.

"Something is wrong, Tara-lin," said Alis. "This is not usual behavior."

"No, it's not," said Tara-lin. "I told you the other day that I am going to have to go with the dryads, and those elves who are willing, to overthrow King Anakrim?"

"Yeah, you told me something like that," said Alis. "What is the new problem?"

"I just learned I'm to be Queen of Elethri! Keller is Anakrim's *older* brother, so, by elven law, *I and Keller* should *even now* sit the throne of Elethri in Frèlin. Once Anakrim is dead, Keller and I will be King and Queen. I just *can't.*"

Alis leaned against Kushon and stroked under his throat. A rumbling sigh of pleasure escaped through his beak.

"Of course you can, Tara-lin," said Alis. "It's not that complicated. Do what you think is right. I'm *sure* you have ideas about how these things should be – how rulers should behave, what kinds of laws are just or unjust, what kinds of behaviors are not rulers' problems to govern, right or wrong, and what kinds of behaviors are. Goodness, this goes back to our first meeting, and to many things you've been saying since then. And I don't think you're concerned about Keller...."

"No," said Tara-lin. "But what if I make a mistake? What if I'm wrong? Or what if I just make a mistake that plunges Elethri into war? Or lets some traitor have influence and position? Don't you know about the Valor Hall?"

"You're making excuses, Tara-lin. No one can find a ruler who's guaranteed to never make a mistake, even a catastrophic one." She paused for a moment, then said, "I'm sure I wouldn't like it any better than you do, if it turned out *I* was the one who was going to have to be Queen, but someone has to, right? And I don't see why it's so bad for that someone to be you and Keller. Certainly, it wouldn't be better for it to be someone who doesn't recognize that he might get things wrong? For then, he'll get *more* things wrong for *certain*, since he won't admit he might be wrong, so he won't be willing to think or learn. Right?"

"I suppose," said Tara-lin. "But I ... don't know where to start. I *can't.*"

Alis stopped stroking Kushon and leaned against his shoulder. He sighed again, clearly pleased with her attention. Finally, she said, "You don't have to start now. Didn't you tell me that on our first quest together? When you were worried about the fact you didn't know what you would have to do, and the dryads told you the knowledge would come to you when you needed it? I think that applies here, too."

"But this isn't singing ... or even any sort of magic!" protested Tara-lin.

"No," said Alis, "but, tell me, do you even have enough knowledge yet to know where to start?"

"I guess not," admitted Tara-lin. She stood, walked over to Kushon, and began to scratch him in the spots Alis had shown her that he liked.

After a few minutes, she said, "I really should go back to Keller...."

"Would you like Kushon to take you down so you don't have to make that climb again?" asked Alis, with a twinkle in her eyes.

"Sure," said Tara-lin. "I'd like that." She looked the gryphon in the eye and said, "Thank you, Kushon," then mounted him when Alis directed her. After all, he was Alis' gryphon.

The valley was in shadow when Tara-lin reached the elven-style tree-house which she and Keller shared.

She found him sitting with his legs over a branch. She climbed up to where he sat and settled herself a few feet away.

He looked up at her, then said, "Tara-lin, are you mad at me?"

"No! Of course not! It's not *your* fault that ... how could it be your fault? It's been horrible for you all along. It's got to be awful. First you were born to a kidnapped princess and a wizard who quickly hated you! I don't know half of what happened and I'm sure I don't want to ... and, now, you find out you have to be King of Elethri! How could I be mad at you?"

"I just wanted to make sure," said Keller, smiling sadly.

Tara-lin moved across the space between them and hung herself about him. "I won't leave you, Keller. Not even if it means I have to be Queen."

"You're more upset about it than I am," said Keller.

"You said yourself you don't even have a concept of it," said Tara-lin.

He nodded. "I really don't. I can't even believe it." He sighed.

Tara-lin kissed him. "Can you believe I'm not going to leave you?"

He kissed her in return. "Yes, dear Tara-lin. I believe you're not going to leave me."

.·❋ ❋ ❋ ❋ ❋·.

Later, that night, she sat on a branch looking up at the stars. *Another thing is that I don't want to live in Frèlin. It might be the prettiest, nicest city I've seen yet, but it's a city, and cities just ... aren't quite right.* She shook her hair, feeling like crying. She remembered telling her parents she would talk to them soon. *Maybe first thing tomorrow,* she thought. *They're almost certainly asleep with Lyan by now.* Lyan was her younger brother. He would probably be her only other sibling ever, at a little over twenty years younger than herself. Even though he was ten years old, Alis said he looked and acted more like six. Like Tara-lin herself, he was a half-elf, and so no one could know ahead of time how quickly he would grow.

In the morning, Tara-lin and her father took a stroll through the valley. Only when Eldor questioned her did Tara-lin share how she felt. "I went and talked to Alis, last night," she said. "She tries to make me feel like I can do this. Like I know things that should be done, and others that shouldn't be done, and that I don't need to know what to do ahead of time. How could I even know until I see the situation better – until I *am* Queen? But really!" She stomped her foot for emphasis. "What do I know about being Queen? I'm beginning to think there should be no such things as monarchs! Too much decision-making and responsibility resting on one – or two – people! An innocent diplomatic mistake could plunge nations into war and kill thousands! A misunderstanding, a placing of the wrong person into an office, a failure to grasp how to write and implement laws, all could cause untold suffering!"

Eldor nodded. Tara-lin really felt like he listened to her, even when he silently considered what she had said when she was done speaking. "All your points are valid, Tara-lin," he said, "but, if you're worried about the impact of decisions – men will make bad decisions. I don't know if it would be better if there were no monarchs, but if you and Keller do not rule, I do know someone else will try to do so. For all your mistakes, for all your imperfections, even if your own pride and fears interfere with your ruling, you will not cause nearly the problems that result when men like Anakrim and those in the Valor Hall rule. But I'm not sure how much comfort to you that is. As regards wars – I think you imagine you are responsible for things for which you are *not* responsible. Innocent diplomatic mistakes do not *cause* wars. They might be the excuse or catalyst for someone who has bad intentions to start a war. If those on both sides have even remotely good intentions, a war will not erupt out of a few mistakes. Understanding will be sought. Peaceful resolutions will be sought. I think what you really mean is that you are sure that you and Keller are not up to the task of handling these things perfectly, and that if you were up to that task many evils would not result, that will result because you are not perfect. You're asking in this, though, for a perfection that I'm not sure it's even possible for an elf or a human to attain, and, even so, even if some *can* attain that perfection, there is no fault in you for not having that perfection, and not having that perfection does not and cannot make you at fault for the evils intended and done by other men. But I understand that none of this will make you comfortable with the situation thrust on you. And that's okay. It is a very uncomfortable situation."

Tara-lin nodded.

"You look like you want a hug," said her father.

"I do." She stepped into his arms. *I really feel so overwhelmed.*

"I'm nothing like mature enough to be Queen, and I don't think Keller is any more mature enough to be King," said Tara-lin into her father's shoulder.

"I love you," he whispered.

Chapter Two – Magic of the Dryads

Tara-lin rode, side by side with Keller, at the vanguard of her strange army. Around her moved a forest of dryads, appearing one moment to be the densest imaginable thicket of trees, branches and leaves all swaying before a fierce wind, and next moment to be a company of humanesque shapes that yet appeared very inhuman and which varied greatly from one another in coloring, in shape, in height, and in the way they moved. Tara-lin did not know how many dryads were with her, but she knew that dryads from across all of Ellenesia had come, and that she was the anchor point for the magic that allowed them such strong manifestations so far away from their resident trees.

Off to one side flew a company of gryphon riders. When they first rode into the valley where they had lived for the last ten years, Alis had whispered to Tara-lin that there had to be a better way of taming gryphons than that generally known among elves and humans. Tara-lin did not know if anyone else could pull it off, but Alis had succeeded in convincing the gryphons to allow some elves to bond to their young.

Amongst and behind the dryads rode a host of elves, many of them young. Almost none of the younger generation of elves, among which was Earnrìl, Tara-lin's friend, had ever seen a dryad. Many of them, and even a portion of the older elves, joined with Tara-lin's company upon seeing the host of dryads. An instinctive loyalty to the dryads, an innate affection for them, was still present in the elven blood. Thus, as Prince Keller and Princess Tara-lin rode through Elethri, none of the elves had yet taken up weapons against them, and many of the elves followed them. Tara-lin felt as though she lived in a dream. It all felt very unreal, as if it were not happening at all or, if it were, it was happening to someone else.

Before her rose the walls of Frèlin, pure white and delicately carved and engraved with silver. Nostalgic grief passed over her, as she remembered the last time she had ridden into this city beside her father, Sir Eldor. Over the last ten years, he had aged, while she had merely completed the last inch of her growth. She would almost certainly live more than a century more, and perhaps many centuries more, but his hair was now more gray than black and his face was showing the accumulation of the years. Her heart was grieved, both for herself and for her brother, Lyan, who seemed to be growing a little slower than she had grown. If Eldor lived a long lifespan for his race, he would die when

Lyan was barely full-grown.

Tara-lin looked up and saw, upon the walls, archers and swordsmen posted. She held up her hand and the confused ranks of dryads and elves halted. The distance was still so far that even elven arrows would not reach across it.

Around her, the dryads assembled. She looked towards Keller and shared a smile.

"I'm ready," he said, and she knew what he meant. He had prepared the spells he would be likely to need in the confrontation before them as well as he could ahead of time.

The fact was that they had no clearly defined plan. Tara-lin was acting in concert with the knowledge of the dryads, and she barely understood their knowledge and plan at all. However, there were spells useful in neutralizing many forms of casting magic, and the simplest of these Keller had prepared, since they were all that lay within his power.

"What do we do now?" asked a young elf riding up behind them. His name was Akanë, and he was a friend of Eldazìn's.

Tara-lin did not answer at once. Her eyes were closed as she concentrated on the world of the dryads. Instead, Keller answered. "We wait. It is not really we who lead, you understand."

"I do understand," said Akanë, "but it *is* she and her mother who speak to the dryads."

Tara-lin held up her hand, palm straight out before her, and began to sing in a strong, level tone. The resonance rose and hung in the air, and her voice continued, the vocal focus point of power far more than her own.

The elves on the wall stood there, as if uncertain. Their faces displayed many different kinds of uncertainty; some were terrified by the dryads, others were enchanted by them. Some of them simply did not know what the force below them was doing or what was going on. Keller thought to himself, *Anakrim must have known we were coming for days at least, probably more like weeks.*

Then a shiver ran through the wall beneath their feet and the white and silver gates swung open, as if of their own volition.

The elves with Tara-lin cheered. She cringed at their cheers. *Do they not know that if we charge through that gate, our blood stains the stones? We will make it, but their arrows will take many of us first,* she thought grimly. Then she thought, more grimly still, *In war men die. We all know that. And with the gates open, far less would die than storming the walls. Still, such a charge was never my intention....*

As Tara-lin paused, glancing first at the indecisive, frightened elves on the wall, and then at Keller, Akanë hissed, "Don't we charge?"

"No," said Tara-lin. "We have not come for bloodshed. We have come with the dryads."

"Then what is the use of opening the gates, if I may ask?"

Tara-lin said nothing. Dread overwhelmed her. She would do nothing but make a million mistakes, and some of them would be deadly. Perhaps, this was already such a deadly mistake....

Keller spoke, and his voice, magically enhanced, resounded over the city of Frèlin. "We have come in peace, not to make war. We have come to request a peaceful transfer of the throne, seeing as we are the presumed-dead eldest son of the Princess Ithrìl, only child of King Orenduil, the Crown Prince and Rightful King, Keller, and the Princess and Rightful Queen, Tara-lin, spouse of Keller, Singer of Elethri, Friend of the Dryads."

Tara-lin heard the collective gasp that went up from the walls. This they had not heard from Anakrim. She wondered why. Would he not perceive it as a weakness to let her and Keller announce it? Why not better to announce it, and explain why it did not matter, himself? She wondered if he was not very intelligent. Then again, she was pretty certain she and Keller were not very intelligent, either. She certainly did not feel intelligent.

A moment later she saw Anakrim, or something that must have been Anakrim, rise out of the city. He rode upon an armored gryphon and he was once more surrounded by various winged creatures, some of which, Tara-lin was certain, were of the nightmare, but which were partially concealed by magic.

"Keller, now!" hissed Tara-lin. Then she felt the waves of the dryadic consciousness in the back of her mind. She knew now what she was here to do, realized she had known, in some sense, for a very long time; she thought for a moment that she herself might have been the inspiration for this idea, that it had first been born in her mind. Then she joined with the hosts of the dryads and her thoughts were all committed to the song, the greatest she had yet sung.

> Shadow of another world
> Born of magic beyond the world
> Bound by magic sought beyond the world

Radiance of the shadow falls

Waves of light in other realms
Tides of life in another realm
Tides of shadow in another realm
Sweeping under the moon of dawn

Dawn's rays from the dreaming sun
Changing to stone beneath the sun
Change of coming life beneath the sun
Motion of stone, shadow of dawn

Twilight in another world
Spell of twilight beyond the world
Life of twilight sought outside the world
Captured by the evening dawn

Magic bound flows in blood unbound
Captured dreams enthrall sleep unbound
Searching roots through the whole earth unbound
Airs of the deepest regions move

Earth moves on ethereal airs
Binding life from ethereal airs
Born of life in the ethereal airs
Dreams swell under mountains fast

Shadows of rain, colors of cloud
Melted in rising, formless mists
Fallen in dream-colors and forms of mists
Taking earth into sky and deep earth

As her song and mind became the vehicle of mighty magic, exhilaration passed through Tara-lin, unnoticed as she was caught up in the dryadic consciousness, merged, for the moment, with the song. The winds moved around her, almost swaying in rhythm or counter-rhythm to her song, adding at times their own keening, howling voices, or their soft, whispering, breathy voices to the song. Primal, dreamy life surged through the earth and through the realms of dryad-thought, and Tara-lin entered as fully as she ever had yet into the world of those bright, colored shadows and dim, radiant mists, a world both dreamy and wakeful.

An image burned with almost blinding radiance in Tara-lin's mind: a tree with branches upraised and roots diving deep. It was a double image: in one image, the tree's upswept branches seemed burdened, its dark leaves were wilted and curled and drying, its bark was almost peeling. In the other image, the tree's dark bark was smooth, its leaves were a dark, rich green, shining a little and held to the sky, the whole tree, dark as it was, almost glowing with health.

Brighter and brighter the image of the tree burned before Tara-lin. Around it washed shifting shadows of the brilliant dream-colors, melting into each other and swirling back and forth, brushing the edges of the tree's branches and roots as they passed.

Full understanding of what was being done now possessed Tara-lin, but she was too absorbed in the magic to think about it. Then, as the full magic of the song was realized, Tara-lin became once more attuned to the world around her.

"Thank goodness!" It was Keller's voice and he sounded near collapse. "That is done! I did not think I could much longer."

In sudden bursts of realization, Tara-lin took in her surroundings. With the final, binding stream of power, the dryads had all gone, their materializations returning to their heart trees. She saw, taking to the four winds, what could only be a great many drake-lizards and finally realized what some of those shimmering wings she had seen around Prince Anakrim were. Somehow, he had captured and enchanted the rare drake-lizards. No one really knew how rare the drake-lizards were, but they were not social creatures, like the gryphons, and the females hid their eggs even from those to whom they were bonded, despite the closeness of the bond they formed.

Immediately around her, there was much noise which it took a few moments for Tara-lin to process. Elves were screaming, "Charge them! They killed our king!"

The host with Tara-lin grouped themselves together, calling out in fear and confusion. Very few of them were, after all, trained warriors. Some of them fled in fear. They cried out, wondering where the dryads had gone, for they had hoped for the power of the dryads.

"Keller," said Tara-lin.

"Yes?" he said, moving in closer to her so that they could hear each other.

"Can you cast a spell to amplify my voice?" she asked.

"I think I can manage it," Keller said.

"How quickly?" asked Tara-lin.

Keller did not answer. Tara-lin suspected he was already engrossed in the spell. She raised her voice, hoping that her own magic would be enough to influence the situation. "We have not killed Anakrim! Anakrim is not dead! We do not come in war! We are not come for bloodshed! Anakrim is not dead! Anakrim is now a dryad!"

Tara-lin felt Akanë's touch on her arm. "Should I have them throw down their weapons?"

"Perhaps," answered Tara-lin. "I know no better than you. I should have just had Keller yell himself. Perhaps you can do so?"

"No," said Akanë earnestly. "The spell has taken effect. Cry out yourself!"

Tara-lin closed her eyes and concentrated on her voice. "Anakrim is not dead. Anakrim is a dryad. He is alive and well! We have not come in war. We do not come for bloodshed. We have come in peace! Anakrim is not dead."

At the same time, Akanë spoke to the elves and had those who were armed lay down or sheath their weapons or otherwise make it clear they were not a threat.

"I can do no more," said Keller quietly. Akanë reached out his hand and supported the half-elf mage as he slipped off his horse. He slumped against Akanë.

The charging elves drew themselves to a halt. "Not dead? You have not killed our king?"

"No," responded Tara-lin. "We have not killed your king. By the magic of ten thousand dryads, he is now a dryad himself, and his dryadic life will heal the tree with which he is now one."

An elf who seemed to be of some importance in the hierarchy of the defense rode up. "So then King Anakrim is blessed of the dryads?" he asked.

"No," said Tara-lin. "Dryads are peaceful and not violent. This was the best way to deal with the threat he posed to them. He took magic from the dryads in order to gain power for himself. That magic needed to be returned to the dryads. The best way to do this, from the viewpoint of the dryads, was not to kill him, but to make him a dryad himself. After all, if he so much desired dryadic magic that he stole life from the dryads in order to acquire it, maybe he wants to be a dryad himself. And, as a dryad, he can use the magic only as dryads can use it, which limits the evil he can do with it."

"You are saying our King Anakrim was evil?" asked the captain.

"You must surely have noticed that the forests of Elethri are less healthy than they were ten years ago. Moreover, Anakrim knew that he was not the proper heir to the elven throne. He knew – as Princess Ithrìl did not – that his older brother, Keller, survived. It is Keller who should have been King of Elethri. It is I who bear the blessing of the dryads, as is witnessed by how they accompanied me to this point, and by my song," said Tara-lin.

"Where – which – is Keller?" asked the captain.

Tara-lin turned and saw that Keller's horse was now held by another elf, who had also dismounted. Akanë, too, had dismounted, and his horse was held off to another side by another elf. He supported Keller, who slumped against his shoulder, hardly the image of a prince or a king!

Tara-lin wished for someone to give her advice. She dismounted, handing her horse's reins to another elf, then stepped sideways and behind Akanë and appeared on the other side of Keller. She placed her hand on his arm and said, "This is the Prince Keller, but he is thoroughly exhausted by the spell to amplify my voice."

The captain turned to an elf who stood beside him and lowered his voice. He and the other elf conferred quietly, then the other elf rode off towards the city.

Tara-lin was tired, too. Even though most of the energy had come from the dryads, it had still exhausted her to give it form and to understand it. She was not ready to think through all the implications of what she now knew and the magic of which she had now been a part. Lowering her voice as well, Tara-lin almost whispered, "Keller, are you all right?"

He straightened and stepped away from Akanë's supporting arm. He swayed a little at first. "Yes. It's just magic." His words were slurred and almost mumbled and he paused for a moment, focusing, then continued in a slightly stronger voice. "It was all I could do to hold the magic against Anakrim. Then the amplification spell drained the last of my reserves. I'm a little better already, but not enough to cast another spell. It's much harder if you have to do it in a hurry and you haven't prepared the spell beforehand."

"Well, the day isn't over yet," said Tara-lin. "Akanë?"

"Yes, Tara-lin?"

"Send someone back to let everyone know I don't expect a battle

– unless you do expect a battle. I'd like the companionship of my friends, and I'd be interested in any advice Eldazìn might have."

"You need not be concerned for Eldazìn's advice. He has prepped me quite thoroughly. But I will relay your message," replied Akanë. He turned to the elf who had been holding his horse and took the reins, then spoke in soft tones to the elf. A moment later the elf was back in the saddle and riding through the disorganized lines of Tara-lin's company.

Chapter Three - The Palace—Tomb

In a few minutes, the captain of the defenses of Elethri called across the distance between his line and that of Tara-lin and Keller. "I offer truce. May I approach?"

Keller drew himself together and responded. "Your truce is accepted. How many do you wish to bring with you?"

"Two companions," answered the captain.

"Then you may come and bring them with you," replied Keller.

The captain approached.

When he was a couple horse-lengths away, he dismounted and performed an elven curtsy. "Greetings, Prince and Princess. I am Erenvin, Captain of the Guard of Frèlin."

"Greetings, Erenvin," said Keller. Akanë once more stood beside him to offer Keller any support he might require.

"I do, however, have a question for you, good Prince and Princess. How is it possible that Anakrim is a dryad? Can an elf really be made a dryad?"

"When a singer and ten thousand dryads work in concert, an elf who has already stolen dryad life and magic can be transformed into a dryad. You might even say that Prince Anakrim began the transformation, and that we completed it. After all, the elves are descended from dryads and men in the ancient days," answered Tara-lin.

"Pardon me for questioning you, good Princess Tara-lin, but how do you know this?"

"I am a singer and have spoken often with the dryads. Many of them live lives as much longer than an average elven lifespan as an elven lifespan is longer than a human span. They remember," answered Tara-lin.

Erenvin nodded. "I see." He turned and conferred softly with one of the elves who had ridden out with him, a female who appeared to be his sister or at least a close relation of one form or another. Then he straightened. "We acknowledge that you, Keller, appear to be the son of the Princess Ithrìl and, therefore, Prince and Heir to the Throne of Elethri. We invite you and your spouse, the Princess and Singer Tara-lin, into Frèlin. We will not resume hostilities towards you without due warning a minimum of two days in advance. We do not foresee having any reason to resume hostilities."

"No, that we do not," said the elven woman. Her voice was soft and musical, like the cadence of bugs singing in the evening. "We would, however, like to see the tree that is now Anakrim's home."

"That is not a good idea," said Tara-lin. "An angry dryad can be dangerous, and I'm sure Anakrim is very angry, though it will probably take a while for him to adjust to his new mode of existence."

Both Erenvin and his presumed-sister nodded. She spoke again. "We were led to believe that King Anakrim was the elder of Princess Ithrìl's sons. How is it, then, that you, Keller, are the elder?"

Tara-lin and Keller glanced at each other. "What?!" formed on their lips. Keller turned back to the two elves. "Really?" he asked.

"Yes," said Erenvin. "Not that I care. Anakrim is a dryad, now – though, like Arilim here, my sister, I would like to see this – and so cannot rule us. If the dryads choose to make him a dryad, who are we elves to dispute their choice? We certainly cannot undo it, and that leaves you, whether the elder or the younger son, as the Heir."

If they insist, I suppose I must show Anakrim's new state to them, but I would rather not do it now. I am too tired to fight dryad-magic right now, though I suppose it might be best to show them as soon as possible, for it is not possible that Anakrim will have yet adjusted to being a dryad. She smiled to herself as her thoughts went on. *Though this is so strange. Not a full elf, but a half-elf, one with only half the dryadic blood of most elves, is found to be a singer and learns her art from the dryads themselves, and is called 'Dryad-Friend' and given secrets which the dryads have never before revealed to any others. Yet another half-elf becomes not even a singer but a dryad himself! This world is very strange.*

Then again, thought Tara-lin, *if he is not yet adjusted to his new mode of life, it may be impossible for the elves even to be convinced that he is there at all. I would know, but that does not mean others would.*

Keller turned to her. "When do you want to show them Anakrim?"

"I want to speak to the other dryads about it first," said Tara-lin. "Perhaps tomorrow."

"Very well," said Keller. "We will ride into the city now."

Tara-lin and Keller mounted their steeds and a company hand-picked and trained by Eldazìn and Namdon formed up around them. Erenvin rode ahead of them with his two companions.

The crowd of elves who had come with them to Frèlin erupted into cheers. "King Keller! Queen Tara-lin!" they began to cry.

Tara-lin turned to Akanë. "What? I'm not even Queen yet. No one has yet accepted or crowned Keller King."

"They are announcing *their* support of you as King and Queen," said Akanë.

"I don't like it," said Tara-lin. *I don't like it at all,* she repeated to herself. *It all feels wrong.*

She and Keller rode into the city, and the Guard of Frèlin went before and behind them. As they passed through the open white and silver gates, cheers erupted from within the city also. There were cries of "Singer! Singer! The Singer of Elethri!"

Tara-lin wanted to hide from all the noise and clamor. She would have wanted to hide even if she were not the object of attention. Now, she wanted to run to the other side of the world. She wanted to hide in the deep, dark recesses of some forest closed even to the elves. She remembered being embraced by a dryad and drawn almost into the dryadic mode of existence and wished for a moment that she, like Anakrim, could become a dryad.

The atmosphere felt volatile to her. She could almost feel the elven complacency she and Eldor had discussed years earlier when they had ridden together into this very city, the first time she had ever seen a city. They might laud her. They might be thrilled to have a singer again. They might even be thrilled to have this singer for their Queen. But there was no real conviction in their hearts, no real understanding of what made a monarch good or bad, no interest in the question even. They probably *would* support her and Keller against any other contestants, and they might mourn her if she were killed, but they would easily accept another. Many of them accepted her and Keller now no differently than they had accepted Anakrim ten years earlier.

For the first time, as she rode through the city, Tara-lin hardly noticed its beauty. They climbed the terraces and crossed the rings of water, but she was scarcely aware of it. Amidst the cheers of thousands of elves, Keller and Tara-lin rode with their honor guard into the outer courtyard of the palace.

"This is so strange," said Keller to Tara-lin.

"I'm glad you finally realized it," she retorted.

* * * * * * *

Keller and Tara-lin gave an address to the elves who crowded the streets and meadows of Frèlin City. Tara-lin did not remember what either of them said once they were finished. She, Keller, and their inner counsel, including her parents, Alis, and Eldazìn, crowded into a large room in one wing of the palace.

"Keller," asked Eldazìn, "are you up to setting a ward to prevent anyone outside this room from hearing a word we say?"

Keller shook his head. "I don't know. If I could manage, I wouldn't be able to hear a word you said when I was done."

Eldazìn nodded. "Perhaps we should all take a nap and talk afterwards."

"You have news I don't know about, right?" asked Tara-lin.

Eldazìn looked at her sharply. "That's for after your spouse sets the ward."

Tara-lin nodded. "I wasn't asking you to tell me right now." She paused and fingered her dress. "Well then, why don't we find a couple different rooms? I don't think everyone here would be comfortable sleeping in the same room."

"There's no need to find a room for me," said Alis. "Get me when you're ready. I'm going with Kushon to look for a good eyre for the gryphons."

"Very well," said Eldazìn. "Thank you, Alis. For the rest of you, try to fit into as few rooms as possible. I'm a bit short-handed at the moment."

There's definitely something I don't know about, thought Tara-lin. She caught her father looking at her. Her brother was romping around the room playing with the Princess Elisa's son, who, while about the same age as himself, seemed half his age. *It probably means Oranë and Elisa and their son shouldn't be here yet. Dad and Mom and Lyan shouldn't be here yet. Why did they all follow us? But I remember that conversation. 'If Anakrim is victorious, no one will be safe long. He will hunt us out and destroy us. There is no where we can hide long,' they said. But, still, how does it help for them to be here* now? *Then again, I sometimes really like their advice. I trust Eldor as I don't trust Eldazìn, and I think Eldor even knows more. And they thought they might actually be less safe in the valley than with me, for once I and the dryads and many others departed, they would be vulnerable in the valley to any hunters sent by Anakrim to find and destroy us. Still, I don't like this. I don't like this at all. And I do not want to live in this palace for the rest of my life! Indeed, I am not going to. Once I am installed as Queen of Elethri, this city changes. I am going to sleep in the trees as I have done all my life. If this tower comes down, so be it! But I don't want to live in a city at all. Too many people too close together. Cities don't belong in the world. Nations don't belong in the world. Kings and queens don't belong in the world. Unfortunately, however, I am literally just a few steps away from being a queen myself. I might as well be queen already. It's just not official yet. Already, to judge from Eldazìn's comment, I am going to have to deal with the troubles of ruling.*

Anyway, we should at least make ourselves comfortable. Whatever bedding is used in this palace we might as well accumulate in whatever room or rooms we are going to use.

.. * ＊ ＊ ＊ * ..

As tired as she was, Tara-lin did not feel like sleeping. After some bedding had been found and arrangements had been made for those who wished to sleep, Tara-lin found herself walking back and forth along one wall. Keller snored against the other, and occasional vibrations in the stone told her that Lyan and Anuil were playing, probably with their parents, in the next room over. She wondered if she should join them, then thought better of it. She was deeply disturbed and, if she went over, she would only interfere with the fun by trying to get someone – probably her father – to engage with her problems.

Yet more problems with being Queen! Tara-lin thought, hissing under her breath. *I must find a way to deal with all these problems and still be able to play. No one is meant to be King or Queen. No one! I don't think humans are made for the role. I know dryads are not made for the role. I cannot imagine humans are made for the role. I know I am not. And the feelings of the elves for me are not quite right. It's just ... wrong. Never mind the fact I don't* want *to be felt about, one way or another, by so many people. I am not a fit receptacle for their loyalty or applause. I don't know if the problem is that men and elves want to be ruled when they should not want to be ruled, or if the problem is that they want to be ruled by another of their kind, instead of being ruled by Shallim-Araldor. I've heard it said he is the King of Dryads, but the dryads hardly seem to know enough of him for him to be their king. At least, it seems so to me. Alis seems to have some sort of a relationship with him. I can't say that I do. It's all very strange. Anyway, either way, I am not meant to be Queen of Elethri. There is not meant to be an elven king or queen. At least, the elves are not meant to feel and think about their monarchs the way they evidently do, and I am not meant to be Queen. But my father says no one else is more suited for it.* She spun on her heel and marched back across the room. *But the elves will have a queen, and will have me for that queen. I don't know if they will have me for Queen because I am married to Keller, or if they will have Keller for King because he is married to me, but either way, here we are, and we must rule Elethri. But I'd better not growl too loudly under my breath or I might wake Keller.*

Suddenly, Tara-lin realized she was thirsty. She went to the door and opened it slightly. In the hall, she found their honor guard standing at attention. *This is all so strange! I* must *know what is going on here! I* must *know what has possessed Eldazìn, what it is he knows that I don't. I* must! She screamed inwardly.

"What is it you wish, Lady?" asked Akanë.

"I'm thirsty. And hungry, too," said Tara-lin. "And I'm still Tara-lin. I shall always be Tara-lin, even when I am crowned."

"I am sorry, T-tara-lin," said Akanë. "I will order refreshments brought to you. Is there anything Keller would like?"

"Last I knew, Keller was fast asleep," replied Tara-lin. *What I really want is to talk to the dryads. But here I am, feeling like a prisoner. I'm supposed to be Queen, and I feel like a prisoner. Maybe I should just announce I'm going out into the woods? I should have gone with Alis! How could I possibly be so stupid? Oh yes. I am so stupid because I am tired and overwhelmed and over-stimulated. That is why I am so stupid.* She sighed and tried to fight back tears. Should she simply announce she was going to ride out and talk to the dryads? If she did so, they *would* doubtless let her. Either that, or she would know herself betrayed by Eldazìn, or at least Akanë. She would know that she was to be Queen of Elethri in name only, that someone was scheming, that the treachery of the Valor Hall had somehow entered even into that secluded valley among the magic of the dryads.

Was her reluctance to ignore her advisors' expressly-stated wishes a result of fear that they were traitors and a desire not to face it if they were, or was it a result of consideration that they might actually know something she did not, something important?

There's got to be some secret tunnel somewhere in this place that connects to the forest outside the walls. And in that forest there has got to be a dryad who is not so damaged by Anakrim's witchery that he or she can't talk to me, thought Tara-lin. *All this stone around me feels like a tomb! How did the elves ever end up building such a palace for themselves? Perhaps this, right here, in which I stand, is the beginning of our decline as a race. It will be torn down!*

Tara-lin was about to make her way out of the palace, when she thought something else. Even if they let her, would she miss knowing whatever it was Eldazìn was going to reveal? Never mind! Let them get her when they wanted. It was not like she was going to disappear and never come back. It was not like she was going to leave Keller.

Tara-lin addressed Akanë. "Never mind. When the refreshments are brought, let whoever wants eat them. I am going to go visit with friends."

"What do you mean? Aren't all your friends here? Will you be able to find Alis?"

"I am going to go visit with friends. You forget that the trees and dryads are friends to me as they are not to most elves. I am going outside Frèlin."

"Very well. I will detail a portion of our guard to accompany you," said Akanë.

"No!" said Tara-lin. "No, you will not. I go to speak with the dryads *alone*. I am Queen, or am I not? If I am not, I am not!"

"But, Lady, Tara-lin, Princess, Queen, Your Royal Highness, whatever I am to call you, it is not wise for such a personage as yourself to do this."

"It is perfectly wise," answered Tara-lin. "I am the Singer of Elethri. And if there is danger, what will *your* guard do? No. I command you not to come after me." With that she spun and ran down the corridor.

Tara-lin pulled the hood of her elethrian cloak over her face. Yes! That was the way to do it! She had to slip into an unoccupied room with a window and get out that way. She did not fear being stopped, but she did fear being followed.

.. ✳ ✳ ✳ ✳ ✳ ..

Once she was out of the city, Tara-lin found herself making directly for Anakrim's tree. She approached the tree, which stood somewhat apart in a medium-sized glade. Other trees were nearby, but it was not overcrowded.

The whisper in the tree's leaves spoke to her. "You! You who have imprisoned me, bound me in this tree," it seemed to be saying.

"Don't get your hopes up, Anakrim," said Tara-lin softly. "You will not best me. I have lived through encounters with corrupted dryads who had ages longer than you have lived to hone their skills, and that was when I was inexperienced and did not know what I was doing. I will not make that mistake again, but you are a fool. I have not imprisoned you. The prison is all of your own making."

"No. It is your making. It is your revenge." Tara-lin clearly understood the sentiment behind the quivering of the tree.

"What have I to take revenge upon you for, Anakrim? Nor do dryads take revenge. It is outside our nature. When you sought our life, when you sought our magic, you opened yourself up to this. You must know by now – you are descended of dryads as well as of men. You fought against your own existence. Had you succeeded in stealing all the magic of the dryads you likely would have killed yourself. What was it you were hoping to achieve? Was it power merely, or did you desire also the life of the dryads? Well, that life you shall now taste. Unless some misfortune befalls you or your tree, you shall live many hundreds of years. Perhaps, you will learn to know peace. Perhaps here, in the heart of Elethri, bound body and soul to a tree, you can begin to be cured of the curse of Nightshade into which you were born," answered Tara-lin. She gathered her thoughts together and sang. She still did not know how much he had acclimated to his new existence, how easily he would be able to shift the energy of his life in order to understand her when she spoke after the fashion of men.

Unhappiness raged all through Anakrim's leaves, and Tara-lin tried to make him understand she meant him no harm, not that he would be likely to believe her since he considered his new existence a kind of harm. *Perhaps,* she thought, *being so connected to the world he can begin to know life. What a deadening horror it must have been to grow up buried in Nightshade Castle! Not that it is any certainty being a dryad will lead him out of corruption, for dryads have been corrupted themselves. Still, I hope it will be a beginning for him.*

At last, Tara-lin turned from Anakrim and raised her arms to the sky. A very mild sweet wind blew through her hair. All around her she could hear the soft rejoicing song of the dryads and their trees, as the magic Anakrim had stolen flowed back into their realm. Despite all the questions she still had, she felt her weariness lift as the energy touched even her. For a moment she was reminded of standing on a ridge of the Icecrown Mountains, looking down on the Icecrown Vale and on Nightshade Castle, and knowing that where that horrible monstrosity now slumped something good and beautiful and full of life was meant to stand. In that moment the world felt so right that Tara-lin hoped the estrangement which her dryad friend Aumoura had said would arise between the dryads and their elven kin might not come to pass, but that the wound between them would be healed.

Tara-lin managed to sneak her way back into the palace shortly after night fell. As she made her way through the city she could not escape the sense of wrongness. She *hated* the place. It was *much* more beautiful, much nicer, than any of the human cities she had seen, but she felt more strongly than ever that she did not want to live in such a place. When she had been in human cities, even in Astri, it had been only for a short while, only to visit. Now, with the prospect of having to rule Elethri from this place before her, she knew she could not live in a city. She most definitely could not live in that intricate chamber of stone they called the palace. She hated to leave the woods, too. She felt like they were calling to her. But she had to go back. She would not want her friends, her parents, or her spouse to worry about her. She definitely would not want Keller to feel like she ran away and left him.

She *did* want to run away from Elethri, though.

Tara-lin entered the room where they had all been gathered earlier that day. Keller was sitting on the edge of the bed. Eldazìn sat on one side of him. On the other side sat Eldor and Lìrulin. Oranë sat next to Eldazìn, and Akanë was seated upon the bed right behind him. Alis stood against the wall. Somehow her gryphon had managed to squeeze through the doorway, and he stood next to her. Tara-lin surveyed the whole room, picking out Namdon and Cuthlin also, and asked, "Where's my brother and Elisa and Anuil?"

"Elisa is playing with the children in the room next to this," answered Lìrulin.

"Oh," said Tara-lin. She was aware of Eldazìn's gaze boring into her. "Where should I sit?" she asked.

Eldor and Lìrulin shifted themselves on the floor, making an open spot right next to Keller. Tara-lin immediately made for it.

"Is the ward set, Keller?" asked Eldazìn.

"Yes, the ward is set," said Keller, "but a wizard could definitely break it. I don't know about a singer or a dryad."

"It is enough," said Eldazìn. "We fear no evil from the dryads. I doubt there is any wizard in Elethri yet. I have my men posted here to guard us and they are also guarding the portal." He shifted so that he could look into Tara-lin's eyes. "Why did you do leave?" he asked.

Tara-lin was silent for a moment, considering her response. She could feel Keller sitting beside her. She could almost feel his confidence in her. "Why do you ask me that?" she asked.

Eldazìn let out a huge sigh. "I did not think you were this foolish, Tara-lin. It was dangerous."

"You refused to tell me what you knew that I did not. I did not see how it was dangerous and still do not see how it was dangerous. And all this stone around me feels like a tomb."

"Were you aware that you were followed?" asked Eldazìn.

"Did you then follow me?" asked Tara-lin. "I am not surprised."

"Tara-lin, I am not your enemy, but you are a fool," said Eldazìn.

Keller spoke then. "Eldazìn, do you really know that? I know none of us here know whatever it is you wanted to say to us yet, but if she does not know something, she can hardly be called a fool for not taking it into account. She is the Singer, and I doubt *you* have a full appreciation of her needs or capabilities."

"She might be able to lose almost any human without trying, Keller, but she is not such an exceptional woodswoman among the elves. All of us here know that she has skills which far surpass even my comprehension, but I have skills which far surpass hers — and so do many other elves, some of whom may be her enemies."

"No one doubts, Eldazìn, that you have skills I do not," said Tara-lin, "but you should tell us what you know instead of suggesting that your Queen is a fool. You explain yourself to me; then, perhaps, I shall explain myself to you."

"Very well," said Eldazìn. "As you wish. I have captured many of those who participated in the assassinations surrounding Anakrim's rise to the throne, but I am certain that I have missed some of them. They may be lurking even among Erenvin's Guard."

"I presume," said Tara-lin softly, "that you are short-handed because you have committed many of your men to guarding these traitors? Or have you killed them yourself? How do you know no spies lurk within your own, I seem to recall you once called it impromptu, organization?"

A cloud passed over Eldazìn's eyes. "If you must know, some of these assassins I have killed. I had no other choice, when I was trying to get Oranë and Elisa out of the palace alive. However, I am an elf, and, as such, possess an aversion to violence and bloodshed. You are correct in assuming I have many of them under guard. As for how I know that I have no spies within my own ranks, if you must know, I did, and at first I did not know it. But I have tried to learn. The extent of the corruption you, Sir Eldor, and Namdon, and Cuthlin, found within the Valor Hall, made me reconsider the loyalty of those whom I had working for me. I *hope* I have successfully ferreted out all the spies."

"And what did you do with them?" asked Lìrulin.

Tara-lin caught Alis looking at her with approval. Then she returned her attention to Eldazìn.

"If you must know," he said, very quietly and gravely, "I killed them."

Now I know why he was so insistent that the valley was not safe. Doubtless, he had traitors in his ranks who might have reported our location to our enemies! And, even now, I don't think he's sure he has all traitors out of his ranks. If he is telling the truth, now. He should not have hid this from Keller and myself.

"And," said Keller, "why are you bringing this all to our attention now, and not earlier?"

Eldazìn hissed between his teeth. "While you were fighting Anakrim, *I* was hunting and capturing spies and assassins. I did not have anything to do with them previously, but when you fought Anakrim it was clear that we would either lose or win. If we lost, it would not matter if I revealed myself. If we won, I would finally have a place to guard the captured spies and assassins."

"And how does any of this have anything to do with why I should not go out to hold concourse with my dryad friends?" asked Tara-lin.

Eldazìn moved in a blur and came to a rest crouched with a small knife in his hand. "If I wanted you to be, you would be dead right now, Tara-lin. I believe that I may be the best among the elves, though I have practiced these arts because they appeal to my sense of excitement and vanity, and not out of any true desire to kill, but there are others who are nearly as good as myself. Some of those others may have escaped my attention. Some of those others may desire your death."

Tara-lin laughed and shook her head. Her ruby hair, the color of new leaves, swirled about her light brown face. "Eldazìn, I know better than to let my life be ruled by fear. I have been into Nightshade Castle itself. I have fought and vanquished three wailing wights. I know better than to fear. I had to, I had to learn; else I would not have survived. *Might. May. Death.* These are the words of fear. Fear will take your life; fear will kill you; fear will drag you into the depths of Nightshade. And if I am to rule Elethri, fear will never make me a good queen."

"No," said Eldazìn, "but over-haste and recklessness will make you a dead queen before you start. It is not fear I advocate, but caution."

"It is fear," said Tara-lin. "Fear that would entomb me. This palace was never made for elves to live within. It is no place for the dryad-kin."

At that moment, someone rapped a distinctly-patterned tattoo on the door. Eldazìn stood.

"What is it?" asked Lìrulin.

"A signal of mine," said Eldazìn, going to the door and opening it.

An elf known to Eldazìn – and whom Tara-lin had barely seen before – entered. "I've just received a message that a personage from the Valor Hall has come through the portal in the tower. We have apprehended him."

Eldazìn nodded. "Thank you. Do you know anything else?"

"Very little. This personage knows that something has changed in Frèlin. He wishes to know if there is a problem and expresses his wishes that King Anakrim is alive and well. I know little else," answered the elf.

"I thank you, again," said Eldazìn. "I will send for you when I require it." With that, the elf closed the door. As soon as it was closed, Cuthlin, who had already gotten to his feet, said, "What is that about? I wonder how the Valor Hall has sold it to the peoples of the Alliance that their arch-enemy Anakrim is now King of Elethri and part of the Northern Alliance."

"They may not know," said Namdon, "that Anakrim and Elethri were allied with the Valor Hall. It may have been unofficial. Furthermore, there are all kinds of things they might have said. They might have cast Anakrim in the light of one who has changed from his father's ways. Perhaps, when he was at last free of Falkur's power, he changed his ways. We know that is the story he has told in Elethri."

"But what about that stuff about how he had to be stopped because he was doing something, stealing some life or something, to make himself a wizard?" asked Tara-lin.

"The common people may never have known it," said Eldor. "Most even of the nobility may not have known the details. Besides, the Valor Hall could say they were mistaken if anyone did get suspicious."

"We have to do something!" said Cuthlin. "We have to let the people know!"

"First," said Eldazìn, "we need to decide what we are to tell this diplomat or what we are to do with him. *This* is where Elethri stands on the brink of war." He turned to look at Tara-lin and Keller. "This is also where the elves may decide you will not make a good King and Queen if your leadership draws Elethri into war."

"Why not just tell him the truth?" said Tara-lin. "Tell him the dryads were unhappy with Anakrim's magic and raised up a singer through which to make him a dryad in reparation for his crimes against the trees, and that his older brother, the Prince Keller, is now Heir Apparent to the throne of Elethri."

"Let us tell him that," said Keller. "Let me tell him that. In fact, bring him here before me. Then, we will have to figure out what to do with that portal. I do not like having it there."

"I've already decided we need to tear this whole place down. Elves were never supposed to dwell entombed in stone," said Tara-lin.

"By the deep forest, I like that idea!" said Keller. "Did we not also receive an invitation to dinner?"

"Yes," said Eldazìn, "and that dinner begins in a few minutes."

"Send one of your men to tell the elves to prepare it on the sward. I and Tara-lin will speak to them again after dinner. Meanwhile, bring the diplomat to us and we will speak to him," said Keller.

"As you wish, my lord," said Eldazìn, bowing after the elven fashion. "However, I would advise you to prepare a more formal arrangement for your audience. Tell any of the guards and he or she will ensure the diplomat is properly conducted to the hall of your audience." He then departed.

"I want a room with a window that looks out on the forest that clothes the side of the mountain," said Tara-lin, rising.

"Then let us make such ready," said Keller, rising after her. "Let's also entertain him ourselves."

"Very well," said Tara-lin. "Why?"

"You're concerned about war, right?" asked Keller.

"Yes," said Tara-lin.

"What happens when the diplomat carries word back to the Valor Hall that Alis Luela is here?" asked Keller.

"Oh!" said Tara-lin. "Yes, I see your meaning. Still, it will have to be dealt with sooner rather than later."

"It will," said Eldor, "but better when you are firm on the throne of Elethri than now. It would look too inviting to try to ruin your reign before it has begun."

Both Namdon and Cuthlin nodded.

"Well, let's find a fit chamber for our audience," said Tara-lin. "Rooms with no windows are evil."

"Do you really think so?" asked Keller. "I find myself that it reminds me too much of Nightshade Castle, but I did not know whether that was just because I'd never been in any other building. I was too exhausted at first to notice, but since I woke up I have not liked it."

"I don't know about evil, exactly," said Tara-lin. She had opened the door and moved into the hallway now, and she interrupted her conversation with her spouse to inquire if anyone knew of an appropriate room. Returning her attention to Keller, she said, "As I was saying, I don't know about evil exactly, but certainly not fitting for the children of dryads. And if it reminds you of Nightshade Castle, that is certainly very interesting. I am so sorry. That must have been horrible."

"Let's just say I fully endorse your plan to rip this place down. I'm not sure what we will put in its place, for we will need some kind of a place to hold court and have audiences," said Keller.

"We will figure something out. We do not have to figure everything out tonight," said Tara-lin.

$$. \bullet \; \ast \; \maltese \; \maltese \; \maltese \; \ast \; \bullet .$$

Tara-lin and Keller had barely seated themselves in ornate elven-crafted chairs, their backs against the window from which a breeze flowed into the room, when Akanë escorted the Valor Knight who had been chosen as a diplomat into the room. The Valor Knight saw Keller and Tara-lin seated and executed a bow in the fashion of the Valor Hall. "Greetings, fair lord and lady," he said. "May I ask to be introduced?"

"Yes," answered Keller. "I am the Prince Keller and Heir Apparent to the throne of Elethri, the firstborn son of the Princess Ithrìl, only child of King Orenduil and Queen Alaria. This is my spouse, the Princess Tara-lin, Singer of Elethri."

"It is a pleasure to meet you, Prince Keller ... Princess Tara-lin," said the Valor Knight. "My own name is Kennor. May I ask what is the meaning of this audience? How are you come to be here as Heirs Apparent of Elethri?"

"It is the work of dryads. The previous King of Elethri, Anakrim, had offended against them, by improperly using their magic, and they have decided that he should be a dryad himself in order to atone for his crimes. They have done this through my spouse, whom they gifted with their magic. Anakrim can no more be the King of Elethri, and so the crown now falls to me, the rightful Heir," answered Keller.

"I see. It is indeed a pleasure to meet you," said the Valor Knight. "On behalf of the Valor Hall, I wish Anakrim well in his life as a dryad, and I wish you well in your reign. Have you any message to the Valor Hall and the rest of the Valor Alliance for me as the new rulers of Elethri?"

"Not yet," said Keller. "We will send word when we have it."

"Very well. We at the Valor Hall will eagerly await your word. Shall I feast with you now, or shall I return to the Valor Hall?" asked Kennor.

"You may return to the Valor Hall," said Keller.

When Kennor had left, escorted by Akanë, Tara-lin looked at Keller and said, "This business of being King and Queen is *really* strange."

"It really is, isn't it?" said Keller, returning her look and laughing. "It is *so* weird."

"Well," said Tara-lin, "now we have a banquet to attend, and you said that we will speak, and I don't know what we will say, and then we have to deal with Eldazìn's prisoners, and who-knows-what-else, before we can even begin to get to the things which interest us."

Keller rose and took Tara-lin's hand. "No. We begin to get to the things which interest us tonight, my dear. Tell the elves about *your* vision for Elethri. Tell them how *you* will lead them back into friendship with the dryads. Tell them how you will lead them back into the legacy and glory and magic of their race. Tell them how you will tear down this palace, which is modeled on human cities and palaces, and will instead dwell in a manner suitable to a Dryad-Friend."

"Sure, I guess," said Tara-lin. "I'm not sure I know how."

"If you don't know how, then sing to them," said Keller.

"That I'm really not sure about. Did I ever tell you what happened the first – and only – time I've ever sung to an audience?"

"No, I don't think you did," said Keller.

"It was *horrible.*" Keller did not immediately respond, and Tara-lin went on to say, "And how are you going to talk to them? You've never done anything like this before!"

"There's a first time for everything," said Keller, laughing again. "And I feel so rejuvenated by your plan to tear down this palace of stone. I think you called it a tomb."

"That I did," said Tara-lin.

Just then, their paths crossed that of Lìrulin, who was trailed by Lyan. "How did the audience with the diplomat go?" asked Lìrulin.

"Fine," said Tara-lin. "Keller did all the talking – quite well, actually. He's probably back in the Valor Hall by now. We're going to have to guard the portal until we find a way to dismantle it."

Lyan ran up to Tara-lin and threw his arms around her. "I've missed you all day, Tara-lin!" he said.

"I know, Lyan," said Tara-lin, running her fingers through his dark green hair. "I've missed you, too. We'll have to find a good place to play tomorrow."

"That will be fun!" said Lyan.

"Right now, though, I have to attend a banquet and take care of the business of being Queen."

"I forgot you were a queen," said Lyan. "It's really weird. What's it like being Queen?"

"It's annoying. Not fun," said Tara-lin. "I know. It is really weird. I'm going to forget it myself one of these days. And I'm not Queen yet. Not quite. But I might as well be. I'll play with you tomorrow. If I can't figure out how tomorrow, I'll make sure it's the day after that."

Chapter Five – Call of the Forest

"Elethrians!" Keller's voice carried far on the night-breeze with his first word. Tara-lin, who stood beside him on the wall of the palace, reflected that he was no longer the frail-looking thin man, as light as a plant that has seen no sun, whom she first found on Anakrim's witchery table. He was tall – not tall for an elf, but only a little short – and broader than most elves. He had darkened, as well. His eyes were the same blue she had first seen, but his hair, though still light and silvery, was much darker than it had been, and his skin was darker as well, though still substantially lighter than her own skin. "Elethrians, in the space of only a little over a decade much evil has befallen you. You learned that your Princess, Ithrìl, my mother, was dead. Shortly thereafter, your King and Queen, Orenduil and Alaria, died, along with most of the royal family. Anakrim rose up to rule you, offering himself as one unfortunately arriving in the nick of time and in a time of tragedy, and as one who could teach you anew the lost secrets of your magic. You then learned that he had lied to you, that his magic was not the restoration of your ancient magic which worked in concert with the dryads, but that his magic stole life from the forests and dryads and harmed them. Many of you may now wonder if more harm is coming to Elethri, now that another half-elf and his half-elf spouse stand in line for the throne and prepare to rule these ancient and beautiful forests. I do not think that I can assuage your fears without time showing that I am not like he who ruled before me. I can tell you my own past, one which I shudder to remember and which still haunts me in nightmares, one where I was cut off from my mother at an early age, tormented by Wizard Falkur for reasons I could not understand, later tormented by Anakrim, my brother, as he sought the magic with which I had been born, and which I did not understand, for himself. But anyone could say these things, nor would the fact that I fell afoul of him who kidnapped my mother and of my younger brother necessarily warrant that I would be a different kind of man.

"Perhaps, you accept me as your future King because I came to you in the company of ten thousand dryads. Many of you mourn the lost days when elves and dryads were close, when it was not the event of a lifetime for an elf to sight a dryad. Many of your hearts thrill within you, for just this morning you saw, not a dryad, but hundreds upon hundreds and thousands upon thousands of dryads. You had hoped, but without certainty, to someday see and speak with a dryad, and while you have not yet spoken to a dryad, yet you have seen not one dryad but many dryads.

"I now suggestto you what may be a reason why the dryads and the elves have grown apart for so many years. Have any of you wondered why we have banqueted in these lawns, instead of in the central tower of the palace?

"Yes. Elves were never meant to live in halls of stone. When we try to live like humans, it damages our connection to the dryads. When we erect halls and palaces of stone, as do the humans, we become more like humans and less like the dryads. We insulate ourselves from the song of the dryads which, inaudible, sweeps at all times through the forest. We erect barriers between ourselves and the wild, fey, and living magic of our birth. Slowly, that barrier begins to affect us, to cut us off from our own selves, to make it harder for us to touch the world of the dryads which is one with the world of our magic. It renders it difficult, it renders our capability to see and hear and feel the magic and life of the dryads weak and dull. For that reason, Oh Elethrians, one of our first acts when I and Tara-lin are crowned King and Queen will be to tear down this palace that is the symbol and beginning of our decline and estrangement from the dryads. Do not worry! The ancient light that hovers above the tower will be preserved. Perhaps we will even learn anew how to make them.

"But now I will step aside and the Princess Tara-lin will speak to you."

In the moment of applause that followed, Tara-lin leaned in close to Keller. "Could you manage another of those amplification spells?" she whispered. "I don't think my voice will carry as yours does."

Keller shook his head. "I can't materialize magic in my mind at all right now. Just say a few words, or sing. I've heard you sing enough, I think your song will float very nicely on the wind. Even if they can't hear your words, they'll hear your song."

"I know *that*," said Tara-lin. She pulled herself together. "I don't know if you can hear me, but I don't have anything to add to what my spouse has just said!" she yelled. "Instead, I will sing to you." *This is so strange, this is* so *weird*, Tara-lin thought. She closed her eyes and reached out. She felt the whole forest as if it were a living, breathing thing, but also a community of living, breathing things, hundreds and thousands of dryads and even more trees, and whatever teeming millions of living things made their homes with the dryads and the trees. She selected a single note on which to start and held it for a long moment, starting steady, then allowing her voice to warble a little. When her breath ran out, she selected another note and did the same thing with it.

Slowly Tara-lin began to sing, not now trying to work magic. She was, after all, a bit tired for that. She tried only to join the dryads in their song. As such, her song had a very slow rhythm and beat to it, corresponding to the slowness of the life of the forest and the lives of trees and dryads. The song by which she had transformed the mode of Anakrim's life had further deepened her understanding, and though she had not had time to process this deepened understanding, it entered into her singing and her ability to hear the dryads. She had developed a new ability within her ability and could sing with the whole forest.

Tara-lin became aware of Keller's hand gripping her shoulder. She stopped singing and looked at him. "What?" she asked, then almost shrank at the applause of Elethri. She had almost forgotten where she was and what she was doing.

"You have sung long enough, and I don't want you to wear yourself out," whispered Keller.

Tara-lin nodded.

.。* ✸ ✱ ✸ *。.

When they descended from the wall a few moments later, Eldazìn stood before them. "I heard that as well as any elf, Keller," he said. "Where are you going to sleep? How will you be guarded?"

"We will figure something out," said Keller. "Right now, we need to go to sleep."

"Inside the palace?" asked Eldazìn.

Alis stepped out of the shadows. "No. But they can certainly sleep in the eyre if they wish."

"That way there will be no reason for your guard at all, Eldazìn. You can all rest and amuse yourselves as you please," said Tara-lin.

Eldazìn bowed. "Very well, but make sure you come down early tomorrow. I was not able to discuss half of what I wanted tonight."

"Kushon does not usually like to carry anyone other than myself, but he will be happy to oblige you tonight," said Alis. "Follow me."

As they followed Alis, Keller said to Tara-lin, "Eldazìn is ... irritating."

"That he is." Tara-lin paused, ensuring that he had not followed them and was not going to overhear what she said next, then spoke quietly. "He thinks he knows better than we do. He thinks he's smarter than we are. I did not notice this bent of his in the valley."

"Neither did I, much," said Keller. "We are going to have to manage him."

"His behavior makes me doubt his trustworthiness," said Tara-lin. "Sometimes, I feel like he is trying to intimidate me."

"I noticed that. I don't think he means us any harm, but I do think he thinks he knows better. I think his point there was what it sounded like. He did not want you to fear him, but to fear others – others whom he, in some measure, fears himself."

"Well, I realize now, why he could not make a good king for Elethri. He is too ... he fears too much, and I think ... I think he is not well-aware enough of how much lies beyond his experience and knowledge. I still ... don't feel like I can fully trust him," said Tara-lin.

"This thing about being King and Queen is so tricky and complicated," said Keller. "I suggest we be together and sleep and take it up again tomorrow."

"That sounds like a great idea," said Tara-lin. She laughed.

"It really does," said Alis. "And, really, ask me for my opinion more!"

"What did you have an opinion on, Alis? I'm always interested in your opinions. You know that."

"Well, I think you need to make sure Eldazìn doesn't boss you around. He has gotten very bossy. And I think you shouldn't *just* rip down the palace. I think you should build a tower or re-do the tower, or some-thing. It should be tall, and sturdy enough to support itself, but it should be open to the wind. The air should blow through it. And I think you are right about Eldazìn and fear. I think your description of the palace as a tomb is apt. I don't feel it the way you do, but I do feel it. It seems Eldazìn wants to enclose himself in a tomb. He's afraid, of treachery, of daggers, of intrigue, of whatever it is, and he wants to wall himself up to protect himself. Maybe that is why he has gotten bossy, but I think he has his own ideas of how to do things in his head, and I think he thinks you two are naïve and inexperienced and do not know what you are doing. Of course, I think his fear and his ideas are related. But I think you did not notice he was bossy in the valley because, well, you, Keller, had not even developed a concept of what was going on and what you were doing, and you, Tara-lin, talked a lot about how incompetent and unsuitable you were – not to mention, about how he seemed much more competent and suitable. And, well, I think he's willing to accept that you can sing and he has to accept that the magic of the dryads works in such a way that he cannot understand what you are doing, certainly not ahead of time, so he was willing not to interfere with or advise you, and certainly not to try to boss you on that. But I think he is certain that neither of you have any idea how to rule.

"But I like your idea of how to rule much better than his," said Alis, laughing. She motioned for them to stop. They had now reached the rocks of the mountain that rose up behind the palace and the tower. In the relative quiet, Tara-lin heard the soft brush of Kushon's wings on the air as he glided towards them.

When Kushon landed, Alis stepped up to him and stroked him under his mane and wings. Then she said, "He's not well-pleased, but I trust him to behave. He will carry Keller and Tara-lin to the eyres. Then we'll figure out which cave they want to have to themselves."

At that moment Tara-lin remembered something. "What about the others? Mom and Dad and Lyan? What about Oranë and Elisa and Anuil? I'm *sure* Lìrulin doesn't want to sleep in that palace. She's not a singer, but she's as close to the woods as I am."

"That is taken care of already," said Alis.

"Care to tell me about it?" asked Tara-lin.

"Lìrulin is even better at sneaking around than Eldazìn," said Alis. "Which of you wants to go first? Kushon is impatient to have done with this."

"I don't really care," said Keller. "But I wanted to tell you that I really like your idea about the tower."

"Well, thanks," said Alis. "It was pretty obvious, and I'm sure either one of you would have thought of it tomorrow morning, after you've had some rest."

.．＊ ＊ ＊ ＊ ＊．．

Tara-lin lay awake. The stars shone in the sky above her. Their beauty beckoned, as they twinkled above in stately glory, white and red and blue and green fires in their hearts. They looked cold but not cold, hot but not as she knew hot. They spangled the sky with untold glory. Questions and thoughts raced through Tara-lin's mind. The winds. She had felt as if the winds sang with her, sang in her song. Did the winds have any personality? Were they, too, some kind of spirit? Now she looked at the stars. Far away and far above, were they wholly unlike men and dryads – indwelt by spirits of magic and glory? Hints, bits and pieces of understanding of the song she had woven with the dryads, teased Tara-lin's mind.

She laid the covers aside and stood, carefully so as not to wake Keller. Weariness, or something like weariness, and the desire to sleep were strong upon her, but she could not sleep. She did not want to sleep *here*. She stood still and felt the night-breeze wrap its cool fingers around her. Above her the stars twinkled in all their glory and magic. Below her, shrouded in darkness, lay the forests of Elethri, their trees and dryads, all in slumbering wakefulness, in a soft song of dreams, bright and shadowy and dim and colorful with all the life of that world, a world which called to itself images of the under-sea. It felt as if the forests called to her; or else, her soul called to them. Down there, she could sleep as her mind and body desired to sleep. Up here, she could only recover some strength. Down there, she could rest in the songs of the dryads. Up here, she could only dimly sense them. Down there, her mind and body could be rejuvenated in the life of the earth, could receive into itself new life from the earth and sky.

Never again would Tara-lin sleep away from the trees and the dryads if she could help it. She had not known how horrible, how unsatisfying, how impossible she would find it, for she had once been able to sleep in the Valor Hall. But now that she knew the songs of the dryads, now that she felt their world and was a part of that world, she wished never again to leave their forests behind for long, never again to sleep far from the roots of a tree. She wondered, too, if she had been closer to the trees in the Valor Hall garden than she was now to the nearest trees, for all around these eyres were only rocky cliffs and treeless stretches where perhaps a few blades of grass or scraggly bushes held on to sheer rock, cut in places by the torrents that flowed down during storms or, at the end of summer, from the snows above. But Tara-lin knew it was more than that. She was much closer to the dryads now, much more in touch with her dryad nature. She felt its call and its needs much more keenly now, she gained life through it much better and more directly. Before, she hardly knew them, hardly listened to them, and so she could not feel a restless emptiness at their absence. Now she knew them and felt restless apart from them. And, more than sleep as humans knew it, she needed that contact with the dryads that came in her dreams, that brought their dreams and awareness into her sleep. Only that could cure the exhaustion that came from singing their songs and could help her to incorporate into herself the knowledge and understanding she had learned.

If she were separated too long from the dryads and the trees, she would wither. Either she would die or her life would wither until her power was that of a human, until at least most of her song was gone. Separated from the dryads, she would no longer be perhaps the greatest singer in elven history. She might not even be a singer at all.

Something in Tara-lin said she would rather die. She wondered if she felt about the forests as dragons and their riders felt about each other in the stories. Either way, tomorrow she was going to sleep among the dryads. No one would convince her otherwise.

Chapter Six – Magic of the Trees

Tara-lin stood between two trees, a hand on either one. She felt good that way. It had been a trying day. She and Keller had managed to convince Eldazìn that they could wait to try and judge his prisoners until after the coronation. Much of the day had been spent in conversation and planning with what remained of the elven aristocracy. Never before in elven history had there been such a situation as this. It was elven tradition for the king and queen to abdicate in favor of their child some number of decades before their death, which meant that the coronation ceremony involved the previous king and queen crowning the reigning king and queen. There had been an occasion in which the king had ridden to war and been killed, and it was left to the queen to crown their successors, but never had there been neither king nor queen to crown the new king and queen, except in the recent case of Anakrim. Anakrim had been crowned by an older elf, an aged and distant relation of King Orenduil, who had now died. Even so, no one wanted a precedent set by Anakrim.

More of the day had been spent trying to figure out how to deal with Erenvin and Arilim's request to see Anakrim. Tara-lin was extremely reluctant to show Anakrim's tree to the elves. She did not want him disturbed. She was certain that if she showed the tree to any of the elves many more would flock to see it. She did not want him to become a tourist attraction. For one thing he was a subtly dangerous tourist attraction, but, for another, she did not think being a tourist attraction would help him to recover from the madness of the nightmare.

Yet more time had been spent on an argument with Eldazìn, who insisted that Tara-lin and Keller not sleep in some random part of the woods. "Random!" Tara-lin had said. "As if there were anything random about choosing a dryad to sleep under!"

"I may be an elf," Eldazìn had said, "but I do not share your connection to the dryads. It is random to me."

"And who cares if it is?" Tara-lin had retorted. "I don't need you to guard me! I don't need you to try to keep me safe! Say whatever you like about how you're sure you haven't found all the assassins. Say whatever you like about my lack of skill. I just don't care!"

"You're not acting like a queen right now," he had said.

"I don't *need* to act like a queen right now. I need to get away from you! Your concerns would turn the whole world into a tomb if you were allowed to run it! They're the exact opposite of what dryads are like, and what I want to be like. And you're not going to tell me anything about what I have to be like in order to be a good queen. I shall be the queen *I* want to be, whatever you think about it."

"Very well," Eldazìn had said, bowing. He spoke quietly and courteously, but in a way which irritated Tara-lin beyond endurance. *As if I were a tree and beetles were crawling around under my bark,* she thought.

Tara-lin had snatched up a dinner which she ate quickly. She had told Alis to tell Keller that she just needed some time alone, and then she had lost the elf Eldazìn had sent to follow her. It had taken some doing, for the elf was really very good, but she had succeeded. Climbing among the branches of the trees left no tracks, and she could manipulate her Elethrian cloak so that it did more than mask her appearance and repel the eye, but truly took on the hues and patterns of her surroundings, as well as increasing the strength with which it slipped underneath the attention of any searching mind. She was lighter than most elves, which meant branches bent less under her weight and that flimsier branches could support her. It had taken hours before she was confident she had lost her pursuer, but she had succeeded. *I am going to confront Eldazìn about this,* she thought angrily, *and if he doesn't quit, I'm going to find something to do with him. Probably have him thrown into prison along with all the traitors he caught. Because I* need *this to stop, even if he thinks he's doing me a service and protecting my life.*

She could lose Eldazìn's trackers. She knew that Keller could not do so. But, even so, it was a waste of precious time and energy for her to spend hours losing the elves Eldazìn sent to track her. She was not a child who needed to be guarded or watched over! Neither was Keller. Eldazìn *had* to learn to respect their wishes. Otherwise, she would have to either figure out how to exile him or have him thrown in prison. But this was not what Tara-lin had come out here to think about, and yet here she was thinking about it, due to his attempts to stick his branches where they did not belong.

Tara-lin ran her finger-tips over the irregularities in the bark. Something about the pattern soothed her. This was where she belonged, out in the woods, surrounded by the song of the trees. She wished she could speak more easily and often to dryads like Aumoura and Beririri-kirkirkitira and Elkanakur and Alai-ie-a. As it was, their trees were far away on the other side of the Malaitha Mountains and she had to take a long journey over the mountains to meet with them. She had spoken to them a little, of course, when all the dryads of Ellenesia gathered together to take Anakrim with her, but though Tara-lin understood very little of how they had been able to move and sing so far from their trees she knew it was not an every-day thing. It was a once-in-a-lifetime event, once in the lifetime of a dryad, possibly a long-lived dryad such as Beriririkirkirkitira, not the lifetime of an elf or a short-lived tree. Perhaps, it was not even a once-in-a-lifetime event. Perhaps, it was one of those things that could – or would – happen only once in the history of Areaer.

Yet she wanted to ask them questions, and she thought that only Beriririkirkirkitira might even have an inkling as to what the answers to those questions might be. Beriririkirkirkitira had lived longer than most dryads ever lived, and she had been young and attentive to the world around her for all those years. As a result, she knew things about Areaer which no one else knew. From her, Tara-lin had learned that once dragons had flown the skies and that, in all likelihood, dragons again flew the skies over another continent. It was a curse that had brought their race to the brink of extinction and that curse had been lifted recently – from the view-point of Beriririkirkirkitira, that was. From Tara-lin's view-point, it had happened long ago, but to Beriririkirkirkitira, it had not even been all that long since dragons flew over Ellenesia.

Just one question was, how had she been able to sing Anakrim into the existence of a dryad in such a short time? Even with the strength of ten thousand dryads, such a spell felt like it should have required days of singing. In fact, Tara-lin's own memory confused her, for in her memory the song went on and on and on, as if days should have passed within it, yet it had only taken a few hours, for she had ridden up to the walls of Frèlin in the morning, and it had been high noon when it was done.

Tara-lin breathed in deeply of the air of the wood, laden with the scents of life, most of them mild and almost imperceptible, though now and then one would blow by which almost startled Tara-lin with its vibrancy. She felt the life of the trees through her hands on their cool bark. Above her, between their branches and needles, she glimpsed, here and there, a star or two. She was so tired. She ought to go back to Keller, but she did not want to. She wanted to remain out here, alone, with the forest and the sky. It was not that she would have minded Keller's presence. In a way, she wished he were out here with her.

.. * ✳ ❋ ✳ * ..

A thicket of deciduous trees surrounded Tara-lin. In the darkness, she saw clearly the form of Beriririkirkirkitira. Her mind felt illuminated by a strange kind of clarity. *"Where am I? Am I dreaming?"* Tara-lin thought or asked. She could not tell which.

Beriririkirkirkitira answered in her soft, husky voice. "You are here. And you are dreaming."

"How? What?" asked Tara-lin.

"I would have thought you would understand, daughter of dryads. In your dreams you are open to this world in ways you cannot be open when you are awake. From our perspective, we neither sleep nor wake, as human-kin understand it."

"I know that," said Tara-lin.

Beriririkirkirkitira laid her brown hand on Tara-lin's arm. "I am probably one of only several dryads who can call to you in this way. I felt you reaching out to me, and I chose to answer."

"Well, thank you," said Tara-lin. *"I'm glad to be here."*

"I know you are. And, frankly, I am a little surprised this is even possible. We were quite surprised to discover that you can share in the consciousness of the woods. We had thought that our ability to know and to a lesser extent move and sing, across space came through the trees, that the trees are connected to one another in this way and that we share this through our trees. But you are not one with a tree, so I do not know why you manifest this ability. Nonetheless, it is extremely beneficial."

"It is nice," said Tara-lin. After a long moment, she added, *"So no elven singer has ever manifested this talent before?"*

"No. Other elves have been able to hear us both in their waking state and in their dreaming state. Other elves have been able to hear us sing. But we have never known of an elf who could delve into our united consciousness, who could be aware of the world directly through us and our trees. As I said, we thought it was not something directly of our dryad nature, but that it was something of the trees which we shared because of our oneness with the trees, but you are not one with a tree, so there must be something we did not take into account."

"Could it have something to do with the Starweave? I don't think I experienced it until I donned the Starweave," said Tara-lin.

Beriririkirkirkitira tilted her head to one side. After a moment she said slowly, "I don't think so. The Starweave might strengthen this connection for you, but curiosity has made me delve into your presence in these regions. You were already manifesting this when you lead the

Valor Knights into the Icecrown Mountains, before you donned the Starweave during your battle with the wailing wight."

"*I remember that,*" said Tara-lin. "*They wondered how I knew so well the best route by which to lead them and where to find good places to rest. I did not know how I did it, but I knew it had to do with you – with the dryads.*"

"Wasn't there something else you wanted to ask me about?" asked the dryad.

"*Oh yes,*" said Tara-lin. "*Many things. Ever since I sang with all the dryads, I've felt like ... like there's more knowledge I have but that I don't know. It seemed to me that the winds sang with us. Do you know if winds are – well, I don't know how to say it. As if there are spirits of the wind.*"

"I think there are," said Beriririkirkirkitira. "Sometimes, I feel as if the wind is singing to me, or as if the wind is using my tree to make its own music. I also think whatever spirits there are in the wind, or whatever spirits make song with the wind, they are more different from you and I than even dryads and dragons are different. The relation of the spirits and the wind is probably equally incomprehensible to both of us. You have to remember, Tara-lin: for all the years of my life, all the years I have watched and lived with Areaer, there is still *so* much I don't know. Your own talents demonstrate this very well."

"*Indeed. I have another question, and perhaps it is something you do know about, for it consists of dryad magic.*"

Beriririkirkirkitra laughed – a whispering sound, like leaves and twigs rubbing against each other in a light, unsteady breeze. "There is still so much dryad magic I do not know. I thought I just reminded you of that? But ask."

"*Why did it take me – us – a few hours to sing a song that should have taken days to sing, all the strength of all the dryads notwithstanding?*"

"Time," said Beriririkirkirkitira. "You know that we tend to experience the flow of time differently than human-kin do, that our lives are slower, as if time whirls and flows around us faster. You know also that we have some ability to shift our place in time, so that we can understand and speak with you, so we can see the world in the frames in which you see it, perceiving it closely enough to the way you perceive it that we can both be of some help and be able to communicate. This ability to manipulate our connection to time is what allowed us to sing as we did."

"*I ... see,*" said Tara-lin. It was a lot to consider. It made her head spin. Yet it made sense. She remembered when a cedar dryad in the Ice-crown Mountains had pulled her into her own frame in order to hide her from orcs. The more she thought about it the more it fit, since the song was one of shifting modes of existence. She could almost see the threads and rhythms of the song anew in her mind, the contrasts and loops of it.

"*You don't manipulate time in a really direct way, do you?*" asked Tara-lin.

"I'm not sure what that question means," said Beriririkirkirkitira. "Does time exist in a direct sense? I don't know what that means. I know this is related to how we guide our trees, and that most elven singers have a very limited ability to work this kind of magic. But I don't know if time is a misleading word. Time is just perception and the speed of our lives."

"*That makes sense,*" said Tara-lin. For an indefinable moment, silence – a rich, dreamy silence, full as it were of a silent sound – reigned in the dark grove. Then she said, "*You told me, when we first met, that you wished to know more of Shallim-Araldor. Have you met Alai-ie-a?*"

"Alai-ie-a? A dryad?" asked Beriririkirkirkitira. "No, I have not."

"*Yes,*" said Tara-lin. "*She knows nothing of the name Shallim-Araldor, but she sings a song of such surpassing beauty and such surpassing happiness that its loveliness, its fearlessness, and its gladness was the only thing I could hang on to, sometimes, in my battles with the ice-wraiths. She lives close to men and sings to them.*

"*Doubtless, you also remember my friend, Alis. She has some knowledge of Shallim-Araldor. She thinks he has directly guided her. She told me that when she met him she knew that the horrible gods she had been taught about were false, and that, compared to him, none of us are much.*"

"Stop," said Beriririkirkirkitira. "I appreciate the thought, Tara-lin, but this is of little use. If you could tell me what you yourself have known – even then it might not be knowledge to me. Remember when the dryads berated me for sharing about Shallim-Araldor with you at all, remember how I said I could not say what I meant. I think they were wrong in thinking I should share nothing with you, but their thoughts are not without solid roots. And, with regards to Alis' knowledge, you know it not at all. Even if I could hear it from her lips, I cannot hear it from your mind. When you tell me about Alai-ie-a, and her song to which you clung, there is something there, and I get an echo of it from you. When you tell me about Alis, you tell me nothing."

"All right. Can I tell you about my life as to-be-Queen of Elethri?"

"Of course, Tara-lin. Tell me."

Tara-lin told Beriririkirkirkitira about her feelings, thoughts, and actions as best as she could.

When Tara-lin had finished, the dryad said, "I think we should quit this dream soon. I do not know how much time has passed. But let me say a few things first: it is easy for me to agree with you about fear. Whether this Eldazìn is motivated by fear or not, whether what he does is all right for him or not, I cannot say, but I see nothing wrong with your desire to be free of his interference. I cannot imagine what it would be like to be ... haunted, like that. It goes against the solitude and peace of our nature. I am certain that you are right that living in stone buildings, away from the free air and the earth and the trees, is not good for the elves, and is definitely not conducive to remaining in touch with their dryad nature. As for being Queen, as for whether monarchy is bad or not, I do not know anything about these things, only that we have no such things, or even the thought of them, among ourselves. I think you and Keller will be good for each other."

"Thank you for your thoughts," Tara-lin began, when softness closed in about her.

She woke to birds singing in the trees and chipmunks flitting around her. One ran over her calf. The forest was alive and happy, and Tara-lin had slept through the night. She still felt tired. At first, all she remembered of the night was a womb of living and dim glowing green-ness, waves and pulsations of life that made her imagine what the tides might feel like underneath the sea, but yet which seemed to have more of air and earth than of the sea in them. Then, in a strange flash, as of a dream both clear and dim, both crisp like a cloudless morning and muted like light shining through mist, she remembered her meeting with Beriri-rikirkirkitira. Feelings of surprise and strangeness and even curiosity that she had not known in the dream-meeting flowed over her at the memory.

Then Tara-lin thought of Keller. Was he worried about her? Was he lonely? Had he found some place in the forest to sleep, or had he spent another night in that miserable stone palace or in some cave far away from all trees? She needed to find him!

Chapter Seven - This Night Together

"Keller!"

"Tara-lin!"

The two of them embraced. "How did you sleep?" asked Tara-lin. "What took so long?" asked Keller. "You didn't feel lonely, did you?" asked Tara-lin.

"Nothing went wrong, did it? I hope you slept well," said Keller.

"We need to talk in private," said Tara-lin.

"All right," said Keller. "Where? When?"

"As soon as possible," said Tara-lin. "Do you think you can cast a spell of warding?"

"You mean to protect us from being overheard? Sure. It's not that hard," said Keller.

"Yes," said Tara-lin.

"It's easier if I can do it in a room. Otherwise, I can cast the ward, but nothing prevents someone from stepping inside the perimeter and hearing what we say."

"That's fine. Having a conversation in a stone room is one thing. Living and sleeping in it is another. Anyway, how did you sleep?"

"When I couldn't find you, and you didn't come back, Lìrulin assured me that you were probably involved in a conversation with dryads or had just fallen asleep. She invited me to where she and Eldor and Lyan are staying. I agree with you; there is something much nicer about sleeping in the trees. I didn't mind the eyre at all, but there's a special kind of peace in the forest."

.. * ＊ ✹ ＊ *..

When the ward was set, Keller turned to Tara-lin and said, "What is it you wished to talk to me in private about?"

"Eldazìn," said Tara-lin. "He *must* stop having us followed everywhere. That might be why I was out all night: I succeeded in losing the tracker he sent, but it took me several hours, by which time it was already late. I wish I could go out into the forest and be alone, just with you and the things of the forest, but it's hard enough for me to lose his trackers. He wastes valuable time and energy."

Keller held up a hand. "You don't need to go on, Tara-lin. I understand the problem. Can you explain why you wanted the room warded to have this conversation?"

"Because I don't want him listening in on our discussion. I don't want a report going back to him of what we said, or what conclusions we came to, or by what means," said Tara-lin.

"Ah, yes. I understand," said Keller. "And what will we do to make sure he behaves?"

"That is part of why we are having this conversation," said Tara-lin. "It *must* stop. We are not children to be guarded and watched. If we are to be King and Queen, then we will be King and Queen, and he must not act like ... well, like we are his subjects. Even if he *thinks* what he is doing is best for us, he must obey us in this regard and desist."

"I understand, Tara-lin. I truly do. The problem is ... controlling someone of his skills, to put it crudely. Exile is the only appropriate consequence if he persists in his misbehavior, but I don't think that would be very successful. Someone of his skills could simply sneak in and do much as he wishes in the shadows," said Keller.

"It is a problem though! I will *not* be Queen-in-name over another Valor Hall-in-the-making."

"Are you trying to be funny?" asked Keller.

Tara-lin shrugged. "I guess this is my fault. I used to complain about how useless I would be as a Queen. So, I guess it kind of makes sense if Eldazìn believes me and thinks he needs to help me be Queen." *This is the second time I've done it,* she thought. *A decade ago, I disclosed, in the ear-shot of potential enemies, that I intended to follow my father up into the north, thus inviting those enemies to realize where I had gone and what I was doing and so endanger our lives and mission. A month ago, I talked about what a useless, ignorant Queen I would make, and how much better of a King Eldazìn would make, thus inviting him to try to force his ideas on me and rule through me.*

"We'll go together and tell him he had better leave us alone when we want to be left alone and not send trackers to follow us," said Keller. "If he does not desist, we'll think about what to do then. I agree with what you've said earlier. I and Alis were talking about it this morning. His thinking is wrong. If it's not fear, it's still wrong. He's *using.* He's willing to try to *use* us to rule Elethri as he thinks best, and he needs to understand we will take none of that, even if you were a little stupid a month ago."

Tara-lin smiled at him. "I'm so glad we have an understanding."

"That's definitely to be hoped, if we're to do life together."

"But it feels good to know you've chosen *right,* not that I really had any doubts."

"If we'd had doubts, we never would have slept together. Now, let's summon Eldazìn, unless you have more you want to talk about."

"No, not right now," said Tara-lin.

They called Eldazìn to them, and he came. When he had heard their demand, he bowed and said, "Your wishes, my lord and my lady. However, I beg leave of you to permit me to express my concerns that you are making a very fool-hardy choice in not permitting me to protect you from any who seek your deaths. I entreat you to reconsider, but I will acknowledge your commands."

Now, thought Tara-lin, *it remains to be seen whether he will do as we say, or whether he will try to find a way to follow and guard us without letting us know it.* However she said none of this while she and Keller accepted his acquiescence.

Eldazìn left, then returned to them a moment later. Tara-lin and Keller looked at each other. *What does this mean?* "I am sorry to disturb you," he said, "but the guards at the portal have intercepted and detained another diplomat from the Valor Hall."

"*Another?*" asked Tara-lin. "I thought they were going to give us some time...."

"The Valor Knight will not tell us what message he was sent to deliver, only that he will deliver it before, and only before, the united Council of Advisors to the Sovereign of Elethri. I told him we have no such thing at present, and if he wished to deliver his message he had to deliver it to you and Keller. What do you want to do? I can have him searched and take whatever missives he carries from him, if that is what you desire."

"No," said Tara-lin. "Just make sure he goes back to the Valor Hall and *stays there.* Perhaps write a missive stating that we desire no more interference as we move towards our coronation ceremony. We will have a talk with the Valor Hall sometime *after* that is done." She turned to Keller. "We need to destroy the portal."

"Eldazìn, have someone write the reply and bring it to us so that we can read and seal it." As the elf went, he turned to Tara-lin. "I know, but I don't know enough wizardry."

"Well, then, we'll have to employ Eldazìn to get more volumes on wizardry, specifically on portal wizardry, for you. I'm sure it's much easier to render a portal unusable than it is to make one."

"Probably," agreed Keller.

Tara-lin stood. "I want to talk to Alis, and I promised my brother I would play with him yesterday, and that I would make sure I played with him today if I didn't get to it yesterday. You can look over the message and know if we like it or not, and seal it, unless you want me to stay? I do like you," she said, resting her hand on his shoulder.

"I like you, too, Tara-lin. We need to make sure we have this night together."

"We will," said Tara-lin. "Is it all right if I go?"

"I'll go with you and just make sure one of those elves, who are no longer following us around since Eldazìn received our royal command, instead comes and gets one of us when the letter is ready."

"That sounds like a great idea!"

As they walked down the hall, their Elethrian cloaks swinging behind them, for they were moving quite exuberantly, Keller said, "You know what?"

"What?" asked Tara-lin.

"There's a really easy way to render the portal unusable."

"Huh?"

"Take down the tower," said Keller.

"There're a million problems with that idea," said Tara-lin. "For one thing, we don't want to destroy the orb. For another, were we going to take down the tower, or were we going to modify it so that it's a light, airy thing, and only destroy most of the palace surrounding it? For the third thing, is the portal tied to the *space* or is it anchored to a stone in the tower? If it's tied to the *space*, it'll still be there in the Valor Hall – only, anyone who comes through it will fall to his death. The Valor Hall will think we're murdering their ambassadors and declare war. If it's anchored to the stone, it might still exist, wherever we put the stone. Or it might half-way exist, so you can step into it on the Valor Hall side, but then you just die in the portal. Unless you know something about portal magic that I don't?"

"I don't know anything about portals," said Keller. "I've never been through one. Never even seen one."

"In that case, you should climb up the tower and look at it sometime. Maybe you'll know enough to know how we can safely dismantle it just by looking at it," suggested Tara-lin.

"It's worth a try, but I don't expect it to work. Certainly, right now is a good time to get away from all this nonsense and have fun. I'll look at the portal later."

"Exactly what I was thinking," said Tara-lin.

. • ✳ ❋ ❋ ❋ ✳ •.

Night had fallen. Both Keller and Tara-lin had climbed up and sat with their legs dangling on the branch of a sturdy birch tree. Around them spread the forest with its thousand shades of green. Above them the white bark and five-fingered leaves of the birch gently swayed. Through these and above the horizon on all sides sparkled thousands and thousands of stars. The lingering rays of sunset barely kissed the sky between the peaks of the Malaitha Mountains. Areaer's smaller moon, which would escape the notice of anyone who did not pay attention to the skies since it was only barely bigger and brighter than the brightest star, hung less than a hand-span above the eastern horizon where lay the sea.

"Do you ever wonder if people live in the stars?" asked Tara-lin. "I think they do."

"Do you mean like people live in Areaer, or do you mean like dryads live in trees?"

"I was thinking of dryads living in trees. Do you really think it might be possible that people – like us and humans – live in stars?"

"We don't know what the stars are like. By all the trees, we don't have any idea how far away or big they are. I'm sure they're a lot bigger than they look, but how big? As big as Areaer? Maybe." Keller shrugged. "I don't know what might live there or whether it's possible for anything to live there."

"It might be something so different from us that we wouldn't even know it was something – or someone – at all. Did I ever tell you that I think there are spirits who – well, I don't know if the winds are their bodies or their songs, or if some winds are their bodies and others aren't, but are made some other way, or whether any of what I'm saying even makes sense – but that I think there are spirits of the wind?"

"I don't know," said Keller thoughtfully. "I don't think so, but the last several days have been so busy and weird I might have forgotten something, even if it was something you said."

They sat there for a while, looking at the stars and at the dark forest and feeling the wind. Somewhere not far from them night insects were chirruping. They leaned against each other a little and felt the branch sway gently beneath them. Keller said, "How did you enjoy your night, last night?"

"Very much," said Tara-lin. "I think most of it might have been spent talking to dryads, but I don't think I can share much of the conversation with you. It was mostly about their secrets, which they charged me not to share with anyone else, and I think that might include you. I'm sorry about that."

"There's no need to be, my dear Tara-lin. I don't need to know about that. I'm just glad you enjoyed it."

"I almost *always* enjoy conversing with dryads," said Tara-lin. "As long as the dryad isn't twisted or corrupted like Zànalin ... or Anakrim. Also, I like it better when they don't need me to do something to save the world! But as I seem to have finally finished doing that, and I usually avoid dryads like Zànalin and ... well, there are no other dryads *like* Anakrim ... anyway, it's going to be really great now, I'm sure."

"That'll be nice, since this business of being the Heirs of Elethri is going to be one nuisance and problem after another, and it won't get any better after the coronation."

"Let's forget all about that, while we're out here. As if it never happened and never will happen and never could happen."

"Didn't I say something like that only the other day?" asked Keller.

"Yes," said Tara-lin. "It wasn't last night, but the night before that."

"I'm surprised you remember."

"How could I not? Last night I spent with the dryads. The night before that is the one we spent up in the eyres." To herself, she thought, *How is it that almost three whole days have passed since we defeated and transformed Prince Anakrim – why do I still call him that? – and were declared the Heirs Apparent of Elethri? It's been crazy! I don't know whether it feels more like it's been a few hours or whether it feels more like it's been months, but it definitely does* not *feel like it's been* three days. "It's strange, too," she said softly.

"What's strange?" asked Keller.

"Oh – the way we are served. When I was a child, living with my parents, now and then we would store up some food, but mostly we went out and gathered what we wanted to eat when we grew hungry. Sometimes, my mother – or another of the elves in the neighboring woods – would hunt something. If it was small like a rabbit, the elf's family, in my mother's case *we*, would cook and eat it ourselves. If it was large, like a deer, then we'd invite all our friends and neighbors to share it. If it was someone else, they would invite us. Then, in the valley, we did much the same."

"I remember that," Keller interrupted.

"And when I was on my way north, to Icecrown, I mean, yes, the dryads brought us food, but somehow, it did not feel so strange. We were always moving, always traveling. You know what else? I think I am an exceptional elf. Almost every elf knows how to use the bow and hunt. Or trap. I *don't.*"

"I don't know how to do those things, either."

"Yeah, but it's different for you. I wonder, though. What do the city elves do? Do they go out to forage and hunt? I've never really thought about what it's like, living in a city. Humans have farmers who live outside the city and grow food, and bring it into the city, and maybe a few of the houses in the city have little gardens – I saw some of these when I was in their cities. But, mostly, those who live in the cities make *things* and sell them in order to be able to buy food. Then, I know that elves must make *things,* too. Perhaps some of them make bows? And the armor and swords used by the Guard have to be made, too. And the Elethrian cloaks, though I think I could do that now myself. But maybe a different way than other elves make them. And our other clothes. Those have to be made, too. Though, I know Lìrulin knows how to make her own bows. Many of us who live out in the wild woods know how to make and do most of what we need for ourselves."

An owl flew past them, almost within reach of their fingers if they had stretched out their arms.

"I don't know these answers," said Keller. "I preferred the conversation about the stars and winds. But I'm not sure if I want to talk right now at all."

"That's fine. I'm not sure I want to talk either." Tara-lin snuggled up against him and together they enjoyed the night for a while. Then they strung a small sheet of the elven cloth used for tree houses between several branches of the birch tree, and climbed onto it. There they slept together, rocking gently in the night wind under the stars, the whole forest alive around them.

Chapter Eight – The Coronation

Side by side, Tara-lin and Keller rode up the road that lead through the wide-open gates of Frèlin. Over their shoulders hung their Elethrian cloaks. Tara-lin wore a dress of deep emerald green, with light highlights interspersed throughout. It shone the bright color of new leaves where the light fell on it, but was as dark as the shadows of the deep wood elsewhere. Keller wore a dress of crimson and maroon with green threads woven through it. It was somewhat untraditional dress for the Crown Prince of Elethri on his coronation day, but it was what Keller had picked out and Tara-lin, of all people, was not one to argue.

Ranks of elves lined the side of the road, cheering. *Why do we have to have a coronation?!* thought Tara-lin, as elves waved unstrung bows and cloaks in the air and cried out in what sounded to Tara-lin like a cacophony of sound. "The Singer-Queen! The Singer-Queen! The Dryad-Chosen!" they cried. *The crown only even comes to me through Keller,* she thought, though in elven tradition the distinction between the Heir of the royal family and his or her spouse disappeared on coronation. Both would rule in concert. The Heir had no more authority or power than his spouse. She knew it could not possibly be so in the nations of the Northern Alliance, among the people from whom her friend Alis had come. She wondered if there were any human nations that took the elven view of men and women, or of the union between them.

Before and behind them rode two honor guards each, and Tara-lin had persuasively argued that one of these pairs should be gryphon riders. With greater difficulty she had succeeded in persuading the Council that one of these gryphon riders should be her human friend, Alis. She would have chosen her oldest elven friend, Earnrìl, also, but Earnrìl's gryphon was being moody and unpleasant. She did not like moving her eyre while hatching an egg – an egg which was due to hatch any day now. Instead, an elf Tara-lin barely knew rode beside Alis.

Tara-lin squirmed as they rode through the gates and into the bulk of the city. She cringed at the cheers that rose from the assembled elves. Their whole attitude towards her felt wrong! *Wrong!* The noise was just too much! How could the children of dryads possibly sound like this or make this great wave of noise? It was so utterly unlike the forest, quiet at times, or visited with the sounds of animals at others, or even with all its boughs tossing in a strong storm-wind! It was not *elven*. She would discuss with Alis later whether the woman thought it was *human* either. It was strange thinking about Alis. She grew so much faster than Tara-lin. *It's almost a curse. Earnrìl grows and ages so much slower than I do. Not so long ago she was a kind older elf who took interest in a curious child. Now, she's younger than I am. I am married, and she has hardly changed since I knew her. With Alis, it's the opposite. Yet I almost wish they could both ride, side by side, in front of me, Kushon and Welri.* But Tara-lin's thoughts could not be distracted from the adulation of the elves. *It feels almost as if they* worship *me! It is as Earnrìl told me. They do not seek to explore the world, or to know it. Isn't this how the humans became what they are, with their horrible civilizations and horrible religions?*

I think the dryads are wrong. They do not need to withdraw from the elves. They need to try to help the elves. I think they would have been better to fight the elves' unconscious withdrawal from them, to speak to and build relationships with those elves with whom they still can do so. I don't know if it would have changed the course of Elethrian history, but I think it could have changed the course of individual elves and families. I think it would have been right and well, and would have done no harm. Anakrim did not pursue evil because he was too close to the dryads.

Tara-lin was torn from these thoughts as they proceeded higher into the heart of Frèlin. They ascended the terraces, their horses mounting long stairs up the terraces and crossing bridges over the rings of water at the backs of the terraces. Everything was decorated and splendorous. Ribbons adorned the edges of the bridges. On the rings of water beautiful boats rowed or sailed to and fro, and the elves within them cheered their new King and Queen. Tara-lin shuddered again. *They worship my talent, instead of seeking what it represents. They worship my song, instead of singing themselves.*

At last, they reached the top of Frèlin. Seats and thrones were erected on the stairs that mounted to the royal tower. Tara-lin had argued that she did not want to be crowned in that tomb of stone, that palace that was the symbol of the fall of the elves from their dryadic legacy. If her reign was to lead the elves back into harmony with their own nature and with the world around them, she did not want to begin it by being crowned and enthroned in the symbol of that disharmony.

At the top of the stairs, next to the waiting thrones, she saw her father and mother and her brother, Lyan. Pain shot through her heart, as it often did when she looked upon her father. He was well over fifty years old now, and gray streaked his hair and beard. Next to him stood

Lyan, a young boy, by Alis' measure not more than about six or seven years old despite the fact that he was ten and a half. Even if Sir Eldor lived to quite an old age, Lyan would be scarcely full-grown when he died. Tara-lin would miss him, too. She was just coming into the fullness of her own adulthood, and he was already old. Her mother stood tall and proud beside him, but Tara-lin grieved for her as well. Lìrulin was still very, very young. She was not yet two hundred and fifty years old. If her life was not short by elven standards, she could live three times as long as she had yet, and Tara-lin doubted her father would live more than another twenty years. She would miss him so much! All of them would miss him so much. His voice ... his embrace ... his counsel ... his wisdom ... playing with him. Already he could not play as he had when Tara-lin was young. Her brother would never know a father in the peak of his strength.

Tara-lin shoved these thoughts aside. Such self-pity would do no good. Happiness was before her. She could see clearly that Lyan and Eldor loved and enjoyed each other. It would do no good to darken the present with shadows from the future. After all, Eldor was still capable of doing a fair amount physically, and while Tara-lin knew he had not the strength and energy of his youth, for she remembered him from those days, Lyan knew no such sorrow. He reveled in playing with his dad and in learning the things his dad could teach him.

A hush fell over Frèlin, and with it a relief so massive Tara-lin almost felt like she would faint. At the foot of the stairs she dismounted and handed Vonë's reigns to Earnrìl, who stood waiting. The elf smiled at Tara-lin, her green-blue eyes flashing something between encouragement and excitement. Beside her Keller also dismounted, and his horse was taken by a waiting elf.

Up the stairs Tara-lin mounted. She wondered what the assembled crowd of elves was thinking. Had they just now realized that hers would be no normal coronation, for there was no suitable member of the royal family to crown them? Instead, her mother and father would crown them, for they had argued that as she was elevated to the same authority as Keller, so, in this exceptional case, her parents could almost be considered as royalty, as father and mother of the Heir.

Tara-lin hardly remembered the coronation proper. The moment came when she and Keller rose as one, hand in hand, to face the assembled elves. The cheer that rose up from them made her flinch, but she smiled out at the assembled crowd. Then they came forward, first of all elves such as Akanë and Erenvin, then others of some import or significance, to swear their allegiance to their new sovereigns. Tara-lin remembered when, days before, Eldazìn had approached them to swear his allegiance, saying he did not want to do it at the accustomed time, directly after the coronation, for two reasons: one of them was that he did not wish to become such a public figure, and another of them was that he might not be present, having been committed a mission by them. She had taken his hand and told him to rise. "You are not to give your allegiance to *me!*" she almost hissed. "Your heart, your soul, your life, your conscience, none of these can ever be *my* property – nor Keller's. Your obedience in affairs of state – that we require, else we are no King and Queen. But beyond that, your life is your own! You may quit our service at any time you should desire – only, you are required to give us the courtesy of letting us know and, also, of continuing to protect any secrets you may have from us. But I do not, and never shall, own you! I, like you, must serve Elethri and, indeed, all of Ellenesia. I am no greater than yourself, of no more importance than yourself. I have no authority over your soul, no right over your heart. I have not made you, do not sustain your life, do not know what is best for you. I am a creature like you."

She had not spoken to him of Shallim-Araldor, doubting he could yet understand. He could only do wrong by spreading the worship of a deity, a worship which might someday disintegrate into something like the religion of Alis' people. Long before it got that far, it would still be a shame on the real thing, on whomever it was Alis knew. In Eldazìn's own mind, and doubtless in the minds of most of the elves who now almost worshiped Tara-lin, such worship would be a disgrace. It would not be living reality, however dimly perceived, but a statement worshiped where instead open receptivity to the unrevealed reality should be maintained, along with acknowledgement of one's own lack of knowledge. But Tara-lin thought that, even if she had never heard of Shallim-Araldor, the King of Dryads, the Sustainer, she still would have known that the way the elves looked to her now was wrong. It was so clear that she was one of them, gifted perhaps in a special way, but not in a way that set her apart as a different category of being or gave her dominion over their souls.

Now, Akanë knelt before them and began to offer his oath. "No!" said Keller. "Not to us."

"Then to whom?" asked the young elf, looking completely

bewildered. "How else do I do this? How else do I make it clear that I am your loyal subject, that I will serve you unto death, that I will not oppose your reign or work to install another in your places?"

"You don't have to serve us unto death unless you *want* to," said Tara-lin.

Akanë looked like he swallowed a thousand questions with his next breath. "Okay, but how do I announce the rest – and, what if I do want to, how do I announce that?"

"You don't need to announce that you do want to in any special way," said Tara-lin. "Just tell us if you don't want to, and leave our Guard. And it isn't really us, but all Elethri, that you should defend, and if you think we're doing it wrong, then, well, you should let us know, and you should do what you think right."

Utter chaos expressed itself on Akanë's face. Tara-lin could almost hear his thoughts. *How will you rule at all that way?* She was glad Eldazìn was not here to scold and interrogate, that this conversation had already been had with him. Keller said, "Just tell us. Tell us that you won't oppose our reign or work to install another in our place. But don't give your allegiance, as if your life, your body, your heart, your soul, and your conscience belonged to us. It doesn't. Being King and Queen doesn't mean we own you, or any other elf.

Akanë nodded solemnly. He looked like he had been bitten by an ant on the back of his tongue as he spoke. "I will be your loyal subject. I acknowledge you as my King and Queen and will not oppose your reign." He stopped, then continued. "As a Captain of your Guard, I swear to serve and protect you unto death." Then he rose, uncertainly and awkwardly, completely thrown off by this twist of events. *But, really,* thought Tara-lin, *he has been around us so much that he ought to have seen it coming. He's listened in on enough of our conversations and observed us relate enough that he ought to have known, or at least guessed, or at least been suspicious, even if he's rarely conversed with us directly.*

Akanë moved aside. After considering for a moment that this process was likely to be repeated with almost every other elf in the line, he moved down the stairs, hoping to make things go along faster and to ease the discomfort of many of the elves by explaining to them beforehand what awaited them at the throne and what their new King and Queen wanted, even though he was plagued by severe misgivings. Who would follow his King and Queen if this was what they advertised?

Who would obey them, especially if Elethri were dragged into war? How would they enforce their will? How would the elves respect them? Perhaps, more pressing, how would the human nations of the Valor Alliance and of the south respect them? He had learned enough about human society from his master, Eldazìn, and from the previous Valor Knights, Eldor, Namdon, and Cuthlin, to know that this would be considered a great weakness if ever word of it reached their palaces, and word of it certainly would reach their palaces. Surely they had one or two spies throughout all of Elethri. Surely disloyal elves, such as those who had served Anakrim and betrayed King Orenduil and Queen Alaria, were still free in Elethri. A human tourist or visitor could be a spy, too. The human nations would see it as a perfect opportunity to sow unrest and disloyalty throughout the elven nation.

However, Akanë kept these thoughts to himself. It was not for him to question his King and Queen, and certainly not so publicly. They must rule as they saw fit. He wondered, too, if there was a hidden wisdom in their actions, however strange they appeared to him.

.. * * * * *..

A few days later, late at night, Eldazìn returned with a volume entitled *Introduction to the structure of portals and other such wizardry objects.* Even though it was late, Keller opened it at once and paged through it. Seeing the expression on his face, Tara-lin asked, "What? Do you know how to do it?"

"I think so," said Keller. "I remember when we walked up to look at the portal, and if my memory is at all correct, I think I know what to do. It should be very simple, really."

"Should we do it tonight?" asked Tara-lin.

"Yes," said Keller. Together they rose from where they had settled down to inspect the book. Still carrying it, they proceeded towards the tower and up to where the portal opened at the very top. The leader of the watch politely asked them, "If I may ask, what are you doing here at this late hour?"

"Seeing if my idea will work," said Keller. He was too excited to stay and explain himself, but rushed up the stairs to the portal. Tara-lin skipped behind him, almost as excited herself. This was so much better than a miserable coronation!

At the top, Keller pushed himself between the guards, ignoring their startled looks. "Aha!" he said. "I thought correctly."

"What?" asked Tara-lin.

"It's tied to the frame. After reading what I have in this book, I know that when I disrupt the frame the portal will cease to function. Both openings will be non-operative. If the frame is ever properly placed again, it could reconstruct itself, but there's an easy way to make that impossible. If we burn or crush the wood no one can put the frame back together, though if they could do so the portal could reappear. Unfortunately, this is going to take a lot of strength," said Keller.

"You can't do it with wizardry?"

"No. My wizardry abilities are not yet that advanced." He turned to one of the guards. "Get the whole Watch and assemble here."

"It will be done," the elf said and hurried down the stairs.

"Can we try by ourselves and those who are still here?" asked Tara-lin.

"Yes," said Keller, "but four of us won't be enough. Also, we will have to be careful no one falls through the portal in the process."

"No, Keller. Like this," said Tara-lin. She drew her elf-sword and stepped toward the portal. A moment later he joined her. Their elf-swords impacted the wood frame.

The jeweled frame lay in pieces on the ground. Tara-lin staggered backwards. It felt as if her bones were ringing, but the portal was no more. After taking a few moments to recover, she and Keller alerted the Watch that the task for which they had been called was done. It was no longer necessary to guard the top of the tower, but the jewels should be taken out of the frame and the rest of the wood burned or otherwise destroyed. For themselves, they were going to go out to their tree and go to sleep after the tiresome events of the day.

The next morning, Keller and Tara-lin wrote a missive addressed to the Valor Hall, alerting the Valor Hall of Elethri's formal withdrawal from the Valor Alliance. They then commanded Akanë to see that it was sent and delivered to the Valor Hall by gryphon rider or fast horse.

Chapter Nine - Lizards and Dragons

Eldazìn appeared before them just as Keller and Tara-lin had finished writing the missive and giving instructions about its delivery. He bowed and said, "I have a surprise for you. I was going to share it with you last night, but you were so excited over the book and ran off so quickly. If you will come with me now...."

"We will. What kind of surprise is it?" asked Tara-lin.

Eldazìn flashed her a cheeky smile. "Drake-lizards."

"Drake-*lizards?* As in multiples of them?" gasped Tara-lin.

"Well, no. Only one of them is a drake-lizard. The rest are still eggs."

"How many?" asked Keller.

"Well, only one egg and one drake-lizard," said Eldazìn. He tilted his head in an odd gesture, and Tara-lin thought he could have said more, but she was not sure how to press. After a moment, he spoke. "Actually, the egg is hatching, so if there's anyone you want to be a lizard keeper, we should get that person as quickly as possible."

Keller and Tara-lin looked at each other. "Who?" they asked simultaneously, and then simultaneously answered their own question. "You."

"No, really," said Tara-lin. "And I don't care to be. As exotic and cool as it might seem, I don't care to be."

"I know. You're exotic enough already, Queen," said Eldazìn. "But, really, hurry up and decide. The longer you take, the less likely the drake-lizard will attach at all."

"Lyan!" said Tara-lin suddenly. "Is that okay with you, Keller?" When he nodded, she spun around and yelled, "Somebody get Lyan! Tell him to come as quickly as possible! He's going to love it for sure!"

Lyan soon appeared, running ahead of his parents. "What is it?" called Eldor, panting.

"No time!" said Keller. "Come!"

In short order, Eldazìn unlocked and swung open the door of one of the rooms in the palace. Immediately a scarlet drake-lizard with brown wings flew in his face and attached its small body to his shoulder.

Lyan gasped, as Eldazìn pushed him through the door. Tara-lin stood, watching from the hallway with her parents and spouse. It appeared that the drake-lizard accepted the boy. It flared its orange wings wide as Lyan approached, but did not fly away when the boy stretched out his hand to touch it.

In a low voice, Tara-lin asked, "What is his name?"

"Lyan's lizard? I don't know," said Eldazìn after a moment's pause.

"No, I mean yours."

"Oh. *Her* name," said Eldazìn. "Runi."

"How did this happen?" asked Eldor.

"I happened upon a drake-lizard nest. I took both eggs, meaning to give them to you to do with them as you wished, but Runi hatched yesterday night – less than an hour before I arrived," said Eldazìn. "Your daughter and her spouse decided her brother would make a good lizard-keeper. Actually, it's a little more complicated than that. I urged them to make up their minds quickly, since if a lizard doesn't bond immediately after hatching they get completely wild and reclusive. Tara-lin thought of Lyan."

"I know about bonding with drake-lizards," said Eldor. "It was the appearance and the choice I was asking about."

"Oh yes, I forgot," said Eldazìn. "You used to have a friend who was a lizard-keeper."

"Yes," said Eldor, with a touch of sadness.

"Here, Lyan," said Eldazìn. "You should feed her, now." The boy had the drake-lizard curled up against his chest, nestled in the crook of his arm. He deftly caught the chunk of meat thrown his way by the older elf. As it sailed towards them, the drake-lizard stretched herself out and shook her wings. She stretched her tiny quivering nose towards the meat and made a pitiful chirrup. "Here, here, I'm giving it to you, right now!" said Lyan.

"Now that that is done," said Eldazìn, "one of the next things should be to pass verdict on our captured criminals, unless you think otherwise?"

"I think now is as good a time as any," said Tara-lin.

"Yes," said Keller, "bring them in."

"And ask if Alis is willing to join us. No command, just a request from a friend," Tara-lin added.

.．＊＊＊＊＊＊．．

The first to be brought before them was Fizzer. Tara-lin gasped when she saw his face.

Keller turned to her. "Do you know this elf?"

"Yes," said Tara-lin, "and I'm not surprised to see him here ... not really ... I suspected him ... I just never thought...."

While Eldazìn stayed behind him and did not speak, another elf Tara-lin had often seen with Eldazìn presented him. "This is Fizzer, brought before you, O King and Queen of Elethri, on charges of treason."

Tara-lin nodded. "What did he – you – do?" she asked.

Fizzer's expression displayed resigned outrage. "I only served the best interest of Elethri faithfully. May I hear of what I am accused?"

"That is what will now occur," said the elf whose name Tara-lin did not quite remember. Tin-something perhaps?

A long proceeding followed, as Tin-mar and Eldazìn interrogated Fizzer in front of her and Keller. The details bored her at times, though at other times she found herself interested. She tried to listen and to pay attention, but she already had no doubt in her mind that the charge was true. Too much fell too readily into place. At first, Fizzer seemed inclined to argue with Eldazìn and Tin-mar's questions – Tin-mar did most of the talking – but then he maintained complete silence. Tin-mar slapped him once in the face, simultaneously with his question, doubtless hoping to jerk something of an answer from him, but the look on Tara-lin's face and the tenseness of her muscles, and a corresponding tenseness in Keller, indicated that both sovereigns were ready to leap to their feet and stop it if it continued. Both Eldazìn and Tin-mar nodded towards them, acknowledging their wishes. The questions continued, Tara-lin surmised, for her benefit and Keller's, to give them some appreciation of the general situation and events surrounding Anakrim's rise to power. Unfortunately, it was mostly lost on Tara-lin, though she did not know about Keller. However, she did piece together and note a few things. For one, it seemed that many of the elves who had had contact with Princess Ithrìl upon her return had connections to the deaths of various individuals in the Elethrian royal family. Another thing she noted was that Fizzer had had some connection to some of these elves.

Despite the sadness on Fizzer's face, Tara-lin felt no compassion softening her judgment. She knew this elf had been at least complicit in murder; she more than suspected that he had tried to ruin her own chances of helping Keller and defeating Anakrim. She discussed the judgment for a moment with Keller, then they commanded that Fizzer be taken to the dungeon and kept there for the rest of his life. As the guards turned to carry out her command, she said, again mostly to Keller, "But we must make a way for them to have trees or little gardens even in their confinement. It would be too cruel to entomb a living elf, to keep him away from all trees forever. It would be better to execute him than to torture him so."

Alis nodded from where she sat beside the thrones. "I agree, Tara-lin. I don't experience what it is to be an elf, how your kind feels about the trees, but it seems to me that it would be like taking a human from the sunlight forever. Or like never letting me touch a gryphon again. Or even any animal."

"Don't speak of being taken from the sunlight," said Keller. Pain made his voice taut as if he were angry, which perhaps he was.

"Oh. Sorry. I ... uh, I forgot," said Alis.

"Eldazìn," asked Tara-lin, "will all the interrogations take as long as this one?"

"Perhaps some will be a little shorter," he answered.

"How many are there?" she asked.

"Over a dozen," he answered.

"Is there any way to make them shorter?" she asked.

Eldazìn shrugged. "If you're willing to simply take my recommendation and condemn them all to life imprisonment."

"I don't want to do that. Fizzer, him I am comfortable condemning. I know, from my own sources, in my own way, that he is guilty. Your ... evidence ... corroborates that. The others? How do I *know?* Even after your questioning ... unless they confess ... how would I *know?* Not to doubt your judgment, or your work on my behalf, but I wouldn't feel comfortable condemning someone so harshly without ... I mean, what if you picked up the wrong elf? Maybe a twin? Or a cousin who looks almost identical? Or something neither of us have ever thought or dreamed of!" Tara-lin said, her voice rising.

"I have no advice to offer here," said Alis.

"I *strongly* advise against releasing any of these elves back into elven society. Or even back into the world," said Eldazìn.

"Why?" asked Tara-lin. "Couldn't some of them have served Anakrim only because they were lied to? Now that there is no Anakrim to offer them a lie about restoring elven magic, they might still be very bad, but not such a threat that they need to go to prison for the rest of their lives."

"They cannot be trusted," said Eldazìn. "They cannot be trusted not to, say, collaborate with any attempts made by Valor Hall, or even the southern nations, to kill you or Keller or destabilize Elethri. Yes, they may be no worse than many other elves, but they have shown themselves capable."

Even as he finished speaking the door opened, and Tin-mar brought in another of the suspects.

.. ＊ ＊ ＊ ＊ ＊ ..

Tara-lin, Keller, and Alis passed their notion about what to do with the elves by Eldor and Lìrulin, who thought that it was not their domain and so they had no business endorsing it, but it was a fine enough decision. Lyan positively shouted his agreement. Tara-lin and Keller decided to keep all the suspected elves in prison until they decided what to do. They also decided that, as soon as possible, each one must be provided with a seedling or sapling to tend and grow. Any who might be released would get to take their tree with them if they wanted. They decided to leave a wing of the palace intact as quarters for Namdon and Cuthlin and any other human visitors or guests who would prefer similar accommodations, but arranged for much of it to be torn down. They would decide how to handle the Tower proper later.

After all this was done, Tara-lin was still uncomfortable with what seemed to her to be a decision made out of fear. Nonetheless, she and Keller prepared to tour Elethri, visiting all the cities, and most gathering clearings throughout the forests, to see those whom they could not think of as their subjects. Alis chose to go with them, as did Earnrìl, since her gryphon, Welri's, egg had hatched. As Alis and Earnrìl told Tara-lin just the morning after the hatching, they had both decided, along with Welri, that it would be good for Keller to bond to the gryphling. Thus, they traveled through Elethri, visiting their people and singing to them, with a young female gryphling, yet unnamed by Keller.

.. ＊ ＊ ＊ ＊ ＊ ..

Half a day's ride from an elven seaside city, the four (seven including the gryphons) stood on a promontory, overlooking the sea. Tree branches arced high over their heads. Before them was a ragged, rocky, line of cliffs. Beyond that lay the sea, dark but streaked with light as it moved under the moon. In the east, beyond the sea, dawn glowed along the horizon.

"This is one of my favorite things in the world," said Earnrìl. "I feel like I like both the dawn and the sea more than most elves do."

"That's fine by me," said Tara-lin. "My other best-friend isn't an elf at all." She nodded towards Alis. "And my mate is as half-elf as I am, and a wizard like human wizards. It's weird to be the iconic Queen of Elethri and yet be so different – and have such different friends."

"I guess that would be weird," said Earnrìl.

"I think I'm more different than you are," said Alis softly. "How many human girls run away into the forests because they don't want to marry or join a monastery? How many human girls are not only gryphon riders, but can talk to all gryphons? As far as we know, I'm the only person to be able to talk with any gryphon."

"I don't know if you *are* so different," said Tara-lin. "You only had the courage to run away because you met me and I convinced you. As for the gryphons, what do you think humans might be capable of, if they weren't entombed in such a horrible religion?"

Alis laughed dryly. *"Entombed,"* she said. "I guess that *is* what it's like. And I guess you're right, too. We have to do something so that more girls can ... well, can choose their lives, if they're willing to choose to do so ... to 'risk the wrath of the gods and the netherhells,'" said Alis, mocking the things she had once thought she believed but acknowledging the very real fears – even though the things feared had no existence – to which she, and so many other humans, both male and female, had been enslaved.

"I like the dawn and the sea, too, Earnrìl," said Keller. "I really feel something for or about the dawn. Something nameless. I can't speak it, but the feeling is so strong sometimes. As if ... I don't know. It just calls to me."

As they spoke, the rim of the sun rose, slowly but perceptibly, over the ocean. The whole world was flooded with ruddy light. The waves of the sea flashed, blue-gray on the light side, green-gray in the shadows, with lines and streaks of reddish light running along them. Where Keller and Tara-lin stood, the world was streaked in long, narrow patches of shadow and ruddy light. Every moment, and then every few moments, the patches grew thicker, as the shadows receded and thickened towards the objects which cast them, as the sun rose higher.

"What is that?" asked Earnrìl, squinting.

"What? Where?" asked several voices at once.

"Against the sun," she said. "It looks like wings. Not quite against the sun," she added. "A little off to one side, but still within the glow."

"Anyway, I don't think it's a threat," she said, after a few moments. "Probably just a bird. Maybe it's a migratory bird. Alis, you want to go for a swim in the sea?"

"Sure!" said Alis. Kushon woke at the excitement in her voice and stood. In a moment, she leapt onto his back and buried her hands in his mane. Earnrìl sat astride Welri, her arms outspread even as her gryphon took to the air. Only her legs, hooked under Welri's wings and clasped tightly to the gryphon's belly, held her to the beast. Some female gryphons did not have the fluffy manes anyway.

They glided and dove towards the sea. Tara-lin and Keller drew nearer to the cliff-edge to watch, wondering if the gryphons would actually swim.

Before long, it became clear that the approaching flier was a dragon. The grown gryphons and their riders got out of the sea and came to where their friends waited. It was soon clear that the dragon had white wings and pink and purple splotches all over his or her body.

"Much more colorful than the drake-lizards," said Alis.

"I'm not sure if pink-and-purple-splotches is more colorful than reds and golds and oranges," said Keller.

"All right," said Alis. "I'm just shocked to be seeing a dragon at all. That is what it is, isn't it?"

"I *think* so," said Earnrìl.

"It certainly... well, it's certainly no bird. And look! There's a rider on its back!" said Tara-lin.

"Well," said Alis, "all the stories suggest that dragons are just like bigger drake-lizards. Still, how can it be that there are *dragons?!*"

"Let's wait and see," said Tara-lin. "Maybe it's not a dragon, but something else."

"It has wings like a drake-lizard," said Keller.

The sun continued to rise higher into the sky as the flier approached. "Is there any way to get it to notice us?" asked Earnrìl. "If that's not a *dragon*, I don't know what is!"

"You and – or – Alis could fly up on your gryphons. I bet that would get its attention," suggested Tara-lin.

"Or, it might be dangerous," said Alis.

"You never know until you try," said Keller. From the sound of his voice, he had no interest in which way the decision went.

"Why don't you just call out, Welri?" Earnrìl suggested to her gryphon. Tara-lin thought the beast gave her a questioning what-kind-of-stupid-idiot-are-you look, but she also knew that Earnrìl did not need anyone to tell her what her gryphon thought.

"The gryphons – or at least mine – don't like that thing," said Earnrìl. She sounded annoyed.

"It looks like the kind of thing that could *eat* them," said Tara-lin. "Hopefully, if they notice us, the rider is respectful enough, and has enough control over that beast, whatever it is, to keep that from happening."

"Keller could do something," said Earnrìl, casting him a look.

"Maybe," he said. "I'm really not much of a wizard yet, but I'll do my best to prepare whatever spells I know that might help with such a situation."

"Running would just draw its attention," said Earnrìl.

"Besides, we don't even know what its intentions are," said Tara-lin.

"Oh. I forgot. You might be able to protect us too. Just a little," Earnrìl added when Tara-lin threw her a dark look.

As they watched, the creature angled in, preparing to land on the promontory. It looked huge to Tara-lin. The rider, who sat astride its neck, turned out to be quite a large human, yet he looked smaller than a child on a gryphon compared to his beast. Its whirling eyes glowed an eerie shade of blue. Tara-lin had no idea what it was thinking as it passed over her at a low altitude, but she was sure it saw her. It had no scales, just shiny, smooth skin. The wind from its wings buffeted them.

"It has to be a dragon, even if it doesn't look much like a drake-lizard," said Earnrìl. "Do any of the legends or stories suggest that dragons might eat gryphons?" Her voice sounded near panic. "I don't think we can fight that thing. It's huge! And what if it *can* breathe fire?"

"No," said Tara-lin and Alis, both together. "I've never heard a story to suggest that dragons eat gryphons. And," Tara-lin continued, "from all I know, dragons are so close to their riders that they wouldn't eat something their riders wanted them not to. I don't just know about this bond from legend. An ancient dryad confirmed it to me."

"Well, then," said Earnrìl, "shall we meet this human from across the sea? Oh. Welri says to make sure you keep her gryphling safe, Keller."

"Tell her I promise I will," said the half-elf wizard.

"By the way," said Alis, as they walked in the direction the dragon had landed, "that creature *does* look more like a gigantic drake-lizard than anything else we know, even if it's the wrong color, doesn't have horns, does have the weirdest-looking chicken-crest, does have spines, and doesn't have scales."

They found the rider leaning against the dragon, digging his fingers into the dragon's chest as if to scratch the huge beast. He turned as they approached, the two gryphon riders astride their companions. The dragon swung its head to look at them with those eerie eyes that again sent chills through Tara-lin, and the rider made a strange bow and said something in an incomprehensible language.

Frustration and impatience seethed through Tara-lin. *We won't even get to find out* anything *until one or the other of us manages to learn a whole new language.*

Tara-lin caught the dragon looking at her again with one of those over-sized blue eyes. Oh, yes, that was another thing about how dragons and drake-lizards were different. Their eyes.

"Do *you* understand me?" she asked the dragon.

The dragon's eye whirled faster. After a moment it nodded.

"But you can't talk to me."

The dragon nodded again.

"So you can tell your rider what I say, but you can't tell me *anything?*"

The dragon paused, then nodded a third time.

Tara-lin sighed. This was so irritating!

No! Wait! There had to be a solution! There *was* a solution. Dryads were not hindered or constrained by human language. They used it as a courtesy. It was neither how they heard nor how they spoke to humans. Tara-lin was almost a dryad! Surely, this power of theirs was not beyond her. Hadn't one of them hinted to her that she, too, could learn to speak and hear as they did? If she manifested dryadic powers which they had thought impossible to any who were not true dryads – one with a tree – surely she could speak as dryads spoke. The only question was, how? She suspected it was a simple matter of knowing how.

Probably she could learn it from almost any dryad in a few hours, a night at most, *maybe* a few nights. This was still frustrating. She wished they could learn why the human and dragon had come here and what they wanted here *right now.* But at least, there was a way that would not take months or even years. Still, there was the problem of managing this one interaction.

The dragon and rider were looking at each other now and seemed to be conferring with one another about something. Tara-lin did not think they were thinking about them anymore. She turned to her friends. "I have an idea how we can fix this language problem."

"It's only a one-way language problem, apparently," said Alis mischievously.

"A one-way language problem *is* a language problem, even if it's not a two-way language problem?" said Earnrìl, as if this last was in doubt.

Doubts assailed Tara-lin again. *What if he can't hear me? It seems some humans can't hear dryads at all. Maybe this won't work at all.*

But it will work. A little. I will be able to hear him, and his dragon can hear me. That way we'll have some *mutual communication, though I don't know how satisfactory it will be.*

Chapter Ten - Speech of the Dryads

Tara-lin sought a tree whose dryad she thought would be pleased to accommodate her. She sat down, her back pressed against the trunk, and sought that dream-like but waking consciousness, the earth-sea in which dryads both were rooted and swam. *Beriririkirkirkitira. Aumoura. Beriririkirkirkitira. Beriririkirkirkitira. Aumoura. Beriririkirkirkitira. Aumoura,* she thought, turning the names into a dreamy chant, trying to remember how to send out her thoughts, like ripples through that thick, dreamy, colorful sea, so utterly unlike the real sea, and yet so reminiscent of something underwater, to those whose company she desired.

Tara-lin could not tell whether it was before her eyes or within her mind that she saw the forms of the two dryads she had called. The world around her seemed both thick and lucid, dim but full of bright and soothing colors and moving shapes clothed in those colors. Yet it was also as if she saw a forest of many trees, prominent among them Aumoura's tree and Beriririkirkirkitira's shrub-tree – or as if she felt them, for at times it seemed more like feeling, like bark and leaves and the shapes of the trees on her finger-tips than it did like sight.

"Greetings, Tara-lin," said Aumoura. "For what do you ask?"

"Someone indicated to me once that I could learn to hear and speak as the dryads do – unaffected by human language. There is a Dragonrider from across the sea, and while his dragon can hear me, I cannot hear his dragon, and the language he speaks is unknown to me. I want to know how to hear him as dryads hear."

"You don't know?" asked Beriririkirkirkitira, sounding more than a little surprised.

"No, I don't."

"That is a surprise," said Aumoura, "for you are clearly capable. I suspect your mother could do this, at least enough to understand the foreign language. It is a skill I thought was common among elves. Isn't it?"

"It used to be," said Beriririkirkirkitira. "I don't know if it is anymore. But I agree with Aumoura. I think you have not tried."

"I don't know how to try," said Tara-lin.

"I thought you would have learned by now!" said Aumoura. "Your notion of trying and of knowing how is altogether too human – if it is human. I don't know much about humans. You wondered how you would know what I had taught you, and I told you that when you needed to, you would find out. That is still your problem, apparently. How is that you can speak to us through the dreams of the trees, but you cannot do this?"

Beriririkirkirkitira said, "She dreams. I think she can do a lot, if she's not thinking in a human fashion, and once she has done it in her sleep enough, she begins to have enough feel for it that her human ways of thinking don't get activated when she wants to do it. I don't know how to help her with this, though."

"That's why I came here," said Tara-lin. *"You first taught me how to really touch my dryadic heritage, Aumoura. I learned so quickly and so well from you. You told me you're certain that we are cousins of some degree and that might have something to do with it."*

"I think it does," said Aumoura, in her resonant voice. "I think you know how, too. I think you just think about it too much. But come. I will try." She reached out her rough, brown hands, and Tara-lin took them. Dreamy ecstasy flowed over her at the touch of that bark-like skin.

A moment later, Tara-lin felt as if waves were folded over her – waves of forests with tall, solid trees, of leaves whispering in the wind, roots drinking up water and nutrients deep in the soil, waves of song, deep and fresh and wordless. "Sing," said Aumoura's voice, deep and resonant. "Sing in the depths of your being. Sing always. Do not forget that you are a singer, nor that your song does not require the words of men or elves. You have sung before now without words. Learn to sing always in the depth of your being. Learn to live in song, and you will be attuned to song, and your song will be attuned to your understanding and your will."

Then all words passed away into imageless resonances, flowing melodies intertwined with a gentle harmony, then something deeper yet. Tara-lin felt lost in a world so far beyond her own imaginings. A stab of cold, rushing fear cut through her for a moment, then slowly the pain and cry of fear faded. It was still a world of feeling and sound, but feeling and sound perceived so differently that Tara-lin felt bewildered, without anything to hold to. It was not really feeling or sound anymore. She felt like she was drowning in a void that was full of something that was yet void to her. Then, she recognized Aumoura beside or around her – with her. Her fear and confusion was softened as she recognized that this was the same Aumoura she had always known. Aumoura was not different.

Finally, some kind of stability was reached for Tara-lin. She sent out a questing thought for Aumoura and knew it was acknowledged. How was she able to go so deep in dryadic power and thought without knowing it – without really going there?

She had been there and not there. It might have something to do with her humanity. Her humanity might actually have helped her to dive deeper and faster than one with only a dryad nature could do, but it did not help her to breathe the air of that world. It did not make her at home there.

I'm still not all the way there, am I?

Aumoura's thought answered, *No.* Tara-lin might be as far as one so human could go. But who knew what could be after another hundred or so years? After all, she was barely over thirty. Furthermore, who knew what lay deeper within the world, beyond the sky?

It took a moment for Tara-lin to understand. *Death! Right?*

Her thoughts went down another line. What did the dryads think? Had she done wrong in keeping the elven traitors in prison for the moment? Was it motivated by fear – the fear of death, fear of the victory of the nightmare, that very fear with which the wailing wight had almost succeeded in freezing her soul?

Aumoura and the dryads had entrusted her with the task of trying to prevent Anakrim from killing and destroying them. It did not *seem* wrong to her.

Beriririkirkirkitira had wondered if that choice of the dryads would lead them nearer to corruption.

Perhaps it is better to discuss this with Alis, thought Tara-lin.

.. ＊ ＊ ✳ ＊ ＊..

It was late in the evening when Tara-lin opened her eyes. A soft whisper of her friends' voices reached her, and she soon picked out their forms some way across the forest. She stood and walked towards them.

Desiring not to startle them, she walked around them and approached them from within their field of vision as they stood speaking to one another. Keller looked up and spoke first. "Hi, Tara-lin."

"Hi, Keller," said Tara-lin.

"Did you find what you were looking for?" asked Alis.

"I ... *think* so," said Tara-lin. "It seems I've always had it, but not quite. It's all strange, and I don't know if I can tell you about it very well."

"Cool," said Keller. "I think the dragon and rider bedded down from the night somewhere not too far away. Hopefully, we can find them in the morning before they fly off."

"Perhaps, now that they've found land, they're in no hurry to move. They might want to make contact with us, or, I guess, they might just want to live by themselves. We'll see. If they want to be by themselves, that's not really any of our business, though with the gryphons we might be able to follow and arrange contact," said Tara-lin.

"If that's settled," said Keller, "we were just discussing a name for my gryphling. I wanted to know if you like it."

"What is it?" asked Tara-lin.

"Kellia," said Keller.

"I *do* like it!" said Tara-lin. She caught Alis and Earnrìl looking at her. "No, no, no. I don't want my own gryphling. What I am is satisfying, and I'm not sure how compatible with gryphon riding it is."

"Let's find a good place to spend the night," said Earnrìl.

"Anything will do, really," said Tara-lin. "Alis, what do you think? Do you think I sentenced Fizzer to life imprisonment because of fear, or because I think that would be better for him than whatever nasty deceitful plans he might have? Do you think I decided to keep the others in prison until I know what I want to do with them or because I'm afraid of them and what they'll do? What do you think I should do?"

"Do you mind me interrupting?" asked Earnrìl.

"No. Go ahead," said Tara-lin.

"What's so terrible about throwing someone in prison because they might cause harm to yourself or to others – the people you're obligated to protect?" she asked.

"I –" began Tara-lin. She stopped, began again, and stopped again. "Because fear, fear is, well, it's the weapon of the nightmare creatures. It's what makes you do or be things you really don't *want* to do or be because you're afraid of something else. What else is it? That's exactly what it is. I don't want to do or be things that aren't *good* because I'm worried about something else happening if I don't. I want to do or be what's *good*. I want to rule Elethri in a way that's good for *all* of Elethri, instead of in a way that's driven by evil. I ... fear is the weapon of the nightmare. Fear is the beginning of corruption. It's what makes dryads go evil, fearing the dissolution of their life in this phase of existence. Some of them think fear might be what makes human death so horrible. At any rate, the whole structure of fear – or at least the fear to which I'm opposed, some kinds of evil are even *useful* for fighting orcs, like the kind that makes you able to use your sword better – is that it, well, the whole structure or meaning or action of it is to make you do what you *don't think is GOOD*, it's a motivation to do something for some reason other than because it is *good* or *happy* or *beautiful*. It's the exact opposite of Alai-ie-a, but you've never met Alai-ie-a, Earnrìl. I think you should, sometime. Alis has, though, so she knows what I mean."

Alis laughed. "A little. Maybe. I don't know. I think we both kind of, but not all the way, know what the other means. As for what you should do, what do you think, Tara-lin? I can hardly tell you. I know you're thinking about their good when you ordered that they be given trees and flowers or whatever is their favorite plant. I know you pitied Anakrim and thought he should be rescued instead of killed, and, perhaps, that is why he is now a dryad in the woods of Elethri not far from Frèlin. I don't know what your motivation or thoughts are right now. I *thought* you ordered the rest of them kept in prison for the moment because you don't know what to decide and were just putting it off."

"Or maybe because I'm afraid of what they might do if I let them out," said Tara-lin. "So I'm putting off making a *final* decision, not that any of it is really final. As long as I don't kill them – which I won't – I can always pardon them. In another way, it is final. Every day or hour they spend in prison is a day and hour they spend confined, not doing what they wish as free elves. Keller, really, I should be asking you what you think, since you are King. Maybe, since I don't know, I should just give this whole issue over into your hands?"

"Or not," said Keller. "Maybe I don't think about these things enough to be a good person to decide them. My own thinking would be that I doubt Eldazìn is wrong. I don't think he is *that* kind of untrustworthy. I'm certain they are guilty as charged. So why not follow his advice and throw them into prison for the rest of their lives? They certainly deserve it. It's no unfair punishment for their crimes."

"Oh, you're not as unfeeling as you say!" said Tara-lin.

"Not to you," said Keller. "But them? I tell you, I don't really care."

The dryads said Shallim-Araldor is merciful and that there needs to be more mercy among humankind. I know, for myself, that fear is at the very heart of the Nightmare and all Corruption. If Keller is willing, I think I will pardon and release them. But really? Would it be better for them to be alone with a tree, and maybe a dryad, for a long time? I don't know. Is it mine to decide? What does it mean to be Queen? What decisions am I supposed to make, and what is none of my business? At any rate, I need not decide tonight.

"Hey, I think these trees right here make a good place for us," said Tara-lin to her mate. Several firs grew close together. It would be easy for them to climb up the trees and attach their house-cloth to the trees to make a good, tight hammock for them to sleep in.

. . ❋ ❋ ❋ ❋ ❋ . .

The next morning the gryphons flew out and spotted the Dragonrider. He and his beast had taken up residence on the shoreline below the cliffs. It looked like they were building a fire-pit in the sand. It looked like they were in no hurry to move on.

Tara-lin and her friends found a way down the cliffs – a narrow, winding ravine, narrow and rocky enough to be easily and safely navigated. The adult gryphons followed them in the air, and Keller's Kellia was passed back and forth when they came to particularly difficult spots.

As they drew near the place where the dragon and rider worked, both stopped and turned to approach them. Tara-lin whispered to Alis, "Aren't the dragon's eyes eerie?"

"I suppose so," said Alis, shrugging.

The rider spoke, and Tara-lin tried to let go of the ordinary way in which she perceived the world. It felt like trying to stop swimming in the middle of a deep lake or the sea. It felt like letting go of a branch when one has climbed most of the way to the top of a tall and ancient fir.

She turned to the dragon and thought, *Ask him to repeat himself.*

The dragon stared at her as if not understanding. She spoke out loud. "Ask him to repeat himself."

The dragon's eye whirled slowly and intently. Alis stepped forward and said, "She said 'Ask him to repeat himself.'"

The dragon nodded, and the rider spoke again. "Hello. We have come to your land from across the sea. My name is Klaisen and this dragon's name is Sugarfly."

Tara-lin nodded. "Tell him that he has come to the King and Queen of this land. My name is Tara-lin. I would know why he is here. Did he come here on purpose? Was it an accident?"

"Shush! That's as much as I can do at once, since it seems the dragon only understands me now," said Alis. She directed her voice to the dragon and repeated Tara-lin's words.

Before she finished, Klaisen bowed in a strange, awkward fashion and spoke again. "I do not know the courtesies of this land, but I expect you know that already. I am glad to have met you, Queen Tara-lin. I am here because the land from which I come is hostile to dragons. Not long ago, almost all the dragons were killed, but a dragon-keeper and a Warrior of the Dragonriders arose. There are now many dragons in Aneri, the land from which we come, and the wild spaces are not big enough. In the south, there are still laws in effect ordering that dragons and Dragonriders be burned alive if captured. In the north, the people are not exactly friendly, and will turn against us if they perceive that the dragons are eating their rightful prey. Sugarfly learned from birds what islands she could use to cross the sea, and that is how she brought us here." He paused, then bowed again. "Are we welcome in this land, Queen Tara-lin?"

"You are welcome if you abide by our laws," said Tara-lin. "You and your dragon must not burn the trees, for the dryads who live in them are our friends and allies. You may hunt the wild deer and animals, and you may take deadfalls or low branches for firewood to cook. We will be happy to teach you how to forage in these forests so that you can feed yourself mostly on the food they provide. You must not threaten or harm our citizens or destroy anything that is theirs. I think that is all, or at least enough for now."

When Tara-lin's response had been summarily passed through the dragon, the rider bowed again. "Have I and Sugarfly leave to pass to our friends instructions on how to cross the ocean to this land and to invite them to do so?"

"Tell your friends how to come across, if you wish. I cannot forbid them to begin the journey, but before you tell them they will be welcome here, I will wish to converse with you more, to learn more about you all, and also to know how many of you there are who wish to come to Elethri."

The information was passed, and the rider bowed again. "I thank you, gracious Queen. It is good to meet the elven people and to know that you are real, but that you do not keep my people as slaves, as the stories we have in Aneri say. It would be nice if we could find a more convenient way to converse," he said.

"I think I shall soon be able to speak your language,

Dragonrider," said Tara-lin. "But if you wish to dwell in Elethri, you must eventually learn our language so that our people can speak to you more easily."

When the information was again conveyed to the dragon, Klaisen bowed again. "I shall be pleased to learn your language, Elven Queen."

"Then this audience is finished for the moment. Stay here, on this tongue of the land, until I speak to you again. If you will, let Sugarfly hunt mostly in the sea, so that she will not eat too many of the land-animals and make it harder for my people. I will speak to you again soon, Klaisen," said Tara-lin. *So dragons and dryads really do have a hard time speaking to and understanding each other,* she thought. *The dragon understood me fine yesterday, and, while I think she understood me only a little today, she understood me far less because of the dryadic thought. I guess it makes sense, even though dragons and dryads are similar in that they need no language to speak and are not affected by space quite as humankind are in their communication. After all, dryads are of the trees, and dragons are beasts of fire. What in Areaer could be more different? How could anything be more different from the thoughts of trees – free though rooted in the earth, with a lifeblood of cool sap, whose lives wax and wane with the seasons, and the dryads who dwell in them – than the thoughts of beasts who soar upon the wind and in whose bellies dwells a fire which they can breathe out, and who bond to human-kind with all the fierceness of more-than-human emotions?*

When I live and think after the pattern of the dryads, there's probably not enough animality in my thoughts for the dragons to hear me well. After all, dryads, while they can appear, and apparently even marry and have off-spring with humans, have very different bodily functions from those shared by humankind and dragonkind and all the kinds of beasts.

She shook herself, trying to shake off the slowness, almost, of the dryad pattern of life. She felt a strange quiver. It was not weariness, but something else entirely, yet it almost felt like weariness in her limbs. "Let's go and get some food now," said Tara-lin to her friends, turning back towards the ravine. "We'll return to Klaisen and Sugarfly after we finish visiting our people."

Looking over her shoulder, Tara-lin caught Sugarfly looking at her. "Do you understand me now?"

The dragon nodded.

"Did you understand anything at all when I was focusing on

being able to understand your rider, earlier today?"

This question seemed to confuse Sugarfly. Klaisen rose and spoke, and Tara-lin was a little surprised to understand him a little. He said that Sugarfly had known she was there, but did not understand her. At least, that was the simplified gist of it. Tara-lin knew there was more to it. Sugarfly nodded her head, then shook it, nodded it and shook it again, in an attempt to answer Tara-lin.

Tara-lin shook her head a little, trying to clear it of what felt like a dream. Already, her conversation with Klaisen felt dreamy and strange, as it had been had in another world or another realm of existence. She held onto it, not wanting to forget it, as she suspected she forgot much intercourse between herself and the dryads in her sleep. Then she continued moving after her friends.

Klaisen has blue eyes. Like his dragon. I wonder, is there a reason for that? Are the two related? I've never seen blue eyes on a human before. His skin is light, too.

Chapter Eleven – Shadow of Night

Several months later, Tara-lin rose in the middle of the night from the trees where she and Keller slept. The thicket grew on the ridges of the mountain up against which Frèlin was built, and Tara-lin was able to descend the incline. She made her way to the sward surrounding the Tower of Elethri. She stood for a while on the grass, looking up at the shining globe that glowed above the spire of the Tower. Much of the palace around the Tower had been torn down, and gardens were being planted where once stone had lain upon the ground. Most notable of all there, some ways behind and a little to one side of the ancient tower, a tree had been planted. The tree had been found by her mother, Lìrulin, and Tara-lin could tell that it was a special tree.

Treading softly, she approached the tree. As she did almost every night, she placed both hands side by side on its bark and sang to it. She did not really know why she did so. She knew that the tree had no dryad, or at least not yet. Perhaps it waited for whoever was right to appear. Perhaps it was made for something else; she knew some trees never did have dryads, and she knew also that this tree was unique in Areaer. Sometimes she wondered if this tree were somehow related to her ability to reach into the consciousness which the dryads associated, not with their own nature, but with the trees. Perhaps it was to trees something like what she was to dryads. She did not know these things. She did not have any reason to think them. She did not even exactly suspect them. She just wondered sometimes.

When Tara-lin was done singing to the tree, she did not return to Keller's side as usual. Instead she stayed there, enjoying the cool air and the solitude. Sometimes she felt like she needed quiet and silence and nothing else around her in order to think or to sort through her thoughts.

Footsteps alerted Tara-lin to the approach of another. She turned and saw her father crossing the sward towards her. She ran towards him. "Hello! What are you doing here at this time of night?"

He smiled at her. "Coming to see you," he said, then added, "You often seem kind of sad. Are you sad right now?"

"I wouldn't say *I'm* sad," said Tara-lin. "But I look at you. I love you. I want you to stay with me. I get to play with you so little, now that I'm Queen, though it's been more often recently than it was at first. I love your advice. But you're getting old. You're so much older now than you were when I was young." She swallowed, then began again. "I'm sad for Mom and Lyan, too. And I think I'm sad for you. There's so much you're going to miss." She was speaking very quickly now, but slowed down a little to say what she had to say next. "And I think, for all I know, and for all the dryads have taught me, I fear death. When I think of it, there's a cold emptiness in my heart. So I think I'm sad and afraid for you, too," she said, speaking more quickly again, and then, a little more slowly, "but who am I to talk to you like this? It should be the other way around. I don't have the business to feel this way. Why am I asking you to comfort me?"

He closed the distance towards her and took her hands in his. He kissed her lightly. "I love you, Tara-lin. I want to comfort you and be with you."

She nodded, tears spilling from her eyes. "I love you, too, Dad. But I don't know how to love well when life is so short."

"I know, Tara-lin. I know you love me. And sometimes I don't know how to love well with such a short life. It's weird to think about. But let me tell you something, since you asked me. Shall we sit down first?"

Tara-lin shrugged. He took her – she clung to his arm – over to the tree, and they sat down under its eaves. She leaned into him, relishing his closeness. "Tara-lin, I'm not afraid of death. Ever since the first time I walked into Nightshade Castle, I haven't feared death. I just have not. I did fear Nightshade, and I can still hardly believe that I walked into Nightshade a second time."

She nodded. *You didn't exactly* walk *into Nightshade the second time. You were captured and taken,* she thought, but she did not speak. It was irrelevant.

"Neither do I think often of it," Eldor continued, meaning death. "I try not to. It fills me with a fear of a different sort, or maybe it's only sadness. I love you. I love Lyan. I love Lìrulin so much. It's why we were so drawn to each other that she went into Icecrown with me. It's why I married her. I cannot call it foolish, even knowing the sadness that comes of it. We were, and still are, so in love with one another. It is a love which has only grown and burned brighter as the years pass. What would have been foolish – perhaps even a victory for the nightmare – would have been for us to think ahead, to foresee a sorrow which is not even yet upon us, and so not to follow our hearts, not to follow love and joy. But I can't even imagine doing that. How could we not seek to be one? We were in love!"

"I kind of understand," murmured Tara-lin. "And I think it *would* have been a victory for the Nightmare if you and Lìrulin had stayed apart out of fear, instead of coming together in love, Dad. But I also think if you hadn't been the people you are, people who *would* fall in love, you wouldn't have survived Nightshade at all." *And,* she thought to herself, *I think the Nightmare has won a victory in the choice of the dryads to estrange themselves from the elves. Hopefully, before I die, the dryads will re-think their decision, and more like Alai-ie-a will rise.*

"I'm sure you're right, Tara-lin," said Eldor.

The moment hung between them for a long time. The night was still, the city was bright. It was quiet, except for a few muted woodland noises. Time might as well not have passed. Then Tara-lin shifted. "I should probably go back to Keller, now," she said.

"And I should go back to Lìrulin and Lyan," said Eldor. They both rose and he smiled at her.

"Am I weird?" she asked, holding her arms out.

"I think everyone is weird. How do you mean?" asked Eldor.

"I'm married. I love Keller. I could be pregnant one day, myself. Yet I still love you, and I don't want to miss you. I *will* miss you," said Tara-lin.

"I don't know if that's weird or not," said Eldor. "I love you, too."

"I love you, Dad." She smiled back at him, then turned and walked back up towards the mountain.

Tara-lin paused on the breast of the ridge. Outlined against the stars was a pair of wings. She looked closer and thought she discerned a rider between the wings. If it was a dragon – and the motion of the wings looked a little strange for a dragon, though she knew different dragons had very different strokes – then it would have to be a young one, for a human, or even elf, would not be as large compared to a dragon's wings as this rider was. There were not any young dragons in Ellenesia. It must be a gryphon rider. Tara-lin wondered if it was Alis and Kushon, whom she missed, or if it was another of the gryphon riders.

A part of Tara-lin hoped it was Alis. She missed Alis, even though she had only been gone for a couple months. Another part of her hoped it was one of the other gryphon riders out for a night ride. If Alis was coming back this soon, it was probably because something had gone wrong.

Tara-lin remained there for a few minutes, watching the beat of the gryphon's wings. Then she continued towards where she and Keller slept. She would not be able to tell which gryphon it was by the wing-stroke. She might be able to narrow down which dragon it was, but not which gryphon. For some reason, dragons had a variety of different wing-shapes, many of which Tara-lin had seen, as more of Klaisen and Sugarfly's friends had arrived from across the ocean.

.. * * * * *..

Tara-lin lay awake on the cloth, rubbing it between her fingers. The pre-dawn light filtered through the branches above her. A gentle breeze blew down from the mountains. Beside her Keller slept soundly, but she could not sleep. She ought to have been tired, she thought, but her mind insisted on listening to the forest around her, at the same time that thoughts buzzed through it. She could not wait to find out if that was Alis and Kushon she had seen flying through the night or simply a gryphon and rider going for a night flight. Both seemed improbable. Gryphons tended to be mostly day-creatures. It would be unlikely for Alis and Kushon to choose to travel at night, but it would also be unlikely for a gryphon rider to take a pleasure ride that far out from the eyres at night. That it was Alis and Kushon seemed to Tara-lin the more improbable of the two options, but she had to know for sure.

If she got up now, Keller would wake soon, and he would wonder where she went and why. She knew that he still had nightmare-panic-flash-attacks about being abandoned, and she did not want to do that to him. It was really miserable for him, and there had been enough of it already.

Tara-lin's ears caught the sounds of gryphon wings heading in her direction. *Is that Alis, wanting to see me, or knowing I can't wait to see her, or is that any one of the gryphons, possibly bearing his or her rider, heading down to whatever business they have in Frèlin or the surrounding woods?* thought Tara-lin. *Would Alis even know how to find me at this hour? Would she even know where or how to find anyone who could tell her how to find me at this hour? If it was her flying in late last night, almost this morning actually, would she even be awake, or would she and Kushon sleep for most of the day? If she was flying so late, maybe there was a real problem, and they've been flying so long and hard they could both sleep for a week. Would it be the kind of problem that would keep them awake so they could tell me about it as soon as possible, or* would *they sleep until hunger and thirst woke them up?*

Only a few more minutes, thought Tara-lin to herself. *Maybe more like half an hour. Not more than an hour. If it's more than an hour before he wakes up, I'll leave anyway. He'd expect me to. Or I'll wake him. That's probably a better idea. Only a few more minutes! Then I can find out! It probably wasn't even Alis last night.*

The sound of wings receded as the gryphon passed over her, and, before long, she heard more wings coming down from the eyres. This was normal. Many days she was not awake at this hour to listen to it, but other times she was awake to hear it. It went on for a long time in a somewhat staggered fashion; on most days, a few riders would not even fly down until it was almost noon.

Tara-lin smiled to herself, imagining Alis looking at the torn-down palace wing and the gardens that were being grown in its place. Then she thought of how irritated Eldazìn would be to discover the lack of the structure, which he thought of as a defense, as something protective, both against deadly violence and against eavesdropping. How in the world did he not understand that it was a tomb? How could he be what he was and do what he could do, and not feel a need, like hunger or thirst, for the trees?

Tara-lin did not want to worry about death or violence. That struck her as the wrong way to rule or think. She certainly would not go against the needs of her nature and magic in order to be safe. She would never trade in life for safety. However, without walls, eavesdropping *was* an issue, one for which she and Keller were working on finding a solution that did not involve too much inconvenience or potential pitfalls. Perhaps, they would be able to work one out by the time Eldazìn returned. Otherwise, he would be very unhappy about the present situation, even though he knew to expect it.

If he returned. For a moment Tara-lin felt a brushing tendril of fear. What he was doing might not be nearly as dangerous as sneaking into Nightshade, but it was still potentially dangerous. She did not know all the details of it. She knew far more about Alis' plan, but it had to be dangerous. Trying to spread, in whatever way Eldazìn thought best, the news that the King and Queen of Elethri welcomed fugitives was not the safest thing in the world. If the Valor Hall captured him *or* Alis, it would probably kill them – unless some other fate were chosen for Alis, which Tara-lin could imagine, especially if she were recognized as Alis Luela, which was not improbable. Of course, if that happened, Elethri would go to war to free her! Tara-lin amended that in her mind. She would not try to make her people do that. But she *would* find a way to rescue Alis.

Another tendril of fear brushed against Tara-lin's mind. She could not imagine any way to keep Elethri out of war with the Valor Alliance, sooner or later. Surely, the Valor Alliance would not tolerate what she and Keller were doing with Elethri. Namdon and Cuthlin, with some help from her father, had decided to look for a way to publish their experience and knowledge of the corruption in the Valor Hall, in the hope of gaining the support of any Knights who cared about their oath at all. Tara-lin was not quite sure about all the details of their plan, but she was sure Eldazìn was helping them, and that some at least of the gryphon riders and the Dragonriders from across the sea would also be interested in helping them. She was not sure what she thought of the plan, except that she did not think it was in her rights, even as Queen of the nation they were using to stage it, to forbid it. For one thing, she did not even think it was likely to be the deciding factor in whether the proverbial tree fell. It might determine *how soon* the tree fell, but the Valor Hall would not be likely to tolerate her and Alis offering girls – and others – a way to escape the tyranny of their religion and society. That is, *if* anyone took, or tried to take, the way of escape, and she did not think the Valor Hall would want war with Elethri if there were *no* effect to what Namdon and Cuthlin were doing, either. While she suspected those who ruled in the Valor Hall were confident of their ability to crush the elven nation if they so chose, she knew also that they might know that it would be costly, and would potentially leave the Valor Alliance open to an assault from the south, especially if the southern nations chose to unite in such a war effort.

Sometimes, Tara-lin wondered if she was wrong to use Elethri to try to influence other lives for the better. Was it betraying her relationship with the elven people as their Queen to use the resources that came from being their Queen in order to do something, however good in itself, that she suspected would bring war onto their land? Was she right to risk their lives and well-being – and, possibly, the entire nation, for while she knew Elethri had advantages the Valor Alliance could not know about, she did not know if they would be enough to turn the tide – for this enterprise, however good and well-intentioned? At the same time, she was Alis' friend, and she knew that while she had an opportunity to give others like Alis a chance of freedom she could not refuse to try.

Hot energy burned in her veins. She could not just lie here! She got to her feet, grabbed a branch of one of the trees which anchored and upheld her and Keller's little tree-home, and thrust herself up into the tree.

Below her, she heard Keller's voice. "What are you doing, Tara-lin?"

"Climbing a tree," she answered, then, suddenly concerned, "Did I wake you up? Are you still tired?"

"Why are you climbing a tree, though?" asked Keller.

"Because I'm upset and couldn't just lie still any longer," said Tara-lin. "I'm sorry. Did I wake you up before you were ready?" She looked down below her.

He was sitting up and rolling his shoulders. "No, I think I'm pretty much ready to wake up. I think I was just waiting for the breeze. But why are you upset?"

"I think I've talked to you about this, before, Keller. I know I should not be afraid. I know I'm thinking like Eldazìn instead of thinking like myself – which I don't do very well, anyways; Eldazìn can think like himself, but Tara-lin shouldn't – but I fear. I fear whether what we're trying to do for others will bring Elethri into war, and whether it's a betrayal of our people, of the trust of being King and Queen, to risk bringing war into their lands like this."

"Why is that bothering you, this morning?" asked Keller.

"I saw a gryphon rider flying during the night, and I thought of Alis," said Tara-lin.

"Oh," said Keller. He bowed his head, so that she lost contact with his eyes. "You know my own fear."

"I do," she said, disentangling herself from the branches and landing with something of a thump on their bed. "You fear being thrown into a dungeon and abandoned, alone, again, if we lose." Her eyes filled with tears as she said it. "But really, that's not likely to happen. If we lose, and we're captured, instead of being able to escape from some useless human woodsmen, we'll probably be executed fairly promptly. And I don't think we'll lose. After all, we might have much less resources, but we'd be fighting a defensive war. Elves – and some Dragonriders – fighting to defend Elethri is a *lot* easier than bumbling humans trying to take Elethri. And, even if we are captured, it *won't* be Nightshade Castle."

Keller nodded. Tara-lin knelt next to him and touched his shoulder lightly. He was shaking. "I know," he said, "but I'm *so* afraid of being alone, in the dark, even for a few moments. I guess it's silly, but it doesn't seem silly. I don't even think it's silly. And, Tara-lin, it *could* even be in Nightshade Castle itself. Nightshade still stands. Who knows what's there? And who knows how much they'd hate us?"

Moved by emotion, Tara-lin jumped to her feet, making the whole cloth bounce and vibrate, while Keller went on. "And if I'm taken into Nightshade again, I think I really *shall* go mad. I think the childhood madness I endured protected me. Stripped of that, what would I become?"

"*Not* a monster," said Tara-lin. She stomped her foot, forgetting for the two-thousandth time how ineffective stomping was on a sheet of cloth stretched between trees. "And we *won't* be imprisoned in Nightshade. And Nightshade *shouldn't* exist. If they take us prisoner and take us into Nightshade, I'll – I'll *destroy it!*"

Keller was shocked into raising his head and looked at her with his sky-blue eyes. "What are you saying, Tara-lin? *How* will you destroy it?"

"I just *will*," she said. "I have the Starweave. I – Nightshade Castle can *not* hold us, and I would *never* leave you behind."

"Like my mother, but I don't know if she knew," said Keller under his breath. More loudly, he said, "Tara-lin, I'm not sure what I should think of your declaration. But I do think we don't need to have this conversation right now."

"I agree," said Tara-lin. "I need to go and see if that was Alis flying in last night, or someone else going for a night flight." She swung herself over the edge of the sheet, hooked her feet on the tree branches, and undertook the descent more rapidly and carelessly than usual.

Keller followed after her, using a ladder made of elven cloth and tied to the trees. Half-elven as he was, it was not exactly safe for him to have to always descend the trees with no aid, no matter how he felt. He had never had the opportunity to climb a tree until about eleven years ago, and while his woodcraft had improved greatly, it was still not up to elven standards. Tara-lin herself did not have the perfect, natural ease in the trees of most elves, which meant that even sick, exhausted, or both they could climb safely. Sometimes Tara-lin thought her deficiency was because she had had less time to perfect the art; if she were an elf, she would still be a toddler, and so it was only natural that she lacked their ease in the trees. Other times she thought it was because she had less dryad blood, that because the human blood in her was more direct and immediate it affected her woodcraft, even though in many ways she was more dryad than most "pure-blooded" elves.

As she neared the forest floor, Tara-lin spun and jumped down. She almost instantaneously recovered from the fall and sped down the hill. The whole way down her mind spun with imaginations of how it probably was not Alis at all, or anything really, except a night-loving elf taking his gryphon for a ride, and how she would then have wasted so much time wondering and worrying about it being Alis when it wasn't. Then she thought, even if it was Alis, wondering would still have been a waste of time.

Chapter Twelve - Magic of the Elves

Tara-lin burst out of the woods that clothed the mountain-ridge to see people gathered in the sward around the tree and the Tower as usual and, as was less usual, a human woman strolling through the newly-planted garden, examining the foliage.

It could have been one of the female Dragonriders, but to Tara-lin the form and attitude looked like that of Alis. Tara-lin altered her course but did not slow down at all. "Alis!" she called.

Others stopped what they were doing to turn at the sound of her voice. Alis straightened up from examining a plant and looked in the direction of Tara-lin. "Hi, Tara-lin," she said.

"Something went wrong, didn't it?" asked Tara-lin.

Alis shrugged. She looked a little sad and more tired. "I don't know about *wrong*, exactly. Things go wrong all the time. Since I ran away with you and confronted the wrong, instead of letting it stomp all over me, I've noticed that things are *always* going wrong."

"Get to it," said Tara-lin. "Please. I want to know what's going to happen. Is the Valor Hall sending a diplomat right now to deliver a declaration of war?"

"I got chased. I was just, you know, spreading rumors. Pinning papers onto walls and street corners. Having these Elethrian cloaks really helps. I can sneak around cities in the dark, and I might not be as good as an elf, but from the perspective of the city-folk and guards I might as well be! Stopping during the night to have little conversations with people in various cities and hamlets and farms. Well, so, I get discovered by these Valor Knights roaming around, and since I'm not as good a woodswoman as I would be if I were an elf, I can't completely lose them, so I do what I can, and then call Kushon, which of course means they know I'm a gryphon rider, though I still don't think they know I'm Alis Luela unless they have elven spies. Which I suppose they might. Well, before long, I notice that I'm being chased by another gryphon rider. So I, well, I suggest to the gryphon that she doesn't really want to interfere in the affairs of a different tribe of gryphons. I think she was quite confused between my suggestions and her rider's commands.

"Well, it was still quite a chase. I fled towards the mountains and I called the wild gryphons. Several tribes answered my and Kushon's call. I think they see the Valor Hall gryphons as slaves, but they think of Kushon as a 'free gryphon' with a human, and they were happy to help one of their own. They harried the Valor Hall gryphons – she had been joined by another two – and provided enough of a distraction for me and Kushon to escape far into the trackless skies." Suddenly, Alis laughed. "I'm no elf. I can't leave the earth trackless. But I am a gryphon rider, and the skies are trackless!"

"But I presume they will know you're Elethrian," said Tara-lin.

Alis tilted her head dramatically. "Because why else would I be spreading news or rumors about Elethri? The fact I fled towards the Malaitha Mountains means nothing. Where else would a renegade gryphon rider go?"

Another worry occurred to Tara-lin. "Do they know you can speak to all gryphons?"

Alis shrugged. "If she told them, they might, but who knows what their relationship to their gryphons is? Who knows if she *would* tell them? They're rock-headed enough they'd probably just think I was a witch and that it was a spell, and I might do it again, but I can't *always* speak to *any* gryphon." She stopped speaking, then said, "And I can't, not the way a Dragonrider would understand it. Space isn't a factor for the dragons."

"I know you can't speak to other gryphons if they're far away, but can you and Kushon speak across any distance?" asked Tara-lin.

"I've never been out of range from Kushon. But I don't know if it would happen if I went far enough," said Alis. "Gryphons have a longer range over which they can communicate with each other than I had, at least at first, with anyone except Kushon." She sat down on a rock that had been placed beside the garden path.

"You're tired," said Tara-lin.

Alis shrugged.

"You want to talk?" asked Tara-lin.

Alis shrugged.

"You *are* tired," said Tara-lin.

"I suppose. Kushon is hungry. So am I. I'll wait to sleep until after breakfast."

"Breakfast is soon," said Tara-lin, sitting down on the path next to Alis. "Is the Valor Alliance full of rumors about the Witch-Queen of Elethri now? Sometimes I wonder how this will work at all. They will teach them all that I am secretly mated to the High Demon or something like that. And how will the girls run away and find us if they *want* to?"

"Who cares what they say about you?" said Alis. "Will it even matter? Either they will be afraid of being cast into the netherhells for running away and defying those who are supposed to guide them, or they won't believe a word of it."

"You didn't believe *I* was evil. You weren't even afraid I was evil," said Tara-lin. "How would I have been able to make friends with you and convince you to run away with me if you thought *I* was evil, instead of just being afraid *you* were ... well, I'm not exactly sure what you were afraid of, but whatever it was. The netherhells."

"We're doing the best we can," said Alis. "There's at least a chance, an opportunity, for some of them, now. If anyone does win through to Elethri, you've taken care of that, right?"

"Yes," said Tara-lin, "I and Keller have arranged that if any human strays into Elethri, they're to be aided and guided to us. We're setting watch-posts in the more uninhabited regions of the border."

Alis yawned, muffling her attempt to say, "Good."

"Really, you need to sleep," said Tara-lin.

"I need to eat," said Alis.

Tara-lin rolled her eyes dramatically. "You're *always* hungry. You've *always* been hungry."

Alis giggled. "It does seem to be that way," she said, yawning again and muffling her last few words.

"Come," said Tara-lin, rising and brushing dust off her dress. "I'll get you what food's already available, and then you can eat in quiet and sleep wherever you want until Kushon comes to take you up to the eyres or whatever it is you want to do."

Keller was standing, waiting for them near the tables. "Hi, Tara-lin, Alis. How did it go?"

Alis shrugged. "I got chased back."

"She's tired and hungry, Keller," said Tara-lin. "I'll tell you."

.•*＊✳＊*•.

Days passed and turned into weeks, and weeks passed and turned into months. Eldazìn returned, alive and well. He was proving to be more of a helper than a nuisance now that he had accepted that Keller and Tara-lin intended to rule as they saw fit, and while they would hear his advice, did not require it. He now accepted their word as absolute, even if it went against his instincts and preferences, or even strong leanings. While Tara-lin and Keller learned to appreciate him, his thoughts on some subjects and his aid in other areas, and his sense of humor, they did not know how to respond to his loyalty. Tara-lin thought that to Eldazìn she was something of a goddess. Of course, it seemed to her that she was something of a goddess to most of the people of Elethri. Some of them seemed to revere her more as an attraction, distant, interesting, but unimportant, their reverence rather empty, while to others of them, like Eldazìn, she was more of a religion, for whom and on whose word they would fight and kill or suffer and die like martyrs for their faith. There was a fine line between the two kinds of loyalty and worship, one blending into the other in various degrees, with some elves' attitude being on one extreme and other elves' attitude being on the other extreme, and Tara-lin was not sure which she hated more. She was disgusted by both, and tended to be most disgusted by which ever one was most recently presented to her, though she thought she was more disgusted by Eldazìn's almost-religious loyalty. She did not know how, knowing her as closely as he did, he could still see her as a goddess. She was so clearly elven, even if she represented the epitome of what elves desired to be.

Tara-lin traveled the border of Elethri, singing songs into the air and earth with the intention of encouraging and guiding any fleeing refugees to places where the elves would find them and be able to take care of them. Keller often went with her, but other times she went with only Alis or Earnrìl. Once, she went alone, and another time she went with her parents, and her brother and his drake-lizard.

The last time when she returned to Frèlin she looked in amazement at the tree. It grew as no tree had grown before. It was continuing to grow through the mild Elethrian winter. It was beautiful, but not quite like any other tree Tara-lin had seen before. She found her mother and said to her, "How did you get this tree?"

Lìrulin smiled. "Some instinct made me pick up a seed from the ground when your father and I were sneaking into Nightshade Castle. It quickened in Nightshade Castle, but I planted it in the forest of Elethri and watched over it. When you and Keller were talking about the problem with the palace, I thought of it, got it, and transplanted it. This is clearly where it wants to grow."

"How come you never told me?" asked Tara-lin testily.

"You are still *very* young, Tara-lin," said Lìrulin. "I haven't told you *most* things, yet. It did not seem important for me to tell you. Why would I tell you about something the importance of which I don't understand and which I don't see as having any connection to you? I mean, I do tell you such things, but how would I ever tell you all of them?"

"Are there more things like this you haven't told me?" asked Tara-lin. *This certainly has some connection to me. It's growing in my capital city, and, for some reason, whenever I'm around it, I choose to sing to it. There's something important here,* she thought.

"Exactly like this? No, of course not. Are there things I know, but haven't told you, but may sometime turn out to be far more than I currently know them to be? Probably, but I wouldn't even know which ones they are." Lìrulin raised her hands in a "What can I do?" gesture.

"Does Eldor know?" asked Tara-lin.

"Yes," said Lìrulin.

"If he could know, why couldn't I?" asked Tara-lin.

"I was with him when it happened, Tara-lin. You're being silly right now. Why? There's some importance or significance to this in your mind that I can't see."

"Yes, there is!" said Tara-lin. She stomped her foot lightly, almost a tap, on the ground. "I *sing* to this tree whenever I'm around it."

"That's really curious," said Lìrulin. "I sing to it, too."

"You *sing* to it and you didn't think it was important enough to tell me about? And you *sing* and you didn't tell me?" asked Tara-lin.

"I *don't* have the talent you do," said Lìrulin. "I have something else, and this tree calls to me in a special way. I didn't know it called to you, also. That is really interesting. But I couldn't have known, and I *can't* tell you everything of importance in my life. Really, Tara-lin. This is quite silly. Why are you like this? Why are you *still* like this?"

"I'm not – usually. Am I?" asked Tara-lin.

"No, you're not, but this is ridiculous," said Lìrulin, "and it inclines me to think you know something you're not telling me."

"I really don't. Not that I can think of," said Tara-lin.

"Well then," said her mother, smiling strangely, "let's leave it at that I may have felt the same way. I just didn't think you would need to know. I *can't* tell you everything, and you are married. You ought to know there might be things you and Keller know just because you live together that you might not tell a child for decades – if it ever does occur to you to tell him or her."

"You're right," said Tara-lin. "I just –"

"The tree seems so obviously important, and so obviously significant to you, that you wonder how I could have neglected to mention it," said Lìrulin.

"Yes. It seems there's a lot you and Dad never told me. For example, I found out that he had a tangle with an ice-wraith and never told me until after I'd met them," said Tara-lin.

"There's more in any being's life than can ever be told another being. We have to be selective, Tara-lin. You'll find that out, soon. I bet it's already happening in your relationships with your friends, and even with Keller," said Lìrulin.

Tara-lin nodded. "Anyway, that is *really* interesting about the tree." She glanced at its silvery branches and shining scaly foliage that now towered above her, though it was still much shorter than most of the trees of the forest. It felt like something was about to click together in her mind, like she had or almost had the piece necessary for something to make sense, like something important, foretold but not seen, was about to reveal itself to her. *What is it?* she thought. Then she turned back to Lìrulin. "Sorry, Mom. I –"

"It's fine, Tara-lin. You would just do well to learn how to say what you're thinking or what you think is important instead of getting strangely upset about things only incidentally related. I love you." She offered her grown daughter a hug.

A few days later, Tara-lin woke in the morning to find Keller already sitting up on the bottom tarp. She opened her eyes to see him sitting with his eyes half-closed. He was gently humming. "Good morning," she said.

"Morning, Tara-lin," he replied. "Is there anything you want to do this morning?"

She shook her head, making little ripples move through the tarp. "Not in particular."

"Then let me show you something I've discovered recently."

He resumed humming and added words which sounded to Tara-lin like they belonged to some strange inhuman language. In a few moments she recognized it. "A *spell*," she breathed almost silently, watching. *Singing? A spell? Is that a wizardry thing? Or is Keller a singer, too? But it doesn't have the rhythm of my song. And it's hard to imagine Keller a singer. He doesn't seem to have the connection. But could he? My mom is ever so close to the dryads, but she's – well, I don't know what I think. She's apparently something of a singer. And maybe different singers have very different rhythms or harmony to their songs. Or maybe it's because he discovered his wizardry first....*

Tara-lin felt the air move around her. Energy was being sucked into it. She felt wind patterns form and collide and form again into a more complicated pattern of building power. *Definitely not the dryad song,* she thought. *The manipulation of the elements is like wizardry in form and substance ... or at least, as like wizardry as I can tell. It's definitely not the dryad song.*

Suddenly, the wind broke in a gust. Tara-lin gripped the tarp and lay as flat as possible, trying not to be tossed out of the tree-house by the wind flying in every direction and shaking the boles and leaves of the trees.

"Sorry," said Keller. "I should have warned you."

"It's okay," said Tara-lin. "But let me guess – you've discovered that you can work magic better if you sing it."

"Yes," said Keller. "Somehow, it's easier and works better – I'm not sure if more efficient is the right idea – if I sing the spell."

"That is *so* interesting," said Tara-lin, "but it's definitely wizardry, not the singing talent." She thought for a moment. "It actually makes so much sense and fits really well in with my theory that human magic is dryadic in origin. Maybe singer and wizardry are different primarily in degree. No, that's not right, but there's something in the idea. After all, the elves in the day of their glory made many artifacts that have power that's as similar to human wizardry as it is to my song."

"You're right," said Keller. "Hmm. Yes, I see it. A lot – not all – but a lot of the lost elven arts are as human in tone as dryadic. Even the art of making the glowing globes, that's not really dryadic ... but you can sing light if I remember the story correctly?"

"Brighten existing light. Steady it. Expand it," said Tara-lin. "But how *do* the light globes work? We've never really studied them. It might be ... it might be a surprisingly similar song."

Keller looked at her expectantly.

"What if you could sing to the globe so that it absorbs the light and shines again with the right pattern of radiance?" asked Tara-lin. "We reflect light. Trees get their energy from the light – and reflect light, too. Some living things glow. There might be a way ... Still, I think our thought is on the right track. I think the emergence of so much magic and the building of the Tower and the palace might be two sides of the same effect. They happened at about the same time, too. What if, in order to work magic of certain sorts – the light globes might not even be a particularly good example of it – an elf has to learn to use his mind and work his song in a way which is more human than dryadic? What if the era of magic among the elves carried in it its own doom? What if in order to work the magic an elf had to start a process that would begin to sever his ties with the magic – maybe not for himself in his lifetime, but if the way of thinking were continued and, so to speak, perfected, then for his descendants or students, until the art of practicing the magic finally estranged the practitioners from the magic they sought?" She sat up suddenly, leaning on her arm, thrilled with her thought. It fit so perfectly! It just *felt* right!

"That's an idea," said Keller. He paused, considering. "Do you think I should stop using wizardry lest I estrange myself further from the forest?"

Tara-lin shook her head vigorously, throwing ruby curls everywhere. "No! You're half-elf. You were born with the talent innate in you. It *is* how you think. I don't know if you can grow towards a more dryadic magic, or even if you should. But I think, as a whole, the elves should seek to be a woodland people with a woodland magic. I don't mean individuals here and there shouldn't pursue whatever art of magic appeals to them, but I think it shouldn't it be seen as characteristically elven or as the summit of elven magic. I think the woodland magic should be seen as the *elven* magic. And I think," said Tara-lin, softly, to herself, "it might even be a matter of degree and tone whether an elf is a singer or not. My mother now ... I think the dryad magic runs in all of us in one way or another."

She needed to pursue this thought with other elves.

Chapter Thirteen – Across the Malaitha Mountains

It was not long thereafter before Alis returned from a sudden call into the mountains, four days after she left and with two wild gryphons following Kushon, both bearing human riders. Tara-lin and Keller, who knew about Alis' arrival because Kellia sensed the approach of Kushon, waited under the magic tree that had first quickened in Nightshade Castle, while the gryphons swooped down and landed. Alis' face shone with what looked to Tara-lin like the widest possible grin in the world. She leaned over Kushon's neck and crooned some wild and happy tune into his ears while the other two humans, one male and the other female, dismounted their wild mounts. As soon as they were safely on the ground, the wild gryphons turned, flicking them with their tufted tails, spread their wings, and were flying back towards their lonely eyres.

At once, Tara-lin guessed that these were refugees from the Valor Alliance. Both wore, under heavy cloaks, what looked to have once been fancy garments, though they were now dirtied and torn so that, while still quite suitable clothing, they no longer appeared worthy of a palace. Both looked to be from one of the far northern nations, though there was enough mixing of the royal houses of the Valor Alliance that it was hard to be certain. The girl had dark reddish-gold hair, light skin, and light brown eyes. The boy had skin and eyes of a very similar shade, but his hair was darker and had less red in it. They both looked nervous and uncomfortable. They stood, looking at Tara-lin and Keller, and then averted their eyes, realizing they were being rude.

Finally, the girl curtsied in the Alliance fashion. "You're the Sorceress, right?" she asked, straightening.

"Sorceress?" asked Tara-lin. "I'm the Singer, the Queen of Elethri."

"I didn't know what you would like to be called, your majesty, sorry," said the girl. "Honestly, I don't – didn't – know who or what you are, or what customs are observed in the Land of the Five Rivers, only that we – well, I think my friend here should be talking, but he tends to be a bit shy in the presence of royalty or even lesser nobility."

"Then tell him – umm, don't be shy. I wasn't born royalty at all. What are your names? Mine is Tara-lin," said Tara-lin.

"My name is Keller," said Keller, right on her heels, "and I was born in, umm, a dungeon actually, so ..." He rolled his eyes and shrugged, making Tara-lin want to laugh at him.

"You guys are all being silly," said Alis, finally realizing what was going on. She slid off of Kushon's shoulders, laid her face against his for a moment exchanging some kind of communication with him, then stepped between the nervous fugitives and the equally awkward King and Queen. She curtsied to the pair of fugitives in the Alliance fashion. It looked strange done in her riding clothes. "I'm Alis, Gryphon Rider of Kushon. I'm guessing that you two are here because of some nonsense about arranged or forced marriages, and you heard that we don't do those kinds of things here in Elethri and that we accept any humans who want to come live here and be free – like myself. I'm the first girl Tara-lin helped escape a forced marriage. Come with me. There's no need for an irritating, awkward audience. I'll make you comfortable and explain everything to you, and you can explain as much or as little as you want to me." She beckoned to the two to follow her, shared another knowing look with her gryphon, and then lead them across the sward.

When they were gone, Tara-lin turned towards Keller and laughed.

"What is it?" he asked, catching her.

"Alis. She used to say that she was completely socially inept. She's doing so much better than we are with this, though."

"It helps that she has more in common with them, instead of being the absolute rulers that people are probably telling horror stories about. Also, did you listen to the way she talked? It might be great for putting those two at ease, but it sounded nothing like the court-language we've received from the Valor Hall's ambassadors so far."

"You're right," said Tara-lin. "I can't imagine any noblewoman or Knight's lady talking in court or in public or at a first introduction or in front of royalty like Alis just did. Though, the in-front-of-royalty doesn't really count. She knows I *despise* that kind of thing, and we've always been friends, just friends, who didn't care a rootlet when I was going to become Queen. Still," she said, collapsing into giggles again, "she remembers the curtsy."

"Well," said Keller, "let's take care of the other things we need to do today, and hear all about it from Alis when she's done with them."

"That sounds great," said Tara-lin. "I only wish they weren't scared of me."

"It might have helped if you'd said, 'I don't know about the Sorceress; I'm the elf here who receives visitors,'" said Keller.

"You don't think I — well, I guess you're right. Elven royal fashion isn't as exceptional as human royal fashion is, and we don't flaunt elven royal fashion or luxury, and what would a human know about how elves dress?"

.. * * * * * ..

That evening, Alis told them the whole story. From her side of things, it was very simple. An elf with a young gryphon had been flying through the Malaitha peaks and seen the two climbing up into the foothills. He had flown down to investigate, found them, asked Kushon to come and bring Alis, and convinced his own beast to carry the humans, one at a time, a little farther into the mountains, where the search-parties would not be likely to find them quickly. Alis and Kushon had gone immediately, even though they did not have a clear idea what it was about, and Alis had convinced some wild gryphons to help them.

The human fugitives had a longer and more complicated story. The girl's name was Coriann and she was a princess of one of the far north nations. She and a page from her father's court had fallen in love, while she was absolutely opposed to marrying any of the men her father considered suitable suitors. Both she and the page had known the other loved them, but they had only ever been able to fetch a few secretive moments together and both had despaired of ever having a life together, until the page, whose name was Valmor, had heard about Elethri's offer of sanctuary. He had been doubtful if it could possibly be true, but had known he had to try if Coriann was willing. He had successfully convinced her that they ought to try — whatever would happen to her if they failed or were caught or were sent back would hardly be worse than being forced to marry a man she disliked over the one she loved. Coriann had countered that if it was the will of gods she marry one of those men then it was best for her soul and for the world; besides, she cared about Valmor, and if he were caught spiriting her away he would be executed without trial. Eventually he had succeeded in convincing her — from his perspective, if they could not be together he would not mind dying trying to be together — and they had planned and plotted how to escape. They decided that they had to wait for the annual gathering at the Valor Hall, and that, somehow, they had to ensure that Valmor was one of the pages who was sent to attend the family. He told Coriann that he would figure out how to sneak through the portal, either with the royal retinue or after it, and find a way to meet her, but that had not been necessary.

Their escape from the Valor Hall and Astri had been similar on some counts, but different on others, from that of Tara-lin and Alis. They had chosen a festival day when the adults would all be most busy and it would be most likely Coriann would be not missed for the longest. Not knowing how long it would take them or what they would encounter in their journey through the mountains, Valmor had packed a great deal of food and extra cloaks into two packs, one larger and for himself to carry, the other smaller and for Coriann to carry. Instead of fleeing in the night, after everyone had gone to sleep, they had disappeared during the courses of the banquet, getting themselves into the streets of Astri and out of the gate in all the confusion of city-folk and rustic farmers from the countryside gathered together for the banquet. Many of the farming families were rushing to get out of the city so they could be back at their farms at the same time Coriann and Valmor were also leaving the city. Foreseeing that a search for Coriann would be begun at about bed-time, though the first conclusion would probably not be that she had fled Astri with Valmor in an attempt to win through to Elethri, they bumbled through the hills and woods all night. When the elf gryphon rider saw them in the morning they were already thoroughly exhausted. They had to wait another an entire day, night, day, and night again before Alis came with gryphons who could carry them all the way through the mountain passes and into Elethri. The elf had scouted constantly, ensuring that if any search parties neared their hiding place he and his beast would have time to get the two humans away to a new place.

It took Alis a while to tell the story. When Tara-lin had heard it all, she said, "So, we've had some success."

"And our idea of having watchers on our less heavily populated borders has turned out to be a very good one," said Eldazìn. "I wonder: did the fact that Alis was discovered as a gryphon rider who fled towards the mountains help with this? Did Valmor know about that incident and did it influence his decision about the best way to try to reach Elethri?"

"I don't know," said Alis, yawning. "I could ask tomorrow, I suppose. I hope if this happens a lot we find a better way to do it than having me fly out there and persuade wild gryphons to help. For one thing, they're cheerful if they only have to help a little, but they'll get very tired of this if it happens every couple of months."

"There's an easy solution to that," said Tara-lin. "Send a Dragonrider next time. A dragon can easily carry three people. And they owe it to me for living and eating in Elethri. It's not that much to ask."

"Of course it's not much to ask," said Alis, yawning again. "But there's another problem. Kushon and Odombra were almost out of reach of each other. Kushon only barely received a vague sense of urgency from Odombra. If we're any farther apart, it won't get through at all, and gryphons don't talk to dragons well. They can do it a little, but it's not helpful. The gryphon to dragon range is much shorter than the gryphon to gryphon range."

"You should go to sleep," said Keller. "We can talk about these problems tomorrow."

"That sounds like a good idea," said Alis, rising. "By the way, Earnrìl, can you thank Welri for me for hunting for Kushon?"

When Alis went, Tara-lin turned to Earnrìl "What's that about? Can't Kushon thank Welri himself?"

"He can and does, but it's how gryphons like to do things," said Earnrìl.

Tara-lin nodded. She probably could not understand everything about gryphons. It probably took a gryphon rider to understand everything about such intelligent and interesting beasts. *Actually,* she thought, *probably none of us understand everything about any animal. We just notice it with the gryphons because of the gryphon riders.*

"By the way, Keller and Tara-lin," said Earnrìl, "I don't think there's any need to re-build the Tower. It makes an excellent guesthouse for us to house those who are not yet ready to experience more elven accommodations."

"Or might not *ever* enjoy such accommodations. Most humans don't have enough dryad blood to matter," said Tara-lin.

"Of course," said Earnrìl. "I did not mean it like that – to come across snotty or anything."

"We know," said Keller. They all stood, and he whispered a word, allowing the wards to lapse and remain dormant until the next time he activated them. They had developed something of an enclosed area by using several different plants to create a screening hedge which would probably reach a good twenty feet in height and was already taller than Tara-lin. Keller had found a permanent warding spell and tweaked it in order to permit them to ward the area and to provide a perimeter to the ward which would alert him whenever anyone strayed into it and which was wide enough that it could not be physically breached before he could warn whoever was in council with him. It was not like Tara-lin was even strictly opposed to ever using stone rooms for private conversations, but this made things easier and simpler. "Also," Keller explained, "I can adapt this spell to be temporary, and allow us to have some privacy almost anywhere. So it's well on that account alone that we've figured this out."

. . * * * * * . .

That night, when Tara-lin went out to sing to the tree, Coriann came and stood outside the door of the Tower, looking at her. When Tara-lin finished singing to the tree and turned to go back to Keller, she saw Coriann walking out towards her. The human princess curtsied. "Hello, Tara-lin."

"Hi, Coriann. You seem suddenly less afraid of me."

"Yes," said Coriann, still hanging back and a little shy. "After talking to Alis, I realize you're not that different from us, even if you're twice my age, and a half-elf, with magical powers, who's a Queen."

Tara-lin nodded.

"So I just wanted to say hi and to say thank you."

"Well, thanks," said Tara-lin, "but it's really quite unnecessary."

Coriann came a step closer. "It might be unnecessary, but ... but you're why I and Valmor have a place to go, a chance to make our life together. It all started with you helping Alis escape, and now ... how can I not thank you?" She smiled shyly.

"I guess," said Tara-lin. She tilted her head. "Do you feel uneasy about me because of things you've been told, or what? And why did you think you should call me 'Sorceress'?"

"I think it's a combination," said Coriann. "I might be the princess of a minor kingdom, but you're the Elven Queen. That's ... that's a big difference. It's weird to think about what it is like to be you. As for the stories, you're rumored to be evil and to be able to control the spirits of the trees. I don't know what you really can do, but it's definitely something, isn't it?"

"Yes, but I don't control the dryads. They choose to work with me or not. Most often, it's I who choose to work with them."

"That's so strange," said Coriann. "Even stranger than being an Elf Queen, I think, to have that kind of relationship with *dryads*. And I've always been a little shy, but I think I might like to be friends with you."

"Well, I'm willing to be friends with you, Coriann, but I won't feel hurt if you're not interested another day. A person can only have so many friends, myself included. One of the things about the Singer-Queen is that most of the elves think of me ... well, it's really weird. You're probably right that my position among the elves is ... more exalted than your own previous position, but it's not by my choice. I *hate* it."

Coriann nodded. "I ... I can just hardly believe we're actually here." She looked around with an odd, bewildered look, as if she could not believe her surroundings.

"Well, you are," said Tara-lin. "As long as Elethri stands, you can do whatever you want here ... within reason."

"Of course," said Coriann, blushing. The rose color showed strongly on her lighter skin tone. She looked very awkward for a few moments, then ventured a question. "What were you doing just earlier?"

"Singing to this tree," said Tara-lin. "I don't really know why I do it, but it's a magical tree. Anyway, it's nice to meet you, Coriann."

"It's nice to meet you too ... Tara-lin."

"We can talk more tomorrow. I should go back to Keller."

"He's the King, isn't he?" asked Coriann. "I mean, he was the Crown Prince, the Heir, right?"

"Yeah," said Tara-lin. "What do you mean?"

"Well, you seem to be, well, the Queen. As much the Ruler as he is. How is that so, if you're not the Crown Princess? Wouldn't he be primary Ruler even if he had married you for the throne? What's your relationship like?"

"In Elethri it's like that. When we marry, we form a team. If we're King and Queen, we either rule together or whoever is more suited or interested in it rules. It no longer matters who was born to the throne and who married into the line."

"How ... interesting," said Coriann.

"Well, I need to go," said Tara-lin. "I'll gladly continue this conversation with you tomorrow, but, really, I should go back to Keller."

"Bye, Tara-lin," said Coriann softly.

"Bye, Coriann," said Tara-lin. As she turned towards her and Keller's tree-house, she remarked to herself, *Coriann does not seem to me very much like Alis.*

I wonder how many have tried and been caught. She and Valmor are the only ones to have made it so far. Have they been the only ones to try, or have others tried and failed ... or are others on their way right now, not having yet failed?

Chapter Fourteen – Land of the Five Rivers

Though they did not find any easy or perfect solution to the issue of how to efficiently and reliably transport refugees across their border, Tara-lin and Keller regularly visited different cities of their nation and frequented festivals. They, along with their elven friends, wanted to teach the elves their discoveries about the nature of elven magic. Both of them spoke to the elves, and Tara-lin often sang at the festivals. Afterwards, she would give speeches like the following:

"Elves of Elethri, children of dryads, it is not I only who can sing! We are each gifted to express our dryadic heritage in different ways and to different degrees, and it is possible, though not certain, that none of you can spontaneously sing and dramatically change the weather or otherwise alter the world around you. Yet all of you have an innate connection to the forests and to dryadic magic, and for many of you one of the ways through which you can discover your legacy is your song. I do not, however, urge you to sing if you do not feel like it, but let nothing make you afraid to sing! Seek whatever it is that resonates with you – the sound of the waves breaking on the shore – the whisper of the leaves before dawn – the feel of the earth after the rain. Whatever it is, do not be afraid to follow whatever draws your heart. Learn to love and feel with the earth, if that is your desire. Sing with the wind and the rain if that is what makes your heart soar! Sit in the woods and listen to the silence of the trees if that is what pleases you. Walk along a stream and learn its song, if that is where your heart runs! Whatever it is, do not be afraid! Do not be afraid to try what you do not know! We may never attain the magic arts of old, but that is because we are not the elves who lived then. We are the elves who are alive now, and we are no less elven if the arts of our magic are suited to us rather than to those who lived before. We are the children of dryads, and our magic is the magic of the woods and the world in which the woods thrive. It does not have to flash and sparkle to be elven! Indeed, the greatest expressions of our elven legacy may be much quieter and subtler or very gentle indeed. As dryads are different, so are we. If your heart sings with the streams, then sing with the streams. If your heart sings with the wind, then sing with the wind. If your heart sings with the sea, then sing with the sea. If your heart sings with the dawn, then sing with the dawn. Do not be afraid to find your own song, your own art of magic. Even if it isn't a song, don't be afraid to find it! It does not make you any less elven, any less a part of this beautiful world of nature. Dryads themselves do not sing as we who are human-kin sing! We think of it as song because, for most of us, song is the closest thing to it we know, the thing that brings our human thought most into harmony with the dryad thought. For some of you, your dryadic heritage may be such that song is not a part of it for you. This does not make any of you any less or any more elven, any less or any more children of nature!"

The applause and the attention always made her feel strange, even icky. She was trying to change the way they thought, to give them an understanding of the world which would free them of whatever it was that made them worship her and her talent, but she felt that they did not believe her words. It was not that they consciously or deliberately disbelieved her; it would never have entered their minds to doubt her words. Instead, their reverence for something of which they made her the embodiment rendered them unable to understand her, so that they thought they believed and agreed with her while doing exactly the opposite. She knew that Earnrìl thought they behaved this way because of laziness. She was not sure what it was. There was certainly an element of something that looked like laziness associated with it: they did not seek their own talents, their own songs, whatever it was that would have fulfilled their nature, their inheritance of dryadic magic. But was the cause laziness, or was it only something that looked like it that was one of the results, and the cause was something else altogether?

Tara-lin tried to talk it over with Alis, but her human best friend maintained that she had no thoughts on the matter and she was not one to understand or speculate why people, human or elven, did or thought the things they did. Tara-lin understood why Alis felt this way, having never been at home among the other humans. She had been different from the rest of the human girls when Tara-lin first met her at the Valor Hall and, since coming to know Coriann, Tara-lin realized that Alis was very different even from other human girls who had the courage to flee their previous way of life in search of their true desires. Alis was far more rugged than Coriann. Tara-lin could not see herself having the friendship with Coriann that she had with Alis. She wondered if she and Coriann would have even been drawn to each other. Coriann certainly did not have the drive Alis had to get as close to animals and the wild as she could. If they were elves, Tara-lin supposed Coriann would have kept a delicate garden, while Alis would have had her home in a tangled thicket.

It's not like I'm like other elves any more than Alis is like other humans, though, Tara-lin thought. Nonetheless, she could not blame Alis for her lack of interest in the problems of ruling. One of the things Tara-lin liked about Alis was that she was always supportive of Tara-lin and of Tara-lin's choices, and when she did have thoughts to share she shared them, but she was not embroiled in Tara-lin's life or problems as Queen. When Tara-lin was with Alis, even when they were discussing the problems of Queenship, she might as well not have been Queen. Far from being frustrated with Alis' lack of emotional investment in her problems as Queen, Tara-lin was glad about it.

The walls of Frèlin rose before them. Tara-lin reined in her horse and stopped, her eyes searching the trees and sky above her for nothing in particular. Keller stopped beside her. She could feel him wondering what she was thinking, but she did not elect to speak. She wondered if Alis and Kushon had returned to Frèlin. They had arranged for Alis to engage in what they jokingly-but-also-deadly-seriously called her 'subversive missions' in the Valor Alliance at the same time as Tara-lin visited other cities and festivals of her Kingdom. That way, they could be together as much as possible. Kushon, like most gryphons, was not a nomad and wanted an eyre to call home, though he would travel with Alis whenever she really wanted. *And please, please, please,* Tara-lin ordered herself, *do not freak out if Alis isn't in Frèlin when you get there. She's been late before. Nothing is perfectly predictable.* She struggled not to worry about Alis being captured or killed. For one thing, Tara-lin could not imagine life without Alis. She would miss Alis so much, and she would not know how to be Queen without Alis' unique friendship and support. For another, if Alis were captured, Tara-lin thought she would go to war with the Valor Alliance if they did not release Alis to her. Tara-lin did not think that it would be the right choice to lead all her worshiping elves into a war that would probably be the end of most of their lives and of their nation, in order to rescue her friend.

Even if Tara-lin were not certain that Elethri did not stand a chance at successful invasion of the Valor Alliance, she still would not have thought it was right of her to spend the lives of those who seemed eager to place their fate in her hands in such a way. Nonetheless, she was not at all certain that she would hold to these convictions, or even that she would hold these convictions if Alis were captured. Certainly, she would do all she could to free Alis by herself, even if it meant almost certain failure and death, and doubtless Keller and Eldazìn would help her. *This whole business of being Queen is crazy,* thought Tara-lin. *It makes me not know what is right or what is wrong.* Then, steadying herself, she remembered the advice she had received many times over from various dryads. The situation was not upon her. She did not need to know right and wrong in a situation which was not hers, and which might never be. Was it even possible to know right and wrong outside the present situation?

Shallim-Araldor, she thought, *whoever you are, help me, if you can hear me. I fear, and I know I should not fear, but I do. I wish I did not fear, but I don't know how to love without fearing. Even if I knew what lies beyond this phase of life, even if I knew that beyond this phase of life is only perfect contentment, how can I not fear losing the company of those I love?* As it was, the impression she had received from the dryads was not a conviction of perfect contentment beyond this phase of existence; some of them seemed to have notions heading in that direction, but their thoughts suggested to Tara-lin more a continuance of existence in an as-yet-largely-unknown realm, which might contain possibilities of failure and grief similar to those in this world. That they believed that life would ultimately lead to perfect contentment Tara-lin did not know, but she was not at all certain that they believed that perfect contentment was right on the other side of, so-to-speak, death. Even if it was for dryads, Alis was a human, and Tara-lin's own understanding of these things was muddled and confused and she rarely thought about it because she could not think about it. *But even if I knew Alis was perfectly happy, it would be no balm to me. How can I love and not fear to miss the one I love? Yet I know fear is the power and heart of the Nightmare and all evil.*

In a hoarse whisper, Tara-lin said, "Let's go on."

Together they rode, as they had many times, through the gates of Frèlin.

When they reached the highest level of the city, the royal terrace, they found Akanë waiting for them. Tara-lin leapt off of Vonë's back and kissed his nose. Her arm still around his neck, she said to the elf Captain of the Guard, "What is it? You look like something has happened."

"You have a diplomat from the Valor Hall waiting to speak to you. He's been here for five days already," said Akanë.

"Hmm," said Tara-lin. "I wonder what about."

Keller shot her a look that shouted, "You are not this stupid!

Even I could guess!"

Akanë said, "He's told us already. The Valor Hall wants to know if Elethri knows anything about the whereabouts of the missing Princess Coriann or Page Valmor, who disappeared during the same festival, or about the whereabouts of the Lady Asana. The Valor Hall also requests that Elethri hand over their forsworn Knights, Namdon and Cuthlin, for trial and judgment within their country. The Valor Hall is deeply aggrieved that Elethri has allowed them to use it as a base from which to slander and malign the Valor Hall, and notes that this will strain future relationships between the Nation of the Five Rivers and the Alliance."

When the elf paused, Keller asked, "They did not ask for her father, Eldor, too?"

Akanë replied, "They acknowledge that he is her aging father and so she would not wish to relinquish his company, and ask only that she ensure that he has no further opportunities to slander or malign the Valor Hall or to betray his oath – basically, that she can keep him in a beautiful prison."

"Well," began Tara-lin, speaking loudly and about to stamp again, when she felt Vonë tense and shy under her arm. Relaxing her pose and voice she said, "Sorry, boy," and stroked his ears and face. Deliberately keeping her voice lowered, she continued, "Well, they can drown in their own run-off for all I care. I wouldn't do a thing to drain their soil for them. They dug this pit for themselves, and they can live in the bottom of it if they can." She tried to stroke her horse reassuringly since he continued to pick up on her tension.

"Do you want war, Tara-lin?" asked Akanë.

"Is there any other choice? I absolutely refuse to acquiesce to their illegitimate demands. If they wish to go to war with Elethri, even though we haven't done anything except offer asylum and refuge to refugees, then they can have war. There's nothing I can do about it. I certainly can't give them my friends, and I can't rule Elethri out of fear. If I'm Queen, I have to make Elethri what I think is a good country, right?" She tilted her head and gazed at Keller.

"Yes, my lady," he said. "But I think Akanë is inquiring if you think that is the best way to say it."

Tara-lin shrugged. "It's how I feel it. Will it make a difference as to whether the Valor Hall decides to go to war or not? As I understand it, war is pretty expensive."

"War certainly is expensive," said Akanë, "but how you tell them to keep their branches in their own space and out of yours could certainly affect their inclination to honor your request."

"That sounds like something Eldazìn would say," said Tara-lin.

"It is," said Akanë. "I have been trained and tutored by Eldazìn, though I daresay I am not an expert on every available weapon as is he. To be honest, I prefer being the Captain of the Guard to my previous position with that estimable elf, but I certainly respect him and have learned from him. And I can perhaps talk to you about how you might want to reply in such a way as to say what you mean without being unnecessarily confrontational, though," – and this he said with a smile – "I suspect the meaning of elven insults would be *mostly* lost on them."

"They'd certainly understand if I *said* it," said Tara-lin. "Even if I said it in Elethrian, I'm sure they would know they were being insulted, even if they didn't understand the insult."

"I'm sure they would, too," said Akanë. "When would you like to talk?"

"After I ask if Alis is back and find Vonë a pasture," said Tara-lin.

"Alis is back," said Akanë, "and just as prone to making insults as yourself, though I daresay they don't tend to be Elethrian and would probably be more understandable to the other humans."

"I can imagine," said Tara-lin, and she could. *What matters, though, is this: Elethri is a free nation and, as such, a haven for all who wish to be free! I won't tell them if we know where Alis, or Coriann, or Valmor, or Asana are. They don't need to know that, though, even before* – Tara-lin stopped and turned back. "Akanë!" she called.

"Yes, Queen?" answered the elf immediately.

"Have scouts – gryphon riders, Dragonriders, ground patrol, I don't care, whatever you can, however you think is best – sent out. If they're asking us if we have Asana, we can only guess she *might* be coming here, and if she is, we'd rather find her sooner than later, especially if they're going to start patrolling the border to try to keep their people on their side!"

"As you wish," said Akanë.

.. ❋ ❋ ❋ ❋ ❋ ..

After composing a response and sending the diplomat back with it, Tara-lin sought Alis' company. They climbed up the mountain and sat down on a rock overlooking the forest. They could see all Frèlin spread out below them, and miles and miles of forests extending to the horizon, and one of the rivers (for which Elethri was named Nation of the Five Rivers in the lands of men) winding through the forests on its way to the sea. "You wanted to talk about something, Tara-lin, didn't you?" asked Alis when neither had spoken for several minutes.

"Yes," said Tara-lin. "Fear lies at the heart of the Nightmare and is the beginning of the Corruption, yet ... Alis, I fear. I fear losing you, and I don't know how it's possible not to fear missing someone if you love her. Love is what defeats the Nightmare, I know. Love is what is uncorrupt, I know. So why does love seem so bound to that which is corrupt?"

"I think you're being silly, Tara-lin," said Alis.

"How? I mean ... I suppose I *know* I am, but how not to be?" asked Tara-lin.

"As if I know all the answers?" asked Alis. "I remember when you were yelling about how evil the gods of Valiance are, and trying to get me not to be afraid of them." She pulled her knees up to her chin and put her arms around them. Tara-lin glanced up and saw Kushon gliding towards them. She had made room for the great furry, feathery beast to land on the rocks without hurting her with his wings. She turned her head to look at her friend. "I love you, Tara-lin. I like being with you. I like doing things with you. I like investigating the forest with you. I like listening to you talk about all the different plants and animals. That black grass was really interesting! I love Kushon. I like flying with him. I like sleeping under his wing or burying my face in his mane. I like being with him and conversing with him. But what am I supposed to say, Tara-lin?"

"I don't know! What would you do, how would you feel, if I or Kushon were in danger? If you didn't know how we were?" asked Tara-lin.

They were silent as Kushon glided in, folded his wings, and settled on the rocks. Tara-lin felt tense the whole time. Even though she knew that he knew what he was doing and would be careful, she could not feel completely at ease with such a large creature landing so close to her.

When he had settled, Alis said, "You seem to have forgotten something I'd thought the dryads had successfully taught you by now."

"That's what I was thinking earlier," said Tara-lin. "I just want to know how to stop doing it. What the right way to feel is. I – would it feel like I didn't love you if I wasn't worried about you?"

Alis shrugged. "I'm glad you care about me, but I don't need you to worry about missing me." She was silent for a few seconds, and then spoke again. "I seem to recall you telling me about a conversation you had with your father, or something you thought, or something. Something about him and Lìrulin loving each other without regard or fear for the loss that would inevitably come of love between a man and an elf being a victory over the Nightmare – that, if it had been possible for them not to love each other, for them to turn down and kill the joy of their love, because of the sadness and loss that would come, *that* would have been a victory of the Nightmare. I *think* – but this isn't how I think at all – but I think maybe you should not see it as that when you love you necessarily fear losing the friendship or love, instead when you love someone you disregard the fear of losing that person, you disregard the potential for sorrow. But tell me if I said it all wrong."

"No, I just don't know how," said Tara-lin.

"It seems to me you worry that you don't know how instead of just doing or being a great deal!" said Alis, her voice blushing with friendly laughter. "Isn't that what you said the problem was when you couldn't figure out how to do the elf-dryad thing about understanding someone speaking in a language you hadn't learned?"

"All right, Alis," said Tara-lin. "Thanks for talking me through this."

"It's nothing," said Alis, "but I'd like it if we can leave such conversations for the moment and just be together and watch the afternoon."

That's a lovely idea, thought Tara-lin. *But how can she put things away so easily? Does it help to have that telepathic bond with an animal? She has to know about the message from the Valor Hall! Why else would Akanë mention her insults with regard to it?*

Far below them, the trees swayed slightly in the wind, the lights and shadows at their branches and needles moving in an almost hypnotic pattern and rhythm. It was both like and unlike light on water or on the bottom of a very clear pond. *They're so free, swaying in the wind, their roots stationary in the ground*, thought Tara-lin. *I used to wonder how the trees and dryads could be rooted in place and yet be so free. I think I started to understand it a little when I learned that there's more to what they are than being rooted in place – they're all together. Is there more to it, though? Like Alis, not in the least concerned about the problems of my Kingdom, even though she's actually pretty involved, considering her attempts to help others be free. Then again, Keller's never been as worried about ruling as I. So it can't be that I'm Queen and she ... well, isn't.*

Then again, she probably doesn't know what I'm thinking right now, and, while some dragons would know, I don't think Kushon does.

C'mon! You're supposed to be enjoying the afternoon with Alis, not spending yet more time thinking about your problems and the threatened war.

Chapter Fifteen - The Warded Forest

Several weeks later, Eldazìn returned. His report confirmed the seriousness of an implicit threat the Valor Knight diplomat had made. It appeared that the Valor Alliance was mobilizing for war. "Though," Eldazìn said, "I cannot yet *confirm* that we are the intended target. They could have their sights on one of the southern nations as well. I know no more than anyone who knows where to listen and where to watch and how to put one and two together."

"That's probably not true," said Keller. "You are exceptionally good at sneaking about."

"It is true, my King. If you order it, I can sneak into the Valor Hall itself and listen in on their most secret conversations, but I do not do this as a matter of habit. If I do it too many times, one day I will be caught and executed, and if I am not captured, I will still one day be discovered and much of my advantage will be gone even if I succeed in fleeing."

"That makes sense," said Keller.

"You mentioned the southern nations," said Tara-lin. "I'm thinking we should send a diplomat to – what's the name of our southern neighbor? Akeesh?"

"It is Akeesh," said Eldazìn. "What are you thinking? Elethri has usually had rather little relations with any of her neighbors, even during the days when we were technically part of the Valor Alliance."

"There's no reason – I mean, I don't want to get embroiled in the politics of the southern nations, but why shouldn't we trade with them? It would be profitable for both of us, and it might prove helpful in dissuading the Valor Alliance from attacking us, or convincing them to abort, or at least blunt, their war effort. We're not strong enough to threaten them, but if they've never had good relations with the south, and the south *is* big enough to threaten them if all those tiny nations would only work together," said Tara-lin.

"We don't want to create a southern Valor Alliance," Earnrìl piped in.

"I agree," said Eldazìn, "but I think Tara-lin's idea has merits in it. Good diplomatic relationships with Akeesh could be beneficial to both of us – they may have goods we might like. Also, it would signal to the Valor Alliance that Elethri is not completely alone. If they crush Elethri, the southern nations will fear that they will crush them next, and may form a united war effort. At the same time, a trade agreement with Akeesh is not the beginning of a new Valor Alliance. After all, all those little southern nations have diplomatic relationships; some of them tend to be on good terms with each other, some of them tend to be in a state of near-constant conflict, others of them switch back and forth a great deal. Elethri did not create the Valor Alliance, and this won't substantially change the nature of southern politics."

"I didn't think all that," said Tara-lin.

"You thought they might have swords we could use?" asked Eldazìn.

"Our magic swords are better, but we don't have that many of them, and we don't know how to make them," said Earnrìl.

"No, not that, either. I'm hoping not to need too many swords," said Tara-lin. "I'm really not violent."

"What then?" asked Eldazìn. "You do know you can't win a war by not killing?"

"I'm the Dryad-Friend," said Tara-lin. "I have ideas that might minimize that side of things. I – just – I'd like to send a diplomat to Akeesh. Just an overture of friendship from the new King and Queen of Elethri and an invitation to trade."

"Whatever is your will," said Eldazìn, "but we will have to choose a diplomat and also to discuss what items you're interested in trading and what terms interest you. The discussion will get long and complicated."

"I trust you to choose a diplomat, Eldazìn," said Tara-lin. "Keller?"

"I also trust Eldazìn in this."

"Then tell us what you think about items and terms," said Tara-lin. She pressed her fingers to her forehead trying to fight back what threatened to become a headache merely at the thought of such conversations and decisions.

.. * * * * *..

The next day Tara-lin went out in the forests seeking a fir tree with a dryad by the name of Kalithalias who had some degree of prominence among the dryads of Elethri. In Tara-lin's theory, some of the older dryads were capable of receiving and synthesizing the over-all intention of the entire forest in which they lived, and so they ended being something of a spokesperson for the surrounding dryads. She was not sure if they had something of a leading influence among the dryads of the area, or if it just seemed that way because whichever dryad ended up taking the role of spokesperson tended to be one who stood by the general consensus – a dryad at odds with what most of the other dryads thought or wanted would probably not volunteer to speak for them.

Tara-lin dismounted her horse and took the last dozen steps alone. She placed her hands on the old fir and said, "Kalithalias!"

Out from behind the tree flowed and materialized the form of the dryad. Her skin was white, freckled and streaked with flecks of brown, similar to the bark of her tree. Her hair flowed down from her head and covered most of her body like a robe or a cloak. It and her eyebrows were a deep emerald green. Her eyes were amethyst in color. "Hello, Tara-lin," said Kalithalias.

"Hello, Kalithalas. Usually I seek you out just to learn about the forest from your perspective and sit with you. Today I have something of greater import to bring before you all," said Tara-lin.

"I might differ with you about the importance of the thing, but tell me, Dryad-Kin."

"I do not yet have a formal declaration of war from the Valor Alliance, but I expect that one will be forthcoming as soon as their diplomat has time to return to the Valor Hall, and they compose a response and send another. I'm harboring fugitives from them: a few Valor Knights, and a princess who came to us so that she could marry the man she loves instead of one she doesn't," said Tara-lin.

"I know about them already," said Kalithalias. She waved her hand in a dismissive gesture and her whole tree shivered from top to bottom – it was a subtle shiver, but Tara-lin barely saw it. "You don't need to tell me about them. What have you come to tell me?"

"Will you and your kin be willing to help us defend Elethri? We're a small nation, and without your help, I don't think we'll be able to turn back the invading armies," said Tara-lin.

"What are you thinking, Dryad-Kin?" asked Kalithalias. "You know that we are bound by the ancient Pact. We will not, and we do not desire, to hurt humans. So what are you asking from us?"

"I warded the valley where we took refuge during the reign of Anakrim until the time came when we could change him," said Tara-lin. "I am wondering if I could do something similar to the whole forest, with your aid. I feel a great dread, for I do not know how to defend a nation without deaths on the parts of both armies, and I do not wish for death, but I am asking you: if we kill only when our defenses are breached, if Elethri fights this war entirely defensively, will the dryads be willing to support my wards?"

Kalithalias stood for a few minutes as if listening. Tara-lin waited. "Yes, we will do that, Tara-lin. It will be our pleasure. We support your effort to offer freedom to those humans who desire it. Furthermore, if Elethri is taken by the humans, it will not remain the forest that it is. Most of it will be taken and turned into farmland. We hold no grudge against the humans for farming, but, at the same time, we would like to continue living in this forest. It will be no problem for us to support your magic: but, what are you thinking of exactly?"

Tara-lin stepped away from the tree and sat down. The tall dryad sat down facing her, keeping one hand on her tree. "I have not thought it all through exactly. I am wondering if I could sing a differentiating sleep ward: one that repels those who enter with intentions of invasion and slowly lulls them into a deep sleep, but which guides those who enter seeking refuge and safety to place where they can be found after they fall asleep."

"That is definitely an option," said Kalithalias, "but there are other possibilities as well. Have you thought of singing a spell to confuse the senses and send invaders around in circles and back the way they came – out of the forest?"

"Could the two be combined?" asked Tara-lin.

"Certainly," said Kalithalias. "We will all be glad to help you with this."

"Thank you very much," said Tara-lin. "It is such a strange thing to me to be Queen. I thank you for your help, for being my friends, and, now, for helping me protect my people – though it is my own actions which have brought this war upon us, for I think it was no idle threat the ambassador made, and this suspicion has been confirmed by Eldazìn's report."

"Always, Tara-lin. You are our kin, though you walk in the world of men. We consider you one of us," said Kalithalias. "But now you must learn a new skill."

"I know," said Tara-lin, nodding vigorously. "I know. I struggle to sing one man into sleep and not cast the spell on others with me, let alone sing a ward that will differentiate when I'm not there to sing and direct it. I know I sang the wards for the valley of refuge, but I know those anchored around the direction of the dryads there. I don't know if that will work here – with armies and masses of men and all that?"

"Differentiating magic is not a skill easy to a dryad," said Kalithalias. "Few of us master it fully, and there are some of us who never achieve proficiency in it. The song will have to be a group effort, and we will repeat some of what you did for the wards in the valley. Dryads will help to direct it, but to deal with what we will be dealing here, the original song needs to be fairly well-differentiated. I will seek out the dryads who know this skill best and who are likely to have most rapport with you, and then I will call you, and we will work on this together."

"Thank you so much, Kalithalias," said Tara-lin. She tilted her head. "Would Beriririkirkirkitira be one of those, perhaps?"

"Beriririkirkirkitira?" asked Kalithalias.

"An ancient bush-dryad in the Malaitha Mountain Range – the west side of it," said Tara-lin.

Kalithalias shook her head, and the hair which fanned out from her face and clothed her whole body rippled like waves on the sea. "No, that's not what I meant. I was just wondering what made you think of her. She can do this, but, for a dryad her age, only passably. If you want, I will call her, but you will need others, I'm sure."

"Whatever you think best," said Tara-lin. "Maybe Aumoura can help, too. She's the one who first taught me to sing and I've learned well and easily from her. Thank you so much."

"There is no need for thanks, Tara-lin. It is our own which we protect, and, besides, this is no cost or difficulty to us, though most of us would rather dream in the sunshine and listen to the stars and maybe try to capture wind."

"Well," said Tara-lin, rising and placing her hand on the trunk of a nearby tree, "when first the dryads spoke to me and taught me, I was doing something for you, though it was something that coincided with a direction in which I was already headed. Now, it is you who are doing something for me."

"We do not think of it that way," said Kalithalias, smiling. Tara-lin thought the expression looked interesting on her face. "As we have told you before, you are Dryad-Kin. You are as one of us. Your life and ours are inextricably intertwined."

..* * * * *..

Tara-lin spent most of the next several weeks in the forest with the dryads, much of that time in the dream-state in which she connected most easily with her dryad nature and the rest of the dryadic world. When the dryads decreed that she was ready – Tara-lin herself had no sense for it, perhaps because she was the one who was learning, not the one who already knew, or perhaps because she was still not fully in touch with her dryad nature – she rode to the northern border of Elethri with an escort consisting mostly of friends. Elethri lay between the Malaitha Mountains and the sea, and thus shared only one accessible border with the Valor Alliance. While it would be possible to mount an offensive through the Malaitha Mountains, it would be certain slaughter for the invading humans. There was no way of sneaking through the mountains and falling out of them in a surprise attack since the gryphons and gryphon riders would surely discover any army long before it reached the peaks. In mountainous terrain, much of the lower reaches of which was heavily forested, the humans would be at an almost insurmountable disadvantage against the elves, and the gryphons would be most in their element. While the humans had some gryphon riders, Alis had insisted to Tara-lin that she and the wild gryphons would be able to convince the humans' gryphons not to fight as long as they and their riders were not attacked. Even so, there were not *that* many Valor Hall gryphons. The elven gryphon riders alone outnumbered them, and Alis told Tara-lin she was confident that the wild gryphons would fight if an invading army approached their home. Furthermore, there were the dragons, who also fought well in mountains; at worst, the terrain did not hinder them. Thus, Tara-lin went to ward her most vulnerable border first, the border which would see the first and bulk, if not all, of the Valor Alliance's assaults.

One day, Tara-lin walked across the main road entering Elethri from the north. She halted on the path. Overhead a narrow strip of brilliant blue sky alternating with streaks of cloud was visible between the tops of the trees that grew on either side of the path. It had been raining only the afternoon before. "This is such a wonderful place," she said, "but it is a weakness. Much more is required to turn a man unwittingly from a path upon which he can fix his eyes than to lose him in a wild wood and send him back the way he came."

"Isn't there something you can do?" asked Alis, who had decided to come with Tara-lin. She liked traveling the woods with her, even if it was not Kushon's favorite thing. "Couldn't we turn the path into some sort of a bog or fill it up with wild vines or something? It's fairly overgrown as it is. In the Valor Alliance lands, this would never be recognized as a main road, hardly as more than an animal trail. It should be pretty easy to fully cover it up enough that they will lose it and not be able to find it again, I should think."

"You are full of wonderful ideas," said Tara-lin.

"And to think once I thought I was stupid – except I didn't *really* think I was stupid," said Alis. "I only thought I didn't know anything useful. But then again, I didn't, did I? Because I'd never had any opportunity to learn."

.. * * * * * ..

That evening, as Tara-lin was falling asleep, she felt a tingle, an almost ticklish sensation. She paused between the half-dreams to concentrate on it, then realized it was her newly-sung wards acting. *Will I always feel them?* she thought, feeling a touch of panic at the thought. *What will it be like when it acts on a whole army of ten thousand men instead of just a small retinue?* She stood and looked for a moment at Alis. Should she wake the sleeping human? No, probably not. She could take care of herself in the wood at night, and Alis did not have nearly her night vision.

"I'll be back," she said, addressing Kushon who had taken his head out of under his wing and was examining her with one eye. That said, she gathered her cloak around her and disappeared into the night. She wanted to get to them and send them back before her spell took full effect. Furthermore, she knew that Eldazìn would not like conducting them all the way to Frèlin and hosting them there. Even though the secret of the Dragonriders could not be kept for long, he wanted to keep the dragons as a surprise for as long as possible.

Tara-lin found the Valor Hall retinue setting camp on the side of the path. She looked down at the path for a moment. *Tomorrow I will fix this,* she thought to herself. Then she stepped out of the shadows and addressed them. "Men!"

They paused in their work, startled. She saw them look around frantically, trying to pick her out of the scenery.

"You have come from the Valor Hall," Tara-lin said. "For what?"

The men looked around, confused. Most of them had spotted her now, but she knew that they could not see her well, except perhaps for a splash of her red hair, between the shadows of the forest at evening and her elethrian cloak. "We are ambassadors to the Court of Elethri," one of them said. "Who are you?"

"I am the Queen, Tara-lin. You may give me your message," said Tara-lin.

Tara-lin could tell that they were unwilling to do this. It was out of protocol. And was she the Queen of Elethri? Even so, she was not the King. The men of the Valor Alliance could not possibly understand her and Keller's relationship, either as spouses or as the Rulers of Elethri. She stepped forward and placed her hand out in the light of the fire so that it gleamed on her signet ring.

"I am the Queen of Elethri. Give me your message.... This is elven land. Our customs are not yours."

The man nodded. He still seemed nervous. "Then here is the sealed missive for you."

Tara-lin took it and ripped it open. Quickly her eyes scanned over the writing. It was what she expected: a formal declaration of war. Elethri had unambiguously declared itself to be an enemy to the Valor Alliance by keeping the children of Valiance royalty from their parents and by harboring traitors to the Valor Hall within its palace. This left the Valor Alliance with no other option than war.

"Go," said Tara-lin. "Go back and tell the Master of the Valor Hall that he will *not* invade Elethri. He may try, but he *will* be turned back. Make camp after you have left the borders of Elethri. You are no longer welcome here until you come in peace. Henceforward the woods themselves will reject you. Now go!"

Tara-lin stepped back into the shadows and tuned her mind to the ward-song, willing it to encourage the retinue not to sleep until they had passed out of the forest. She watched them pack up and go and saw the terrified looks they cast around them. After all, they had been taught that the Queen of Elethri was a witch who controlled the spirits of the trees. Part of her enjoyed their discomfort. Another part of her wished they could be other than what they were, and that she could help them to be other than what they were.

She wondered if her diverse feelings expressed the attitude of the forest around her.

Her eyes glanced down to the missive she still held in her hand. She wanted to rip it up right now and stamp it down into the earth. But should she bring it back whole for Keller and Eldazìn to see?

Chapter Sixteen – Between Fear and Laughter

When Tara-lin had encouraged the plants to overgrow the path and finished singing the border wards, she went back to Frèlin. *I wonder,* she thought as she rode, *will it prove to be a boon or a curse that Frèlin is situated near our northern border? It means I will be able to reach the border quickly, very quickly if a gryphon or a dragon will take me. It also means that if we can't hold the Valiance army at the border, it's a short march for them to our capitol. I suppose I wouldn't care if it weren't for the Tree. Cities don't matter that much, and we're elves. We could abandon the city and survive in the forest with little difficulty. As far as our cities go, Frèlin is fairly defensible. Those terraces almost work like a series of castle walls with moats below them. It would be slaughter for their own army to take Frèlin from us, but not more slaughter than it would be to fight us in the forest.* It was a well-known fact of warfare that elves were at a distinct advantage in the forest and in mountains but did no better defending a city than did humans.

I just wish we didn't have to fight a war at all. I wish we could do this without any slaughter at all. Most Queens would be happy with minimizing the slaughter of their own people, but, somehow, I'm not, but then again, most Queens aren't named Dryad-Kin. And when has what 'most' would do or be ever been part of my life? Well, that is *what I am working on – a tactic for minimizing the slaughter on* both *sides, and, hopefully, convincing the Valor Alliance it's not worth it to take Elethri,* without *substantial killing.*

I hate this. I hate being Queen. Is it even possible to do the right thing when you're Queen?! Is there a right thing to do?!

When she reached Frèlin, she found Keller, ran up to him, and threw her arms around him. "What is it, Tara-lin?" He asked. "I missed you."

"I did too, kind of. Anyway, it's good to see you again."

After hugging her for almost a minute, he let her go and they stepped apart from each other. "What is it? Did you ward the forest?" he asked.

"Yes, I warded the forest. But our fears are confirmed." She drew the missive out of her cloak and handed it to him.

"We expected this," said Keller when he had read it. "Why are you so upset?"

"I don't know!" said Tara-lin. "I still want to rip it up and stamp the pieces into the soil. I just – why do I *not* want to kill the enemy?"

Keller shrugged. "Because you think some of the soldiers in their army might be people like Cuthlin or Namdon – or your father – who haven't been around long enough, or thought enough, or met the right people, or seen enough, or whatever it is, to know they need to run away from the Valor Alliance and request haven in Elethri?"

"Alis is of the opinion that any of those three, given what's going on now as opposed to the state of things ten or twenty years ago, would have found their way out of the Valor Hall already, and that we might have found the three exceptions who hadn't yet been killed in the world," said Tara-lin. "She also doesn't like Coriann and Valmor very much," she added irrelevantly.

"But that doesn't mean that's your opinion," said Keller.

Tara-lin shrugged. "I don't *have* much of an opinion. My theory is that it's because I'm as much a dryad as I am a human. Who knows? Maybe I am bound by the Pact to some degree, even though I don't know what it is or how it came to be very well. But I don't think Alis is any keener on killing people than I am."

"No, I don't think so either," said Keller. "Now, Eldazìn – he would assassinate the Master of the Valor Hall – or anyone you asked him to – if you asked."

"I don't want to," said Tara-lin. "And I don't think the dryads would like it. And, while I don't love him like I love you, or like I love Alis, or even Earnrìl, or my parents, I don't want to send him into that. It would be too close to sending him to his death."

"Unless we surrender," said Keller, "and I, for my part, will not surrender, but unless Elethri surrenders, we will have to send elves to their deaths. I don't think the Valor Hall is going to turn back at your magic. They'll find a way to get in and try to attack us. They'll use their wizards. Sooner or later, we will have to fight, and some will die."

"I'm not going to force anyone. Those elves who *want* to defend Elethri can fight on the border or the walls," said Tara-lin. She paused for a moment. "You don't really think asking Eldazìn to assassinate people will change that? They'll elect somebody else and then attack us."

"It will throw them into disarray," said Keller. "No, I'm not suggesting that. Eldazìn has been proposing it to me."

"He wants to?" asked Tara-lin. Then, after a moment's pause, "He meant it when he told me he was the 'Assassin!'" She paused again. "It'll just make them mad. I want to see if they *can* be turned back by facing the magic of the dryads. If they do enter Elethri with their army, then – I don't see what harm it can do, so if he really wants to, he's free to do so. I won't tell him not to." She went on thoughtfully. "If he gets himself killed, I'll miss him. I've grown to like him now that he's not trying to push his ideas of how to rule on us, even if I can tell he wants to grovel."

"Anyway, enough of this!" said Keller. "Let's go do things together. We'll tell our people and discuss war tomorrow."

"That sounds like a good idea," said Tara-lin.

.. * * * * * ..

The next day Tara-lin and Keller announced to the people of Frèlin that the Valor Hall had formally declared war on Elethri. "As of yet, there is no immediate threat. When there is something you should know, we will tell you, and when the time comes to defend our land, we will call on those of you who freely desire to join us," they told the elves.

"If you are afraid, I understand," said Tara-lin. "My desire is to defend Elethri in such a way that as few people as possible, especially as few of you as possible, die. I cannot simply hand over my friends and those who have fled to us in order to have freedom to the Valor Hall in order to be killed or made into the slaves of husbands and fathers. I hope that you will stand with me in this, even if you are not willing to fight, that you will not reject me for bringing you into this war. I believe that fear will not help us, however. I believe that fear is what has made the human society the horrid thing it is today, a place where those who seek justice and truth are murdered and branded traitors when they speak against the murder of the innocent, a place where women are dominated and controlled by men, and where men are dominated and controlled by those who claim to speak for the gods. I have been deep within the Icecrown Mountains and into the heart of Nightshade Castle, and I believe that fear is the source and beginning of the Corruption. Fear will make us try to hate and dominate each other if we give in it, especially if we give into it when we know another way. Fear will make us all slaves in the depths of Nightshade. It may be that fear will make us wailing wights if we allow it to dominate our hearts. I have chosen not to be afraid to stand against the tyranny of the ironically named Valor Alliance, and I hope that you too will choose to love instead of to fear! Again, I reiterate: unlike other nations have sometimes done in times of trial, I will *never* try to force you to serve me or to fight for me. You may rest assured that I will die for you all before I try to use fear to control you, and before I allow my own fear to make me try to control you. The Valor Alliance can take me prisoner before I will try to force any of you to follow my lead or orders." She stopped, her voice faltering. She was crying. "Keller," she said hoarsely, when the applause of Frèlin went up.

How can they greet me like this? How can they applaud me like this? she wondered, cringing. A part of her was glad that the news of war had not disheartened them. Another part of her was sorrowful, viewing their loyalty as something vain and insubstantial. She hoped one day that loyalty would be attached to the thing for which she tried to stand and not to her own person.

I never liked lots of people. When I first rode into this city I thought there were too many people too close together! I want to run away! Tara-lin did not know what made her feel like running away more: the war or the city.

I cannot do this. I cannot do this. I cannot do this for another century or two or however many it is!

When the applause died down, Tara-lin fled and sought Alis. She found her grooming Kushon on the rocks behind the Tower.

Alis turned from polishing the gryphon's feathers and greeted Tara-lin. "What's wrong, Tara-lin?" she asked.

"I – I don't know how I can do this! I can't do this! I just can't! I don't think I could manage this for another human lifetime, let alone multiple centuries. I can't stand all the people standing and calling my name and clapping and waving their cloaks in the air! It feels like, I don't know, it makes me feel like my head is going to explode! It makes me feel like I'm going to melt and fall apart into different pieces. I just can't!"

"Maybe you should get a gryphon or a drake-lizard if someone finds an egg again, Tara-lin," said Alis. "Somehow, I think an animal's companionship would help you deal with this."

"You might be right," said Tara-lin, stepping past Alis to stroke Kushon's flank. "Of course, I help Keller groom Kellia all the time."

"It's not the same," said Alis. "You know it's not the same. You like your horse, I can tell. You know that with these empathetic beasts it really matters to be the one bonded to them."

"I think drake-lizards might be capable of bonding to multiple people. Lyan's Shobura talks to me sometimes. Usually to remind me when I told Lyan I would play with him and then forgot to do it. But I don't think I can. I don't have time for a drake-lizard or a gryphling. I barely have time for Lyan and for myself. If I have to take care of a gryphon on top of all this, how will I find the time to wander alone into the forest and sing with the whole forest?" asked Tara-lin.

"Well, maybe I'm wrong and it wouldn't help," said Alis, putting her arm over Kushon's shoulders. She heaved a sigh. "I suppose I really have no idea what it would be like to be Queen. *I* can't imagine being able to stand all that chaos down there. Not even for one day. All I ever wanted was to ride gryphons and hear owls."

"I *like* the fact that you're the way you are, Alis," said Tara-lin earnestly. "I like the fact you don't *care*. I *like* that you can't imagine. I like that you are so far removed from all of it. I like that you –"

"You don't need to go on," said Alis. She leaned her head back against Kushon's neck. "I think you'll do fine. Take it one day at a time. And, really, if ever you *do* decide to abdicate and run away from all this, I'll take you some far away place and we can live in some mountain forest with gryphons for the rest of our days. If Keller wants to come with you, I can easily arrange that, too."

Tara-lin laughed. "Now you're the one trying to convince me to run away with you?"

"Oh, you could run away without my help and you know it," said Alis.

"I probably could. I could probably evade even Eldazìn if I chose to," said Tara-lin. *I wonder if this is where the elven custom of the parents crowning their child in their place before they die comes from. Elves trying to pass the crown off to another and escape from it as soon as possible. Of course, the tradition became a tradition, with the crown passed off only when the King and Queen grew old, but I wonder if that's how it started ...* Tara-lin spoke her thought out loud to Alis.

"Maybe," the human agreed. "I wouldn't really know, though."

"Well, I'm glad to be here with you and Kushon. Can I help you groom him?" asked Tara-lin.

"Of course!" said Alis, smiling. "I told you, you would do better with a gryphon friend of your own."

Tara-lin shook her head. "No. I do best being your friend and interacting with your gryphon from time to time. I think that's best for me. Remember, I get to be friends – a little – with both Kushon and Kellia. And Welri," Tara-lin added, thinking of her elven friend and her gryphon. They were an interesting pair, always flying down to the sea.

Tara-lin was beginning to wonder if the next time she mated Welri would roost in the some of the cliffs overlooking the sea on the peninsula.

.. * ＊ ＊ ＊ * ..

Tara-lin and Keller sent out a declaration to the rest of the elven nation to gather at Frèlin if they wished to hear the royal pair speak to them and the Queen sing for them. She would have asked Keller to speak to them for both him and her, but while she was certain that he was naturally a little more comfortable with the crowds and noise than she, he was at least as scared by them as herself, probably due to his horrendous upbringing.

Before the date set for them to address the nation, one of the Dragonriders flew in from the north with news that an army was being massed not many miles, at least from her dragon's perspective, from the forest's northern edge.

Oh, great! thought Tara-lin, not certain whether her thought was sarcastic or not. *I get to prepare them all for my strange, weird, and innovative – even from an elven perspective – battle plan at the same time as I tell them the news for the first time! I wonder, how will that go over? Will they like my plan? Will any of them want to help me? It won't work if none of them want to participate.*

The Dragonriders have to participate whether they want to or not. They're essential for this to work, and it really isn't very dangerous.

She imagined Eldazìn's response when he heard. "You can't fight an enemy army without *killing* them," she knew he would say, even though he respected her and Keller now. She wondered how many other elves would say the same thing.

"Keller," she said, as she lay next to him that night, "what do you think they will think when I tell them what we're going to do? Do you think any of them will want to come to the border with us?"

He brushed her hair back from her face and whispered his reply. "I think they'll all want to come. I think they'll be thrilled."

"Good," said Tara-lin. She drummed her fingers on her thigh. "How do you think the Valor Generals will react? How do you think the High Master will react?"

It was a question she had asked him many times before. Imagining it thrilled and excited her.

"I have no idea," said Keller, "but I think they will be furious."

Alis thought they would be furious too. She had almost fallen over herself laughing when Tara-lin told her the plan and asked her how she thought the false-Valor Knights would react to its execution.

Alis loves it. The dryads love it. Maybe I really am an elf. A half-elf. Human and dryad. Queen of the Wood, thought Tara-lin. Laughter ran through her mind like butterflies chasing each other through a flower garden as she imagined the austere and scheming Valor Knights foiled and embarrassed by her plan. It was so unlike their own murderous scheming and *so* like herself and her friends, dryad, human, and elven. They had spent so many hours laughing over it and perfecting it.

Chapter Seventeen – Warfare of the Dryads

Tara-lin felt when the invading army entered her forest, for *hers* it now was, bound to her with the spells she had sung, spells which were still beyond her understanding. The tingling shot through her whole body, and she swung herself down from the horse she was riding north. "Wait," she said. "Or go on without me. I don't care. I can't – I must –"

"What is it?" asked Keller, worried.

"My spell. I'll be fine, but I must – dream." She threw herself on the floor, feeling the root-entangled soil of the forest under her palms. Her mind almost felt like it would wither before the demands of the spell, but she knew she only had to release herself into the dreamlike consciousness of the dryads and the magic would be as natural as breathing, or even as the beating of her heart. She released herself into the state, feeling the whole forest breathe, feeling the myriad tendrils and waves of life and thought snaking and weaving and rolling through the world. Her thoughts passed beyond all words and even images deep into that other mode of consciousness, and the distinction between herself and her song faded. The two melded and, one with her song, one with the whole forest, with its dryads and its even more numerous trees, she took the invading army one by one and led them wandering into the lands of enchanted sleep.

A day later, Tara-lin lifted herself off the ground and sat up. Elves were sitting around her watching with mixtures of curiosity and concern on their faces. It took her a few moments to realize their concern. "No," she said. "It is all right. Didn't I tell you, you could go on? The beasts of this forest would not hurt me. It's just the ward. I'm one with the ward and with the forest and I – I don't think I could explain it very well." She shook her head, trying to focus herself back into her normal state of consciousness, then stood.

"Let's go on. Where's my horse? Oh!" She took the reins, bent forward, and blew into the horse's nostrils. The horse blew back. After a few passes of this, she stepped forward, patted his neck, and then swung herself onto his back. Trotting briskly she led the company on through the forest.

Hours later they reached the region of the forest where the men of the Valor Alliance lay sprawled and dreaming, scattered among the trees. Tara-lin had already given the elves instructions on what they were here to do. First of all, all weapons were to be taken from the sleeping soldiers. Then, when all the weapons had been taken, they would progress to removing the men's armor. The instructions had included that each elf could take for him or herself whatever weapons or armor he or she found and desired. The rest were to be taken and laid in piles, sorted based on type. The Dragonriders and gryphon riders were to fly over the forest, back and forth, allowing the quick transport of weapons and armor from the front where the elves were taking them to a location deeper within the forest where the soldiers would not find them at once upon waking.

Tara-lin smiled, thinking of how much of a genius she was, as her company split into various sections to comb the forest. The weapons and armor the elves did not want would still prove to be a great boon to Elethri and, at worst, they could be thrown into the sea where they would lie forever beyond the reach of their enemies. She did not foresee having to do that unless they had to quickly get the armaments out of the reach of their previous owners, and the sea was the nearest place where they would be beyond that reach. Otherwise what was not wanted by the elves would be either sold or traded to Akeesh or smelted down to its base alloys and metals and re-forged by the elves into whatever it was they wanted, possibly including elven swords, some of them possibly even imbued by new elven magic! She knew the human swords were less than optimal weapons for the elves, being weighted wrong for elven fighting, but they were better than no swords, and the elves did not have an abundance of swords. Most of the other weapons would be discarded for elven use as they now existed, as would most of the armor. Elves never wore more than light chain-mail, which was what was worn by the Guard of Frèlin and the Guards of other cities, since it was relatively non-restrictive and provided substantial protection, and thus was optimal for defending a wall, for it would stop stray arrows from penetrating unless one was unlucky. Heavier armor was never worn by an elf willingly. It weighed them down and restricted their motion so the extent that they lost all of their inhuman grace and speed, usually becoming clumsier and slower than similarly armored humans. There was simply no way for an elf to develop his or her body in such a way as to be able to wear such armor. Even if the human armor were shaped for elven wear, there was no way very much of it would be taken for elven use. Some helms, perhaps, and some bracers and greaves, Tara-lin thought might be considered fitting and beneficial armor by some of her elves.

She stuck a banner into the ground to mark a location. "Bring back what you find and do not want for yourself here. A dragon can land right in the clearing, so this is a good staging place for the dragon to pick up what you get. Now, make sure you can get back here quickly and go! Have fun disarming the men who dare to bring weapons into our peaceful wood!"

The younger elves whirled away, hooting and laughing. The older elves moved quickly and efficiently but more sedately. Many of them were also laughing, but more quietly.

This is so much fun, thought Tara-lin. *How disappointing that this is probably not our only battle and that they will use their wizards to make things much harder for us in the future. I wouldn't mind if this were our only confrontation, though. Not that it even qualifies as a confrontation, much less a battle.*

Alis flashed a smile at her, and Tara-lin knew what she was thinking even before she spoke. "I agree, Tara-lin. This is fun. Funny, too."

"Does Kushon think that?" asked Tara-lin.

"Yes. A shame I won't be part of the fun part, though. Kushon is a little grumpy about our part in this, to tell the truth."

"Oh-h." Tara-lin rolled her eyes in mock frustration. "I'm going to go get started myself!"

"You think I can do *one* fun part before I have to cart armaments to wherever Klaisen and Desën have designated?" asked Alis.

"Sure!" said Tara-lin. "Come!"

She led Alis in an almost unerringly straight path towards where two human soldiers lay sprawled on opposite sides of a bramble thicket. Looking down on one, Tara-lin thought, *No wonder I don't want to kill them. Some of them might even be drafted peasants. Some of them might be young men who just joined a wing of the Valor Hall or a local militia with the idea of protecting their city against bandits or of guarding the border against the southern nations. They don't deserve their rulers. They don't deserve to die. I just wish I could free them all.*

She stooped and unbuckled his sword-belt. She took his small shield also. *But if they come into my forest to kill us, and not to seek refuge from us, sooner or later we will kill them. They will not stand a chance. For every one of us they kill, ten times more will die for entering our forest than if they assaulted a human city with a similar number of defenders. We cannot hope to match them on an open battle-field, where they are armored and we cannot be. In the forest, concealed in the shadows, darting out of the trees and leaping on their branches, they cannot stand a chance. We can kill them in droves without ever being seen by them.*

Tara-lin straightened. "Do you have the other's sword?" she whispered across the thicket to Alis.

"Yes."

"Then let's go!"

This isn't so much fun, she thought. *If I thought this would be the end of it, I would be struggling not to laugh so hard I couldn't do my work, at the idea of disarming peasants who probably did not want to fight us in the first place, of disarming violent men and emerging victorious without ever having met them in battle, without ever having struck a stroke of the sword, taking their weapons from them while they lay in sleep on our forested floor. There is something so wonderful about it, if only it could always be like this!*

Laying the weapons down, Tara-lin thought, *We won't get all of them. From the reports I received there are so many of them we probably won't even get all the weapons before they begin to stir, but at least we will get enough that they will turn back unarmed, defeated not by slaughter but by life, not by weapons but by the lack of weapons. We won't get all of them, but we will get at least half of them, probably many more! That alone will be a great blow. Metal is costly, and smithing weapons and armor is skilled and long labor.*

.. ⁕ ✳ ❋ ✳ ⁕ ..

Tara-lin's whole body was sore and aching several hours later. She paused for a couple minutes to draw refreshment from the forest and then continued, her weariness and aches only slightly alleviated. She noticed that some of the elves had disappeared. Once they had grown weary and aching, and the excitement of this strange kind of warfare had worn off, they had left. Others still continued, and these she encouraged when her paths crossed theirs. To one she said, "I am so glad you have come! The more of us help here the greater the blow will be dealt their war effort, without a single life having to be taken!"

A couple hours after that Eldazìn found her struggling with a sword-belt. "Here, Queen. Let me take that from you," he said. "I advise that you stop and focus on encouraging the others instead. You're so small and this is quite heavy for you. May I tell you what I found?"

Tara-lin nodded. "Tell me," she said wearily.

"I've found the Commanding General. I know you don't want us to kill them, even though we could do so and amplify the damage we're dealing to their war effort a hundred-fold, though I am not *that* fond of killing. It would go against nature. It would not even be like assassinating my traitors, which I didn't exactly enjoy. However, may I have your permission to kill the general?" asked Eldazìn.

Tara-lin knew his arguments without him having to speak them. The Commanding General could not be innocent or half-innocent. He could even have been one of those to gave orders to send honest Valor Knights, such as her father, or Namdon, or Cuthlin, into death-traps. "I don't know," she said. "If you can find Keller and he gives you permission, I cannot overrule it, but it is not in my way. Not until this fails, not until they enter our forest and shed elven blood, can I allow theirs to be shed. This is my pact with the dryads, or else my share in the Pact of the dryads as the correlation to my share in their nature and magic. Perhaps it must be so. With magic comes the requirement to use that magic in accord with its nature, to live in accord with the nature of the magic, and this is that requirement, even though I can't say I fully understand it. I'm not sure even the dryads understand it. They simply know that it is so."

"There is no need to go on, my Queen," said Eldazìn. "I understand."

She wondered if he really did understand, but she followed him back to the staging site, wondering if he was right. Should she lay aside actively helping with the work, and instead wander among the elves, offering them words of encouragement? No, she could not do that. She could encourage those she saw as came naturally to her, but that she could not do. She could not stand the worship and loyalty they offered her. She could not be part of bolstering it in them. But perhaps she *could* sing to them a song that would refresh their bodies and minds?

Tara-lin collapsed at the staging site. Eldazìn was right. She was worn out. She did need to stop. She sat down against a tree and pulled her knees up to her chin, trying to recollect herself enough to sing to her people. Then an elf came bursting through the trees and threw the armaments he carried down. "Oh, it's you! Queen! I think they're beginning to stir."

"Then it is time to call the others and to make sure we get all these piles of armor out of here. I don't really know how this spell will work. It may be some will wake now, while others will not wake for a week. It may be those who wake will be able to wake those who would still sleep for days ... Enough of this! I am tired and distracted. We need – you heard what I said. Help me make sure the others know. The goal is now to get the armaments away from here!"

"Yes, Queen," said the elf. He darted back in the direction from which he had come.

Let me see, thought Tara-lin. *Yes, I will wait here, until the next gryphon rider or Dragonrider flies by.* She stood and walked out into the clearing to signal one down if she saw any passing in the near skies. A gryphon rider would not be able to communicate the new directive to the other gryphon riders as effortlessly as a Dragonrider, but it would be a beginning. She would wait until she had signaled both a gryphon rider and a Dragonrider before she considered what to do next, unless further and unexpected developments occurred. Once all the Dragonriders and gryphon riders knew, they would tell the elves whenever they saw them, and the final stage of this strange defense of Elethri would be quickly begun and done.

Tired as she was, Tara-lin laughed aloud, dizzy with a feeling of exultation and success.

She wondered where Keller was. He was big and strong, and he was not with the gryphon riders, since Kellia was still young and small. She was not yet big enough to carry her rider. It did not help that Keller was so large, but even if Keller had been a normal-sized man she would not be quite ready to carry him yet.

Then she saw a dragon above the tree-tops. She jumped into the air and waved her signal flag in the sky. When she saw the dragon angle its flight towards her she stepped back, away from the space the beast would need to land. *Maryath, if I remember correctly,* she thought. *The one who looks like Sugarfly, even though she's pink with gold wings instead of being pink with purple blotches.*

The dragon landed, and Tara-lin stepped out from among the trees. "Rider of Maryath!" she called, since for some reason she could remember the dragon's name but not her rider's name. "Tell the others! We're moving to the final stage. They're stirring, so it's time to get their weapons and armor out of here, and then get out of here ourselves."

"I will do that, Tara-lin," said the rider. "There, it is done. Maryath has told the others."

"Good," said Tara-lin with a sigh.

"I still don't understand why we aren't killing them. It would be so much faster than taking their weapons and armor ... If we just went through them killing them, they would all be dead by now. Isn't that what one naturally gets for attacking another country?" asked the rider.

"It might be," said Tara-lin, "but I am Dryad-Kin. If we do that, my magic will fail. Nor can I want to do that. I'll try to explain later. Let's get this stuff loaded up."

How can she think that way? Tara-lin wondered. *I ... just ... want ... to lie ... down and ... go to sleep. But I can't. Not here. Not now. I have to ride out of here somewhere. A horse or a dragon. I think I'd rather a dragon. My horse should follow the other horses out, and I'm too tired to even ride a horse.*

I wonder, she thought, feeling like she was already drifting off to sleep even while she stood, *I wonder, are they stirring earlier than they should because of all that hooting and yelling and laughing exuberance?*

If we must do this again, I need to remember to tell the young elves to contain their enthusiasm.

Chapter Eighteen – Lure of the Sorceress

When they returned, Tara-lin thought that, if anything, the elves were even more worshipful of her. She flinched from the commotion they made as those who rode with her and those who had remained in or around Frèlin met. They cheered as if she were returning conqueror and descending goddess in one. She thought they must love the fact that she had won the first battle without so much as shooting an arrow. The thought, *What will they do when the Valor Hall sends wizards against us and bloodshed ensues? Will they turn against me then?* flicked through her tired brain and then vanished. She was very tired.

When she reached the royal terrace at the top of the city, she saw Coriann and Valmor standing, arm in arm, smiling like the winter sun, in the entrance of the Tower. Next to them stood another woman who looked like she might have been from the southern regions of the Valor Alliance. Her hair was as black as the night between the stars. Her eyes were almost as dark, and her skin was a shade of dusky tan. She watched the proceedings with an attitude Tara-lin found it hard to place, and then she fixed the Elven Queen with a gaze just as inscrutable. Tara-lin wondered what she wanted and who she was. Was she the Lady Asana, whom they had never found, or was she someone else entirely? Tara-lin did not think Akeesh could have sent a female ambassador to Elethri, and even so, it was too early for an Akeeshian ambassador to have arrived yet. Also, her expression was not what Tara-lin would have expected of an ambassador.

Beneath the Tree, her family waited. Lyan was jumping up and down and waving to get her attention. Lìrulin and Eldor just smiled at her. She smiled back, and drew herself together and turned with Keller to give a short speech to her people.

When she turned back to the terrace, she saw the woman she did not know finish crossing the sward toward her and lay herself prostrate not far from her. "Your majesties," she said.

"Get up," said Keller, "and tell us who you are."

She rose to her knees. "I am the Lady Asana. I have come here because I heard that the Queen of the Land of Five Rivers is a sorceress. I have always wanted to learn magic, but it is forbidden for women to learn magic. Only those devoted to the gods may learn even the simplest spells."

"You can stand, Lady Asana," said Tara-lin. "You may also

address me by my name, Tara-lin, just as you would an equal. I cannot teach you human magic, but you are certainly free to learn it if you can.

"Really," said Tara-lin, when the human remained on her knees. "Stand up and talk to me as an equal."

Slowly Asana rose. "C-could I learn elven magic?" she asked.

"Not as I know it," said Tara-lin. "Few elves have much of my talent. If you can get a dryad to talk to you, he or she might tell you."

Asana nodded. She looked disconsolate, but like she was trying very hard to hide her disappointment. Tara-lin imagined it might feel to her like a blow of despair. Somehow, she had found her way all the way from wherever she lived into Elethri, hoping that the Sorceress Queen would desire her skills and teach her if she showed her enough obeisance. Perhaps she had never entertained the hope that she could fulfill her dream of magic, but then when she heard that the Queen of Elethri welcomed any who desired to escape forced marriages, and that this Queen was a half-elf sorceress, she had hoped her dream could become reality. Now, how would she ever find a way to learn?

Keller said, "It's okay, Asana. I have books on wizardry. It's how I taught myself, and I would be happy to loan them to you."

Lines of happiness spread out over Asana's face like rays of the sun reflected on ice. She did not know how to respond to such an offer from a king. "I would be s-so pleased," she said. She looked like she was going to say something more, but then shut her mouth. Tara-lin guessed it was 'your majesty.'

"It's nothing really," said Keller.

Asana's face was a mask of confusion and uncertainty. She bowed low to the ground.

"He means it," said Tara-lin. "We find your displays of ... what's the word for it in this language? ... to be unnecessary. I see you as my equal. So does Keller. Start treating us like equals. We're not any better or more important than you are just because we're King and Queen."

Asana shook her head. "It is how my people express immense gratitude," she said. "I am overwhelmed by your generosity. I also ... did not know the King of the Land of Five Rivers was a wizard."

"It's just as well if those we fight don't know all the tricks we have up our sleeves," said Tara-lin with a smile.

"Oh," said Asana. "That sounds ... like a great idea."

"I am tired," said Tara-lin. "If you and Keller want to talk about magic, that's fine by me, but I am going to sleep."

.. * ✻ ✻ ✻ * ..

The next morning, Tara-lin found Alis. "Did you hear?" she asked.

"Did I hear what?" asked Alis.

"About Asana."

"I heard she was here. What about her? You will remember that Kushon is even more exhausted than you were, and I was tending him," Alis added.

"She wants to be whatever you call a female wizard. I don't know if it's something different, because all the human wizards are male," said Tara-lin. She realized that when she imagined the 'wizards of the Valor Hall' it had always been a mixed group of men and women, which she ought to have realized it could not be, given what she already knew about how the Valiance countries thought of women.

"O-oh," said Alis. "I ... never thought of that before."

"I didn't, either. Remember when I was worrying about whether people would be afraid to come to Elethri because the Valor Hall would publish some rumor about how I was a sorceress?"

"Yes?"

"It seems I was wrong to fear that. It seems the Valor Hall *helped* us with that rumor. It makes women who want to learn wizardry think they can do it here! Which they can, *if* they can."

Alis nodded, radiant. "That is *so* cool, Tara-lin."

"It really is! I thought you would want to know," said Tara-lin.

"I would," said Alis. "By the way, I *didn't* think a rumor about you being a sorceress would hurt."

"That's what I wanted to tell you too," said Tara-lin, hopping from one foot to the other in excitement. "You were *right!*" She settled down, then said, "I bet Mom and Dad already know."

"Probably," agreed Alis. "They were here when Asana arrived, whenever that was. But I am hungry. Let's feast!"

"You're right!" said Tara-lin. "There's going to be a feast! We came back victorious without shedding any blood ... yet. Didn't Keller tell everybody we were going to feast yesterday?"

"I don't know," said Alis. "I wasn't thinking about that at all. I was just thinking that *we* should feast ourselves." She leveled her gaze at Tara-lin. "You *have* to be hungry."

"I am. But I'm so excited, and I wanted to tell you as soon as possible."

Alis laughed. "I'd find out anyways ..." she said as the two friends headed for the tables.

"*I* wanted to tell you, even if you already knew," said Tara-lin.

When they reached the table, they found Asana and Keller standing next to one of the platters, talking. Keller was saying, "My wizardry is tinged with the elven talent of singer, so I don't know how well I could teach you."

"You could teach her," Tara-lin interjected. "Perhaps only the basics. You might only be able to get her started, but you didn't even discover the elven hint to your wizardry until recently. You could definitely help her get started, even though once she gets past the basics she'll probably have to do it on her own."

"It's not as simple as that," said Keller. "I don't know anything about teaching."

"Still, I'm sure you could assist her and give her pointers that she can't get from an inert book that can't watch or comment on her spells," said Tara-lin.

"I suppose that might be true," said Keller. "Or I might mess her up. If she casts differently than I do, I might think she's getting it wrong when she's doing it right. I might not know all the ways in which my elvenness affects my wizardry. I might try to teach her to do it my way when that's harder for her and will interfere with her natural ability."

"Do whatever you think best, then," said Tara-lin. "After all, what do I know about wizardry?"

Asana laughed. So did Keller.

Tara-lin glanced between them. They were going to be friends, she was almost certain.

She wondered what it would feel like to have a friend who was another singer. Then she thought that she could not ask for a better friend than Alis. Earnrìl was a good friend also, as was Keller. Her parents were friends, too. Her brother was still too much of an annoying rascal to be a friend and that drake-lizard of his, Shobura, only made it worse.

Tara-lin grabbed a meat roll stuffed with spiced potatoes and bit into it. Alis followed suit. "These are really good," she said around her mouthful.

"They are, but you always think they are," said Tara-lin.

"I think you never eat enough," said Alis. "In fact, I propose that might be why you've been married for – what is it? three years now –

without getting pregnant."

"I'm an elf – a half-elf," said Tara-lin. "Did you notice how many years there are between me and Lyan? It's well within normal for it to take a decade for an elf to get pregnant after she marries, and it hasn't been half that. My friend Earnrìl was conceived half a century after *her* parents got married, and they were starting to think they couldn't have any children. Besides," she went on, "I'm Queen of a nation *at war.* It's not a good time to have a baby."

Alis chewed and swallowed her mouthful as fast as she could to speak again. "Look, Tara-lin," she said, "I really don't care. I'm not married at all, am not going to marry, and don't particularly want to have a baby. If you and Keller don't want to have children, that's your business and none of mine, not that I'd care anyways."

Tara-lin was confused. *Why does she think I think she might disapprove? Oh! I bet it's one of those things they disapprove of in the Valor Alliance, if a woman doesn't have enough children. Or maybe it's just if she doesn't have any children at all. Maybe it's a sign of the gods' disfavor? I don't know.* "Alis," she said, "I'm not worried about you caring. You should forget the Valor Alliance and that all those cultures within it ever existed. I was just telling you how I think."

"I was *teasing* you with the suggestion that you're not pregnant yet because you don't eat enough," said Alis.

Tara-lin tensed. She felt that familiar tingle course through her blood. Someone was entering her warded forest.

"What is it?" asked Alis.

"Someone ... no, two someones ... are entering Elethri," she said.

"What for?" asked Alis.

"I ..." Tara-lin concentrated, feeling the earth and the wind around her, releasing herself partway into the dryadic consciousness. Withdrawing, she smiled at Alis. "Not to invade, but I can't tell very well. Not from this distance and ... not that way. I only get ... it's too hard to describe."

She discovered that everyone at the table was looking at her. "Could it be more refugees?" asked Keller.

"That's probably what it is," said Tara-lin. "It's just that we've only had three so far ... and I don't want to send any of the gryphon riders right now. The gryphons are so exhausted."

"Then send a rider and horse," said Asana. "Your horses navigate the forest very well."

Tara-lin smiled at her. "I'm glad you're learning."

She gave a weak smile in return. *I wonder what her story is like. It might be so different from those who flee here in order to not marry or to marry. Maybe she misses her family. It wouldn't be their fault she can't learn wizardry in the Valor Alliance. Maybe they even helped her.*

.. * * * * * ..

That night, while Tara-lin and Keller were getting ready to sleep, Lìrulin came to her. "I'd like to talk to you for a moment if you don't mind, Tara-lin," she called.

"Of course I don't mind, Mom. I'll be down in just a moment," said Tara-lin, slipping off of the tarp and onto one of the branches.

When she landed lightly on the ground, she said, "What is it, Mom?"

"I think you'll be mad at me when you find out if I don't tell you something, so I might as well tell it to you even though I don't see why," said Lìrulin tilting her head to the side in an amused fashion.

"What is it?" asked Tara-lin.

"I feel your ward, too. Not like you do. When the invading army crossed the border, I felt only a tingling in my blood. This morning it was only a shiver. I wouldn't have guessed it had any connection to your ward, but when I heard you say someone was crossing, I realized that I'd felt a similar shiver around the time the diplomats with the declaration of war would have been entering, and that the odd tingling I'd felt was about the time the army would have been entering." She paused. "You would be mad if you found out I knew and didn't tell you, right?"

"Not mad at you, Mom," said Tara-lin. "Just... I probably would be upset. I can't figure out why or how *you* would be linked to my ward, but it's very interesting and I'm glad to know. I like to know things like this. That way the knowledge is there in my mind, and if I ever find something else, I might have a clue to something it might someday help to know, if you understand?"

"I do," said Lìrulin. "I just don't like it when you get upset, and I ... there's so much in the world that I can't tell you all of it or even remember all of it. But I did think you would want to know this. Especially since it has to do with a ward you sung."

"I do want to know it. Thank you, Mom," said Tara-lin. *I wonder. When and from where did Asana enter? Did she go through the southern nations and enter from our southern border? I would think if she had entered from the north she would have arrived long before now unless she entered after I warded that border, which isn't possible, because I'd have known it.*

When Tara-lin put the question to her, she said, "I entered Elethri from the north. It was about the time you warded it, so I suppose it must have been just before. I was taken in by an elf who took care of me but was decidedly uninterested in helping me get to Frèlin to request an audience with you in anything I considered a timely fashion. When she received your message about the speech she came and took me."

Oh, thought Tara-lin. *Weird. I thought I made it very clear that I wanted all refugees brought to me promptly. I suppose my people don't understand what 'promptly' means.*

"How old was your host?" asked Tara-lin.

"I have no idea how to tell the age of elves. She didn't look *old.*"

"Thanks for telling me," said Tara-lin. *I'm glad I sent a rider. Otherwise the elf who finds them might dally about bringing them to me.*

"Why do you thank me?" asked Asana. "It was nothing. You are Queen of Elethri. You asked me a question about when I entered your domain and who found me. I answered it. There is no thanks deserved for that, for even if we are equals, it is your kingdom, not mine."

"Because I appreciate the information, Asana," said Tara-lin.

In that moment, Tara-lin discovered what might be the solution to the long-standing problem of how to make sure they would be able to find and get to any refugees who again attempted to flee over the Malaitha Mountains. *I could set a ward in the Malaitha Mountains. Not a strong, active one like that on our northern border, but just something to let me sense those who journey deep into them, some of whom will probably be trappers and hunters who have nothing to do with us. Still, it would solve the problem of how to know, and how to send a rider for them. If I can replicate this, that is. I still don't know why my ward calls to me. But maybe the dryads do and can help me know how to do it again, but without the defensive enchantments.*

The next day she sought out Kalithalias to ask her, but the dryad had no answer for her. She did not know why the ward called to Tara-lin as it did. Somehow, it seemed that Tara-lin was linked into it in much the same manner as the entire forest, and it had not been so with the warding she had sung for the valley, so Kalithalias did not know why. She told Tara-lin she would tell her if any of the dryads knew why, but she did not think any of them would. *Still,* Tara-lin thought, *maybe someday I can figure out why and then figure out how to do it again.* She would not want to even try to sing the same enchantment she had sung on the northern border through the Malaitha Mountains. Hunters and trappers and anyone who might make their living in them did not deserve to be hindered by her songs.

Several days later the new refugees were brought into Frèlin. They turned out to be the son of a minor noble who wanted to marry his father's scullion and that same servant. They had been conducting a secret love affair and trying to come up with a plan that would allow them to be together freely. When they heard about Elethri's offer of sanctuary, they decided to try for Elethri. The man, Livis, had arranged to be gone from his father's house for a while, and he had taken Esyn with him, hoping her disappearance out of the several maids would not be noticed. He had reached the border while the army was massed on it, and found a place to stay to await the outcome of the battle. When it became clear that the Land of the Five Rivers was triumphant, albeit by very unusual means, he had taken Esyn across the border under cover of night. Apparently it had been morning by the time they were far enough into the woods for Tara-lin's wards to sing to her. There they had fallen into the sleep she had designed and been found by an elf. Livis and Esyn explained that Tara-lin's unordinary means of victory further assured them that her sorcery could not be the witchcraft of the devil and of Nightshade. Whatever anyone said, they could not believe someone who stripped the enemy army of its weapons and then let its soldiers go, every one of them unharmed, could be *that* evil.

Thinking about it while sitting with the Tree that night, Tara-lin thought, *I bet it's harder for girls whose families want to force them into marriages or monasteries to run away than it is for men or girls who have someone they can trust or who will support them to run away. I wonder if there is any way to solve this? I'm sure there are more women like Alis who would love to come here but who have no idea how to make it here.*

This is harder and more complicated than I ever ever *imagined. Still, I am glad to do what I can, to do something for some people. Even if I can't yet help women like Alis very effectively, at least I can help people like Asana, and Coriann and Valmor, and Livis and Esyn.* It amused Tara-lin that Livis and Esyn were like Coriann and Valmor flipped. Coriann was the princess and Valmor the squire. Livis was the noble's son and the woman, Esyn, was a kitchen servant.

Chapter Nineteen - Song of the Storm

The summer turned into autumn. Despite the war, it was a peaceful time, and all Elethri relaxed when autumn turned into winter and still no overt act of war came from the Valor Alliance. The winter would not hinder their defense of their forests and cities, but it would hinder the mobility of the Valiance forces. A major offensive in the spring was not improbable, but, for the moment, they had peace. That much the capture of the weapons and armor had bought for Elethri.

Akeesh accepted their overtures and trade rules were worked through with the southern nation. Alis argued for buying grain from Akeesh, if that was one of their exports. "Goodness, if it is, can we convince Akeesh to buy grain for us from the Alliance or anyone who grows it, and then sell it to us?" Tara-lin laughed. "If the price is reasonable, we can buy grain from or through Akeesh for you, and any others of the humans who want it. I don't have an unlimited supply of wealth, though, even though I do own most of the weapons and armor we took."

When Asana wanted to write a letter home to her family to let them know that she was well, Eldazìn insisted that her letter be checked to ensure that there were no references to Elethrian secrets, such as Keller's wizardry or the Dragonriders. Asana protested that she could be trusted, and Tara-lin assured her, much to Eldazìn's chagrin, that she had only to say it contained personal information and Tara-lin would forbid Eldazìn from reading it. His response had been, "Do you really think the Valiance couriers won't open and read it?!" Asana had submitted the letter to Eldazìn. "It's nothing personal anyway, so I don't care," she said. It appeared that Asana's family *had* provided her with help in reaching Elethri, though they themselves "had no interest in living in a forest with a bunch of elves and a Sorceress Queen," as they had expressed it.

The weeks brought several more young women who wanted to learn wizardry to them. One of them had been given to a monastery but succeeded in maintaining a friendship with another girl. Together they had succeeded in fleeing. Tara-lin was not very clear on the details. Apparently they themselves were not sure how they had been successful, either. They had expected to be caught, but, somehow, they had made it. Tara-lin wondered if some of the dryads were helping them. She was sure Alai-ie-a would do such a thing *if* she noticed, but most dryads seemed inclined to completely avoid the affairs of humans and to more or less ignore them.

Tara-lin relished the season. She was almost able to forget that she was Queen for weeks at a time. She and Keller made another house for themselves out in the forest a day's journey from Frèlin, but close to the mountains so that Kellia was happy, and there they spent many weeks. Lìrulin, the aging Eldor, and Lyan made another tree-house a short ways away and often came out and lived with them. Tara-lin showed Alis more of the forest, and went down to the sea with Earnrìl and Welri a couple of times. Sometimes the women who were learning wizardry came out with them, and Keller would spend hours of the day watching them and giving them pointers Tara-lin barely understood and found boring. She did notice that he continually reminded them, "I'm half-elf, you're human. If you feel like what I'm telling you doesn't help you or hinders you, forget it at once." In addition to helping the women with their wizardry – some of whom, it turned out, already had some facility, having secretly studied wizardry prior to coming to Elethri – Keller spent many long hours on it himself. Often, he asked Tara-lin to sit beside or near him while he worked or sang.

Then came a day in early spring when Earnrìl and Welri flew back from exploring the coastline with the news that a huge fleet was headed down the coast of Elethri. As soon as Tara-lin heard the news – which was shortly before the evening meal – she thought, *I suppose I need to ward the coastal forests, too! But that is harder. I don't want it to be hard for my own people, like Earnrìl, to go out to the sea and then return to the forests.*

"What are they doing? Where do you think they're going?" she asked, a quaver in her voice.

Earnrìl shrugged. "Aernoss? They're half-way down our coast. Well," she said, reconsidering, "not half-way down the coast, but they're half-way from our northern border to Aernoss."

"Why do they even think it's *worth* it to attack us?" moaned Tara-lin. "War is a major expense. We're really not a threat, who cares if a few royal children run away to us!"

"They might agree with you if you had turned me and Cuthlin in," said Namdon quietly.

"Still. What threat do I pose?!"

Alis laughed. "You know the answer to that question, Tara-lin."

She shook her head. "Not really. I'm a threat to their way of doing things, but why? Why do they ... never mind, I'm sure none of you can answer me. The real thing to be done right now is to figure out how we're going to defend Aernoss. Also, send a gryphon rider to track that fleet! If it turns off course for Aernoss I want to know as soon as possible so we can respond."

"Who do you want to go?" asked Namdon.

"I don't know," said Tara-lin. "I don't think it matters much. Guard! Astëan, over there!"

The elf turned.

"Go and send a gryphon rider at once to keep an eye on a fleet half-way down the coast from our northern border to Aernoss. I want to know at once if the fleet deviates from course to Aernoss. Also, get the rest of my council. After that, get the King, Eldazìn, Cuthlin, Eldor if you can, and Erenvin. I don't know who else, but that's a start. Oh yes, get the Prince Oranë or Elisa, if you can."

The elf bowed. "Yes, Queen."

Tara-lin turned to Earnrìl and made an exasperated face. "I hate this. It makes it seem as if my life and problems and errands are more important than everyone else's. Yet I have to do it this way. I don't have the time to run around finding everyone myself ... Anyway, what should I know to start with? I wish I could think of a way to defend Aernoss without a slaughter."

"Are you asking me or Namdon what you should know?" asked Earnrìl.

"Both of you! Any one of you!" said Tara-lin. "I don't know what the Elethrian navy is like."

At this, Earnrìl interrupted. "It's non-existent. In the past some trading was done by ship, and Elethri had a few merchantmen and no more warships to dissuade pirates. I don't know if Elethri has any ships beyond the barges or canoes of a few odd elves, but if it does, it's no navy to speak of."

"All right. So I know that now." Tara-lin heaved a sigh. "I don't know if it matters yet. I don't know if I can come up with a good way to defend Aernoss."

"Ship for ship, the Valiance navy is not the best in Ellenesia. Akeesh's navy is better, and so is Abourn's. However, in total power, the Valiance navy is incomparable. It's so much bigger," said Namdon. "Earnrìl, can you tell us more about what you saw?"

"Sure," said the elf. She began to explain in detail. She was often interrupted by Sir Namdon's requests for clarification of certain details. To more than half of these requests, the only answer she had to give was,

"I don't know. I didn't know what I was looking for, so I didn't pay attention to that." While this was going on, the others whose presence Tara-lin had requested began to arrive, first of all King Keller. When he asked what was going on, Namdon said he was trying to figure out what the fleet sent against them was going to be. Earnrìl offered to start over again, but Namdon said that it was better not to. He would summarize and explain his analysis when they were done. In the meantime, Tara-lin explained what she understood of the situation, and what she hoped, to her spouse and to the others as they arrived.

The next day, Tara-lin and Keller explained the situation to the elves in Frèlin and told them that anyone who desired to participate in the defense of Aernoss was welcome to travel to the seaside city and do so. Any who changed their minds later would be free to depart. More privately, she requested that the majority of the Guard of Frèlin to ride to Aernoss. "I will be really surprised if any of them do anything useful if I don't come up with another safe and bloodless defense," said Tara-lin to her council when they had finished speaking to the people.

"You will be surprised, Tara-lin," said Eldazìn. "You may have far fewer who will stick with you through blood and gore than if you could use force like the Valiance Army does, but those who do will be of greater use than they would be if you tried to force them. Your people admire you, Keller and Tara-lin. Even if you cannot always lead us to victory without bloodshed, you have shown that you intend to do so. You have shown that you respect their freedoms. Some will fight for you *because* you offer them the opportunity to change their minds and go at any moment. Many will fight for you because you are the Singer of Elethri and both of you have shown yourselves to be at one with the elven nature."

Tara-lin nodded. She felt intensely embarrassed.

"And you?" asked Keller. It was just the question she had been thinking to ask.

"I fight for you because you are my King and Queen and because you are a good King and Queen," said Eldazìn. "We might disagree about tactics and strategy and prudence, but I have never seen either of you command, or think to command, either that which is not yours to command or that which would be evil."

In that, I think you differ from many others who worship me, thought Tara-lin. *Perhaps that is why you are my friend, but I do not feel like the people are my* friend. *You did not fall for Anakrim. What you would do if you were convinced that I was evil, like the High Master of the Valor Hall must be, I do not know. But I do know that you would* not *obey me. That you will be discerning enough to know if you think something I do or command is evil and that you will not go along with it, no matter how else you feel or think about me.*

The conversation changed then to tactics and strategy of all sorts. The next several days were spent in hectic brainstorming. Tara-lin went to the dryads that night to request their thoughts if they had any. She spoke briefly to Beriririkirkirkitira about her issues. The elder dryad assured her she would help if she could. "It was you who first thought of pitying Anakrim, who saw him as hurt and damaged by Nightshade, instead of as only an enemy. I can only imagine what this dilemma must be to you now," Beriririkirkirkitira had said. "I will think, but I cannot promise a solution." The days were spent in long conversations. Someone (Tara-lin did not remember who, or even if it was herself) suggested sending a message to Akeesh and asking if they would be willing to lend naval support in exchange for metals. Someone else noted that it would take far too long even if Akeesh immediately agreed upon receiving the message and marshaled their navy as quickly as possible.

Finally, they decided to ride down to the city (those who had no gryphons would ride with the Dragonriders) and conduct its defense as best as they could. "If nothing else," said Tara-lin, "I will sing to the waves. I have never sung to the ocean before, but perhaps it will sink their fleet for me. I would rather not; it is such slaughter, but I do not have a better solution. At least it will spare my own people, even if I cannot think of their lives as worth more than those of the Valiance humans." If that did not work, those Dragonriders who were willing (which was many, but not all of them) would burn the ships. The dragon fire would, hopefully, counterbalance the disadvantage of having no navy.

It was with sorrow that Tara-lin bid her parents and brother goodbye. She had no real fear that she would not live through the battle to come, though she was not sure why she was not afraid. Was it because she did not fear defeat or death? Was it because, without any real reason, she did not believe she *could* be defeated? Whatever the reason for her lack of fear for herself, she feared when her father would die. He still seemed hearty and strong for a human of his age, but that age was now nearly sixty years old. She knew that he had reached the age at which men began to die without warning and without violent cause. Thus, she feared that she would never see him again.

They left the human wizards-in-training behind, despite the protestations of some of them who wanted to defend their new nation that had offered them refuge and their dream. Keller insisted that none of them were proficient enough to do much good or to have any chance at shielding themselves if there were any Valiance wizards with the fleet.

As she rode behind Maryath's rider again, her dilemma tormented Tara-lin. How was it possible to be a good Queen? *I don't know if you're listening, Shallim-Araldor. I know you favor compassion, but I don't know what my compassion should look like in this circumstance. Perhaps it is not a problem. Perhaps when the time comes to act I will be shown the way. If you're listening, please make it so. Please show me the way before it is too late. I really don't know how to be a good Queen.*

When they stopped at night, she discussed the issue with Keller and with Alis. Neither of them had much to say. Keller still had difficulty connecting to situations that were beyond his present experience. Tara-lin's dilemma simply did not exist to him. As for Alis, she said to Tara-lin, "It is a shame they will have to die, but all men will die one day, and they *could* refuse to fight for the Valor Alliance if they *wanted* to do so. All of Valiance must know now that you are what they call merciful if they are willing: how else did an army come home, alive and undamaged, but stripped of their weapons and much of their armor? No. If you can, offer them clemency. Offer them freedom – perhaps one of those isles in the bay, in case some of them are spies – if they will pirate their ships, or swim ashore, or whatever is necessary to not fight Elethri. Otherwise, they have willingly joined themselves to the evil of the High Master himself. They have had their chance to see that you are not what their religion would paint women who choose your path, and rejected it. Don't feel bad about the death they chose."

Tara-lin nodded, still feeling unresolved. "Have you been spending a lot of time with Eldazìn?" she asked.

Alis smiled wanly. "Perhaps. He and I work together on my, I think of it as my quest. But I haven't learned to think like him."

"Oh no, I don't fear that," said Tara-lin, laughter coaxed into her voice by Alis' manner and words. "It's just not something I would expect to enter your mind. Or mine."

Alis smiled at that.

"I think it would enter Keller's mind faster than mine, to be honest," said Tara-lin.

"That doesn't surprise me, though I don't think of your spouse and Eldazìn as any more alike than myself and Eldazìn," said Alis.

"They're not. Can you imagine Keller as an assassin?" Tara-lin could not decide whether that thought made her feel more queasy or more like laughing. "Or a first-rate bookthief?" This image was only ridiculous; it did not offend her. "I can't imagine Keller doing half the things Eldazìn does, but he does think of ramifications like these better than I do. He has a mind more apt to dealing with hostile international diplomacy than I do, though I think in most ways he's far more like me than like Eldazìn. We're almost always on the same page as to *what* to do. He just thinks better about *how* when it comes to some things."

"And you think better about *how* when it comes to other things."

"Of course," said Tara-lin. She wondered if she should have these conversations with those Dragonriders who were unwilling to participate in burning the ships if it came to that. She did not think their unwillingness was primarily unwillingness to expose themselves or their dragons to risk; most of the dragons did not strike her as susceptible to such thinking, though she supposed she did not really know. She could not speak to them, but the riders certainly spoke of them as if they knew no fear. No, she thought it more likely they might understand something of what she felt.

Tara-lin stood on the white walls of Aernoss. Since she had ridden into the city thinking of it as the site of a battle it instantly occurred to her that it had not been built with battle in mind. If it had been, it would have been built several miles over in a far more defensible location with a road down to the harbor that would be a slaughter for an enemy army to take. If it was built in the image she saw in her mind the harbor would be no less defensible than it was now, and the rest of the city would be far more defensible.

She watched the fleet sail into the Bay of Summer, short for Bay of Summer Dawn. It was huge, she thought. The sails were huge and bore the ensign of the Valor Alliance. The ships looked ugly and terrible to her, even though the colors they were painted were quite lovely, with a predominance of white and purple. "Now," she said to Keller. Now was the time for his spell to amplify her voice to reach across the bay, over the sounds of the waves, and the flapping of sails, and the oars. The fleet was in battle formation, but still too far to bring its cannons to bear upon the empty elven harbor.

He twined his fingers in hers when he had finished the spell prepared the previous day. Together they spoke to the myriads who came as their enemy, offering freedom and peace to any who dared to accept their offer.

They had scarcely begun to speak when Keller halted and whispered in a hushed tone to Tara-lin, "They have wizards." She knew not to speak or ask him questions, but to let him fight his fight undistracted. She knew he must have been alerted by the wardings he had been placing over the previous days, but more than that she did not know. She did not know what kind of magic it was or if the men on the ships had heard her at all. If they had, they had spoken enough for them to know the offer made them. She desperately wished she knew whether they had heard at all. For if they had heard she would wait for any sign that they might be responding, and if she received no sign, she would work her own magic, not to distract Keller, but to distract whoever might be fighting him.

Tara-lin suspected that they had heard. At least, she hoped so. She had reasons to think so. Unless the wizards had expected to fight another wizard, and for them to take the course they had, the ships would not have been warded against outside words. It would take a few moments for a wizard to prepare such a ward. Also, it might even be what Keller's wards had picked up.

Busy in her thoughts, Tara-lin only now noticed the voice that reached across the waters towards them, as her and Keller's voices must have reached across the waters just previously. In fancy words, it threatened and called for surrender. Tara-lin did not even think of responding. She could hear Keller chanting nearly inaudibly under his breath. She could feel the tension coming from him. She knew little of wizardry, but suspected he might be fighting for his life – or hers.

There was no sign that any of the ships had deviated from course, or that any of the men had gone overboard. *Shallim-Araldor*, prayed Tara-lin, *if any of them have tried, and are held prisoner by their companions, please, have mercy. Stop me from doing what I am about to do or spare their lives in some other way. Please, be listening.* Then she sang.

> Wind of the light and sea in rage churn
> Waves of the sea in fury burn
> Airs, hear my voice, lift your own in howls fell!
> Waters, hear my voice, rise in your mighty swell!

> Rush of wind, come from the east in power!
> Wind, come from the west in descent!
> Meet, fly for me as dancing twins of fury!
> Churn to join with you in chaos the low sea!

Tara-lin knelt and placed her palms on the stone breastwork, seeking greater contact with the earth. She continued to sing, low and desperate, a haunting, chaotic tune.

> Chaos of the winds, I give you my chaos
> Sword of the air, to clash and flash.
> Drive from the east, drive from the mighty heights!
> In cold and fury give the waves teeth to bite.

Tara-lin was about to begin another stanza, when Keller fell against her. Concerned, she rolled out of under him and clasped her arms around him. "Keller!" she called.

He opened his eyes. "It's okay. I – I think I killed one."

She did not know what to say to that. He was breathing hard. His skin felt cold. She did not *think* that it was only the horror of having killed. He had been fighting with wizardry. She guessed the fight had been far more intense than what Anakrim had offered. He might be far more experienced now, but the fight with Anakrim had been one to maintain dominance, to maintain a neutralizing spell. This had been a true duel. "Are there more?" she asked.

He closed his eyes. "Yes. My wardings are still flashing."

"Can you tell what the spell is?" she asked. "I think they're trying to neutralize my storm." *Not good*, she thought with furious speed. *That means they may still try to kill us. I doubt he can fight another trained wizard right now! I wish he had more training. I wish he knew more. But I bet he was right the others are not far enough along to help at all. He might know. I would not.*

When an answer was not quickly forthcoming, Tara-lin turned her mind back to the storm. She got on her hands and knees and took up her song. She poured all her energy into it. If Keller was fighting a wizard again, the greater the storm the greater his chance of success. If the wizard, or wizards, tried to counter the storm, that would be attention and energy with which they were not fighting her mate. If they did not fight the storm, it would most certainly rock their ships and gust around them. She could only hope that, too, would weaken their attention and give her mate the advantage. So she sang desperately to the wind and felt the wind and sea respond. It churned in a whirl of increasing energy and chaos.

Around her there was a flash of blue light. A second later she heard the thunder. The ground quivered in resonance with it. She smiled an odd smile, encouraged by the voice of the storm, and gave herself even more to its song. For a brief moment she thought, *I wonder if the spirits of wind know who I am, or what I am doing, or for and against what I am fighting, and want to help me!* Then such thoughts vanished as her consciousness merged with her song.

Suddenly the song released her. The storm certainly raged over the bay, but not with the fierceness for which Tara-lin hoped. She wondered if this was the result of the wizards' counter-magic on the wind and sea or if it was because the dryads could not sing with her in a song which would be the deaths of men, and she had rarely sung songs of great force without the participation of dryads. She could not tell. The way human wizardry affected the elements was very different from the way dryadic song affected the elements, and Tara-lin both had little ability to sense human wizardry and no instinct for how to fight it. She had not been singing the song to kill, though she had contemplated doing so. She had been singing the song to distract – and not even to distract so that another might kill, though that might be the result, but so that another might not be killed. Yet the song had released her. It felt as if it had almost thrown her away.

She stood, shaking from head to toe with the energy she had sung into the storm. Through the mist and rain she could see that the Valiance fleet had made good headway into their harbor. She turned and called down to the Dragonrider and gryphon rider waiting in the sward below the wall. "Now!" she said.

Even if she could do no more to distract the wizards, the riders could. She did not think the wizards could fight the dragons and gryphons, and Keller at the same time. They might try, but if they did, one or the other would almost certainly kill them.

She wished she knew *where* in the fleet they were, so that the dragons and gryphon riders could attack those ships.

Chapter Twenty - Not Destroyer, Healer

Was that Shallim-Araldor answering my request? Was that why the song rejected me? thought Tara-lin as she watched the Dragonriders and, a little behind them, the gryphon riders rise from the city behind her. *I pray I have not messed it up by sending the riders into the battle now. I suppose I shouldn't be afraid of that. If Shallim-Araldor is listening and acting, then I suppose he can probably do something to fix it if this is a problem, too.*

With another part of her mind, she thought, *So both our secrets are out now. But we expected that it might be so, when we planned this as best as we could.*

The dragons rose higher into the mists and clouds. Soon they were invisible to her eyes. Out of the clouds came their first weapon: huge boulders and rocks torn out of the cliff which they had carried laboriously into the sky. They tumbled from the sky. Where ships were struck, decks and masts were shattered. Where the sea was struck, chaos was added to the waves. The first dragons dove, only a dragonlength behind the last boulders at first. As they neared the sea, they opened their mouths and flame poured out of them, incinerating most arrows which came their way. Tara-lin watched with suspense, hardly daring to breathe. It looked as if the dragons would crash into the ships just as the rocks had done, but then they snapped their wings open, angling their flight. They skimmed over the ships, lighting masts and poops and forecastles on fire, then rose into the air. The rain was light and did not hinder dry masts and desks from catching flame very quickly. It seemed to Tara-lin that they converted some of the momentum of their dive into their ascent. The next wave of dragons did not skim so close to the ships but used their fire to destroy the missiles sent after the first charge. The third wave flew yet higher, defending the second, and so on the forth, until the dragons were high enough to have some mobility in the sky and, therefore, the ability to dodge and defend themselves. Tara-lin gasped, and almost cheered, at the awesome perfection of the maneuver, which was not her design. It was the dragons' or their riders' art.

Keller reached out and grabbed her hand. His own was cold and clammy with sweat. "Tara-lin," he whispered.

"What?" she asked. "Are you losing? *Are you dying?*"

He squeezed her hand tighter. "No. I'm almost out of power. I need yours, if you can give it to me. I think you can; we both sing."

She leaned into him, wrapping her arms around his waist, the fingers of one of her hands intertwined with the fingers of one of his. He began his chant again and she waited for a moment, trying to catch its evasive lilt. Finally, she struck a note of harmony with it and tried to give herself to a totally new way of singing. Somehow, she had to sing her energy, her song, into Keller's magic, his song. She was not here to direct, to weave spells or songs herself. She was here to join her power, a power of the forest, with Keller's, to reinforce his magic with her own power. She did not know if she had enough power, especially after singing the storm. She did not know if what Keller asked was even possible, but she had to try that which she could not even conceive or conceptualize, nor was it the first time she had done something of which she had no conception until she had done it.

A strange tingling flowed through Tara-lin's blood. This was like nothing she had ever done before.

Keller's chant faltered and drifted away. Tara-lin tightened her fingers around his. "Are you okay?" she whispered.

"Y-yes," he said.

"You don't sound okay."

"I am. I really am." He shifted away from her. "The wizards are gone. At least, my wardings aren't being tripped anymore."

"Did you kill them?" asked Tara-lin.

Keller shook his head. "I'm not sure I killed any –" he began, but at that moment another elf came running along the breastwork. "King! Queen!" she was shouting.

"What is it?" asked Keller.

"The enemy is almost into the harbor. What should we do?"

Tara-lin looked out over the sea and saw that she was right. The Valiance fleet was nearly to the harbor. Some of its ships were burning. Others were cracked and slowly sinking, but much of the fleet was still intact. The storm-cloud still hung above the bay, whirling around. The rain had almost ceased, except in scattered torrential bursts, but the wind looked dangerous. The gryphons and dragons no longer flew into the cloud. They appeared to struggle as they flew below it and sometimes through its frayed, draping edges. The gryphon riders circled, using great bows to launch arrows which had been drawn through tar and set ablaze arcing away from their mounts and into the ships. The dragons flew back and forth, dropping rocks on the fleet and sometimes diving with flaming plumes around their heads and necks while the gryphon riders provided cover. Tara-lin wondered how their riders endured the heat from their flames.

"They're going to try to land as soon as they can, I think," said Keller.

The elf runner nodded.

"If the wizards are gone, can you offer them peace again?" asked Tara-lin. The thought that there *had* been no choice for the warriors on board the ships tormented her. A few could not fight their companions or pirate their ships. Even if they did, the rest of the ships would fire on them. How could she know whether most of them could even swim (if they took off their armor that is; no man could swim in the armor they wore into battle)?

"I will try," said Keller.

When he had done so, the elf spoke again. "What are your commands? Our commanders desire your input, since they do not know what you can or wish to do with your magic."

Keller nodded. He twisted his sleeve around his arm as he thought. "I don't know. I really don't know. They can run up the white flag to signal surrender. If they swarm onto the harbor or beach armored and weaponed, drop whatever you have on them. Any ship that fires its cannons at the wall can receive the same treatment. That's all I have to say."

"That won't interfere with anything you plan?" the elf runner asked.

"No," said Keller.

"I plan nothing more," said Tara-lin, trying to keep her voice steady. Even so, it shook with unshed tears.

"Let's go to Aernoss' tower," said Keller. "I'd rather not be here if the walls are struck. Tara-lin, why are you crying?"

"Going to the tower is fine by me," she said, as they strode towards the nearest staircase down from the walls. "I just – I don't like this. I – I feel horrible. I used the dryad song – and I don't know if it's making things harder for the riders, and I don't know if, if I misused it. If it did any good at all." Her words were broken by sobs.

"I don't know why you think it was useless," said Keller. "I don't think I could have withstood their assaults if you hadn't distracted them."

Tara-lin gave him a wan smile. "Well, that is something good then."

"But you don't feel it."

She shook her head.

At the tower they were met by Alis and Eldazìn. "Why aren't you with the gryphon riders? I thought you did not feel like we shouldn't kill them so ... is Kushon hurt?" asked Tara-lin.

Alis shrugged. "I can't draw the elven bows," she said. "Also, I *still* have never shot a bow in my life and wouldn't want to accidentally hurt Kushon ... that stuff is dangerous."

"I agree. I totally understand," said Tara-lin. "I was a little ... surprised, myself, when Cuthlin suggested that plan."

"They were all practicing and he was overseeing the practice yesterday. I decided to give it a try, but I couldn't draw the bow, let alone draw the bow on gryphon back, let alone manage it with that fiery stuff ... safely," said Alis.

"I completely understand," said Tara-lin. "I bet you could learn to shoot a bow, though."

"If it were the right size for me," said Alis. "The elf bows are the wrong size."

Tara-lin nodded. Keller said to Eldazìn, "Why are you here, friend?"

"I don't have a better place to be," he answered. "Runi scours the skies for me and tells me what she sees. It's effortless for her to speak to dragons, so I can readily give my input to the Dragonriders. I ask Runi to tell them whatever Akanë or Lomorì want to tell them, and receive updates and information from them. It's quite useful."

"It sounds it," said Keller.

"It does," said Tara-lin, "but I want them all to know I'm sorry."

All three of her companions stared at her. "You're sorry?" asked Eldazìn.

"Yes. To all of you. I don't think I could – I wouldn't want to – kill. What if I accidentally kill someone who is looking for the first opportunity to get away from the Valor Army? You know, if as a group they decided they wanted to be free, they could be, but if it's ones and twos? Their companions would restrain or slay them! Even a single ship might be destroyed by the rest of its fleet before it could signal us or we could do anything," said Tara-lin, "so I want to say I'm sorry because I've been asking all of you to do for me what I wouldn't do for myself."

At that moment, Akanë strode out of the tower. He looked very young and insecure. "What – do you – another dragon is injured."

"Another?" asked Tara-lin. "I'm so sorry!" She burst into tears.

"Ignore her," said Eldazìn. "She's acting hysterical, saying she's sorry that we're doing the dirty work for her that she wouldn't do for herself. But I don't know any more about war craft of this sort than you or Lomorì do."

"Eldazìn!" scolded Tara-lin.

Eldazìn spun to face her and knelt before her. "If you give me a command, I will obey it instantly, Queen, but there's no room for your emotions in the middle of a battle." He rose and turned back to Akanë. "What do you have to say?"

"This is our third dragon injured or killed," said Akanë. Tara-lin could see in his eyes that he hated this almost as much as she did, if not as much. "We can't keep them from landing. There's too many of them, and the dragons and gryphon riders can't keep steady enough pressure on them. None of us have ever fought a real war before. Whoever built these cursed walls was not thinking about defense! Is there anything you can do, Keller?"

Tara-lin spun to look at him and saw an almost glazed look in his eyes. "Maybe," he said, "but if so, give the signal to the Dragonriders to stop diving near the harbor. They can drop anywhere they want, but I don't want them near the harbor. I also want everyone on the walls to be ready to get down and find cover as quickly as possible."

"That is done, King," said Eldazìn. He snapped his fingers and the elf who had spoken to Tara-lin and Keller on the walls stepped forward. "Relay the message to those on the walls: be ready to get down and find cover if anything strange happens." He turned back to Keller. "Is that good?"

The half-elf nodded. Tara-lin wanted to scream. She looked at her hands and imagined them dripping with blood. She tensed and pulled away from the hand Alis put on her arm.

Keller ran up the stairway, seeking the top of the tower. Tara-lin wondered what he was doing. Her thoughts were so conflicted she could not gather them together or think them. Beside her, Eldazìn replied to Akanë, "Whoever built these walls was as slug-brained as root rot," he cursed. "I know what you mean. They're only a little better than a useless outdoors art exhibition. We can't hold them long if they get any equipment to the walls!"

He sounded angrier than Tara-lin had ever heard him before. "If all this blood and death makes you so upset, why do you do it for me?"

she asked.

Both elves turned to her. Akanë knelt and gently, familiarly, took her hand in his own. "I don't do it for *you*, Queen. I would do it for you, but I do it for all of Elethri. I do it so that we elves may remain free in our forest and continue to offer freedom to the oppressed of Ellenesia – and from across the sea. You know very well that there is not one of us whom you have compelled to this, or even exactly commanded to it. You know very well that every one of these elves knows that he or she can leave if he desires, that even the Guard of Frèlin and the Guard of Aernoss know that they can quit their service at any time."

"Really? They all know that?" asked Tara-lin. She was too stunned to withdraw her hand from Akanë's grip.

"Yes. But do you think there is a single elf here who wants to be ruled by the Valor Alliance? We may kill and die for you, but that is because you are the representative and embodiment of what we want to be. Your choices and decrees as Queen of Elethri are representative of the best of this nation."

"What will you do when I and Keller die, and one of our children sits the throne, one who is not like me? What would you do if you lived under a King and Queen who did not care as I do for the freedom and respect of my people – and of all people?" asked Tara-lin.

Akanë released Tara-lin's hand and drew himself up to his full height, which was rather taller than her own. "I would not obey out of fear – and even if the King is a wizard and I cannot desert into the wilderness, what would there be to fear from a King if death waits for me right out there?" he said, gesturing toward the harbor. "I would not obey evil commands. I cannot say that for all who now defend Aernoss, but I say it for myself, and it is no fault in you if others have not learned to see behind the throne. It is no fault in you if you cannot teach others to think for themselves what is good and to do that."

"And what if we lose, Akanë, Eldazìn ... Alis?" asked Tara-lin.

Akanë knelt again. Tara-lin thought part of it was that he did not like how much he towered over her. He preferred to look up into her face. "I may die, but I will have no regrets. What is it you are asking?"

Tara-lin turned. "You?" she said to Eldazìn.

His mouth was set in a grim line. "Kill, Queen. Stain my hands with the blood of those who rule that nation out there." He pointed toward the harbor, and his teeth were almost clenched as he spoke.

"Is that what you wish to do now?" asked Tara-lin.

"While Elethri stands, I wish to defend Elethri. But if Elethri falls, then I see not what else I can do for that which I love."

Tara-lin looked at Alis.

"Did I not answer long ago when I told you that I would rather die than swear myself to a man or to a god?" asked Alis.

"I suppose you did," said Tara-lin. "I don't want to distract any of you from strategy. Are the wounded dragons being cared for?"

"As well as either we or the riders know how," answered Alis.

"Good," said Tara-lin. She ran past her friends and bolted up the stairs of the tower to find her spouse.

Shallim-Araldor, dryads of the world, dragons of the sky, human-kin, I'm sorry! she thought as she ran. Then she burst onto the open level that looked out over the city of Aernoss and over the sea. Keller stood with his back to her, singing a hypnotic chant. He swayed a little in the wind, but the whole air sang to Tara-lin of intense concentration – and of *fire.*

She stepped out beside him and discerned a magnetic glow above the harbor and the sea. With a shudder she drew back and turned her back. She could not contemplate all the men who would die today nor the deaths they would die. She could not contemplate being a part of it. It felt as if her soul were being stretched almost to the breaking point. She fled down the tower, wishing she could find some refuge into which she could fling herself and, hopefully, into which she could draw the whole world with her.

She should have been more intelligent. She should have been less careless. She should have told the elves to abandon their seaside cities and she should have warded the entire forest. Perhaps she could have figured out how to fine-tune her enchantment so that it would not affect those who had a developed affinity to the dryadic nature. That way her people could go out to the sea and then return to the woods unhindered. If she had done that, there would not be this bloodshed. There would not be these men dying! It was her fault. Why had she been so careless and negligent?

Is there anyone who can forgive me? Tara-lin wondered. *Is there any way for this to be fixed? Is there any way for me to atone, be it in another realm?* This was certainly a huge mistake she had made as Queen! Perhaps it was the first, but that did not diminish its significance.

Something Akanë said hit her then. Had one of the dragons been killed? That was already two deaths on her side then, since dragons and

Dragonriders always died together. Probably there were many more by now, for the fighting was below the walls now, and while ten of the human invaders would die for every elf slain on the walls, still some of her people would be slain.

Tara-lin decided to find wherever the injured dragons were being tended.

It was not long before she did so. Their shiny bulks were easy to see. There were other dragons laying or standing nearby, dragons who would not fight or participate in killing humans, Tara-lin suspected. She approached them.

One dragon, a scaled blue male with white wings, was obviously injured. His head lay on the grass, and against it leaned his rider, an arm and leg bandaged. His wings were bloody, and someone was still trying to figure out to withdraw an arrow from where it had, by a stroke of misfortune, gone between and under his natural armor.

Tara-lin was not crying now. She wove her way between the dragons and riders and elves who were nearby, many of them passing back and forth doing whatever it was they thought they should be doing. She could tell that many of them looked at her for a moment, wondering what she was doing here. She approached the wounded rider and knelt before her.

The rider sensed her proximity and opened her eyes. "Hi ... Tara-lin. What do you want?"

"Nothing," said the Queen of the elves. "I'm here to say I'm sorry. I'm sorry that you were hurt fighting for my country, and I'm sorry that your dragon, your friend, was hurt in the same way."

"Tara-lin," said the rider, "you don't know what it is like in Aneri, do you? There are rumors that it was much worse once, but it is horrible. We are refugees here. Some of us will not kill, but that is because they *will not kill*. We have grown too numerous for the secluded mountains and forest which are alone are safe for us. There, if a Dragonrider is not careful, or if she and her friend are unlucky, they can be captured and burned alive. There are some who teach that the Lord of the Light expects that we never kill other humans or dragons, for that would be to fall prey to the fear and hatred of the nightmare, but there are others who will try to fight if a dragon they know is captured. I am one of those. I and Mounth have killed before. A friend of ours – though we count all Dragonriders friends – was captured. We were too late."

"I'm sorry," said Tara-lin.

"Don't be, singer. It is not your fault, and you have offered many of us a place to stay, to be free. Nor do I think we could be part of this Valor Alliance. I have been talking to the women you have here, and to some of the elves. If they do not permit women to be wizards or gryphon riders, how would they look on female Dragonriders? How would they look on dragons? Would they not be as quick to see our dragons as demons as are the people of Aneri?"

"Probably they would," agreed Tara-lin, "but I'm still sorry the world is this way. And I think this battle is my fault. I think I should have told my people to abandon their seaside cities, and that I should have enchanted the entire border."

"Perhaps," said the rider.

"Is there anything I can do for you?" asked Tara-lin.

"Others have already tended to my needs. If you would know how to extract that arrow from Mounth's neck that would be nice, but I have confidence those who are working on it will figure it out eventually."

"I could sing Mounth to sleep so he won't feel the pain, if that will help them," said Tara-lin.

The rider closed her eyes for a few moments. "Mounth says that is fine by him. But you should talk to them first."

"I will," said Tara-lin.

A few minutes later she stood next to Mounth and placed both her hands on his aquamarine shoulders. *At last I have something good I am doing with my song. Something healing, instead of destructive. Something in accord with my nature, instead of against it. Something that I know is not against the Pact. After this, I will offer my services to those who tend the wounded. There may be other things I can do, as well.* She closed her eyes and sang softly, weaving a melody of entrancing sweetness. The song refreshed her as well as casting a sleep upon Mounth. It was as if the sleep came upon Mounth by first being drawn up through her from the roots of the dryad realm, deep and earthy and full of life, slowly growing, inexorable, ever-healing life that slowly and not the less surely for the slowness healed over every hurt and left the dead and rotten behind.

Tara-lin opened her eyes and stepped back. Strangely, what she sung as sleep upon Mounth was wakefulness to her, not an anxious wakefulness, but a ready, fresh, calm wakefulness, like the consciousness of the dryads or, perhaps, of the trees.

She looked up and saw an incandescent glow above the bay. *Strange. Beautiful. What is it? Should I be worried? I've never seen anything like it before. Should I know what it is?* These thoughts ran through her mind in a detached, quiet kind of way. In her present state, she did not relate to negative reactions or thoughts of fear or worry or anxiety. She felt somewhat curious, but it struck her as the curiosity of a tree. It was not bland, but it was calm and unhurried.

Then there was a blast. Tara-lin felt the sound of it more than she heard it. Flickers of flame rose into the sky above the harbor.

Keller! thought Tara-lin. It was his spell.

She wished she could help their wounded. She wished she could free them from their slavery. For now, she had to help her own people. She wondered if some, who might otherwise die, could live if they were sung into the dreams of trees. It felt so refreshing, so inexorably and unhurriedly healing and alive, Tara-lin knew it was worth a try.

Chapter Twenty-One - The Song in Your Blood

By nightfall, Tara-lin learned that what remained of the Valiance fleet had turned itself back towards the sea. She spent every moment singing healing sleep to the wounded until she fell into the sleep she sang.

The next day she found Mounth and his rider. Something she had said about the 'Lord of the Light' intrigued her. When she found the rider, who was sitting against a bank with her dragon a few paces away, Tara-lin curtsied. "Hi. I remember Mounth's name, but I forget yours," she said.

"Esilien," said the rider. "What interests you?"

"You said something about being taught about a 'Lord of the Light' about whom some teach that he says that one should not fight and kill because that would be motivated by the corruption of the nightmare," said Tara-lin. "I'm interested in what is thought about him in Aneri."

"Among the Dragonriders of Aneri, mostly. I don't think that anyone even knows about him in the civilizations of Aneri, but if someone were to teach about him openly, I don't know if the kings and oracles wouldn't decide he was one of hundreds of demons and declare that any who called on his name were witches. But why? What do you want to know?" asked Esilien.

"Could he by any chance be called Shallim-Araldor?" asked Tara-lin. "*If* it really is wrong to kill, I want to know."

"I don't think it is wrong, and neither does Mounth. I only said *some* think it is wrong and makes one vulnerable to the nightmare. It is said that the Lord of the Light is the only one with the power to defeat the nightmare and that one must surrender to his lordship to withstand the nightmare," said Esilien. "Only some of the Dragonriders call him Lord at all. He is alleged to have messengers called Ellenari, and that he and these were very active in events several generations ago, when a curse that had been laid on the dragons was broken and when the world was saved from an army of the nightmare. What has been handed down to us is that the Lord of the Light is Love, that Love must be ultimately triumphant, and that only by Love can one be free from the power of the nightmare, which is fear and hatred. This is what the Warrior of the Dragonriders and Silmavalien are said to have believed. Some hold that loving, and never yielding to fear and hatred, entails never killing another human. That Love will have the final victory and is the only freedom from corruption makes sense to me and Mounth. I don't know about the rest. Why?"

"I've heard of someone called Shallim-Araldor, who is the King of the Dryads, and is supposed to be the sustainer of life. My friend, Alis, says she has met him. He cares about compassion and mercy. So I was wondering if Shallim-Araldor and the Lord of the Light are the same," said Tara-lin.

"Well, I wouldn't think I was the one to go to," said Esilien. "But I'm not sure if anyone has that much to say. There's little to be told that I haven't told, except for descriptions of the Ellenari and theories about who they are and what they can do. But Mounth tells me there is more to it than this."

"I suppose. I have a solution. I'm going to ask my people to abandon our seaside-cities and ward the forest along the shore so that invaders will be lulled to sleep if they enter. I was a fool not to think about doing that earlier. I'm fairly sure I can sing it so the ward doesn't affect those who have developed an affinity to the dryad world, and you riders can fly over the enchanted border if you want to go out to the sea and come back. I just don't know: is what happened yesterday a victory of the nightmare? Did I, and all of Elethri, serve the nightmare by fighting this battle?" asked Tara-lin.

"I have no answer to that," said Esilien. "Neither does Mounth, except that if there was a better way, one that does not involve so much slaughter, then compared to that victory, this might be defeat. Mounth says it won't help to agonize over having served the nightmare though. You should just take the better way now that you know."

"That sounds sensible," said Tara-lin, "but I feel guilty of hundreds, thousands even, of lives."

"I have nothing to say except: thank you. Thank you for offering us refuge. The dragons thank you also," said Esilien.

"I am truly embarrassed," said Tara-lin, curtsying again. *I can't change the past,* she thought, *but I can change what I do now. I know, too, that the dryads still accept me. I can feel it in my dreams. I am still one with the earth.* She nodded her head decisively and swore to herself. *The future will not be like the past.* "Thank you Esilien ... Mounth, for listening to me and sharing your thoughts with me," she said.

"There's no need for thanks," said Esilien.

Tara-lin nodded and bid her farewell. "I wish you and your friend a quick and full healing," she said. Then she left to find Keller and tell him her plan. If he agreed, which she was almost certain he would, then she would share it with the rest of the elves, and if Shallim-Araldor were willing, they would not spill another drop of blood in the defense of Elethri.

Her stomach rumbled as she went, reminding her that she had not eaten more than a handful of early-season berries and some leaves since her breakfast yesterday morning. Still, she would find Keller first. She had not seen him since before his fireblast. Maybe he had seen her, though. She did not know whether he had been so exhausted he had crumpled up right there on the tower or whether he had come looking for her sometime in the late night and seen her where she slept. Or would it have been almost morning? She was not sure what time it had been when her singing had finally left her asleep.

She found Keller sitting against the wall of the tower. When she approached, he looked up. "Ah! There you are!"

"Were you worried about me? Did you not know where I was?" asked Tara-lin.

"I was assured you were fine. I expected you found a place you wanted to sleep," said Keller.

"No. I fell asleep singing to the wounded," said Tara-lin. "I am so upset. I was hungry, but now I think I am not." She shook her hair back, gathering her thoughts. "Keller, when we get back to Elethri, if you are agreed, I'm letting all the prisoners free." She wondered now how it had slipped her mind. After *deciding* what she wanted to do with them, she had completely forgotten about it and never done it. How? Why? What was wrong with her?

"The ones Eldazìn captured who were involved in the assassinations of the royalty?" asked Keller.

Tara-lin nodded. "Why would we keep them in prison except because we're afraid of them? And why would we fight here and kill here except because we're afraid of what we think will happen if we don't? I seem to recall once saying of Eldazìn, 'If it's not fear, it's still wrong.' I think that's true here."

"Then so be it," said Keller. "What you say makes sense, but I have no feelings about it one way or the other."

Tara-lin paced back and forth. "You're not afraid of losing? Of what will happen to us if the Valor Alliance wins?"

"Oh! That," said Keller. "I suppose. But I haven't been feeling or thinking that recently."

"Oh," said Tara-lin.

"Eldazìn is going to be mad when he hears that you're freeing his prisoners," said Keller.

"Let him," said Tara-lin. "At this point, he knows better than to disobey us about our business. But, uh, are you okay?"

"I am. I'm just tired. Also, on reconsidering it, I don't think *I* killed the wizards at all. I don't know any death spells, and while blasts of the sort I summoned over the harbor certainly have the potential to be deadly, that wasn't what I was doing to the wizards. I was just defending and countering. I don't know what destroyed them – or if it destroyed their lives or only their power," said Keller.

"You've always been a blast wizard," said Tara-lin, making a poor, sad attempt at humor. Then she said, "How many do you think lost their lives in that blast?"

"I don't know," said Keller. "It broke masts, damaged the docks, threw ships backwards towards the sea. Sails were burning. I don't know what happened. Only that shortly after that they went out to sea and disappeared. I had no more power left. That was the last I had. Lomorì was cursing about how any good siege would bring the wall down and crash the gates in. I hope I didn't damage them with my blast. I'm not good at thinking."

"I'm not good at thinking, either," said Tara-lin. "I wonder: why *did* they flee?"

Keller shrugged. "I don't know. I was almost asleep by that time. I woke late this morning and ate. Alis told me you were well but asleep."

"I really should eat," said Tara-lin, still pacing, "but I don't want to. I want to *fix* this. Why did they flee?"

"Maybe one of those rocks hit the Commander of the Fleet on the head and killed him," said Keller.

"You don't really think that, do you?" asked Tara-lin.

"It's as possible as anything else and not *that* unlikely. I think it would have that effect, too."

"I guess," said Tara-lin. After all, a dragon could easily discover who was the Commander of the Fleet, and then the Dragonriders might easily decide to drop a disproportionate amount of rocks on his ship. Upon consideration, she realized Keller's proposal had merit in it. The thought of the extreme effectiveness of dragons against ships gave Tara-lin no pleasure at all. *I do not want good ways to kill. I want to not kill.* "Keller," she said, "I want to abandon the seaside-cities. Everything valuable should be taken into our interior. I'm going to ask the dryads if there's any way for me to ward the coastal forests in such a way that the elves can pass through them without being affected."

"Can it be done?" asked Keller.

"It might be possible to fashion an enchantment that does not affect those with affinity to the dryadic nature," said Tara-lin.

"If you can figure out how to defend Elethri without any bloodshed at all, then do it. We are all for it," said Keller. He stood up, stepped in front of her, and caught her wrists, forcing her to look at him. "But, if you can't, Tara-lin, it's not your fault, nor is the bloodshed on your head. Alis was talking to me this morning. It sounds like you're messing yourself up with worry about the slain. You *care*. I like that about you. But it's not on your head. It wouldn't be right to let the Valor Alliance take our forests and enslave our people and our refugees. At least, *I* don't think it would be, and almost nobody else does, either."

"I understand that," said Tara-lin, looking up into his bright blue eyes, "but I feel like it's impossible to be Queen and do the right thing. Whatever I do, it isn't right."

"Maybe it's not right that there be Kings and Queens," said Keller, "but I don't think you've done anything wrong. We've done the best we know with a situation that isn't perfect. That's all." He lifted his hand and tucked some of her voluminous new-leaf-red hair behind her tapered ears. "But I understand that you are Dryad-Kin, and that makes you unwilling to be part of some things. Rest assured; you are not part of them just because the rest of us do them, and besides, didn't you tell me the dryads said they would help us defend Elethri as long as we did not initiate bloodshed?"

"I did," said Tara-lin. "That's correct. By the way, Keller, I have a really good idea about the prisoners. Let us send them into exile! If they were part of a plot to overthrow Elethri before us, that suggests that they don't really want to be Elethrian, right? So I think we should exile them. They can go find some other forest to live in."

"That does seem appropriate," said Keller. "I still don't think it will please Eldazìn. He'll worry about them causing trouble outside Elethri or sneaking back in to assassinate us."

"It pleases *me*," said Tara-lin. "Does it please you?"

"It does," said Keller. "Are you calm enough to eat now?"

"I think so. I'll try," said Tara-lin. She shook her head slightly. "No. I have a better idea. I want to speak with the dryads. I'll go out into the forest, find something to eat, and speak with the dryads. Now that the fleet is gone, I don't think anything should require my attention urgently?"

"I don't think it should, either. Do you want to be completely alone?" asked Keller.

"I think so. The dryads don't mind you, but it's easier ... by myself," said Tara-lin.

"I understand," said Keller. He gave her a hug, and then she turned and walked away, finding the path out of Aernoss. Her heart craved loneliness, to be with no one but the forest, the trees and the dryads and the wildlife. Furthermore, she still felt weighed down by guilt, the guilt of having used the dryad magic to hurt humans, more, of having entertained willingness to purposefully use the dryad magic to such ends. She did not now question whether or not it was all right to kill in defense. Such questions seemed beside the point to her now, a distraction from the real issue that faced her, something entertained in order to avoid her own guilt. She was counted Dryad-Friend and Dryad-Kin. Her life was bound up with theirs and with the dryad magic. She was bound by their Pact. That was the meaning of what she felt. She could not, must not, use the dryad song to harm humans; perhaps, she could not fight and kill at all, but that was not because it was wrong to fight and kill, but because it went against the magic in her blood. Others it might not corrupt to fight and kill, but *her* it would, for she was almost a dryad. She had wondered once how it was that she could live in both worlds, that of dryads and that of men. She realized now that she could not fully live in both. Gifted with the magic of the dryads, she was also bound with the bonds of their magic. She did not know if it would be possible to forsake the dryad song, but, even if it were, it was not possible *to her.* That magic was her life. Without it, the world around her would be dead to her, if she did not die herself.

She hoped that she could be redeemed. She hoped the forest would still accept her. She hoped she could be as before, that she could be free of the taint her will had embraced.

On her way out of Aernoss, many of the elves she passed regarded her and greeted her. She nodded in acknowledgement, but she could not endure the thought of conversation. Her head bowed, the hood of her cloak pulled over her hair, Tara-lin hastened out of the city.

She walked for a while after she had left the city, gathering and eating bits of edible plants or early-season berries as she passed them, until she found a clearing in the center of which a sapling, as tall as she, was growing up. Around it were ferns and other less vigorous or younger trees. She touched one of its leaves briefly in passing and stepped into the shade of a very large tree growing on the western side of the clearing. She held her arms out, her fingers brushing against the weeping foliage of the tree, and sang.

She sang for hours, joining in the song of the forest, her heart twisting and clenching within her. The forest did not reject her. It accepted her as it always had, but something in herself felt wrong. She could not fully embrace the forest. When the shadows of evening crept across the forest, Tara-lin knelt, and then lay, down on the ground, stretching herself out, to touch as much of the earth as possible. She reached for the roots of the trees around her.

Help me, she pleaded, addressing the forest and the dryads.

Kalithalias. Berirririkirkirkitira. Aumoura. Alai-ie-a. Elkanakur. Enzai. Lanowa.

It was not even to individual dryads she called. Would the dryad magic and song forgive her?

The waves of the dryad consciousness washed over her. They drew her out, like the tides of the sea taking something into its wild, uncharted heart – only this world was not wild like the sea. In many ways, it could be considered almost opposite to the sea. It knew no storms, no chaotic tumult, no alternating rage and calm.

Its voice spoke to her, rich and dark and green, but pulsating as if with light, a light that reminded her of the pale green, almost white, of fresh sprouts.

Dryad-Friend. Dryad-Brood.

Tara-lin knew then that she was still accepted, still one with that world. In the thread, the multi-colored signature of a thousand dryad voices, she picked out the light of Berirririkirkirkitira, strong and dominant in the voice. She reached out to the ancient bush-dryad.

It was as if the dryad's dark, rough hand were laid against her cheek. *It is not impossible for a dryad to fail, to heed the Corruption, and then to grow new and fresh and strong again. The song in your blood still runs true. It rejected the corruption to which you put it and pulled you back from the misuse you attempted. You are not corrupt, Child of Dryads.*

The stomping of feet on the ground woke Tara-lin from her conscious sleep. She sat up, startled, and looked around, then realized that the stomping was farther off than she had thought. Her dream-state of oneness with the forest had caused her to perceive something that was still some distance away.

Tara-lin stood, listening, considering. Probably one – no, two – of the Dragonriders had decided to go for a walk in the forest. There was nothing improbable about it. Nonetheless, curiosity tugged at Tara-lin. She decided to investigate.

Chapter Twenty-Two – Taste of Victory

Tara-lin sprang forward, feeling light and free, like the Sprite of the Woods. It would not be light for much longer. She knew Keller would like to sleep with her this night, but she also knew that he would not be worried, and that he would understand, if she chose to spend the night in the forest. It was easy for her to follow the sounds of the bumbling men. They made so much noise themselves that she knew she could be quite close to them before they would notice her, even if she did not try to move quietly.

So it was. Her cloak swung around her as she came to a sudden leaping halt just to the side of a thicket of young saplings. The men were not Anerian Dragonriders for certain. She knew that at once. The Anerian Dragonriders had been provided with plenty of clothing by the Elethrians, whereas these men were definitely in need of clothes. They did not *look* Anerian, either. And they were whispering to each other. She could not hear their words, but they were definitely speaking the common Valiance tongue, neither Anerian nor Elethrian. They must be from the Valor Alliance.

So what were two unarmored, unweaponed, unclothed Valor Soldiers doing, blundering around in her forest the evening after the assault on Aernoss?

She watched them for a few moments. The expressions on their faces told of weariness and confusion. She drew her elf-sword and stepped forward, breaking the camouflage of her Elethrian cloak and said, "Hail! What are you doing here?"

The men turned, almost as one. One said, "We're lost. We're trying to find Aernoss. We want to...."

"Surrender," the other added.

Tara-lin nodded. "Your surrender is accepted. I am the Queen of Elethri. Follow me. I will take you where you can have a meal and rest." She turned and lead the way toward Aernoss. Behind her, she could hear them whispering, thinking, she presumed, that she could not hear.

"Aderan," said the second, "they *do* still have the Elethrian Flame."

"It's one for you, too, Corostomir," said Aderan. "Their magic isn't evil."

"She looks much more *human* than I expected," said Corostomir. "If this *is* her."

"There's no reason to think it isn't her," said Aderan, "but there's a rumor that her father was human."

Tara-lin smiled to herself. Their conversation was amusing. She presumed that the Elethrian Flame was a reference to the fire on her elf-sword which she carried still, naked before her. It would be dark to human eyes before they reached the gates of Aernoss. "So, what happened? How did you get here?" she asked, glancing briefly over her shoulder.

"When your dragons dove out of the sky, we shed our armor and jumped overboard. Both I and Corostomir – that's my friend – are good swimmers. By the time we made it to the shore we were far north of Aernoss and exhausted. We crawled into the eaves of the forest and slept. In the morning, we decided to look for anything we could eat in the woods, but we are not good woodsman and got ourselves lost."

"Did you find anything to fill your stomachs?" asked Tara-lin.

"It didn't fill our stomachs, but we did find a few berries like those we know at home," said Corostomir. "If I may ask, what is going to happen to us?"

"You're not prisoners," said Tara-lin. "Nothing is going to happen to you. You're as free of the glades of Elethri as any elf."

.•❋ ❋ ❋ ❋ •❋.

It was well after dark when they reached the gates of Aernoss. Tara-lin could have easily reached Aernoss by the time the sun was setting if she had been by herself, but the two ex-Valor Soldiers were deplorable woodsmen. Even Cuthlin and Namdon's woodcraft far outshone that of Aderan and Corostomir. At the gate, Tara-lin spoke to the elf standing guard. "Take these two. Find them quarters suitable to their kind and give them plenty of food," she said. "Thank you." To the humans, she said, "Go with her."

She found Keller already asleep and settled in beside him.

In the morning, his song was her first impression. Gradually, she wakened and realized what she was hearing. She opened her eyes and spoke his name softly.

"Tara-lin!" he said. "You're awake!"

"I am," she said.

"How was your visit to the forest yesterday?"

"Very well. I also found two ... defectors. They abandoned their ship when the dragons dove."

"Would you be interested in hearing what I and the others have surmised happened yesterday?"

Tara-lin shrugged as well as she could while laying down.

"We think the dragons scared them, but any wizards still alive and the officer in charge did not want to turn tail and run even at the sight of a cloud of dragons without doing any damage. The dragons and gryphon riders kept enough pressure on them that getting siege equipment to the walls proved nigh impossible. When the blast hit them and then the dragons all dove breathing fire we presume that convinced them that they weren't going to be successful. We think they had men on the beach and did not want to retreat if they had a chance at the walls, but when the blast ruined that front, they decided to flee. Even we had no idea how effective dragons are against ships." He stared at her. "Tara-lin, this has *not* been a bloodless battle, but it is a stunning naval defeat for them. From any general's perspective, we have done *very* well."

"I'm not any general," said Tara-lin, "and there are men among them who would be our allies if they could. I found and led two of them into the city last night. They abandoned ship and swam for shore. Others may not have been strong enough swimmers to brave that sea, or may have been lost in the currents and chaos and falling rocks, or not been able to swim at all." She rolled onto her side and raised herself on one elbow to look at him. "Don't talk to me about it like that. I'm glad most of our dragons survived. I'm glad only a few of our people died. But I can't take pleasure in even a stunning victory."

"I know," said Keller. "I just wanted you to understand that, in war, mistakes happen, and, for our mistakes, circumstances have been with us. No one could hope to do as well as we have."

"That may be true," said Tara-lin, "but I take no pleasure in it."

"I don't, either, but I don't want you to feel guilty."

"I don't know if I feel guilty," said Tara-lin, "but if I do, it's mostly about ... something else." She sat up. "I want to see Alis. And get more to eat." She smiled thinking of Alis. "I bet she had a good laugh."

"Alis?" asked Keller.

"Yes. I can't imagine her and Earnril *not* laughing imagining the reaction of the High Master when he discovers that Elethri has an alliance with dragons and that what he thought would be an easy victory has turned into a stunning defeat! In fact, *can* you imagine it? This must be so frustrating for him. He sends his army into our forest – and merely hands us his weapons and armor on a platter. He sends his troops against us by sea and discovers that the legendary dragons, the existence of which he probably has never considered, rout his navy! In fact, I wonder what he *will* do when he receives the report? I wonder, what *will* he think?"

"You're strange," said Keller. "I don't understand what upsets you and what doesn't."

As if you were different, but I suppose there's an explanation for why you are the way you are, but not for why I am how I am. Still, it makes sense to me. "Well, I'm hungry," she said, "and I'm going to find Alis." That said, she got up.

She found Alis getting food. The human looked across the table at her from where she was piling various different elven delicacies onto a platter. "Good morning, Tara-lin!" she said.

"Good morning, Alis. I'm hungry."

"Finally!" said Alis.

Tara-lin ignored the comment. "I thought of something I'm sure you would think is really funny."

"Yes?" asked Alis, pausing in her collection of food.

"Imagine what the High Master of the Valor Hall will think when he receives the report from two days' ago's battle! I bet you he doesn't even have a thought in his head that there might be dragons right now," said Tara-lin.

"Ooh!" said Alis. "That is hilarious."

"It is, and you know what else? Two of the Valor Soldiers swam to our shores and have sought refuge here. At least, I think they have sought refuge. They said they surrendered, but they were already unarmored, unweaponed, and unclothed."

Just then Tara-lin noticed other elves waiting and moving around them. "Alis, let's get our food and talk somewhere else," she said.

"I've already filled my platter up. I can share with you and then we can both get more," said Alis.

They found a bank and sat down. While she ate, Tara-lin told Alis about her idea of sending into exile the prisoners Eldazìn had captured and charged for taking part in the assassination and overthrow of King Orenduil and Queen Alaria. Alis thoroughly liked the idea. "I wouldn't care even if you had decided to execute them though, then again, I might care, because if you decided that, you wouldn't be the same Tara-lin that's my friend, but I definitely wouldn't oppose you. However, I like this idea *much* better. Keeping them in prison and giving them a plant was easily good enough for me, but, hey, this way no one has to take care of them, right?"

"It seems appropriate, too. If they don't want to be part of Elethri, they can go somewhere else. There's plenty of wilderness area in the south, and even quite a bit of wild forest all the way along the Valiance side of the Malaitha Mountains and several other places in the north," said Tara-lin.

"The only problem is making sure they stay *out* of Elethri and don't come back in to try to assassinate someone, like yourself, or Eldazìn," said Alis. "I agree, it *is* appropriate."

Tara-lin shrugged. She finished chewing and said, "There is that, but I don't rule out of fear. Besides, I'm not even sure they *want* to assassinate us. I think many of them participated in the previous coup because they wanted something, something Anakrim promised. Without such a promise to appeal to them, I don't think most of them will want to assassinate. They can't enter on the north border, but they might not *know* it doesn't only affect humans. Also, I will appear very merciful to them. We elves are not given to violence, but crimes such as theirs are sometimes punished with death. While burglary sometimes occurs in Elethri, murder is *very* rare."

"The Valor Alliance could potentially offer them something tempting for assassinating you or your, umm, wasn't someone explaining to me something about the nuances of that Elethrian term, 'Night's Edge' to me, Eldazìn?" said Alis.

"I guess you're right," said Tara-lin. "But I don't like keeping them all in prison for centuries. Also, not all of them had the same degree of participation. And what if Eldazìn accidentally picked up someone's twin or look-alike?"

"Do what you want," said Alis. "I'd never try to argue you out of it. I won't disapprove no matter what choice you make."

"I know," said Tara-lin around another mouthful. "But I'd *never* dream of ordering someone killed when there was a different way."

"I know," said Alis. "I wouldn't, either. It's just ... I don't know. Killing an entire family because ... well, for no reason at all ... is fairly bad. If someone didn't want to take care of people who did that or let them go ... well, if you murder people you can expect they might kill you. As I said, I suppose I would care, because if you did things that way, you wouldn't be the Tara-lin I know." She cast Tara-lin a flashing smile, then shoveled more food into her mouth. After she had chewed and swallowed enough to have a chance at being understood around her food, she said, "But I wouldn't criticize a monarch or government for ruling that way."

"Well, it's a moot point, because I'm not killing anyone," said Tara-lin. "I am Dryad-Brood and to destroy human life would be to go against the nature of my magic and corrupt."

For a few minutes there was silence between them as they both ate. The bank on which they sat looked out towards the sea, and dragons of many colors were diving towards the sea and re-ascending. Often they were silhouetted dark against the morning sun, but other times its light reflected gloriously off their scales. "What are they doing out there?" asked Tara-lin.

"Practice," said Alis. "One of the Dragonriders thought that their tactic might be improved to involve less risk to the dragons and riders. Instead of leveling off and re-ascending, the idea is to dive, burn, and then go *under*. On the edges of the fleet this will work very well, because the entire dragon force can dive, burn, and then swim under water, away from the ships. They might have to break water occasionally for them and their riders to breathe, but most of the time they can be under water where they're not easy targets. Hopefully, people are too busy with their burning ships to be thinking about launching missiles at the dragons, anyways, so depending on the extent of the damage done and the chaos, the dragons can go under and then directly fly up again, or swim away first."

Tara-lin shook her hair. "I bet it is really frustrating for the Valor Hall. Do you know what happened to the wizards? Keller doesn't think he could have killed them."

"No. But I suppose the rocks and arrows and dragon fire could have killed them. Or maybe they were distracted by the rocks and dragons and their own spells killed them. I know less than you do about casting magic," said Alis. "But I know what you mean. If they send what's left of that navy against us again, these dragons will make quick work of them. I didn't know dragons were so effective against ships."

"It's been a *long* time since there were any dragons here," said Tara-lin.

Alis nodded. "They're *really* fun to watch."

"They are," agreed Tara-lin.

There were another few minutes of silence while they chewed. Then Alis said, "It's really great, by the way, that you found those two ...

that they existed and that they made it."

"Yes, but I'm sure there's more. I'm sure there're others like them who really can't swim well enough to get through that ocean. We have to make a way for them to come to us, too," said Tara-lin.

"I expect there is one," said Alis. "I wonder what the Valor Hall will do next? Unless they can come up with a really good way to fight dragons, I don't think they're going to try attacking us by sea again any time soon, and they know already what happens when they try to cross our northern border. Do you think they'll try an attack over the Malaitha Mountains? – Anything that's not a sea attack should ... well, it should be easier for people who can't swim to get away."

"I don't know," said Tara-lin. "Can you ask the gryphons to watch that border for us?"

"Of course," said Alis. "They will, anyways. Gryphons are friendly, but a mob of armored, clanking men climbing up the mountains is still sure to be notable, and they consider Kushon and our gryphons their friends, so they'd let them know about anything interesting."

In the afternoon, Corostomir and Aderan requested an audience with Keller and Tara-lin. The royal pair waved away their courtesies and obeisance. "Get to the core of what it is you want," said Keller. "Bowing and fancy words will not make us think more kindly of you or be more disposed to grant your request."

Corostomir swallowed at that. "Then it is this, my gracious King and Queen. Must we remain in Elethri?"

Tara-lin leaned forward from where she sat on the bank next to Keller. "Why? Where do you want to go, that you do not wish to remain in Elethri?"

"It is not that I have any problem with Elethri," said Corostomir, "though it will certainly take some getting-used-to. It is that I know there are others who have no wish to fight you and that the reign of the Valor Alliance has gone too far. I and Aderan know others in the army who will be glad to quit it. We think many in Scanmir will listen to us that it is time to no longer be ruled by the Valor Hall."

"To answer your question," said Keller, "no. You are not held prisoners here and may leave if you desire."

"Thank you," said Corostomir, bowing. When he straightened he seemed very nervous. "Can I – would you receive us back into Elethri if we have to flee?"

"If you cannot secure Scanmir, or you and the Scanmirans do not wish to fight if it can be helped, then Elethri is always open to you," said Tara-lin. "We even have some islands in the bays where we could settle your people if they desire."

Corostomir and Aderan bowed again. Tara-lin and Keller glanced at each other, but chose to let it pass. "Even if it does not come to that, we are forever indebted to your most gracious majesties. May we ask for more favors?" This time it was Aderan who spoke.

Despite the grim thoughts of war and death that his obeisant words, strangely enough, wakened in Tara-lin, she said, "Of course. Ask for what you want, and feel no need to add in words for talking to royalty. They rather irritate me than otherwise."

"Will you supply us for the journey north?"

"Of course," said Keller. "Would you be willing to come with us to Frèlin first?"

The ex-Valor Soldiers declared that they were more than willing to do that. That night, a thought came to Tara-lin. They could send the prisoners into exile on one of their islands in the bay! That way they would be isolated, but not in prison. She told Keller about her idea and about the conversation she had had with Alis.

"That is a good idea," said Keller, "but how would we get them there? We don't have any ships."

"We could always buy a ship from Akeesh and hire an Akeeshian crew for it until some of our people learn how to handle it," said Tara-lin.

The next day they began the ride back towards Frèlin, Aderan and Corostomir coming with them, as well as Alis, most of the gryphon riders, what they had taken to Aernoss of the Guard of Frèlin, and Eldazìn. "I intend to sneak around and see what is going on in the Valor Alliance nowadays," he told them, "but I may as well ride to Frèlin with you first. It is mostly on my way."

Chapter Twenty-Three - A Gryphon's Wisdom

Tara-lin flung herself at Eldor. "You're still alive!"

"I don't feel like I'm about to die yet," her father said, "but I'm glad to see *you* are alive and well." He hugged her for a few long moments.

She stepped back. Lyan rushed at her. Shobura flew circles around his head, her orange wings contrasting with his dark emerald hair. He flung himself at his sister, and said, "Tara-lin!"

She picked him up. "It's good to see you too, Lyan." He wiggled, and she put him down.

"Dad is teaching me how to sword-fight!" he said. "We can teach you too, if you like."

"Sure," said Tara-lin, "but not right now. I'll find some time for that this afternoon or tomorrow. Okay?"

Lyan drew back and nodded. "Okay."

Though, thought Tara-lin, looking at him, *I don't really want to. I'd much rather play with you.* As splendid as she thought her idea of what to do with her prisoners was, she still did not enjoy the prospect of taking them out, one by one, to declare judgment upon them. She also wished she had chanced upon this idea years – was it years? – ago, but thought that she did not have diplomatic relations with Akeesh and would not have been able to get a ship when she first came to the throne.

.. * * ❋ ❋ * ..

Tears fell down the elf's face. He knelt and spread his hands before the King and Queen who were seated on a bank turfed with some plant that brought tiny purple flowers. "I thank you, o most gracious majesties! I cannot hope for such mercy. Wherever in the world you send me, you have my undying gratitude."

The sycophancy sickened Tara-lin. This was the third of the condemned to respond in this way. She examined him, looking him over, wondering what drove him to this. She was certain the previous two who had responded in like manner had not meant a word of it. She had almost felt something dark and nefarious, something nightmarish, in the manner of one. She thought the other had meant nothing at all, much as when many addressed royalty with lavish but empty praise. She tilted her head as she examined this elf. She thought there was something sincere about his gratitude. He was not totally out of touch with reality;

he understood that he could expect life imprisonment or execution, and there was something in the world that he valued. Perhaps he had been lured by the promises of the restoration of elven magic and perhaps he truly believed in and valued that magic. It did not excuse his crime at all. As Anakrim's pursuit of the dryadic magic went against the very nature of that magic, so did his, but at least it was *a* redeeming quality. She was glad she had come up with this idea of exiling them to one of the farther isles. She would want to give an elf such as this one more of a chance to discover the reality than prison was likely to afford him. Part of her almost wanted to keep him in Elethri. She wondered if he was any worse than many of those who nearly worshiped her in what she felt to be a perverse way. It was not like the crime of which he had been accused was especially bloody.

When he was taken away, Tara-lin said, "Don't bring the next in yet. I want to discuss something first."

Akanë acknowledged her request.

"Very well," said Eldazìn. "What is it you wish to discuss?"

Tara-lin turned towards Keller. "Did you notice how some of them acted? Like they're really grateful for the chance to get to make a life somewhere *else?*"

"It would be hard not to notice that, Tara-lin," said Keller, "but I think the first two were trying to manipulate you, and I think this Pìnzuel is not entirely free from such motivation."

Tara-lin tossed her ruby curls back around her shoulders. "I *know* the first two had more or less nefarious motives, and I didn't think Pìnzuel is anything I'd call pure, but I think he's *much* better than the others. How *could* I think him pure or good? He has to have, at the very minimum, turned a blind eye to murder and treason of the highest order, but I think there is still *something* pure in his desires: something he desires for its simple goodness. The hold of the corruption in his being does not seem complete to me. I wouldn't want to hold him in prison forever."

"It's the nature of things, Tara-lin," said Akanë. "They knew when they participated in a rebellion that, even despite the reticence of us elves to kill, they risked execution if they failed."

Eldazìn nodded his agreement. "I tend to think you are too merciful. I would not mind if you kept all of these locked away in prison for life, whether it was by their hand that the King was slain, or that his cousin was poisoned, or whether they facilitated the work of others and purposefully turned a blind eye to it. Exile to a far deserted island is, in my opinion, a barely tolerable way to deal with the situation. After all, there's always the chance someone will manage to get across the sea and cause more trouble."

Tara-lin's face lit up. "That's an idea! I really don't like keeping people in prison forever who *might* just have been really stupid or tired or absorbed in some trouble of her own, but we can keep those whose hands have touched the axe in prison for the moment, and decide what to do with them later, and send the rest to the island. We can always send those who've killed with their hands later, if we want."

Eldazìn sighed. "Some of those I have here are those who helped to organize the slaughter."

"Did you not hear me say 'those whose hands have touched the axe?'" asked Tara-lin.

"I confess I did not," said Eldazìn. "It can be hard to follow your speech when you are excited."

Keller reached over and squeezed Tara-lin's hand. "My thoughts aren't developed in this matter, but I want you to do what seems right to you," he said.

Tara-lin nodded vigorously.

Eldazìn sat, still and stiff.

Tara-lin's eyes sought out Alis, who had buried her head in Kushon's mane. She was here only because Tara-lin had asked her to be present despite her protestations that she knew nothing about such things and would be completely useless. Her arm still wrapped around her gryphon's neck, she turned towards Tara-lin.

"Did you hear my idea?" asked Tara-lin

"The one about sending those who seem less nefarious to the island and deferring what to do with the others yet longer? Yes, I did."

"What do you think of it?"

"It sounds fine to me," said Alis, "but do what you really want to do, not what makes sense to me." She paused, then did not continue, as if she had something she thought of saying but then disregarded.

"Did you have something else to say?" asked Tara-lin, rising and approaching her and Kushon. *It's been such a long time,* she thought, thinking of the day she had first seen Kushon as a cute little dark brown gryphling. Now he appeared cute, protective, fierce, and gentle all in one as he sat, his wing brushing his rider's soldier. He surveyed Tara-lin with an eye in which she thought some sort of intelligence glimmered. She wondered what he was thinking and if he understood anything at all of the present conversation.

"Only that it's strange living with elves. A deferral that is, relatively speaking, short to an elf would consume half a human's life-span," said Alis hesitatingly. "But don't take that as criticism. I know you live and age so much slower."

"Don't worry. I don't feel criticized. It's strange enough for me, being half-elven and Queen of Elethri, I understand where you're coming from," said Tara-lin. She sat down a pace away from Alis.

She watched Alis nod and reach her other hand back to stroke Kushon under the folds of his throat. The gryphon made a strange deep-throated noise which Tara-lin knew denoted pleasure. She found herself glancing into his eyes again. It was not the first time this had happened. When she and Alis were together with him, especially when they were talking about something that affected Tara-lin strongly in some way, he would often look at her with a gaze she could not quite understand, but which she thought conveyed interest. It suddenly occurred to her to ask Alis. "Is – I don't know how to ask this – Kushon sometimes looks at me as if he wishes I could tell him something, or maybe as if he wishes he could tell me something."

"He does," said Alis. "He tends to be interested in things around him and the affairs of humans and elves. He often makes me explain them to him, but his gryphon mind doesn't understand them very well – not that I understand a lot of this stuff either – so I have to tell him what is going on the best I can in terms he can understand, and often it isn't very close. One of the things he doesn't understand well is the concept of 'prison'. Why would – how would – anyone keep some idiot renegades who killed her family, members of her eyre, as if they were eyre cubs? If something is so dangerous you have to keep it penned up, why don't you all get together and chase it out of your eyre-lands for good?"

"Oh my!" said Tara-lin. She looked into Kushon's eyes again. "I suppose I can understand how you would think something like that. It even makes sense. So, do you think I should send them all far away, over the sea, where maybe I can watch to make sure they don't come back, but I won't be taking care of them anymore?"

"Kushon doesn't think in ideas like *should* or *should not*," said Alis. "He would not think of telling you what to do in this. There are some things he understands, and other things he does not understand. He cannot imagine gryphons acting like that in the first place. Why would a gryphon want to kill his family? How would it make him any more of a gryphon to do so? It's hard for Kushon to imagine killing another gryphon for any reason at all."

Tara-lin smiled. "Does Kushon have so elaborate thoughts about everything?" she asked.

Alis laughed. "No. Sometimes when I try to explain to him what we're talking about, he can't understand at all. Sometimes he bothers me, trying to understand when he can't. Other times he gets bored. Other times he eventually understands well enough to conclude the conversation is boring and can't understand why in Areaer you or I would want to have it. This one captures his attention. He identifies with how horrible it would be if such things happened in gryphon eyres."

"Oh!" said Tara-lin. "I wouldn't want to disturb him."

At this Alis laughed and Kushon made a strange rumbling, wheezing sound which Tara-lin interpreted as laughter. "Oh no, it doesn't disturb him at all. Since he hasn't been separated from me, and hasn't had to bounce along on a horse, he's usually quite relaxed. It's not like it's happening in his gryphon eyre or any of his friend's eyres, so why should he be disturbed about it?"

"I will have to ask you what he thinks more often!" said Tara-lin.

Alis rolled her eyes. "No-o! Don't encourage him to try to make me explain impossible concepts to him."

"Does he understand what I say?" asked Tara-lin.

"Only a little, barely. But he picks up on most of what goes through my mind," said Alis. "Really. I've heard the Dragonriders talk about their dragons, but I'm happy with Kushon. Not that he's anything like a dragon."

Tara-lin laughed. "I understand." She rose, then stopped mid-motion. "I ... I really think I *like* Kushon's way of thinking. Prison does seem ... unnatural to me. I'm still a little undecided. Eldazìn's position has merit to it, but it doesn't satisfy me. I don't *like* it." She fully straightened and nodded sharply, like a bird. "Yes, that shall be my decision."

"Oh, Tara-lin?" asked Alis.

"Yes?"

"Since you want to know what Kushon thinks, he understands your idea of letting the mates of the renegades go away with them wherever they're going. He thinks the idea anyone might *not* do that, might separate eyre-friends, really ... strange."

Tara-lin laughed. "That's kind of another reason why I want to send them into exile instead of keeping them in prison, too," she said. "Anyway, thanks so much, Alis. You too, Kushon."

I bet this is only going to make Alis more determined to convince me to bond to a gryphon. If I want a gryphon's wisdom, then I shouldn't burden someone else with explaining my problems to the gryphons or explaining their answers to me. Besides, a gryphon bonded to me would doubtless understand what I'm thinking and feeling better than one who isn't, and would be able to give me far more of their eyre wisdom than one who's only bonded to my friend! And she hates trying to explain impossible concepts to Kushon. Tara-lin smiled and shook her head slightly as she made her way back across the space to where the rest of her present council sat.

"What is it?" asked Eldazìn, looking up at her.

"Just that Alis is going to try to convince me that I should really try to bond to a gryphon, too. She's going to say, 'Now that you've discovered how wonderful gryphons are, don't you realize now that it would be good for you to have a gryphon friend of your own?'" She laughed again. *Maybe, maybe, I'll just maybe take her up on that offer. After this war is over. I'm too busy to raise a baby gryphon while being singer and Dryad-Brood and governing a country and fighting a war.*

Keller looked up at her with a smile. "Just ask me and Kellia for our wisdom, too," he said.

"Or Earnrìl and Welri. You know, gryphons might really have some very cool ideas." She stopped and tilted her head. "Keller – is that why you asked me to make sure what I really wanted to do? Because Kellia doesn't understand the notion of prison, either?"

"She doesn't, but she also tends to be a lot less interested in what our problems might be than it sounds like Kushon is, though I think that might be because she is very young," said Keller. "Everyone is waiting on us. Let's get to the point."

"We're sending them all into exile – if you concur, Keller?"

"I do," answered the King.

"Then," said the Queen, "Akanë, go and fetch someone, or send a gryphon rider, or whatever is best, but get word to all the families, relatives, or close friends of the prisoners that we will be sending them to an island in the far reaches of our domains and that any of their friends who wish to go with them may do so. Also, have communication about purchasing a ship opened with Akeesh. I do not wish to see any more of the prisoners today. Anyone who wishes to go is welcome to do so."

Akanë, several guards, and the witnesses all departed. When they had all gone, Alis approached where Keller and Tara-lin were seated and wished Tara-lin a good rest of the day. Then she leaped on Kushon's back, and the gryphon ran forward, opened his wings and, a moment later, was rising into the air.

Tara-lin smiled after them, a little wistfully. *Maybe I do want a gryphon*, she thought. *That's got to be fun.* Then she turned her gaze to Eldazìn. Surely, there was a reason he had stayed.

He accurately discerned the cue. "I've been speaking with Corostomir and Aderan. They want to go to Scanmir to contact a Valor Knight they know. They hope that, with some of their friends in the army, most of them from Scanmir but some of them from other parts of the Valor Alliance, they can get Scanmir to secede from the Alliance. I would request your permission to go with them and to help them in whatever way I deem best – and in the interests of Elethri. I will provide you with regular reports. Runi will help greatly with this side of things. I will leave a few of my friends here to protect and serve you however you deem best. They will answer to Akanë in my absence, even though to most extents and purposes he is no longer part of my agency. I would, however, like to take some of my friends with me, to aid me in this."

"Your requests are all granted." She turned to Keller. "Unless?"

"It is good. You may do as you have proposed, Eldazìn."

The elven night's edge rose and bowed deeply. Tara-lin did not get on his case. She could tell that he was deeply moved, though she did not understand why this mattered so much to him. This was not, or not mostly, obeisance to a sovereign, but a display of heartfelt gratitude. He was truly moved. Straightening, he inclined his head in another bow. "Thank you so much, Tara-lin and Keller, King and Queen," he said. Even his tone of voice gave away that he was overwhelmed by emotion. As he turned and left, Tara-lin leaned over and whispered to Keller, "I don't understand him. Why does this matter so much to him?"

Keller shrugged. "Do you doubt his loyalty to us and to Elethri?"

"No," said Tara-lin. "Not that at all. I just don't understand him."

Reflecting, Tara-lin thought that much of what Eldazìn was, Akanë could never be. They had found something in common, a common goal, and so Eldazìn had worked with and taught the younger elf, probably deliberately grooming him for a very different position from that of shadowhunter, of assassin, assassin-guard, and spy, night's edge. If Eldazìn was an elf of the night, Akanë was an elf of the day.

Chapter Twenty-Four – Bounds of the Song

As she did almost every night when she stayed in Frèlin, Tara-lin rose in the middle of the night to sing to the Tree of Elethri. When she was done singing to the tree, she still wanted to be alone with the forest, and so she made her way out of the lighted city and into the woods. For a while she wandered aimlessly, listening to the song of the dryads and the trees, walking almost as if in a dream, almost in that world of earth and air and light shadows. It almost felt like a different world, and made it easy for Tara-lin to believe that there might be rank upon rank of existences and lives following one another.

Eventually, she noticed two things. One was that it was early dawn. The other was that she was wandering towards Anakrim's tree. She accepted that for some reason she wanted to see Anakrim, and realized that she had thought of him in her dreams after her misuse of the dryad magic in the battle of Aernoss and her subsequent acceptance by the dryads, being told that her blood remained that of the dryads, uncorrupt. Thinking this, she continued, making her way between the last few thickets and across a meadow towards where Anakrim lived.

Tara-lin stopped just beyond the eaves of Anakrim's branches. She noticed that his leaves were tinged with purple highlights around the edges and on the veins. It had not been that way before. He and his tree were now truly one, after the manner of the dryads.

She stood there for only a few moments before she saw him materialize out from within the trunk of his tree. He stepped towards her, his pale skin – which had darkened since she had last seen him – and his purple hair shimmering with hate. She could feel the thrum of it in the air around her, but she was not afraid. She had the strength of the forest on her side and she knew the magic and what she was doing with it quite well. He could not catch her unaware with the song he had now, when he had not been able to best her before. As he came towards her, her thoughts paused for a moment, and she considered her confidence. She did not quite understand it. What did she know, that she did not know? There was more to her confidence than she knew.

"Tara-lin," Anakrim said, and his voice dripped with bitter envy as he spoke her name. "Have you come to gloat over me? Surely, you know how unfair it is. You have taken from me my power and imprisoned me in a tree, while you have taken power from the dryads yourself and roam free, neither fettered nor hindered by the bonds of a tree."

"Fair?" asked Tara-lin, and her voice shimmered in the air. "There is nothing fair or unfair about it. I wondered once how I could walk so well in the world of men and yet draw up, as if through roots, such magic from the world of dryads. It is not like that. You have defied the very nature of the magic, and apparently, even now, you do not understand the essence of the song. The power I wield is not my own. I wield it on behalf of the entire forest, and I have not sought the power, but received it, in order that, through me, the entire forest could come into its own. Through my magic, the forest and its dryads are strengthened, not depleted and killed. Nor am I unbound, as you say I am. I am bound by the nature of the magic, as are you. I must use the song in accord with its nature, or become corrupt and lose the greater portion of the song, but you have not used the song in accord with its nature, nor ever could, nor ever desired to. You did not sing to heal and nurture and protect. Instead you sought to steal the magic of the song in order to dominate and make for yourself a throne. As I acknowledge and live within the bounds and nature of the magic, so you must live within the bounds of the magic if you would use it. You took these bounds upon yourself in the day you sought to steal song that was not yours, to take life instead of to give it."

"It's not fair!" the half-elf-turned-dryad wailed, and the boughs and leaves of his tree shivered in synchrony with his wail. "You deposed me and have gained what I sought. You took from me my crown, and now *you* are Queen! You declared I could not use the song as I did, that my power was wrong, and you took it from me, and now you wield far more of it than I ever dreamed I could possess!"

"Anakrim," said Tara-lin softly, "I pitied you. I yet do. I hoped that you would learn to love your tree and find sanity. Both you and your brother were raised in the shade of the nightmare, and both of you needed love to find sanity. I hoped you would find it this way, would realize that, while you can still choose the corruption and become part of the nightmare, yet you do not have to do so. You have been bound to the magic in this way in the hope that through it you can find life. Dryads, too, can break the Pact of their magic and follow corruption to death, but it was my hope, and that of the dryads, that you could learn life. Tell me: do you love this tree of yours not at all? Is there no gladness in you that you were not permitted to kill this tree, but that instead you can give it life and receive life from it?"

The dryad howled again, a sound that felt to Tara-lin like it could sheer apart anyone without protection. She felt like it pulled at and cut even her. "Perhaps I would be a little glad, if I had not been forced to this tree in such an unfair and unnatural way. If *you* had not been set above me! Why is it not *you* who are bound to the tree?"

Tara-lin drew herself to her full height. "Because I accept that I am bound to the nature of the forest, instead of working against the nature of the forest. Because I receive my song from the forest, instead of taking it from the forest. Because my song is one with the forest. I *am* bound, Anakrim. I accept that I am bound by the Pact. It is the price of the magic. It is the nature of the song. If I went against the Pact, I would go against the nature of the song, the nature of that which has become my life, and so would corrupt, but you have never even considered the Pact. This was taken as a way to give you a way out of the corruption, the nightmare, into which you were born through no fault of your own. This was given in order to provide you with a way to realize the nature of that which you had taken for your life, and so to be cleansed of your fault. This was given so that what you stole for yourself in corruption might become to you nature and life. It is *gift*, Anakrim! As I said, fair has nothing to do with it. It is such that it can be neither fair nor unfair.

"The Pact does not bind those who do not take its magic for their life, but to those who take its magic for their life, the Pact is the law of their nature. Breaking it is corruption. You have been given a way out of corruption. The song as you took it *was* corruption to you, and a lesser corruption to those from whom you took it, for it was being forced against its own nature, out of life, into death. Did you seek life beyond the spans of men? You have it now, but in a fashion which is corruption neither to the human life nor to the dryad life, for as you would have taken it, it would have been death to your humanity and death to your dryad nature. Now, as a dryad, you can live. Nor are you bound as you think you are. I cannot tell you how often I've looked at the trees and known that they are *free,* and that the fact that they are rooted to one place in the earth does not impede their freedom at all, but is part of it. The dryads share that freedom." She paused, then said, "Learn to sing with the forest. Learn the secrets of your tree. Love it and sing with it, and it will be one with you, and what you never dreamed in your corruption will be yours. Now I will sing to you, and then I will depart, since my presence makes you so envious, though, in fact, neither one of us should envy the other: unless you envy me for being raised by a man and an elf who loved me, while you were raised in Nightshade by a

father who wanted to use you for his own demented purposes? Even so,
I don't know if envy exactly is what is called for. You can call for me at
any time if you wish to speak or sing with me."

Having said this, Tara-lin took half a step back, spread out her
arms, and sang. Low, soft, and slow, she sang with the whole forest of
the coming dawn, spreading its fingers of still-cold radiance over the
horizon and through the airs of the skies. She sang with the waiting yet
never-waiting forest, awake and yet asleep and dreaming under the stars
and the clouds and the moons.

> Golden on the wings of eternity
> White on wings of the dawn
> Soul of this world
> Heart of another
>
> Golden on the wings of eternity
> Silver on breath of time
> Heart of ages
> Shield of the morning
>
> Golden on the wings of eternity
> Dreams reborn out of ice
> Of thousand eyes
> In the heart of dawn

It was not for or to Anakrim that she sang. Almost at once she
was scarcely even aware of the angry dryad's presence. Instead she saw
again Icecrown Valley, lit with the dawn, but this time it was not
darkened with the stain of Nightshade Castle. Where Nightshade Castle
stood, in her song Tara-lin saw the dawn-light coalesce into something
which was, it is true, shaped not unlike Nightshade Castle, but the
overall effect was entirely different. This thing was made of the light of
dawn, and from it power flowed out to enliven all the trees and dryads of
the world. It was as if the thought she had beheld in a vague glance
when she looked down into Icecrown Valley had now taken form. At
once she had both been horrified by Nightshade Castle and known that
there was something very good and important about the valley and that
something else belonged there, and now she knew, after a manner, what
ought to stand in the place of Nightshade. Instead of a monstrous thing
with the nightmare as its heart, there ought to be some being formed of

the light of dawn. The dawn should rest in Icecrown Valley.

She remembered Keller urging them to seek the sun, to go towards the sun. Had he known? Had his urgings been insanity merely, and fear of the dark, or had there been more to it than that? Had the light of dawn not fully departed from its proper resting place? Had what ought to be in Icecrown Valley and she had briefly glimpsed there been what allowed him to survive as an – albeit damaged and insane – elf in the heart of that horrible place?

It was lighter, now. The rim of the sun hid just below the line of the horizon. Tara-lin loved this half-light, the dawn twilight. It was so fresh and cool with waiting life. She smiled, embracing the whole forest as it were, and turned back towards Frèlin. She waved goodbye to Anakrim, but did not reach out to him. If anything more than envy was growing in his mind, she did not want to disturb that process. Yet, she had a feeling that she had not come only because there was something she wanted to tell him. He had called to her, perhaps without realizing it, but called her nonetheless. Would she have even thought of him in the context of her discoveries during and after the battle of Aernoss, except that there was some contact between them after the manner of the dryads?

Tara-lin wandered back towards Frèlin, enjoying the feeling of the dawn twilight. The threads and waves of the song kept flowing through her mind. It was certainly a dryad song, but it sounded like it was also something more: or was the dryad song something more? She remembered Lìrulin telling her about where she had found the seed for the Great Tree, and suspected that Nightshade Castle and the vision of the tower of the Heart of Dawn and the dryads were all intertwined in some way she did not understand but that might have to do with the deepest nature of their magic. It was certainly a very special and unique tree, and Tara-lin had a feeling that she did not know how special or unique. The only unique thing she knew about it, other than that both her mother and herself chose to sing to it, was that it had been found at the doors of Nightshade Castle.

Tara-lin realized that she did not want to go back into Frèlin just yet. She wanted – or at least she thought she wanted – to talk to Keller, and maybe her parents also, about these thoughts she had after singing that song, but she did not know if she wanted to think about them more before she talked to anyone. Whatever she wanted to do about that, she wanted to talk to the dryads. She wanted to talk to her friends on the other side of the Malaitha Mountains. She wanted to hear their thoughts about what she should do with her prisoners, even though she was pretty certain that she had already decided what to do. She wanted to know what they thought about her song and her vision of the dawn-light. After all, they were the dryads and from them came the power of the song.

Tara-lin emerged from a thicket to see the world bathed in the ruddy streaks of light from the risen sun. If she sought out her dryad friends this morning then she could not return to Elethri before early afternoon, and she could easily get lost in their perception of the world and not return until nightfall. What with everything that needed to be done, Tara-lin thought she would be missed if she disappeared for a whole day. The new policy for defending the coast had to be finally and formally decided and the elven people had to be made aware of it. Corostomir, Aderan, Eldazìn, and the men he chose to take with him had to depart from Frèlin for the regions of the Valor Alliance. Akanë might want to discuss what was desired in a ship from Akeesh and what Elethri was willing to pay. The prisoners had to be formally tried and sentenced, and though none of that had to happen that day, it did have to get done. Some of these tasks could be handled quite adequately by Keller, but there was also the promise Tara-lin had made to spend more time playing with Lyan and her father, a promise she really wanted to keep, since her days with her father were so limited. Additionally, she knew it was hard for Keller when she vanished without forewarning him. He was still wounded by being abandoned by his mother, as it had appeared to him as a young child, even though it had not been Ithrìl's choice or intention.

So Tara-lin put off her meeting with her dryad friends for the following night (or day) and returned to Frèlin. Keller would almost certainly be awake before she got there, but she knew he often enjoyed having time to himself in the early morning and that he expected her to not always be right by his side.

.. ✳ ❀ ❀ ❀ ✳ ..

That night, Tara-lin placed her hands on the Tree and began to sing to it. Almost at once she found herself in Beriririkirkirkitira's thicket, but also not in the thicket. She was in the waking dreams of the dryad consciousness, where the threads and waves of each tree or dryad's life met constantly, directed as embroidery through cloth, flowing and ebbing like the ocean tides, directional and separate like its currents. It was strange, too, in that it was as if the earth wherein the Great Tree grew and the thicket wherein Beriririkirkirkitira's bush-tree grew had somehow been transplanted into each other, but Tara-lin only absently noticed the strangeness then.

The whisper of Beriririkirkirkitira's thought was communicated not only by her humanesque form, as it existed within the magic, but also through the air and earth and wind of the magic. "What is it, Tara-lin?"

"I wondered what you thought of some things. And do you mind me coming to you like this? Does it disturb your life, your perception and thought, at all?"

Beriririkirkirkitira laughed gently. "Never, Tara-lin. You are as a dryad-child to me. I am interested in your life. Some things cannot be talked about, or not much, between us, but, other than that, I mind no conversation with you. What is it?"

Without words or language, Tara-lin passed to the dryad much of the occurrences and thoughts of the past day and night.

"I have no knowledge or thoughts about how to deal with prisoners," said the bush-dryad. "All of the ideas I have from you seem to me not unreasonable, but it is an issue wholly outside my experience as a dryad, and utterly alien to me."

"It is utterly alien to me, too," said Tara-lin. *"That is why, I think, I have so much trouble with it, with being satisfied I've found the right solution. It is too* alien. *As if having prisoners is too alien to my nature for me to know what to do with them after I've got them – through no fault of my own."*

Beriririkirkirkitira chucked again. "Indeed. And I think you have settled on getting rid of them. As for this song of which you sing to me, there is no question that the Icecrown Valley was made for something else – or that something else was made for it – than the Nightshade. That this something else should be the Heart of Dawn of your song seems not unreasonable to me. Your mind invents many theories, and I don't know what I should think about them. You think that the Heart of Dawn may in some sense be present in Icecrown Valley, even though Nightshade Castle is there, and that it may have been what enchanted or made the seed that is now growing in the Tree of Elethri?" Beriririkirkirkitira tapped the fingers of one hand against the palm of another. "It seems a quite reasonable thought. I, too, think something of that sort may be the case. There's more there than we know, and I think this is one of those things we can't talk about much, even among ourselves." The tapping of her fingers stilled and then increased in tempo. "It seems to me like it is one of the deep powers of Shallim-Araldor."

"It does have that feel," agreed Tara-lin. Then she said, "I think it is a terrible defeat, a victory of the nightmare, if the dryads withdraw from the elves."

"I think the same," said Beriririkirkirkitira. "It seems more a thing of Nightshade than this song of which you've told me."

"I wonder," said Tara-lin, "is it the kind of thing that might give growth to things like Nightshade?"

"That hardly needs saying," said Beriririkirkirkitira. "It is a ... strange thing, however. The inclination in so many dryads is to withdraw from the elves, apart from the life of you or your mother being present among them."

"Then," said Tara-lin, "I will hope some victory reverses this, or else that such as myself and my mother continue to live among the elves and draw our kin together."

Beriririkirkirkitira agreed. They spoke for a little of other matters, passing quickly over their thoughts on other things, such as Tara-lin's discomfort at the elves' feelings towards her, something Beriririkirkirkitira indicated might not be wholly unrelated to the dryads' reticence towards their race, "though," the ancient dryad said, "what I mean by related and what comes to mind for you may be very different."

"Perhaps," said Tara-lin, "but I think the more I grow to understand and speak in the dryad magic, the less I misunderstand you."

In a long, timeless moment of silence, of darkness amidst the glowing colored shapes, Tara-lin thought of Alai-ie-a. At once, she knew she was with her. She felt, almost saw, the dancing dryad's bower. To many of her questions she felt she had already received all the thoughts Alai-ie-a could offer her from her sense of the dryad and from her previous conversations with her, but now Tara-lin sang the song of the dawn for her. She did not care if Alai-ie-a was aware that it came from her or not, but she had the sense that the dryad would know. The dryads were so much more in tune with their nature, their world, their magic than she was, even now. She sensed, also, that Alai-ie-a would know much more than the song, would know of her confrontations with Anakrim also.

Alai-ie-a's laughter rang like a bell in her mind. "How good it is to see you, Tara-lin!" she said. "What of your friend, Alis?"

"Alis is here with me. I think she's too human to meet as we are meeting. She is very well and is a gryphon rider. I will tell her that you have inquired after her. Perhaps she and Kushon can find a way to go to meet you," answered Tara-lin.

"It is okay if she can't," said Alai-ie-a. "I am well familiar with such things." She laughed again, a sound of such pure joy it seemed it would stop Tara-lin's heart – or turn her blood to sap. "You know, Tara-lin? I am more certain than ever that the nightmare is none of my business." In a flash Tara-lin's entire song was joined to the laughter and voice of the dryad. "It is not. The Heart of Dawn is."

.. ❋ ❋ ❋ ❋ ❋ ..

After a conversation with Aumoura, who thought Tara-lin's ideas about how to handle her prisoners were excellent and, in her words, "very elven," and who, more or less, agreed with her and Beriririkirkirkitira's thoughts about Icecrown Valley – Tara-lin thought she understood parts of the song better than either of the other dryads and possibly better than herself, though she thought the latter was probably true of Beriririkirkirkitira and Alai-ie-a also, and that she herself probably understood the song in some ways better than any of them – Tara-lin wakened to her other way of living. She was still singing, softly and dreamily, to the tree, and it was the coldest hour of the night, the hour before dawn – again.

Chapter Twenty-Five – Fire and Ice

Eldazìn, Corostomir, Aderan, and Cuthlin departed the following morning. Tara-lin was convinced that Cuthlin was one of Eldazìn's 'friends,' and had had his training as a Valor Knight supplemented with training by the elven counter-assassin. She had long had the suspicion that he and Namdon were working together with Eldazìn, though she had not known how closely or permanently. She suspected that *one* reason he went with Eldazìn now was that, if interactions with humans were required, Cuthlin did not stand out as much as an elf. The fact that he was the ex-Valor Knight Sir Cuthlin could be disguised much more easily than the elvenness of Eldazìn or anyone else who might be with him. She also could have guessed that Cuthlin would want a part in what Corostomir and Aderan were trying to do. He and Namdon had been trying to think about how to get something similar to happen for over a decade now, and doubtless they saw it as their long-awaited opportunity. Namdon was probably staying in Elethri because he was as old as Eldor.

It was not long before they received a message, conveyed through Runi, that Corostomir had stumbled upon a dragon egg, doubtless laid by one of the dragons of Elethri, which had hatched for him. The rest of the party would continue to do what they could, but this was going to slow them down and hinder them for a time, since there was much that was more difficult and more dangerous if one had to take a helpless hatchling along. There was a fair amount that could be accomplished in the meantime, but it would take more effort and require more caution, and thus take longer. The message contained no other details. Tara-lin asked the Dragonrider who conveyed it, "Anyway, how long *does* it take for a dragon hatchling to cease being helpless?"

"It depends on the hatchling and the definition of helpless," said the rider. "Like most creatures, they mature gradually. I'd say, typically, a dragon hatchling is flying after about five to six months and breathing fire after more like eight to ten months."

So it will delay them substantially, thought Tara-lin, but she did not give the matter much more thought. She hoped they were successful, and that all went well, but no thinking about it that she did would help them, and it was not part of her life right now.

The months progressed. Another woman who wanted to learn wizardry arrived, along with a brother who did not want to have his talent pressed into service. The wizard trainees progressed, along with

Keller, and one afternoon meal the half-elf wizard king told Tara-lin that he thought some of them had vastly different native abilities to cast spells or provide energy. In the meantime, agreements were made with Akeesh, and a ship was purchased and an Akeeshian crew hired. Arrangements were made for everything the elves would be likely to need to survive on the intended island, and those of their relatives and friends who wanted to go with them into exile were gathered. Others came also, to say goodbye to them. Tara-lin could feel the gratitude and amazement of the elven people, especially of those few who had expected their brothers, or sisters, or mothers, or fathers, or cousins, or friends to be executed – or, at least, spend their entire lives in prison. As it was, Tara-lin had made it clear that visitation with the exiles would be allowed occasionally, and exile to another island was, to an elf, a much preferable life than prison, even if one did get to keep a single tree or flower.

One night, after an audience with her people, Tara-lin stood, lost in thought, next to the Tree of Elethri. *I can almost see why they nearly worship me, I suppose,* she thought. *Is this why? It may be part of why. It may strengthen and encourage it, yet many of them followed Anakrim. I don't think it's all of why. Yet maybe I should be less upset about it. I can't help it, and since this* does *get me all that adulation and worshipful attitude, maybe it's part of it. Maybe I'm what they were looking for.* She looked up at the silvery branches of the tree above her. *Still, it isn't right. I'm not that perfect. And they should be trying to be the elves they should be, instead of worshiping me as the perfect elf. It's not like I even am the epitome of what an elf should be. I'm one elf, trying to be the best half-elf dryad-singer Queen she can be. But should Earnrìl not love the sea? Should Eldazìn not be the elf he is? Just because neither of them is anything like me? No! I wonder: is there a way for me to show them that? I've tried. I and Keller have both tried, many times. But I feel as if only I could find a way to succeed at this, I should have won. And I suppose it is better for them to worship me, as the living embodiment of their dryadic heritage walking among them, than something else. I just don't like it, though. Being Tara-lin is not the only way to be a good elf. Perhaps anyone who bears the dryad power as I do is bound to be very much like me in some ways – thought not all – but even Keller has inherited power from the dryads, power that is so different from theirs that the Pact no longer seems to apply. And I don't think Eldazìn is a bad elf, even though he's very different from me. I think he couldn't be King. I think there are things he does wrong, I think he fears and worries, but I'm not perfect myself. After all, I tried to – I almost did, I began to – misuse the dryad magic! Even if I was a perfect elf, I still wouldn't be everything an elf can be, so it would still be wrong to worship me as the epitome of that. I don't think there can be any one epitome of that. Other elves could go wrong trying to be me when they're not me. Sunlight and clouds, other elves might even be able to fall prey to the corruption trying to be like me, just as if I tried to think or act like Eldazìn it would corrupt me, for it would go against the nature of my life. But to think or act like me might go against the nature of someone else's life! Maybe not as dramatically, but I wouldn't know, since I'm not someone else.*

Somehow, Tara-lin doubted that Kushon, or any of the other gryphons, would have any useful ideas about how to show this to the elves. In fact, she'd bet that none of the gryphons could even *understand* the issue. At all. It was probably *completely* incomprehensible nonsense to any gryphon. She heaved a sigh. Getting every elf to bond to a gryphon was an entirely too simplistic solution to the problem. It might sound great, but it would never work. For one thing, the gryphons would never want it. Goodness, Alis was sure she could convince a gryphon to let Tara-lin be present at a hatching, but Alis *might* be wrong. Both of them *knew* the gryphons would not choose just any elf or every elf for their offspring. It could not be done without abusing the gryphons, and that would ruin it, even if it *would* work otherwise – which might be nonsense. Gryphons who were not protective of their hatchlings would not be the wild gryphons they were. But even so, it might not work. The elves might not be influenced that way.

The wind coming down the mountain gusted, and Tara-lin pulled her cloak closer around her for warmth, suddenly realizing how late it was. She really ought to grab a bite to eat and then go to bed. What she was asking to do was probably impossible. If the elves did not *want* to pursue their own lives there was nothing she could do to force them to it. Just like there was nothing she could do to force the dryads to accept the elves again.

Additionally, while she was in many ways more dryad than most elves, she was also more human than most elves, Tara-lin reminded herself. She had grown far closer to the rate at which humans grew than that at which most elves grew. Changes she might expect to see in months or that would express in her in a few days might take decades to show in other elves. With that thought, she emerged from the shadow of the Tree.

.. * * * * *..

A few days later they rode down to Elenrìr, another Elethrian seaside-city, to see the ship and make sure it contained everything it should, such as all the food and tools, and to meet the ambassador Akeesh had sent them. It was while they were there, just after the meeting with Akeesh's ambassador that Tara-lin felt the familiar tingle that meant someone was crossing her wardings. Then another and another, like a thousand ants crawling under her bark. She closed her eyes and took a deep breath, mastering herself, then said to an attendant, "Get Akanë and the King. Tell them a large group, possibly the Valor Army, is entering the forest right now." She hurried out, found a garden, and sank to the ground a moment later, to give her strength and mind to the enchantment.

Pain jabbed through her like a searing flash of lightning. Then came another, and another. They ripped through her like lightning strikes through the boles of trees, like tongues of fire along a scroll. Blackness pressed in on her mind. She struggled with the sleep enchantment. In the depths of the dryadic pattern of life, it took a few long, long moments before she thought about what was wrong.

Tara-lin let out a scream and flew to her feet. "The forest!" she cried. The forest was burning! Someone in the Valor Hall had had the brilliant idea of setting her forest on fire to overcome her magic! She almost panicked. What could she do? What could she do? She was months away from the north border at an easy pace. She did not think she could sing the enchantments that might be able to douse the fire from this distance. Not yet. Maybe in another century or two. Maybe even in a few decades. After all, she had not yet lived two score of years. But not now!

"Queen, I am here. What is it?" called an elf's worried voice from several paces away.

Tara-lin turned to meet the unusually turquoise-haired elf. "The northern forest is set on fire!" she said. "The Valor Alliance. Get Lyan to me right now! That's my brother."

The elf nodded and ran.

Tara-lin pressed her head to her hand and tried to touch the sleep ward again. If she could slow down the setting of the fires, then that would help her save her forest – and her country. The fear of being caught in the fire should hold off the sleep, but the combination of drowsiness and fear might drive warriors out of her forest before they had accomplished their task.

It felt like only a few seconds before she heard Lyan's voice. "What is it, Tara?" he asked.

She looked past him and saw Keller and Akanë and several others. "I need you to ask Shobura to do something for me. To tell the Dragonriders that I need the fastest or nearest one to Elenrìr here *now* to take me – and Keller – north as *fast as possible.* I also want them to inquire if any of the human wizards have any spells that might counteract fire and, if they are willing, to take them north as fast as possible to fight the fire. Take as many warriors and hunters as they can without being slowed down. They might need protection depending on what's going on and being done." As she spoke she noticed Shobura whizzing above their heads.

The drake-lizard dropped down and twined her tail around Tara-lin's arm while still hovering in the air. The Elven Queen received a clear message: Yes. I have done it.

Thank you so much, she thought back and reached up her hand to stroke the drake's underbelly. A moment later the drake-lizard disentangled her body from Tara-lin's.

"Now what?" she asked.

Keller stepped towards her. "Are you all right?"

"Yes, yes," she said, still breathing heavily. In fact, her breathing rate was not slowing down at all. "I'm not hurt. But the trees are burning! The dryads are dying!"

"And the enchantment is failing," finished Keller.

"Yes," said Tara-lin. She forced herself to take a deep breath. "Let's get some food that'll last a few days collected. It might take a while to fly to the north border even on dragonback."

"After that, see if Earnrìl's Welri is willing to carry you to meet whatever dragon is coming. Otherwise, Kellia is willing to do it, but she's still fairly small and won't be able to fly as hard and fast with you as Welri could."

"Wow," said Tara-lin. "That's unexpected." *I thought gryphons usually did not want to carry anyone except their riders, but maybe it's more like gryphons feel about carrying those who aren't their riders the same whether the gryphons have riders or are 'wild.' So maybe Alis' Kushon would be willing to carry me when there's a need, like the gryphon carried us down from the city wall, or like they carried us into Icecrown, or like they flew with Alis into Icecrown and then carried us out.*

"In that case, let's do this as fast as possible. No. Let's do this at once. Food will only be more weight for the gryphon. I'll find enough to eat at night. Just get me a little water. Shobura?" Tara-lin held out her arm and her brother's drake-lizard hovered over her outstretched hand.

"Let whatever dragon's flying for me know what's going on so she or he and the gryphon can look for each other to meet," said Tara-lin. "And send another Dragonrider for Keller."

Shobura dipped her head in synchronization with the low sweep of her tangerine wings, a gesture Tara-lin took to mean she had done as requested.

Maybe it would *have been a good choice for me to attach her,* thought Tara-lin, *but she and Lyan are happy together and I – I wouldn't want to bond to something like her or a gryphon for reasons of* utility *and not because I* wanted *that relationship.* "Get someone to get Earnrìl," said Tara-lin.

Akanë nodded. "Yes, Queen," he said, and departed. Tara-lin did not mind being called Queen in situations like these. It made it clear he was responding to her request, and that was all it meant, and that clarity was necessary. She did not know if seconds mattered, but they might, and she felt as if they did. She did not want to look for Earnrìl herself. That would be a recipe for missing each other, which was fine when one had half an afternoon to spare, but not in an emergency.

Tara-lin sat down and reached out for the forest again. The way she felt was not helpful. What would be, would be. What was, was. This panic was not in the nature of the magic. It was not in accordance with her nature. It was a disturbance, a disruption. It felt to her more like whatever alienated the dryads from the elves than it did like the song of Alai-ie-a.

Tara-lin opened her eyes and watched, with horror, as a cold darkness materialized out of the air. It was hardly visible, a shade, a minute darkening, but she felt the chill of it, and then heard the high, ear-piercing keen. She knew it at once and wondered, for a moment, before the battle commenced, *Is it the cause of my unnatural panic? Or was it drawn hither by that panic?* A moment later, *Why do I have to fight wights so much? I thought they were rare and that almost no one survives them. Does it have something to do with being a singer? With being Dryad-Brood?*

Then there was no time left for thoughts like those. Tara-lin already had the elf-sword half out of its sheath as the wailing harmonized in a terrible song of fear and horror and despair, of mindless panic and lost life, that Tara-lin knew hung in a pall of cold shade over all of Elenrìr, as if it were an extension of the wraith's non-self.

A feeling of despair and hopelessness, a fierce and senseless urge to give in, assailed Tara-lin, as if the non-being and coldness and darkness of the wraith were drawing all the strength and will out of her. She closed her eyes and the song that came to her mind was the same one she had sung at the dawn:

> Golden on the wings of eternity
> White on wings of the dawn
> Soul of this world
> Heart of another

Seamlessly, the song flowed into another:

> Sun on edges of never-ending night
> Roots deep through winter's cold
> Hold to the life
> In the sun-earth's heart

> Sun on edges of never-ending night
> Roots drink deep of earth's life
> Water of life
> Through the withering blaze

Then the song merged back into the other:

> Golden on the wings of eternity
> Dreams reborn out of ice
> Of thousand eyes
> In the heart of dawn

"Go!" said Tara-lin, raising her hand, and from her upraised hand violet and lilac elf-fire reached out to scorch the wraith. For a moment it glowed there, its form outlined and materialized in the magic flames.

"Go, and never trouble Areaer again! You are a shade of ice and cannot last before the dreams of dawn which *will* walk the earth!"

The flames pulsed and grew, and their shifting purple shades tinged the low-lying edges of the clouds above them. Then, in a flash, they dispersed. Nothing was left of the wailing wight except a circle of violet elf-fire that burned out even as Tara-lin watched. She was surprised to see a circle of purple, just the dominant hue of the flames her elf-sword produced, burned into the ground. *Why?* she wondered.

Then, with a shock, she realized others had seen the battle. The entire elven nation would know her henceforward as the Wight-Slayer. This was the third or fourth ice-wraith she had fought, and she wondered if, perhaps, many more elves and elven singers had defeated the horrors in private, unseen, no one but themselves and perhaps a few trusted friends ever knowing, and that was why the elves thought they were impossible to defeat. Maybe it was even a plan of the nightmare, of the fear and the despair, to nurture that fear in the hearts of the elves that they might more readily despair and be consumed in the nightmare. But she did not have time for these thoughts. Earnrìl had just run up and was standing before her, on the other side of the purple circle.

"What?" she gasped, then said, "Welri will carry you."

"Thank you so much," said Tara-lin, stepping across the circle to embrace her friend. After a few moments she stepped away from Earnrìl and spoke to everyone around her. "For the sake of the world, *please* get the elves to calm down, let them know what's really going on, maybe, I don't know, but maybe they can help. Goodness, maybe they can all get together and help to sing the rain onto our northern border. Or whatever it is they do. Oh, and convince them that I'm not the only one who can slay ice-wraiths – I mean, wailing wights. I'm sure lots of other elves have done it, unknown to anyone but themselves and maybe a few trusted friends."

They nodded.

"I know," said Keller. "I will try." Something in his blue eyes made her think he knew something he had not told her, not that she cared. They embraced, and she said, "Come as quickly as you can." After that, Lyan hugged her. "Goodbye, Tara-lin," he said.

"I'll be back. Love you, little brother," she said, straightening. Next she and Eldor embraced. Lìrulin was out in the forest and, presumably, unaware of what was happening. "I love you," he said. "Stay alive."

"Stay alive for as long as possible," said Tara-lin in reply. "I love you, too."

Then she let another elf attach a water-skin to the woven belt on which her elf-sword hung, and then let Earnrìl assist her in mounting Welri. Then Earnrìl hugged her gryphon and whispered some things Tara-lin did not hear into her ears. She stepped away and looked up at Tara-lin. "My best wishes are with you! Take care of Welri!"

Tara-lin smiled, then gasped and clutched the gryphon's neck as she spread her wings and lurched forward and up. "Thank you, Welri," she half-sang into the wind as they leveled off. She felt strangely uncomfortable on her elven friend's gryphon. She wondered why. Was it because she did not know for how many days she might be flying Welri away from her rider? Welri had never done that before. Still, she had consented, and everything Tara-lin knew about gryphons made her confident that Welri would hold to her consent.

Chapter Twenty-Six – The Wild Ones

Tara-lin had ridden Welri for almost two days before she met the Dragonrider, at which point she continued with him and his dragon, and the gryphon flew back to her friend. Her bones ached with the fire burning in her forest. She spent the days sleeping as well as she could on dragonback. The nights were spent gathering enough food to keep her going, and then kneeling on the ground and reaching out to the forest in an attempt to do what she could to foster wind conditions on the northern border which would work against the flames. She could feel the dryads teaching her and working with her, and knew that her efforts were not in vain, but she did not know if they would be enough.

It was two weeks later when they approached the fire line. For several days they had seen the smoke spreading out above the forest and collecting against the mountains. When they landed a day's flight from where the fires burned, instead of continuing in the morning, Tara-lin climbed to a hill that rose above the surrounding forests. Standing in the shade of a spreading tree, she held her arms out and sang.

> Wind of the sea
> Come to me
> Come to the airs that blow
>
> Wind of the sun
> Glance and run
> Past the waves that billow
>
> Wind of the skies
> That racing flies
> Come to the trees that grow

She began to sing as the sun came up and was still singing hours later as clouds billowed out of the sea and formed in the sky, the light of the sun glancing off their upper sides in blinding white brightness, while their undersides grew ever darker. She gathered them towards her, her song changing as she sang to the elements, if indeed it was only elements to which she sang, if there were not souls or spirits in the winds and waters that could hear her song and sing with her.

Chase now the sun!
Follow the tracks of light!
Water, air, and fire together run
Drawn by the mountain height!

Tara-lin continued to sing, even as the first droplets fell around her, and then gathered into larger and larger drops, falling quicker and quicker. Still she bound the magic around itself, gathering the water, directing its energy. Lightning flashed in the clouds above. For a moment Tara-lin wondered if she should try to do something about the lightning, but then she thought that if her song did what she intended, it would not matter. Lightning might start fires, but she hoped to bring down enough rain to quench fires. This was not a summer squall she called, but a long, steady rain.

When she stopped singing, half-way through the night, she was so exhausted she thought she would faint right there. She took a few moments to gather enough strength from the forest to make her way back to the dragon and rider, and there she slept until the morning. After a drink and a quick breakfast, she returned again to the hill to sing to her storm. When she had spent several hours singing to the rain, she went back to the dragon and rider, and requested to continue flying towards the fire. They flew low that day, to avoid the lightning that might flash higher in the sky and to be able to get out of the sky quickly if necessary. The rain pounded on them, and Tara-lin sometimes heard the rider responding out loud to her dragon's complaints about having to fly in heavy rain. Once, the rider looked over her shoulder and smiled to Tara-lin. "Many dragons like rain, but Neiliesh complains that this rain is too heavy. Also, she would like to *play* in it instead of having to fly and fly and fly. She's tired. Also, I am cold."

"I can appreciate that," said Tara-lin. "I am exhausted and cold myself. But this is war, and this is the *nicest* part of war." *Except for the dryads and the trees,* she added in her thoughts.

"Neiliesh agrees with *that,*" said the rider, "and so do I."

While they flew, Tara-lin sang to the storm and the rain whenever she could gather the strength to reach out to the forest below and sing both while moving and without being on the ground. It was much harder to touch the trees and the dryads and know through them while flying through the air than it was while touching the earth or a tree. It was this that made her reconsider whether she wanted to bond to a gryphon after all. Gryphons were beasts of the air and highlands, not the earth and trees. If she were a gryphon rider, she would have to spend time flying with her gryphon, far away from the earth and forest and from the source of her magic life.

It was afternoon when they reached the fireline. Grief for her burned forest washed over Tara-lin again. They flew over a flooded meadow on the other side of which stood the burnt skeletons of trees. High up on some of them signs of life and a few greenish leaves still persisted. Others were clearly dead. Still others, she would not know until she touched them. Life might yet re-awaken in them when the spring came. Though many of her trees in this portion of the forest would survive the fire, more would not survive. It was not that occasional fires, and the deaths of a few trees due to them, were not part of nature, but fires instigated by men at the height of summer for the express purpose of damaging and killing as many trees as possible were not right. They were horribly wrong. *I'm sorry, dryads,* thought Tara-lin. *I'm sorry for dragging you into the wars of human-kin and into all this destruction and death. I'm sorry.*

She could not help thinking that way, even as she wondered what Elkanakur would have said to her about it, or what Berirrikirkirkitira might say about it.

Neiliesh landed on the far side of the meadow in slushy wet ash and crunching wet charcoal. Her rider dismounted and offered a hand to help Tara-lin down. As the half-elf landed on the ground, the Dragonrider asked, "What would you like now?"

"To eat and sleep," said Tara-lin. "But I'd like to talk to someone who knows what's been going on, so can you ask someone to fly over?"

"Yes, I'll do that," said the rider. "I also suspect they'll have some food, so I'll ask for some to be brought for you."

"Thanks," said Tara-lin.

She looked up at the blackened skeletons of trees above her. Grief assailed her. Why did it have to be this way? Elkanakur might say that dryads could not even have the experience of giving their lives for someone or something else, because the passage from this phase of life to another felt so natural and lossless to them, simply a journey onto their goal, but still ... This was evil. Why did there have to be war? It was not her fault!

Right now, though, she desperately needed to sleep. She did not want to sleep here, on burnt barren ground and ashes, under those stark reminders of life vanished from the world. She turned to the rider and asked her if she and her dragon would carry her across the flooded meadow.

Tara-lin was already fast asleep when a gryphon rider arrived. Her grief dominated her sleeping consciousness. Then, in a moment, the grief was brushed away, as if by a huge root thrusting earth aside. Out of the deep, living darkness a myriad consciousness brushed her own. It felt like a thousand tendrils were trying to draw her into their midst.

Once again it was if it was not one individual dryad who spoke to her, but the consensus of the dryad race given one voice, perhaps even one consciousness: *Tara-lin, Dryad-Friend, Dryad-Brood, Singer, do not grieve. No longer life or better forest would be ours if we did not stand with you against the nightmare-mad humans. We defend you even as you defend us. Do not be overcome by sorrow, for life beyond life awaits us and the forest shall grow again, as is our nature. Rather, fight for us as we fight for you. We remain in peace. Remain also in peace.*

After that, Tara-lin fell into a deep, peaceful, and refreshing sleep. Then a tingle skittered across her skin, and she sat up abruptly. She knew what it was. Enough of the trees remained that her enchantment was singing to her. The Valor Army had entered Elethri. She also knew through the feel of the contact that there was not enough power left in the trees for the enchantment to work its purpose. She could not cast the whole army into a sleep and do as she had done before.

"Tara-lin!" The voice that greeted her with some concern was that of Alis.

She opened her eyes and looked into Alis' face. "Hi, umm," she began, still muddle-headed from sleep.

"Are you hungry?" asked Alis. "That's what I was told, and I've brought food."

"Yes," said Tara-lin. "Thank you. But they come."

"They come? Who?" asked Alis, as she reached for a bag and opened it.

"The army. The enemy," said Tara-lin.

"How close are they?" asked Alis.

"I'd – it'd be hard for me – they won't be here for hours at least," said Tara-lin. Alis handed her a roll.

"Well, then I think you should eat. You've lost weight and you don't look good."

"I'm still really tired," said Tara-lin. She bit into the roll.

"I hope you don't get sick. You've got to be cold in this rain. In fact, you're shivering," said Alis. "What's the battle plan? – Oh yes, you're eating. I shouldn't make you talk instead."

Tara-lin swallowed her bite. The taste of food made her stomach rouse itself and grumble, but she took a moment to answer Alis' question anyways. "The elves will fight from the trees. We do a moving, non-stationary battle line. It's hardly a line at all. Anyway, ask someone else for the details. We're *really* good at it, though. I don't know how the gryphon riders or the Dragonriders can be part of it. Ask them and talk it through among yourselves and with whomever here is in command." She took another bite, and a question formed in her mind while she ate. When she swallowed, she asked, "How did everyone control the fire? They did a really good job."

"Eat," said Alis. "Lots of things. Elgri" – one of the female wizard refugees – "took a flame that she could control and burned out all the undergrowth and deadwood in patches of the forest. We also re-directed streams or pulled water out of the ground to flood meadows. Then we would sit on the other side and watch – the gryphons and dragons were really useful for this – so we could do whatever we could to put out the fire as quickly as possible if it jumped our line. We weren't entirely successful. It helped that it started drizzling every morning."

Tara-lin nodded. "What about the wildlife? And the elves who lived in this part of the forest?"

"As far I know, all the elves got out and are alive and well. Lots of the wild ones got out as well. I didn't know you had so many large bears and cats – and wolves! – in this forest!"

"They're reclusive," mumbled Tara-lin around a mouthful.

"Aren't they dangerous?" asked Alis.

Tara-lin shrugged. "I suppose, if you go walking into their dens. But we all know better than to make them mad." She took another large bite.

"Yeah, don't talk to me, eat," said Alis. "I ... umm, I just found it scary. Not with Kushon, since he's pretty powerful, too, but if I was by myself. And if they weren't more interested in escaping the fire than in prey."

"They don't hunt humans or elves," said Tara-lin.

"Well, in the Valor Alliance, we get the idea that they sometimes kill people. Is that another of the lies we're taught? But, really, I should stop talking so that you eat."

"It won't help me to eat *really* fast. I don't know. I suppose they might ... be more dangerous to humans than elves. Also, they *will* kill you if you threaten something they think is theirs ... their home, or their cubs, or their kills. It's just we elves know better than to do any of those things."

"Or their forest?" asked Alis. "Would they – could they – I mean? The forest is kind of their home, isn't it?"

"I don't think most of them will think of that on their own, though I don't know if they'll feel more aggressive after fleeing the fire, but, yes, that is an idea!" said Tara-lin, her face lighting up.

"Whatever you're thinking of, eat first," said Alis.

"Also, they *can* be tamed. It's rare, but if you go into the swamplands in our southern rainforests, there are elves who've tamed and ride crocodiles. Some elves have cat or bear friends. Quite a few elves have wolf friends. I've known of some elves who live with the pack. We get along with our forest and its wildlife quite well for the most part."

Alis gasped as Tara-lin spoke. "Really? And don't they eat horses?"

"Yes, really," said Tara-lin. "And, no, horses aren't their favorite food, and maybe it's a lingering dryad magic we all have without even noticing it. Anyway, stop interrupting me now. I have an idea."

"Sure," said Alis.

The Dragonrider, who had been standing with her back turned to them for most of this time, turned around and looked at Alis. "Surely, you are kidding with your surprise? You're the human who can speak to any gryphon. You're the human who convinced the Valor Alliance gryphons to disobey their riders and *not attack us!*"

"That's different," said Alis. "Everyone knows gryphons can be tame and good companions for humans. Nobody knows that *crocodiles* can be reasoned with!"

Tara-lin refrained from asking what the Dragonrider was referring to about Alis convincing the gryphons, but Alis elaborated anyways. "Besides, I only *helped* dissuade the gryphons from attacking us. Our gryphons talk to their gryphons, and, really, gryphons don't like to fight each other, or invade each other's homes, or kill each other's eyre-mates. Our gryphons are wild and free. I don't think the Valiance gryphons even really *want* to do as they're commanded to, and most of them don't have the relationship with their riders that our gryphons do.

Remember, they don't give the eggs to people based on their suitability to be a gryphon rider as assessed by the gryphons, or even by someone who knows and thinks about gryphons, but as reward for good service or something like that!"

Tara-lin rapidly finished her food. Her stomach settled a little, but she was still shivering as desperately as ever. She pulled her cloak tightly around herself. "Alis! Zirye!" she said. Zirye was the rider's name.

Both women turned. "What, Tara-lin?"

"I'm not sure how to make sure the wild animals can reliably differentiate between human friends and human enemies. I'm sure I can sing to them so they know not to attack those of us who have a strong connection to the dryad world, which means any elves, but I want you to make sure all the humans know to be ... safe. My people should know what to do but many of yours might not, so make sure everyone knows to stay where they can get out, like into the sky, or ... something."

Both women nodded and voiced their assent. "Neiliesh will pass that on," said Zirye.

"Good," said Tara-lin. She closed her eyes and sang, sometimes low and rumbling, sometimes whistling, altogether very differently than when she sang to the elements, or with the voice of the forest, or to human-kin. This was more like when she had first called a gryphon. She had been pleasantly surprised that had worked. What she sought to do now was a little more complicated than what she had done then, but she was also far more experienced.

The smells of wet beasts pressed in on Tara-lin's nostrils. She opened her eyes to see wolves, bears, and cats gathering around her, furry and wet. She looked into their eyes, one by one, and continued to sing to them. *It is those who burn the forests, who drive you from your homes, whom you may fight. It is those who come over the burnt land. Together, the elves and you will defend the homes we share.* She thought briefly that, if Alis had her talent, Alis would do this better than she could. Alis understood the way animals thought better. Tara-lin was glad she had listened to Alis talk about the way her gryphon thought. Doubtless, gryphons, wolves, bears, and cats all thought very differently, but Tara-lin was sure none of them thought like dryads or humans.

The animals came close to her and sniffed her. Alis *was* right. They *were* kind of scary, at least some of them. Tara-lin stayed very still, though she was not really afraid of them. She had called them, not invaded their home. Then, one by one, they wandered away.

She was left standing under a sky that was no longer raining but was still draped in cloud and fog and mist. The trees around her were dripping. It seemed as if the fog spun around her.

Out of the tattered clouds the form of a brown gryphon materialized. Tara-lin stepped back as Alis and Kushon descended and landed before her. As the gryphon folded his wings, Tara-lin swayed and fell.

She felt Alis lift her up and support her. Worry laced her friend's voice as Alis said something to her which she barely understood through the fog in her mind. She was so tired. It was something about the dragon not being able to land for some reason and Kushon would carry her and, no, he wouldn't fly, and something about going to the dragon and not to worry.

Alis helped her climb onto the gryphon's back and wrap her hands through his mane. He clamped his wings over her legs to keep her steady and leapt into a smooth, rolling gait. She was vaguely aware of Alis running beside them. She clung to Kushon and called down to Alis. "What's the problem?"

"The Valor Army isn't far," said Alis, "and Neiliesh doesn't want to be seen by them. We're going to a clearing to meet her that's far enough she can fly low over the trees without being seen."

Tara-lin did not know how long it was before they reached the meadow and she saw the glittering prone form of the blue, purple, and white dragon. Alis helped her dismount Kushon, and together they walked through the wet grass towards the dragon and her rider.

"Are you coming with me?" asked Tara-lin.

"No," said Alis. "You're going somewhere you can get warm and rest. You're sick and you're running a fever. I am staying. I have to. By the way, I can see how the wolves can make good friends for some of the elves. They're more like gryphons than any other animal I've seen. I don't mean they're *like* gryphons, but they have pack-mates, like the gryphons have eyre-mates. The other beasts don't, do they?"

"The bears and cats we have here?" asked Tara-lin. "No, they don't."

"Well, I have to stay. I'm the only one who can speak to the gryphons, so I think I will be needed, to keep the Valiance gryphons out of the battle – and the sky. Also, I think I have some small ability to communicate to the other wild animals, too, so I might be able to help in a lot of ways, even though I'm still no good with the bow."

They were near Neiliesh now, and her rider had risen and come forward to meet them. "Do you mean you have no bow or that you're not much good?"

"I'm not much good," said Alis. "I got someone to make one for me, but I don't practice enough."

"Then that's fine," said Kirye. "Use your arrows the way we used flaming arrows and boulders at Aernoss. The purpose is to distract, and then those who wait in the sky or shadows can dive or pounce more safely. It's nice if you do some damage with the missiles themselves, but it's not the main purpose, and is bound to happen anyway, when the enemy is packed tightly together."

Tara-lin leaned against Alis while the two women talked. She felt dizzy. Alis hugged her fiercely before letting her go. "Don't worry, Tara-lin," she said. "You've brought us the rain. The forest is so drenched no fire would even start in it. You've brought us the aid of the wild ones. I and the gryphons will help to organize them, in as much as their nature permits, and work with them. You've done your part, and you need to rest now. Go! I'll come back to you."

Tara-lin hugged Alis back. "I love you. I'll be lonely without you or Keller."

"I love you, too," said Alis, "but you won't be lonely. Your mother and father and brother will be there, soon."

Tara-lin nodded. "All right," she said. "Tell Keller I love him."

"I will," said Alis.

Then Kirye took her and helped her to the dragon, while Alis went to Kushon, hugged him fiercely, and then mounted him.

As they were about to mount the dragon, Tara-lin asked the rider, "How is Keller?"

"Coming. He and Akanë will be here soon to take care of the final preparations and the battle."

Tara-lin briefly considered telling Kirye that she would stay. She was too weak to enforce her will, but she was the one who made her own decisions, not to mention the Queen of Elethri. Then she thought that it would do no good. She really did not feel good. She would be a liability, not a help, especially with the way she felt about the lost trees and dryads, and about the deaths of her own people, and even about the deaths of the attacking humans. She would feel horrible even about the deaths of the wild ones, even knowing that they would fare no better in a country dominated by humans.

Chapter Twenty-Seven - Resolution

That night, Tara-lin lay shivering against the warm side of Neiliesh. They resumed their flight towards Frèlin in the morning. It had drizzled again overnight and clouds still overhung the land from the mountains to the sea. Tara-lin shivered desperately, wishing that a summer sun could peak through the clouds to counterbalance with its warmth the cold air flowing past her.

That night, Tara-lin slept, wrapped in many blankets, on the mountain behind Frèlin, in the same elven home shared by Lìrulin and Eldor and Lyan.

Whenever she was awake, Lyan's Shobura gave Tara-lin hourly updates on the battle and the state of her friends – except, that is, when Shobura herself was sleeping, or playing and forgot. The battle continued for days without a clear resolution, but Akanë was certain the elves were winning. The forest was so drenched that the dragons could breathe fire without undue risk of a forest fire, if they were careful. The attacks of the wild ones clearly disconcerted the men. At night they were in their element, and the forest was so wet it was nearly impossible to light even a campfire. Keller wondered if it was possible that the enchantment was still partially active. The humans wandered, losing themselves and being separated easily, and altogether acting confused, and drowsier than would be expected of men at war.

The elves had also taken prisoners. Tara-lin wondered if some of the prisoners might have purposefully gotten themselves captured, not desiring to fight or die for the Valor Alliance, not unlike Corostomir and Aderan. She felt certain the two men could not have been the only ones to come to their conclusions, and they too had been certain there were others like them.

Shobura also relaid that she had spoken with Runi. Runi relaid that Eldazìn had not known that the Valor Alliance Army was staged to invade Elethri, but he had known that much of the Valiance lands were filled with rumors and mixed sentiments about the war. Some considered it the sacred duty of the Valor Alliance to crush Elethri and free not only the Elethrians but all of Ellenesia from the menace of its Sorceress-Queen. Others wanted, even if they were not very vocal about it, to withdraw from the war. Fire-breathing dragons out of the legends were not something anyone wished to meet in battle, and the fact that the first 'battle' between the Valor Alliance and Elethri had been bloodless, due entirely to the choices made by the Elethrians, further inclined many to favor them. Eldazìn expressed his confidence that the resources of the Valor Alliance were limited.

Lyan regularly annoyed Tara-lin. She was sick, cold, and had a headache, but he still wanted to play with her and show her things he could do. He thought this was a wonderful opportunity to have more time with his older sister. When she felt well enough, she watched him play with their parents. She also spent hours chatting with them.

One morning, Tara-lin woke to Shobura flapping her wings in her face and exclaiming that the battle was won! The elves were still ensuring all the invaders got out of their forest, so it would take some time before they and her larger kin – the dragons – returned. When Lìrulin and Eldor climbed onto the tarp to eat with her and Lyan, Tara-lin raised herself on one elbow, and said, "Hi, Lìrulin. I just thought of – or wondered – something."

Lìrulin continued her climb onto the tarp. When she was settled, she looked at her daughter. "Yes. What is it?"

"I was just wondering something. You seem to be ... connected to my enchantment, too. And I think the more you sing to the Tree the better you ... sing."

"I think you're *right*," said Lìrulin.

Eldor clambered up beside them. Tara-lin looked from her Mom's face to her Dad's and back again. "You said the seed quickened in Nightshade Castle. Could we ... Could you have conceived me at much the same time?"

Eldor looked from her face to Lìrulin's. "Yes. That was when we really knew."

"I wouldn't have thought, but, yes. Why?"

"Because, Mom," said Tara-lin, "I just have a feeling. It's as if we're *both* connected to the Tree in some way."

Lìrulin nodded. "As if we both have what no elf has ever had before, but what the dryads do."

"Yes," said Tara-lin.

"What? What is it? What?" asked Lyan, jumping up and down so that the tarp bounced.

"Stop it!" said Tara-lin. "Stop jumping! And, it's not something we can tell you. You'd have to experience it for yourself."

Lyan stopped jumping at once. He sat down next to her. "Okay," he said. "I suppose I'll have to ask the dryads myself?"

"Something like that," said Tara-lin.

.。＊ ＊ ＊ ＊ ＊.。

When the King and Alis and Akanë returned from the battle site, and Tara-lin had sufficiently recovered, council was held. What to do with those who had been captured or surrendered was readily enough solved. Those who wished to return to the Valor Alliance would be held as prisoners of war – and treated fairly – until a truce with the Valor Alliance could be worked out. Those who wished to remain in Elethri and abide by the laws of Elethri would be permitted to remain in the elven kingdom, but they would not be allowed to exchange information with anyone outside of Elethri. Then they transitioned to discussing the battle and the defense of Elethri, particularly how to prevent future burning of the forest.

"There's an easy way to prevent that," said Tara-lin. "I never go south. If I stay near the northern border, I should always be close enough to bring the rain, and we won't lose very much forest next time."

Earnrìl tilted her head, looking at Tara-lin with blue-green eyes. "That *is* a curious coincidence. You spend most of your time in the north of the kingdom. How did they time their strike to coincide with the one time this year you've gone south?"

"Are you suggesting a spy?" asked Alis.

"I'm not suggesting anything," said Earnrìl. "It's just very interesting. Also, are there *magical* ways of spying?"

"Yes," said Keller. "I don't know that much magic. None of the techniques I know of – whether I could work them out or not – should be able to allow them to do that, but there might be techniques I don't know."

"It was a heat spell, too," said Alis. "That might have been all there was to it. They thought the forest would burn best this time of year."

"Well, if I don't leave it can't happen again," said Tara-lin. "But there's still the fact that they've managed to find a way past the enchantment. I can't focus on the enchantment while bringing the rain even if I *am* close." *Speaking of which, I need to re-enchant the border. I want to strengthen the enchantment on the burnt edges of the forest and do what I can to get it to re-grow as quickly as possible. Then I should add layerings of the enchantment further in.* "Even so, I don't like this. It seems every battle goes worse for us than the one before."

"You can't expect every battle to be as easy as the first, or even as the Battle of Aernoss," said Akanë.

"A few more like this, and we will be lost," said Tara-lin.

"Just because it's been a pattern so far doesn't mean it will continue that way," said Keller. "Our wizard-allies are stronger and stronger, and even after our confrontation with some of their wizards this time, I don't think they know what we can do. We don't know what we can do, and it will be more before winter passes."

"What happened?" gasped Tara-lin. "No one told me about this!"

"We're telling you right now," said Akanë, giving her a curious look.

"No. I mean Shobura didn't tell me!" said Tara-lin.

"We fought some of their wizards. I think they were sent to be able to hopelessly outmatch me, but they don't know me – my magic is somewhat unique – and I had others with me, so we killed two of theirs, and the rest fled," said Keller.

"But if they send all their wizards?" asked Tara-lin. "We don't have that many, and they're not that well-trained."

"That is my concern, too," said Keller. "We have to set up wardings and enchantments and traps. We can learn. Wizardry is like anything else. Properly set up, defense is easier than offense. I think we'll be able to manage."

"We're just stupid and didn't think we needed wizardry defense on a border where we had the dryads defending us," said Tara-lin bitterly.

"Well, we're going to try to be less stupid now," said Keller, "and didn't you say that Eldazìn says their resources are limited?"

"That's what Shobura relaid," said Tara-lin, "but if they think they're finally winning, they might throw everything at us anyways."

"Then," said Akanë, "we will simply have to hold them next time, whatever it takes. We can. I and Keller have even talked through ways of dealing with wizards. Appropriate wardings should reveal the positions of any spell-casters so that, if they can't be defeated in a wizards' duel, those of us most skilled in the shadows can reach and kill them that way."

They discussed strategy and defense for a while after that. Tara-lin and Keller arranged to go to the border, with most of the other spell-weavers, to magically secure it in another week. They wanted to be done with that before next spring came around.

In the evening, Tara-lin walked with Alis towards where Kushon waited at the foot of the cliffs. "Alis?" she asked.

"What if we lose?" asked Tara-lin.

"Then we lose," said Alis. "It's better than not trying. Why?"

"Keller says he only *thinks* we can manage defense against their wizards if they send a large entourage of them," said Tara-lin. "Every confrontation goes worse than the last. And so many die, and *will* die if we lose."

"I, for one, would rather fight than not," said Alis. "So do many others. If it comes to that, it's better to die trying this, than to give in to the nightmare from the beginning. Do you disagree?"

"No, I agree with you, Alis, but it's something else: it's all the Elethrians. If we lose, they will lose their forest, their homes, maybe even their livelihood. Elven society may be no more. I know that none of them fight because I compel them to do so. But if our cities and woods are taken, many will die, without choice in the matter. And I *sing* to them. That affects their inclinations. They will worship me even more now that they all know I fought and banished an ice-wraith."

"If there was nothing else you *should* have done, then don't worry about what you've done," said Alis. "It is what it is, and" – she stopped and jabbed her finger towards Tara-lin's chest – "*you* are not to blame. It is those who rule the Valor Alliance and those who *don't* have the courage or integrity to leave behind their religion, and their falsely-sworn vows that are at fault. *Never* you."

"But it doesn't feel that way," said Tara-lin. "Just because they're at fault doesn't mean I've done the best I can."

Alis rolled her eyes dramatically. "Tara-lin! What do you think you should have done?"

"Well, we *could* have defeated Anakrim and abdicated."

"Do you think that would have been a better choice?" asked Alis.

"No. I don't know. It's just – *was* – an option."

"I think you're being an idiot, Tara-lin. It's not your fault the elves half-worship you for being a singer. You're trying to change that. And if you do change that? If the elves do start trying to be themselves instead of worshiping you? What do you think they will choose then?"

"I simply have no idea," said Tara-lin.

"I think many of them will protect Elethri," said Alis. She paused for a moment, considering. "If you're going to decide what's right or wrong based on the expected or feared outcomes, I think you've done the right thing, Tara-lin. Would elven society be a good thing if it was rushing down the path it would without you? Would you feel any better about your life and choices if you had made them differently? Do you honestly think Ellenesia or Elethri would be better places?"

"No. I don't know," said Tara-lin.

"And what would you do if you weren't afraid?" asked Alis.

"I think what I have done ... mostly. I say! Alis, you are right. Remember when you were worrying about what would happen to you for daring to step out of what your society said you had to be?" asked Tara-lin, smiling.

Alis smiled back. "Yes, I do, Tara-lin. But it was a long time ago. Come, let's see Kushon if you want to, and then you can go back to sleep in the forest."

Trudging after Alis, Tara-lin said, "I think I'm still weak. If we do that, would Kushon be willing to fly me down?"

"He says so," said Alis.

"You're such a good friend, Alis," said Tara-lin, "and Kushon, too."

Alis flashed a smile at her.

.• * * * * * •.•

A few days later, they sent messages to the Valor Alliance, alerting them that they had prisoners of war which they might return if the Valor Alliance gave them a peace treaty and paid reparations, since a handful of the men wanted to return to the Valor Alliance. Tara-lin and the wizards then spent what was left of the autumn warding and enchanting the forest. Tara-lin usually sang and worked apart from the wizards, whose work she did not understand. She felt its aura settle over the forest and mix with the aura of her dryadic enchantments. It had a feel that she was certain would be eerie to anyone who did not know what it was and who was not accepted by the dryad realm and magic. It felt a little eerie even to her.

When spring came, Eldazìn, through the drake-lizards, warned them to be ready in case of an attack, but also told them that he did not expect one. The Valor Alliance was in internal turmoil, and there was a growing anti-war sentiment. As costly as last autumn's battle was from Tara-lin and the elves' perspective, it was at least as costly from the perspective of the Valor Alliance. Many men had been slain in the war.

As the year wore on, Eldazìn continued to give them short

updates on what he knew. In the north, turmoil and conflict was brewing. Messages and diplomats were exchanged between Elethri and the Valor Alliance. A truce was made, and argument commenced over what was reasonable in the way of reparations. Tara-lin, confident that she knew nothing about this sort of thing, stayed out of the exchanges and knew little about them. She sang to the forest and to her people, and watched with delight as they began to develop new magic. Her confidence that most elves could get in touch with their dryadic nature and sing, with varying degrees of ease, influence, and power, was confirmed. She was trying to get the elves to move out of the cities as much as possible, and felt that Elethri was headed in the right direction. *I only hope this is enough to sway the dryads from their decision to abandon their kin as soon as I and Lìrulin are both passed on,* she thought one day, looking at the Tree. She was certain it had something to do with Lìrulin's song and affinity for her own enchantment, almost as if her mother was woven into the enchantment the same way as the dryads were. She knew now that, when it was activated, her mother could contribute to its power and guide it. She also suspected Lìrulin's reluctance to leave the vicinity of Frèlin had to do with her bond to the Tree, of whatever sort it was. It was as if her mother was *almost* a dryad. She hoped that did not mean the Tree would die when Lìrulin did.

Tara-lin also spent time with her father and brother. She played with her brother and watched him grow and explained to him what she could about trees and dryads and the magic of the forest. She often sat in a tree near Sir Eldor and talked to him of many things, and listened to him talk to her in turn. She treasured every moment she had with him. She also spent time with Alis and Keller, but though she talked sometimes about what she thought was best for Elethri, mostly their conversations did not have much to do with matters of state. Keller did most of that now, and it was usually with others that he discussed the treaty arrangements.

The next year, the peace with the Valor Alliance was finalized. The 'prisoners of war,' those captives who wanted to return to their families, were returned to the Valor Alliance. Tara-lin still did not know precisely what reparations Elethri received, being uninterested, but she *did* learn that they had gained another ship. Some of the elves were excited about sea-faring, and she encouraged them. *We are not dryad-kin only, but also human-kin. We should each be what we are, and no one should be pressured into the mold or into what is most common. Let those who love the forest love the forest. Let those who love the trees love the trees, and those who love the beasts love the beasts. Let those who love the sea ride it, and let those who love the highlands live there.* So she often told them, and of this vision of hers she often sang to them.

Tara-lin suspected that the internal turmoil in the Valor Alliance, which she was almost certain was the work, at least in good part, of Eldazìn, Cuthlin, Corostomir, and Aderan, had far more part to play in the acceptance of peace by the Valor Alliance than the few insignificant hostages that had been returned. She knew the humans hoped to re-establish independent human kingdoms in the north, and perhaps lead the way for other nations to follow.

Chapter Twenty-Eight - Epilogue

Corostomir and Aderan returned to Elethri, having pirated some of the last of the Valor Alliance's fleet. They had been defeated in the north, but promised by Eldazìn that islands off of the Elethrian Bays would await them if they took refuge there. Thus, for a while, Elethri was a split kingdom of elves and humans, defended at sea mostly by Dragonriders, who grew more numerous despite the disappearance of a few, and by a small but expertly handled navy which worked very well with the dragons. After a time, the human isles and the elven mainland began to split, so that they were more of an alliance than one nation, until, eventually, they split into two nations which long remained closely allied, almost as if they shared one military.

Sir Eldor died shortly after the return of Corostomir and Aderan, and was buried, by the wish of Lìrulin, among the roots of the Tree, from which she never again went far. Over the course of their lives, Tara-lin and Keller had three daughters. They passed the crown to the eldest when they had reigned in Elethri for a couple centuries, and she became the Queen Nazìnil. From her childhood, Tara-lin had watched her form a relationship with the Tree which was not unlike her own and, perhaps, Lìrulin's. She and Keller were glad Nazìnil was their eldest, since they deemed her most fit for the crown especially because of her bond with the Tree. Her coronation was held under the Tree, which dropped a shower of needles on her which rested on her head like a crown. During her reign, Nazìnil and her mate changed the rules of succession. From henceforward, whenever the King and Queen died, the Tree itself would choose, from among their children or close relations, the next successor.

Over the centuries, the Tree entrusted seeds to a few elves, among them a child of Lyan. They treasured the seeds, though they showed no sign of quickening. The Kings and Queens continued to manifest a bond with the Tree which allowed them the power of the enchantments with which Tara-lin, and to a lesser extent Keller, had guarded the forest. The woodland magic of the elves flourished, as did their song, as it never had since the raising of the cities and the gathering of Elethri under a single banner, and the elves had their golden age, their springtime, renewed, greater than before. The forest was full of life and of a magic which repelled invaders and those with ill intent. No contest was ever made for the throne because of the Tree and the magic it conferred on its chosen. However, at long last, both the Tree of Elethri and the Children of Tara-lin faltered together, and the woodland magic of the elves began to fail and the golden age of Elethri faltered. With that, Elethri came to an end, and the race of elves changed from what they had been since they first became a race of their own, separate from the dryads and the humans from which they came. It was as if in the Tree either Tara-lin or Lìrulin had their lives prolonged, and with its death the dryads rejected their elven off-spring. The elves grew then into different peoples, some of them possessing still a magic which, though almost infinitely removed from the dryads, yet still carried hints of its birth.

Among these split tribes, a few of the seeds of the Tree were still kept, and while some forgot what they were, others still remembered, often in the form of legends and myths, a hope that one day the seed might be quickened, and another Tree grow from it and bring their people together with the magical and legendary dryads.

Tara-lin and Keller lived to see their daughter, Queen Nazìnil, change the law of succession so that the future Kings and Queens would not be chosen based off their birth alone, but out of the royal lineage whoever was chosen by the Tree would rule, but not much longer. Tara-lin lived the last years of her life with Keller and closer to the dryads than she had ever been able to be before. Most of the time that she did not spend with him spent with them, learning their deepest songs and mysteries, though Earnrìl was still young and she kept a friendship with both her and Tara-lin's mother, Lìrulin. Interestingly, Lìrulin did not seem to be affected by the years, though one would have thought that by her age she would appear, though still not old, no longer in the very flower of her youth, having completed more than half an elven lifespan. Tara-lin and Keller died within half a century of their daughter and her spouse's ascent to the throne, their lives complete and, overall, happy, though Tara-lin had long missed her friend, Alis, as much as she had ever missed her father. When Tara-lin died, the Starweave was lost with her.

The elves mourned her death, and while they believed that her magic, and maybe a little of her spirit, continued in the Tree and in those of her line who were blessed by it, their legends long after sang of her as their greatest Queen and Singer, one whose like would never come again, even though she had had some small measure of success in convincing them not to worship her but instead to develop their own magic. Whether or not their inclinations were characteristically elven, this development stood them in better stead than they would otherwise have been when both her line and the Tree failed, and they were rejected by the dryads.

Thank you for reading the
Legend of the Singer Duology

If you missed Book One, *Children of the Dryads,* be sure to get it here:
https://books2read.com/legend2

And if you would like more, you can check out all of Raina Nightingale's
books here: https://books2read.com/raina_books
Or here: https://enthralledbylove.com/novels

Sign up to be notified about new releases:
https://books2read.com/r/B-A-OUYQ-HMXXB

Follow me on Goodreads:
https://www.goodreads.com/author/show/20243136.Raina_Nightingale

Follow me on BookBub:
https://www.bookbub.com/authors/raina-nightingale

Or, if you like weekly reviews, ramblings of all sorts, and occasional art posts,
you can follow my blog:
https://enthralledbylove.com

And if you liked *Sorceress of the Dryads,* please leave an honest review on your favorite book platforms. It really helps readers and independent authors to find each other (and what you didn't like can be helpful, too!).